GHOST DAUGHTER

Helen Currie Foster

Alice MacDonald Greer Mystery Series

This is a work of fiction. All incidents, dialogue and characters, with the exception of some well-known public figures, are products of the author's imagination and not to be construed as real. Where real-life historical or public figures appear, the situations, incidents and dialogues concerning those persons are used fictitiously and are not intended to depict actual events or to change the entirely fictional nature of the work. Any legal issues and analyses are fictional and not intended or to be taken as legal analysis or advice. Coffee County and Coffee Creek exist solely in the author's imagination, where they are located somewhere in the Texas Hill Country between Dripping Springs and Fredericksburg.

Published by Stuart's Creek Press, LLC
Dripping Springs, Texas

Stuart's Creek Press

Design by Bill Carson Design
Library of Congress Control Number: 2021911411
ISBN 978-1-7327229-1-0

For Isla, Foster, Lawrence, Emilia and Edward

All My Children

Seven on a June Sunday morning. Off in the pasture of her small Texas Hill Country ranch two of Alice's three burros, heads down, steadily worked through the new grass. The third leaned against Alice's leg while she stroked his elegant ears.

Were burros superior to humans?

Maybe so, Alice thought, recalling yesterday's marathon mediation. She'd settled a bone-wearying will dispute where the dead man's widow and stepchildren were at loggerheads. During one break Alice found herself compiling a mediation playlist: maybe Janis Joplin, *Mercedes Benz. Buy Me a Boat. If You've Got the Money, Honey, I've Got the Time.* But not *Silver Threads and Golden Needles:* "You can't buy my love with money..." On the other hand, her burros routinely demanded apples.

Today she'd have peace. Not go near her law office in Coffee Creek. Instead, take a slow run on a dirt road, alone but maybe not lonesome. Call her college-age kids, John and Ann, in D.C. for summer internships. Call Ben Kinsear, the man she'd said she would marry, who'd taken his two daughters to Puget Sound for Carrie's senior trip.

"When?" he'd asked.

Prerequisites: first, tell her children that she was marrying again, five years after their Scottish father's helicopter disappeared over the North Sea; second, consider options for serene joint family life. Two houses?

Her cell rang. FaceTime this early? Onto her phone flashed the face of Ellie Windom, who preferred calling her lawyer this way ("So I'm sure you're paying attention!"). Ellie looked anxious.

"Alice! I'm back from Santa Fe. I've got to change my will. Something's happened."

Oh, lord. Ellie's current will, drafted by a long-dead Coffee Creek lawyer, divided Ellie's estate equally between her warring sons, Chuck and Don. Simple and clear, thought Alice. Please, no complications. Eight months ago, after Ellie's husband, Woodie, died, Ellie hired Alice for help completing her duties as executor. Later she'd begged Alice to act as her executor. "If I choose either son, or both, they'll fight constantly! Can you help?"

Alice usually avoided acting as a client's executor. She already viewed Don's treatment of his mother as overly entitled, arrogant, and dismissive. Competition between Ellie's sons made the prospect even less appealing. After repeated requests, sensitive to fiduciary issues, Alice said, "If you're serious, hire another lawyer to revise your will and nominate me as executor." Ellie promptly did so.

She took a deep breath. "Ellie, what's up?"

"We need to talk in person. Urgently." On her screen Alice watched Ellie step outside, close a sliding glass door. Ellie lowered her voice. "My children aren't…*all* my children."

What did she mean?

"I've got to talk to you, Alice. In your office." Her bright eyes looked feverish, excited.

"Okay. Ten today?"

"Yes."

* * * * *

At ten sharp Alice stood at her office door watching Ellie hit the curb, leaving her cream-colored vintage diesel Mercedes slightly askew, and stride up the walk. At seventy-three Ellie remained dark-haired and erect, wearing her trademark chino pants and black jersey with an antique gold locket. She'd retired from teaching but still directed summer productions at Coffee Creek Community Theater involving many of her former high school students. She could mesmerize a roomful of them with her bright brown eyes.

Alice had barely gotten her settled when Ellie leaned forward. Then words poured out.

"My first real boyfriend was Roger Preyer. I met him the first day of my senior year of high school. His family was military. They'd just moved to San Antonio. It felt magical, all year.

"He'd been admitted to West Point—his life dream—and had to report to campus that summer. We wrote practically every day. I'd gotten a full-ride scholarship to Trinity; otherwise I couldn't afford college. After my dad died, Mom and I had no money. We lived on what she made as a secretary at the local Catholic high school.

"During Christmas break freshman year my friends invited me for

a riverboat caroling party on the San Antonio River. I heard a familiar voice singing—Roger! He'd surprised me. We saw each other every
night. Then—back to West Point.

"That spring I discovered I was pregnant, due in September. By
then my mom knew she had advanced breast cancer. She was adamant:
I had to finish college, build a future. She arranged for Holy Child
Home to cover all costs and arrange a private adoption." Ellie took a
deep breath. "I had to agree. I couldn't see an alternative. I just counted
the days, waiting for it to be over."

"Did you tell Roger?"

"Yes. Cadets couldn't marry. He said he'd give up West Point and
marry me; I said no. He had to finish West Point; I had to finish college. We couldn't support a baby. My mom begged me to break off
contact with Roger. I told him I agreed with her; it was going to be too
hard otherwise.

"At first he kept writing. Finally he sent a letter saying he understood. His letters stopped."

Alice waited, imagining the tension of the long hot San Antonio
summer, imagining Ellie in labor, no one at her side but her mother…

Ellie went on. "The baby came early, right after my eighteenth
birthday."

"And then?"

"Back to college. Like nothing had happened. No one found out,
not even my roommate at Trinity. I told Woodie, ten years later, before
we married."

"You never told your boys?"

"Never. I didn't want to hear what they'd think."

"And the baby?"

"Beautiful. I got a glimpse when she was born, but the adoptive
parents were waiting. That was my last sight of her."

No baby bassinet in the mother's room, her milk coming in, no
baby to suckle…

"Did you learn the adoptive parents' names?"

"No. I peeked out the window and saw them in the parking lot.
They had kind faces, at least. They looked so happy."

Alice had to ask. "Was there an adoption order terminating your parental rights?"

"Yes. That was the only time I saw my mom cry."

"Did you tell the lawyer who did your will about the adoption?"

"Yes. He insisted I had to tell him all my children. I didn't want to." Typical client, Alice thought.

"Did your adoption order specifically say the adopted child couldn't inherit from you?"

"He asked that too. I told him I thought so. I think he located a copy."

Alice heaved an internal sign of relief. Under state law, without such an order, Ellie's will should name the adopted child and specify any limits on inheritance. Otherwise, the adopted child could still inherit from the mother, like her other children. Of course, if that lawyer was wrong...

"And now? What's happened?"

"Last November, after Woodie died, I flew out to Santa Fe. I went to an exhibition. Gustave Baumann's woodcut prints. When I walked into the gallery, I saw Roger."

"Roger? The birth father?"

Ellie nodded. "We recognized each other immediately. He stood just as erect, had the same smile. He was alone too. His wife, Kristi, was playing golf. We sat in the gallery garden. At first, just awkward chit-chat. 'Do you have children?' 'Do you live here?' After the military he'd been in the foreign service. Then he and Kristi retired to Santa Fe. They have one son."

Alice's imagination whirled, thinking of this encounter. Two teen-aged lovers, over half a century later...

Ellie gazed into space, smiling. "That garden in Santa Fe...after the first shock, seeing Roger, it felt so natural, being with him again."

"Had he learned what became of your baby?"

Ellie lifted an eyebrow. "The fates conspired. Our birth daughter recently did a DNA test and hired a genealogist to help locate her birth parents. She located us but didn't contact us. Meanwhile, Roger's grandson did a DNA test and told Roger the results. That led Roger to our daughter. He hasn't told his wife yet, but that cat's on its way out of the bag."

Ellie dug in her purse and handed a sticky note to Alice. "Her name's Valerie Ames. She's now in Austin—Roger says UT recruited her from Northwestern as associate dean of arts and sciences. I found her address in the county tax records."

"What do you have in mind, Ellie? This could turn out—in ways you don't like."

"I don't want to upset my boys. Having them gang up on Valerie could be even more hellish." Ellie hurried on. "I want to leave her something of value—like cash, maybe, but not a share of the estate. There may be even more now than back when I made my will. Remember my Santa Fe house—the oldest house on Moon Mountain? I bought it some thirty years ago."

Alice remembered. In their wills Ellie and Woodie handled separate property differently from community property, which went into a life estate for the survivor, then to their sons. Each kept control over separately-owned property—for Woodie, his Wildflower Central farm; for Ellie, her Santa Fe house and some Coffee Creek real estate.

Alice lifted her eyebrows. "Why 'even more'?"

"I climbed into a hidden storage area in the attic and found a couple of old packages. Probably there since before I bought the house." She scrutinized Alice's face. "Remember that Baumann print that hangs on the wall in my dining room? Of the bishop's apricot tree? The one you like?"

Alice didn't just like that print; she coveted it. "Ellie! Were there hidden Baumanns?"

Ellie paused. "I'll get to that later." She pulled a folded sheet of paper from her bag. "These are notes I drafted, thinking about a letter to Valerie."

Alice scanned the few lines: "I have missed getting to know you… I know your children are so proud of you… I admire the woman you've become… This gift is only a sign of love… nothing can make up for years of our not knowing each other."

Above "gift" Ellie had inserted handwritten numbers: "$25,000? $50,000?" Then she'd crossed them out.

When Alice glanced up at her, Ellie said, "See what I mean? No amount's right. Nothing can make up for…for what happened. For the lost time, not knowing each other." Ellie's brown eyes met Alice's. "You have kids."

Alice nodded. Her two children were her reason for living.

"After I signed those papers," Ellie said, "I thought I'd be fine. But I started dreaming about the baby. I'd see her sweet face looking back at me from her stroller, and I'd try to catch up with her, and she'd disappear in a crowd. I'd see her laughing with other children in a playground, and I'd run around the fence trying to find the gate, but by the time I got in, she'd be gone."

"Oh, Ellie," Alice said, her heart hurting.

Ellie nodded. "She visited my dreams like a ghost. I'd see that face in nursery school, first grade, blowing candles out on a birthday cake I didn't make. Opening presents on Christmas morning. Or at high school graduation: I could see her from a distance, walking across the stage, but I couldn't get through the crowd to reach her." She shook her head. "After Woodie died, the dreams came back in spades. I'd see her getting into an elevator, and the doors would close in my face."

Ellie sat up, face intense. "When Roger told me her name, and I found her picture online, she looked so familiar! I knew that face from my dreams."

Ellie's cell phone rang. She glanced an apology at Alice, then answered. "Yes, dear?"

Alice heard an imperious voice. "Mom! Where'd you get off to?"

"I'll be right there, dear. Just running errands."

"Well, I'm waiting! I've got a flight, you know!"

Alice frowned, appalled.

"That's Don," Ellie said, hanging up. She made a face. "He's supposedly here checking on my rentals. Not that I need help." Ellie owned three historic properties in Coffee Creek—her own house, the old stable and feed store reportedly frequented by Texas Ranger John Coffee Hays, and a rental house. "Can you draft a short codicil? Right away?"

Alice thought for a minute. "Maybe to be safe we could add a codicil mentioning Valerie and making her a specific gift. Or you could go ahead and give a gift now. But there could be ramifications, once you get in touch with her."

Ellie listened intently, eyes fixed on Alice. "Ramifications?"

Her cell phone rang again. "Mom! What's the holdup?"

"On my way, dear." Ellie hung up and sighed. "Sorry. Look, tomorrow's Monday—I've got auditions scheduled. We're casting the August production for the Community Theater. How about Tuesday at three?"

"Good. Wait a sec—let's amend your old engagement letter." Alice pulled it up on her computer, added a clause about "discussion regarding provision for heirs," printed it, and handed it to Ellie for inspection.

Ellie signed it and hurried out, leaving Alice thinking of the many secrets clients failed to disclose, despite the sanctity of lawyer-client privilege. What was the wisest step? A codicil could protect Ellie from having to reveal the relationship to her boys while she lived, but if Ellie connected with Valerie, which looked inevitable, the boys would likely get wind of their surprise sibling anyway. A codicil might stave off a will challenge by Valerie but could precipitate challenges by the sons, maybe claiming undue influence or lack of mental capacity. Should Ellie simply make a gift now, an inter vivos gift, while still alive?

Alice saw risks looming. As executor she'd have fiduciary obligations to all Ellie's beneficiaries. But Ellie was determined to do something for Valerie.

She began a list of what-ifs to discuss with Ellie—including those "ramifications."

*****

Monday passed peacefully. Tuesday morning began badly and got worse. Before Alice had even reached her desk the president of the Coffee Creek Library Board called. The library's self-appointed smut watchdog had sued again. Would Alice represent the Board again, pro bono? Alice felt obligated to say yes—part of small-town law practice—but pro bono cases didn't pay the power bill.

Silla, Alice's secretary, marched into Alice's office, red ponytail bobbing. "You're way behind on your continuing legal ed," she reminded Alice. "If you don't finish in three days, you'll pay a fine. I've downloaded fifteen hours of courses for you to listen to."

"Thanks." Through gritted teeth.

"And I need you to approve these bills." She slapped the stack on Alice's desk and swung back out.

Alice finished editing the bills, then glanced at the continuing ed courses awaiting her attention. But Ellie came first. She sat down with a legal pad and sharp pencil to think through Ellie's options. Finally, she typed up a draft. Three o'clock. She looked out the window expecting the venerable cream-colored Mercedes to lurch to the curb.

At three-fifteen Ellie still hadn't shown up.

At three-thirty she tried Ellie's phone. No answer.

Alice texted her, then emailed. No response.

At four Silla stuck her head in the door. "Where is she? It's not like her."

Alice tried Ellie's phone again. Nothing. She reluctantly started the first continuing ed video.

At five o'clock the little worry drum was beating inside her head.

Alice wanted to go straight home, check on the donkeys, walk into her own quiet house. She wanted to pour a glass of wine and take it out on the deck to toast the creek, the trees, the sky.

Instead, she told Silla, "I'll swing by her house on the way home."

* * * * *

Ellie lived on twenty acres east of the creek road, outside town, in a high-ceilinged two-story limestone house built in the 1880s. Along the drive stood a pole barn. The old barn and a small corral sat behind the house.

The pastures downhill from the house and barn provided enough grass for Ellie's sorrel quarter horse, Woodie's horse, and the stubby pony originally bought for the grandchildren. Under Ellie's will they'd have equine care until they shuffled off this mortal coil.

Alice punched in the gate code, drove up the caliche drive, and parked under the pole barn next to Ellie's car. She followed the stone path leading around to the front door, with its view downhill.

Summer afternoon; the monotonous rhythmic buzz of cicadas in the air. A light breeze moved the leaves in the ancient live oak in Ellie's front yard. Alice rang the doorbell.

Silence, except for some odd thumps inside. She rattled the door handle. Locked.

Alice retraced her steps around to the back of the house and the kitchen, with its Dutch door facing the corral. She and Ellie had shared tea together in the kitchen in the difficult week after Woodie died.

The Dutch door was open on top, closed at the bottom. Alice stood listening to some remarkable thumps and bangs from inside.

"Ellie?"

More thumps, like iron on wood.

"Ellie? Are you there? It's Alice!"

Frantic thumping.

"Ellie?!"

Alice lifted the latch and opened the bottom of the Dutch door, leaving it ajar. She walked slowly through the kitchen toward the dining room, listening to the desperate thumps.

A horse whinnied. Inside the house.

Ellie's sorrel hurtled into the dining room, snorted in terror, and reared on its hind legs, flashing hooves knocking a dent into the mahogany table. Alice backed into the kitchen, backed around the island. The horse, eyes wild, raced out the open Dutch door, a short, frayed rope dangling from its bridle.

Alice ran over and pulled the bottom of the Dutch door shut.

Once more she called, "Ellie?"

Heart pounding, eyes wide, fearing what she'd find, Alice crept through the dining room into the entry hall. At the foot of the staircase lay Ellie, on her back, face turned toward the stairs. Blood had oozed and pooled on the uneven polished old planks below her. The hair on the back of Ellie's head was matted with blood.

"Ellie?" Alice crouched and touched her wrist. Cool to the touch, no pulse; but had Alice even found the proper spot to check? She wasn't sure. She dialed 911. "I need an ambulance! Head injury. Ellie Windom." She gave the address and the gate code, repeated her own phone number, hung up.

She stood, unsteady, clutching the newel post, then realized she should touch nothing.

"Ellie?" One more time, in case. "Ellie, help's on the way."

The open eyes did not blink.

Alice backed away, returned to the kitchen and stared out the top of the Dutch door. Behind the big round bale of hay leaning against the fence, the sorrel horse was still snorting to itself, skipping back and forth. The gate to the corral stood open, but the horse was back in the corral…

Alice blinked. How long would that last?

Alice feared horses. Despite encouragement from her best friend, Red Griffin, she'd never achieved a gallop, only a brief canter. Red understood horses, talked to her horses, loved horses. But Alice flinched at the thought of those flashing hooves.

She pulled a tissue from her pocket, walked quietly toward the corral, and, tissue over her fingers, carefully secured the gate to the rusty chain on the gate post. At the clanking sound the sorrel snorted and side-stepped, then settled.

She turned back to the house, a house that had seen its share of births and deaths. But a death like this?

Get a grip, Alice! she told herself. She grabbed her phone, called the Coffee County Sheriff's Department, asked for Detective George Files.

"Files here."

"George, it's Alice Greer. I'm at Ellie Windom's. I found her inside with her head injured and a horse in the house. I've called EMS. The horse is out now, but you may want to send a crime scene team."

Silence. "Someone shut a horse in the house?"

"Yes."

"You're alone?"

"Yes. With Ellie."

"Tell the EMTs I'm on my way. Stay there," Files said.

Alice walked back into the house, filled with dread, but knowing she should return to her friend's side.

Sorry, Ma'am

A lice tiptoed back through the kitchen and dining room to the entry hall, hoping against hope to hear a groan, see a movement. Nothing. Ellie's open eyes stared unblinking toward the staircase.

Steeling herself, Alice tried to notice detail, more and more puzzled by the scene. Ellie's skull—hit by the horse's hooves?—no longer leaked blood. Ellie wore the same outfit she'd worn to Alice's office Sunday: chino pants, now bloodstained; black jersey shirt; the old gold locket. Ballet flats, one on, one falling off. Her feet looked sad, forlorn, vulnerable. Alice took a breath and made herself focus on Ellie's face, knowing she didn't want the memory, would never be able to forget it, but had to look.

Ellie looked hurt, horrified, amazed. Mouth slightly open, eyes wide.

Alice heard tires on the driveway, went outside. "I'm afraid she's dead," she told the EMTs. "But the horse is back in the corral."

They looked at her blankly, like…what fresh hell have we here?

"I called the Sheriff's Department too. Maybe the horse kicked her, but…"

The EMTs carried their equipment into the house. Alice followed, standing in the dining room while the blue-shirted techs knelt carefully around Ellie.

"I'm sorry, ma'am," said one. "She's passed."

Alice's throat closed and tears rose, followed by a wave of anger. How had this happened?

Someone would have to tell Ellie's boys.

Alice called Silla and told her what she'd found.

"A horse in the house? Poor thing was probably terrified!"

Alice knew Silla, the Oklahoma barrel racer, meant the horse.

"Listen," Silla said, "Files is going to need those boys' names and phone numbers. So are you. I'll email you their contact info from Ellie's file."

"Thanks."

Alice heard a car crunch up the drive and walked outside.

In the driveway sat a green Subaru Forester with a tall white-haired man inside, staring through the windshield at the ambulance. He saw

Alice and climbed out, face rigid, afraid to hear. "Is she—is it Ellie? Is she okay?" Soft east Texas accent; worried eyes. He wore seersucker shorts and a polo shirt. He looked at the open back of the ambulance, then at Alice.

Alice shook her head. "I'm afraid not. Are you a friend?"

"Yes. I'm Tommy Long. I'm on the board of the Community Theater."

"I'm Alice Greer."

"Ah. Ellie missed our one-thirty meeting today. She was supposed to discuss summer casting. I kept calling but couldn't get her. Do you know what happened? Is it her heart?" His face showed deep concern. "Ellie's our artistic director. We can't do without her."

"She had a head injury."

Down the hill Ellie's gate opened. A Coffee Creek Sheriff's Department SUV rolled up the hill. Alice watched George Files unfold his long legs and climb out, brown eyes on her, then on Long. Files's red-headed assistant detective, Alan Joske, climbed out of the passenger side.

Joske headed inside; Files asked Long to wait in his car and walked Alice over to the corral.

"That the horse?"

"Yes. Ellie's sorrel."

"What brought you out to the house?"

Alice explained Ellie's missed appointment.

"Tell me what happened when you got here."

Alice told him about her arrival, the odd thumping, the locked front door, the bottom of the back door shut. "I went in, calling Ellie, then the horse went wild—and ran out the open back door. Which I closed. I went back to Ellie, tried to find a pulse. No luck. I called 911."

"What about the horse?"

"It had run to the corral. I didn't want it to escape. I tried not to scare it, took a tissue and put the chain back over the gatepost." She swallowed. "Then I went back to Ellie, just hoping…"

"Anything else?"

"I tried not to touch anything. She looked so surprised…"

"Okay. So your prints will be on the Dutch door."

She nodded. "The newel post on the stairs. Maybe on the floor by Ellie, too."

"Who's this guy?" He nodded toward the green Subaru.

"Tommy Long. He serves with Ellie on the Community Theater Board. He says she didn't show for their meeting at one-thirty today. He tried to call but didn't get her."

"Where's her phone? Her purse?"

Alice frowned. "I didn't see them."

"She had an appointment at your office at three?"

"Yes. She wanted to talk about…tweaking her will."

"You were where, before you came out here?"

"At the office all day." She added, "With Silla." Otherwise, he'd ask.

Joske came out the back door. "Boss?"

Files's brown eyes scanned Alice's face. "Okay, I'll call later about the family and the will. You can go."

Alice desperately longed to climb in her car and leave. But… "I'm her executor."

"Oh? I thought you didn't usually agree to that."

"I prefer not. But she kept asking. I need to lock up after everyone leaves. I'll stay out here."

Files nodded. He talked briefly to Tommy Long. Alice saw Long's face change from anxiety to alarm to despair. Long left and Files went back inside. Alice settled herself in her car to wait, gazing at her phone, not seeing it.

Then reluctantly she pulled up Silla's email with the phone numbers. She'd call Chuck Windom, Ellie's older son. She'd last seen him at Woodie's funeral.

Car noise on the phone. "Chuck Windom."

"Chuck, Alice Greer here. Your mom's lawyer. I'm afraid I've got some bad news. Are you driving?"

"Yes, on the way to DFW. I've got a flight to Denver, for meetings. What's the bad news? What's going on?"

"I'm so sorry. Your mom died this afternoon, here at her house."

"*Died?* But Don just saw her! What happened?"

Alice explained how Ellie missed two appointments, first with her theater board, then with Alice. "I came by and found her and called EMS. Your mom's horse was in the house. I called the police. They're investigating."

"Her *horse*? Did the horse kill her? I kept telling her…"

"It's not clear what happened. I expect the police will get in touch with you with more details. Do you have time to call your brother before you leave for Denver?"

He paused. "Yes, okay." He asked if there was anything else he could do. Did she need him to come to Coffee Creek? Maybe he could cancel the meetings tomorrow.

She thought for a moment. "Right now there's nothing you could do. The police are still here, taking samples, dusting for fingerprints, putting up crime scene tape. Silla and I will take care of locking up and securing the house and the contents."

"You'll be the executor, right?" He'd remembered.

"Once the court appoints me. I'll send you and Don the probate requirements. Meanwhile, with the house empty, I'll try to keep the assets secure." She paused. "I am so sorry, Chuck. Your mom—she was very special."

"Yes. Okay, I'll call Don." He hung up.

* * * * *

Two crime scene techs, one bald and burly, one slim and horn-rimmed, came out the back door and walked slowly to the corral, scanning the ground. Bald Tech leaned over, apparently photographing footprints, hoofprints. He shot photos of the corral area. Horn Rims dusted the gate latch for prints. The horse lifted its head, wary, as the men entered the corral. Bald Tech offered an apple, gentling the sorrel. Horn Rims picked up the horse's left forefoot, taking samples of dirt and wiping the hoof with a tissue, all of which went into a sample bag. Bald Tech kept talking softly to the sorrel while Horn Rims circled behind him to the other forefoot.

Curious, Alice tiptoed to the corral. Bald Tech had apparently declared his love and proposed marriage to the horse, which extended its neck for stroking while nonchalantly lifting its hind legs, one at a time, for further sampling by Horn Rims.

When the two men finished, with the sorrel peacefully investigating the hay bale, Alice asked why they were sampling the hind feet. "Just belt and suspenders," said Bald Tech. "My money's not on those hind hooves."

"No?"

"Pay us no mind," said Horn Rims. "Hey, I think we're done inside. Are you the one who closed the gate?" She nodded. "Let's get your fingerprints. And a shot of your footprints." She obliged. That done, the two disappeared into the crime scene SUV.

Alice ducked under the crime scene tape at the back door and located Ellie's purse, a black planner, phone, and keys in the kitchen, on the small desk by the refrigerator. Next to the purse lay a notepad. In Ellie's familiar angular writing, with its dramatic capitals, "Tues auditions 9 am Board mtg 1:30 pm Alice 3 pm." She saw the same Tuesday appointments on Ellie's wall calendar above the desk, plus "Don" scrawled on the square for Sunday. Alice carried the keys to the pole barn and unlocked the Mercedes. On the passenger seat lay a stack of mail topped by a post office mailbox key, bronze like her own, and, like her own, with a ribbon tied to it. Ellie must have stopped at the post office on the way home. Most rural Coffee Creekers had a box at the post office as well as a mailbox out on the road: roadside mailboxes were notoriously vulnerable to late-night swipes by teenaged drivers.

Alice slid into the driver's seat, perforated leather, decades old, and inhaled the faint trace of Ellie's perfume. Classic, like Ellie. Maybe *Joy*? She picked up the mailbox key and the mail in the passenger seat: two magazines, an electric bill, a grocery mailer. On the floor she found a long white overnight-delivery receipt. She relocked the Mercedes and carried the mail and receipt to her car. Silla would set up a file and be sure Ellie's mail got checked and the bills got paid.

EMTs emerged from the house, carrying Ellie's body. Alice watched as they slid the body bag into the ambulance. Her lively client, this energetic, theater-directing, art-loving, horse-riding woman, was disappearing down her driveway, gone forever.

She found Files and Joske in the kitchen. "You ever been here before?" Files asked.

"Yes, once, after Ellie's husband died."

"She lived alone?"

"Yes. Two grown sons, Chuck and Don. Chuck's in Dallas, Don's in Houston. Both married. Don was here Sunday. I think he was supposed to leave that day."

"Can you give Joske their contact info?"

"Yes. Silla emailed it already." Alice picked up her phone and forwarded it to both men.

"What a woman, that Silla," Files said, studying his phone. "Okay, Don's in Houston, married to Danielle. What's he do?"

"Something with a mutual fund. Oil and gas."

"And Danielle?"

"Assistant to a wedding planner."

"What about Chuck in Dallas?"

"I'm pretty sure he's with a medical instruments company."

"Married to?"

"Joanne. An interior designer."

Joske was taking notes.

"Both sons in their forties?" asked Files.

Alice nodded. "Forty-four and forty-two."

"They have kids?"

"They each have a boy. Chuck and Joanne's is Max. Don and Danielle's is Drake. Both in college, I think. I called Chuck. Will you contact both sons?"

"I'll get Joske on it. You said Don called while you and Ellie—Ms. Windom—met on Sunday. Was he here at the house?"

"I assume so. He had a flight to make and wanted to know how soon she'd be there."

"I need to know when he left her house." He nodded toward Ellie's cell phone. "Joske will give you a receipt for the phone. We're taking her planner, calendar and that notepad. Okay, we're outta here. You're locking up, correct? Taking charge of her purse?"

Alice nodded, lifting Ellie's key ring.

"We'll need a copy of the house key."

She nodded again. She'd ask Silla to stop at the hardware store and get one made. Outside, summer twilight, with cicadas and tree frogs. She heard the first whippoorwill just as she called Silla. "If by any chance you're still at the office…?"

"I'm just locking up. I called Uniform Security to see if they'd come out tonight to Ellie's and check what we need in the way of protection. I'll be there in five minutes."

Alice walked back into the dining room. Earlier she'd seen nothing but the horse, then Ellie. Now, wanting to salvage some vestige of beauty from the day, she looked for her favorite picture. But the wall was empty…only a small picture hook remained.

The Bishop's Apricot was gone.

C h a p t e r   T h r e e

I Need Help

S he called Files about the missing Baumann. He grunted. "Let me know if anything else is missing.

By the time Silla arrived it was dark twilight. She ducked under the police tape and met Alice in the kitchen.

"Want to start downstairs?"

Silla nodded. They'd film each room, secure the house, then come back to start a more complete inventory.

First the kitchen: Alice pulled out drawers and opened cabinets while Silla filmed with her phone. Kitchens reflected the owner's personality: Ellie chose bright coral and turquoise Fiesta ware, hefty Mexican glassware, a big earthenware pot holding a couple of hand-carved wooden spoons and a wooden *molinillo* for frothing Mexican hot chocolate.

"She must have really liked to cook Mexican food," Silla said. "Look, she's got a real *molcajete* on the shelf." The basalt mortar and pestle looked lethal but well-used. "I've always wanted one, for making guacamole. And look at these Mexican cookbooks." Silla filmed the bookshelf. "The classics! Diana Kennedy, Fonda San Miguel, Café Pasqual… Oh, look. Julia Child and Patricia Wells too. I'm hungry."

Now the dining room. Alice pointed to the empty picture hook. "Start with that wall. The Baumann print that belongs there is gone." Silla filmed the walls, the scarred table and its formal chairs, the breakfront sparkling with crystal and silver. Alice held open the doors to the buffet while Silla leaned in, filming the china. They tugged open the buffet drawers and unzipped velvety tarnish-proof bags full of silver flatware.

"It's so intrusive, doing this," Silla said. "But I do like seeing what people choose."

She stopped at the dining room archway to the entry hall, pointing at the floor in front of the stairs. "Is that…?"

Alice nodded. Somebody had wiped up some—but not all—of the blood that had seeped from Ellie's head.

They crossed to the living room, with its smoke-smudged limestone fireplace, framed by bookshelves. Silla turned slowly in a circle, filming sofa, end tables, coffee table, armchairs, reading lamps, fireplace tools, and books. She took close-ups of original paintings on the walls. "Some from Santa Fe, but some from here, don't you think? I like this one." Silla pointed to an oil of a mesa above a lonely West Texas valley. "And this." A small painting of a New Mexico pueblo, in earth tones against a brilliant blue sky. Alice was scribbling down the artists' names.

"Upstairs?"

Both stepped carefully over the shadowy stain on the floor at the foot of the stairs. On the second floor, two boys' bedrooms, still with college pennants on the walls. One bed was still rumpled and unmade: Alice guessed it was Don's. Nothing hung in the closets except a couple of high school letter jackets. One guest bedroom with twin beds, chaste and unwrinkled. Closet: Christmas decorations. One bath, medicine cabinet mostly empty. Don seemed to have tossed his towels in the tub.

"Last but not least," Alice said, leading the way downstairs and into a hall that ran from the kitchen to the master bedroom. "We need to see Ellie's desk."

Ellie's bedroom, like her car, carried a trace of perfume. Silla started filming: large mirrored chest of drawers, queen-sized bed with padded headboard. On what must have been Woodie's side of the bed sat stacks of books. Keeping warm at night with bedtime reading material, Alice surmised. One entire wall of shelves held books: drama, novels, history. One shelf held photo albums. She'd look at those later. Walk-in closet: Ellie had kept a few of Woodie's belongings. Ellie's clothes were few but carefully chosen: variations on her usual outfit, the chino pants, the black sweaters, with some bright scarves and shawls. Ballet slippers, high leather riding boots, snow boots.

Bathroom: bubble bath, cosmetics, a scale. Drawers: medication for high blood pressure and cholesterol. Silla took closeups. Aspirin. Vitamins.

Alice stood at the desk by the bedroom window while Silla filmed. Phone. iPad. Computer.

Silla's phone rang. "You're here already? I'll meet you at the back door." She turned to Alice. "It's the security folks," she said. "I'll walk them around while you check the desk." Alice heard her greet the security workers, heard two male voices.

Back to Ellie's desk. Silla and Alice would box up financial and other records the next day for safekeeping. Top drawer: checkbook, pens, and gathered in a rubber band, florists' cards that must have accompanied flowers from Woodie: "Ellie, all my love. Let's have forty more years!" "Okay, Lady Macbeth, Break a leg tonight!" "Happy birthday, my darling!" Alice shook her head. Such love, such loss.

Middle drawer: the boys' childhood artwork, vaccination records, report cards. Bottom drawer: folders labeled Wildflower Central, Community Theater, Estate, Taxes, Insurance, Wills and POA. And, at the back, Family.

Outside the window Silla walked past, pointing at the eaves and followed by two men.

Alice was fixated on the missing print, *The Bishop's Apricot*. She remembered it as bearing Baumann's signature and thought it bore a print number but couldn't recall what. She grabbed the "Insurance" folder, curious whether Ellie had insured it. She flipped through the folder to the homeowner's policy. Yes, Ellie had insured the Baumann and two other pictures. The folder included the invoice from the Santa Fe gallery, showing the date and including the number of a check received from "Ellie Windom." Alice heaved a sigh of relief and took a picture of the print number and invoice.

Then she opened the "Family" folder. Ellie's will. Letters from grandchildren, some old and tattered in sprawling capital letters, some in tentative cursive handwriting, some obviously later: "Gram, thanks for the check. College is expensive! Love, Max…"

At the very back, a folded white notecard. Alice felt a shiver down her spine as she read: "Dear Ellie, Thank you for contacting me. I have followed your career with interest. I attended your production of Macbeth in Coffee Creek—very good. Someday perhaps we can meet and talk. I don't believe I'm quite ready. Very truly yours, Valerie Ames."

Date: just a month ago. No, Ellie had not told her lawyer she'd already been in contact with Valerie Ames…

Silla burst into the room. "Alice, these guys can go ahead and put up security cams tonight if that's okay. At the front and back door and on each corner."

"Good idea," Alice said. "Could they add the pole barn and the corral?"

"I'll ask. They'll be back tomorrow to put motion detectors inside." Silla swept out.

Alice stared down at the notecard in her hand.

No codicil for Ellie's will now…the will-maker, the testator, was dead.

What would the testator want Alice to do? Could she actually do anything at all, other than comply with the existing will? Head aching, Alice called to Silla. "Let's box up these desk papers. Can you get them to the office? Then let's lock the place and get out of here." She took pictures of the notecard before slipping it back into the folder.

She wasn't looking forward to meeting with Ellie's two sons. Had Ellie told them anything about Valerie Ames? If not, should she? Could she? What Ellie told her was privileged…wasn't it?

Silla walked back in, carrying a banker's box with the desk folders. "Tomorrow morning?" she asked.

"Yes. Let's meet here early for the rest of the inventory."

"And to feed and water the horses," Silla said.

Oh, lord, the horses. "I'll call Red," Alice said. She dialed her horse whispering friend, Red. Alice began with the bad news, that Ellie had been killed. Red gasped. "Not Ellie! In her own house? What happened?"

"She was hit on the head," Alice said carefully. Red would refuse to entertain the horse possibility.

"But who? Why?""

Alice sighed. "We don't know."

"I can't imagine Ellie dead. She's so—so alive!"

Not anymore.

"I need help, Red," Alice said. "Ellie and Woodie made sure the horses will have lifetime care. Ellie was taking care of them by herself. Now they need someone to check on them, feed them, water them, whatever's needed." Alice had limited knowledge of horse maintenance. Except for annual shots, her burros took care of themselves. But horses?

"We can handle that," Red said. "I've got a high school senior working part time. She can stop by twice a day, give them some TLC."

"Thanks." She noted that neither Chuck nor Don had asked about the horses.

Alice felt a wave of exhaustion. She found Silla in the kitchen. "Let's get out of here."

Curve Ball

efore they could leave, fierce pounding broke out on the Dutch door. As Alice reached for the handle to the top half of the door, Silla frowned a warning and moved up next to her. "Who the hell are you two?"

Standing ramrod straight at the locked Dutch door under the outdoor floodlight stood a big-boned, hollow-eyed woman of at least seventy, clutching a bucket of cleaning supplies. Her spotless small pickup sat outside.

They introduced themselves and waited.

"I'm Judith Strong. I clean for Ellie every Monday morning." She glared at Alice. "But I saw lights. I thought I might be needed tonight. You're her lawyer? That what you said?"

Alice nodded.

"Do the police" (she said PO-leece) "know what happened? Mr. Tommy told me they were all over the place when he got here." She spoke as though her words needed to reach the last pew of the church balcony.

Alice shook her head. "I don't think they know for sure what happened. So how do you know Mr. Tommy? Is it Tommy Long?"

"Course I clean for him too. On Tuesday afternoons."

Alice unlocked the Dutch door. The cleaning woman ducked under the crime scene tape and moved past her.

Judith Strong cast fierce eyes around the kitchen, scanning in one direction, then the other.

"Huh," she said.

"What is it?" Alice asked.

"Somebody should look into this. It's just…it don't look quite right. It don't look the same. Like something's missing, but I don't know quite what."

"Here in the kitchen?" Silla asked.

"Yes. Here in the kitchen something is astray. Awry. Whatever. I don't see what I should see. Because it ain't here."

Alice looked around, puzzled. On the kitchen counters stood the earthenware jar of spoons, spatulas, whisks, and *molinillo*; blender; food processor; toaster oven; KitchenAid mixer. No blank spaces. She saw everything she'd seen earlier.

"If you remember what's missing, will you tell us?"

Judith Strong nodded. "I will. And if I find out somebody hurt Miss Ellie, they'll wish I hadn't found out."

"You knew her a long time?"

"I've cleaned here over thirty years. Every Monday without fail."

"You were here this Monday? Yesterday?" Yesterday seemed like a long time ago.

"Didn't I just say I was?" She pulled out a handkerchief and wiped her nose. "Tonight I came to clean up after all those people tromped through here."

Alice didn't want house-cleaning until she checked with Files. But Judith Strong was here Monday… "When you were here yesterday, what did you talk about with Ellie?"

"Didn't get much chance. Mr. Don was here. He took a lot of air time. Not too pleasant either."

"How do you mean?"

"He was back in her bedroom, naggin' at her about money. Sound travels right down that hall to the kitchen, y'know. He wanted his inheritance. Said why wait? Said she surely had enough, didn't she want to see her sons happy? Said if she didn't care about him, she could at least help him make Danielle happy."

"Yikes," Alice said.

"Yep. Not real pleasant."

"Didn't she remind him she's got to support herself?"

"Well of course. That's when Don started nagging her to sell Wild-flower Central now and split the money between him and Chuck. She said she didn't want to. Said 'should I just leave everything to the grandkids?' That's when he left to catch his plane."

"I thought he was flying out Sunday."

"He changed his mind, waited until Monday morning. Went storming out." She lifted a gray eyebrow and narrowed her eyes at Alice. "Far as I can tell, that boy's never been grateful. Nothing's ever good enough for Mr. Don. But there was something else eating on him. Ellie threw him a curve ball on something. All I know about that was he made this snippy remark—'Have you already told Chuck? Am I the last to hear this wonderful news?' I mean, the man was yelling. What a drama queen."

"Did Ellie say anything more to you?"

"After he left, she came in the kitchen. I think she'd been crying but she was mad too. 'Sharper than a serpent's tooth,' she said. I believe that's from one of them plays she put on."

Judith Strong grabbed her cleaning bucket and started into the dining room before Alice could stop her. "What in the world?" she shrieked. "The picture's gone! The apricot tree!"

"It was gone when I got here," Alice said. "Was it here Monday?"

"Of course it was here! Ellie loved that picture!"

"After Don left?" Alice wanted to be sure.

"Yes! I know because I polished the buffet Monday after he left. And lord, look at this dining room table. What in the world?" She pointed to the scarred streak in the mahogany finish, left by the sorrel horse.

"The horse did that. The horse got in the house," Alice said.

Judith Strong stared at her, face blank, mouth agape.

"In the house? What evil son of a bitch did that?" she blurted.

"The police don't know. Did Ellie ever have trouble with that horse?"

"No. Quite gentle, she said."

"Listen, Ms. Strong, Silla and I are going to inventory some things. I know Ellie would want you to keep this place nice."

Relief in the woman's eyes. "I'd hate to have to get another cleaning job. Be glad to come every two weeks since nobody's here making a mess."

"I'd like you to do that at least for a while. We'll hold off on cleaning until the police give us the okay."

Silla got Judith's phone number and assured her that she'd get a house key.

Judith Strong teared up. "Ellie. I did love that woman." She wiped her nose on her handkerchief, sniffed. "Let me know if you need anything."

Alice nodded. Judith Strong marched back to her pickup.

Alice and Silla watched her leave.

"You're gonna have your hands full with that Don guy," Silla warned.

"I know," Alice said. Don sounded like an executor's nightmare, likely to second-guess every decision. A man who demanded that his mother give him his inheritance early might also try to find his mother's jewelry for—what was her name?—Danielle.

Thinking about Don, and about the vanished Baumann print, Alice's heart thumped: she realized she needed to secure another house—in Santa Fe. She frowned. She wouldn't ordinarily incur estate expenses before being appointed executor, but she'd promised Chuck she'd try to keep assets secure.

She told Silla what Ellie had hinted about the Moon Mountain house. "So I'll head to Santa Fe tomorrow. Can you be here early to supervise the security folks? We need cameras inside. Let's change the locks too," Alice said. "Can you get Files a key? And let's get going on the application to probate the will and for letters testamentary."

"No problem."

Silla could have organized the Normandy invasion. Piece of cake.

"I'll take care of Santa Fe." Yes. A road trip was in order.

An Old Flame

Early on Wednesday Alice flung a few clothes into her carry-on; located phone, computer, and e-book chargers; grabbed her plastic bags of cosmetics and meds; and loaded her car. Extra key fob, bottled water, jar of peanuts, a couple of oranges. On mature reflection she stuck a bottle of cabernet and a wine opener in the cold bag in case she got to visit with her Santa Fe friend, Margaret. Margaret offered only cheap white. Alice texted Tonio, her sometime ranch hand, who agreed to check the house until she got back. What else?

Music. Road atlas. Ready to go.

With Venus low and bright in the east, Alice rolled out of her gate, armed with a thermos of coffee and Ellie's keys to the Moon Mountain house. Goal: Santa Fe by dusk—about 690 miles in maybe eleven hours, but she'd gain an hour when she crossed the Texas line.

She felt smug, daring, adventurous. Like the Water Rat…like Huck Finn…like Kim with his lama on the Great Indian Road… She would avoid Lubbock and the interstate, taking favorite highways west.

Bloomberg; NPR; depressing news. She switched back and forth between KUTX and Sun Radio, singing along with the radio as she angled up Highway 281. Then she turned west onto the rolling hills and curves of a spectacular stretch of Highway 71, all ranches and steep hills. In early sun she crossed the clanging metal bridge over the Llano River, with a fly-fisherman prowling the rocky banks below. Then Highway 87 to Brady, still saying "no" to goat barbecue, the local specialty. She felt giddy, on a road trip high, flying down the empty roads, loving the place names, crossing the precious rivers, the Llano, the Colorado. She dipped down from the high limestone and red granite of the Edwards Plateau toward west Texas, its blue shadowed ridges on the far horizon. In Big Spring she stopped for gas, then turned north through flat cotton fields to Brownfield, then west again. By early afternoon she'd crossed the New Mexico line heading for Roswell, home of the fabled visit from aliens. Alice pooh-poohed the story but nevertheless was happy to leave Roswell…just in case…

She considered calling Kinsear, wondering how he and his girls were faring. Were they on a ferry in Puget Sound? Kayaking off Bainbridge Island? Were Carrie and her big sister, Isabel, getting along with each other, with their dad? She said a small morning prayer for them and for her own John and Ann, dearer than life.

Then her mind went to Ellie, lying in a pool of blood on the floor of her house, with that dreadful last expression on her face. Again the specter of the first meeting with Ellie's sons: how would they react to the news—which Ellie might've shared with Don—that they had a half-sister? Would he have told Chuck? Would the two sons show any interest in meeting their half-sister? Be furious with their mother? Be indignant at the news that, contrary to their life-long beliefs and expectations, they were not Ellie's first- and second-born children?

Her cell phone rang: Silla, at the office. "Everything's fine, but the security folks in Santa Fe, that's Santa Fe Safety, can't get to Ellie's house until tomorrow at ten."

"Rats. Well, I'll at least video tonight. Everything else okay?"

"Yes. Detective Files wants you to call."

Alice called immediately, got no answer, left a message.

Speeding north in late afternoon, she spied a small herd of antelope, barely visible in the golden grass, and the faint blue line of mountains in the distance. She was promised, at road's end, a room at the El Rey Court, built in 1936 as a roadside adobe motor court in Santa Fe and since renovated. The clerk assured Alice she'd have a kiva fireplace. Not the same as sharing a casita with Kinsear, but convenient to Moon Mountain…

The sun sat low in the west before she reached Clines Corners. By the time she hit Santa Fe, the light was twilight blue. She checked into the El Rey Court, all retro charm, and decided to make a quick foray to Moon Mountain before dinner. She'd film the interior, then come back in daylight to complete the inventory.

Alice climbed back into her Discovery, not ready to be back in the car. She tapped Ellie's address into her phone and set out for Moon Mountain. This side of Santa Fe seemed darker. Where were the damn streetlights? On the way up the Old Santa Fe Trail, using her brights, she finally spotted Overlook Road and started winding her way up the curves. "At the very top," Ellie had said. She passed a cell tower looming above the road and slowed, checking street numbers at every mailbox. Far down the steep mountainside sparkled the lights of Santa Fe.

In the dark street on a leaning mailbox she saw "1702" in uneven white letters, obviously hand painted. Ellie's adobe house stood well off the street. The only car in sight, a darkish Jeep, was parked a few houses down. Alice slowed and parked across from Ellie's house.

In contrast to most houses on the street—large, new, expensive—Ellie's small one-story adobe, with its built-in one-car garage on one side, was built decades earlier. Alice rummaged in the console for a small flashlight and climbed out of the car, Ellie's keys in one hand, flashlight in the other. She sniffed the dry mountain air, with its faint tang of chamisa. Stars were already out, but as yet no moon.

Her flashlight jiggled across paving stones to the traditional covered adobe portal, or porch, on the front of the house. She rang the bell. It echoed inside…then silence. She knocked, just to make sure no one was inside. No answer. Well, she wasn't expecting one, but why was a light on in back?

She left the front porch and followed the sandstone pavers leading to the right around the house. As she turned the corner, a shape jumped off the back portal and took off around the other side of the house. Alice jumped a foot, terrified, banging her ankle on a stone paver. As footsteps pounded up the street, she caught her breath and ran back around her side of the house in time to see someone in dark pants and dark hoodie reach the Jeep. The driver sped back down Overlook past Ellie's, no lights on. Alice managed to get her flashlight pointed at the Jeep but couldn't read the plate except for an 8, and were they Utah plates? The spare tire cover on its rear clearly proclaimed "Rubicon."

Utah plates? Why Utah?

Maybe a recently purchased Jeep that the new owner had so far failed to register.

Heart still pounding from the surprise visitor, Alice walked cautiously back around the house. The back door stood open. She reached inside, flipped on the lights, and scrutinized the door: intact, no sign of jimmying. So who had a key?

She took two steps through the back door. On her left, a door into the one-car garage, quiet and clean. Laundry room straight ahead, kitchen to her right. No sound but the hum of the refrigerator. The faint light she'd seen came from the laundry room. She looked inside:

cabinets ajar above the washing machine and dryer, pantry door open, broom closet open. The intruder was looking for something, but she didn't think he'd carried anything away. Yes, she was sure the running figure was male…

In for a penny, in for a pound. Alice locked the back door before checking the kitchen. More of Ellie's vibrance here: open shelving with bright dishes, a rustic breakfast table by the windows looking out over Santa Fe. A few open drawers, open cabinets… unlikely hiding places.

The kitchen opened directly into a dining area/living room with a traditional corner fireplace, piñon logs stacked inside ready to light. Kachinas stood on the small shelf built into the chimney breast. Bright artwork on the walls, Navajo rugs on the sofas. No Baumanns.

Another hall led from the kitchen to a bathroom on the left, a small study/guestroom on the right, then a master bedroom with bath. Both bedrooms had views of Santa Fe. Alice felt sudden envy at this retreat high above the world. An adobe house, shaped by hand, curved, with the portals front and back providing shade and shelter, felt human-scale to her. The clear air, the violet mountains on the horizon, the tawny hills…maybe before their respective kids got home for Christmas, she and Kinsear could find a place, sit on the plaza with hot chocolate, listen to carols in the crystal air…

Focus, Alice! she told herself, realizing her phone was sitting idle in her pocket. She returned to the back door and started over, phone on video: garage, laundry room, kitchen, living room, hovering over the art work and rugs.

In the master bedroom, a couple of vivid landscapes on the wall: one of cottonwoods golden in the fall; one of a canyon, russet stone marked with winter snow. Sheepskin rugs on the terra-cotta floors by the bed. Closet, nearly bare: a purple windbreaker, sun visor, hiking sticks, and a dusty pair of women's hiking boots. On the floor, a backpack. Alice imagined Ellie hiking up a canyon, lifting her face to the sky.

Nothing of Woodie's remained: Ellie must have cleared out his clothes long ago, knowing he'd never return to their Santa Fe eyrie.

No desk in the master bedroom.

The small guestroom felt comfortable, welcoming, with some

watercolors of wildflowers. The closet shelves held a motley collection: pottery vases, an elaborate Christmas creche including pueblo buildings with tiny figures, cardboard boxes of puzzles, Scrabble, Clue. Leaning against the wall next to the desk stood a rustic ladder of cottonwood poles laced together with rawhide. On the ladder's steps sat what Alice thought might be three Hopi coiled baskets with lids. Alice videoed it all, then pulled open the desk drawer: a ten-year-old phone book, notepad from the Broadmoor Hotel with some scribbled notes, pencils, pens, reading glasses. In the cabinet beneath, one book on Baumann's prints and several brochures from Santa Fe galleries. Alice pocketed the brochures. She planned to track down any art dealer or art appraiser Ellie had talked to.

She could not see any pull-down door to the attic in the bedrooms or hallway. She walked out the rear portal and shone her flashlight on the adobe wall above the kitchen. Nothing. So how to get into the attic? She'd try tomorrow in daylight. Maybe then she'd spot the way in.

Before leaving, Alice called the Santa Fe police to report unauthorized entry at Ellie's. No, she couldn't see that anything was taken, but she wouldn't necessarily know. No, she couldn't identify the burglar, didn't know the license, didn't know who might have a key. Big help.

She was starving. She double-checked that the front and back and garage doors were locked and wound her way back down the mountain. Nearly eight: she needed fortification, delivered with casual kindness and a margarita. She called Café Pasqual. Yes, they could squeeze her in at the community table. Well, all right. Even if she was alone.

*****

Not for one second did Alice regret leaving the hot early summer nights of Coffee Creek for the astringent cool air of Santa Fe. The color and fragrance of Café Pasqual made her smile. A big group had taken over one end of the community table; she scored a chair at the other end, gratefully accepted a menu and the proffered margarita, and let her eyes roam around the room. Pictures everywhere; talavera tiles; *ristras* hanging from the ceiling. Alice felt she had only a glimmer of understanding of Santa Fe: centuries of history, native Americans, Spanish conquistadores, American adventurers. The landscape, so spare, so distinctive, prevailed. Green or golden cottonwoods on streambanks, pink-orange dirt of adobe, flat violet cutouts of mountains on the horizon.

Her waiter materialized. "*Cochinita pibil,*" Alice requested. He smiled and whisked away the menu. She retrieved the brochures from Ellie's nightstand and started examining them.

A voice at her left. "Excuse me."

She looked up at a man with steady hazel eyes in a weather-worn, serious face. Dark hair, turning gray. But she knew him…knew him from decades ago…UT Law.

"Francis?" she blurted. "Francis Blake?"

The serious face broke into a smile. "Alice MacDonald!"

"It's Alice MacDonald Greer now," she said.

He looked at the empty chair across from her.

"Please sit!" she said. "I'm by myself."

The waiter reappeared. "You don't mind?" Francis asked.

"Of course not," Alice said.

The waiter took Francis's order for enchiladas with *mole* sauce.

Then it was catch-up time, covering more than two decades. Alice recited her history, marriage, kids, and moving her Austin practice to Coffee Creek. Francis said he'd made enough money with a plaintiff's firm in Houston that one day he'd just said goodbye and headed west. Now his only law work was pro bono. Was he married? No. Was she? She explained about being widowed and now engaged to another classmate of theirs. He laughed. "I remember Kinsear. Lucky guy!"

And what was Francis doing now?

His face reddened a bit. "I paint some. Landscapes." Then, with equanimity, "I'm pretty involved with the art scene here. Some teaching, some work with tribal artists." He pointed at the art gallery brochures. "What brought you to Santa Fe? Are you on a buying mission?"

"Sadly, no. A client died, back in Coffee Creek. I'm executor. I've got to secure her house here, up on Moon Mountain."

"Moon Mountain? Who is it?"

"Do you know Ellie Windom?"

His eyes widened, his chin dropped. "Of course I know Ellie.

Whenever she's here she calls and we go together to hear the Desert Chorale. She's a big supporter. We're buddies. What happened?"

Once again she saw Ellie, lying at the foot of the stairs, eyes staring, blood pooled around her head…

"I don't know yet. She had a blow to the head." Alice looked at Francis's face, the sensitive mouth, the unblinking concern in the eyes. "Her horse was locked in the house with her."

His eyebrows shot up. He watched the waiter set down Alice's *cochinita pibil* and his enchiladas with *mole* sauce. Then he said, "Sorry. I just can't imagine Ellie dead." He stared past her, eyes unfocused.

Alice let the silence play out. Then Francis said abruptly, "How'd that happen?"

"I'm waiting to find out. I doubt the head wound was the horse's doing."

He pointed at the brochures. "So…?"

Could she trust him? He'd been a straight shooter in law school. They'd argued against each other in moot court. He wasn't slimy.

"She had a Baumann print at her house in Coffee Creek. *The Bishop's Apricot.* It's disappeared."

Again his eyebrows lifted. "Original woodcut print? If so, that's worth thousands."

"I think so." She wouldn't yet mention Ellie's mysterious attic trove. "But I needed to talk to someone knowledgeable about Baumann's work. And the values."

"Got it." He gazed off toward the end of the table, then turned back to Alice. "I can give you names, if you want." Then he surprised Alice. "I spent an evening with Ellie back last November, after Woodie died. That hit her hard. She flew out here for a little R&R, she told me. We went to dinner and to a Desert Chorale concert. Incredible music that night." He paused. "How's your *cochinita pibil*?"

"Wonderful."

He put down his fork and watched her face. "During intermission Ellie told me about meeting an old flame in a gallery here."

Alice felt chills running up her arms.

"Guy named Roger Preyer. She'd known him in high school."

"Do you know him?" Alice asked.

"Yeah. We play poker once a month. He's a tough poker read, not many tells—that foreign service work, maybe. He's also got season tickets to the Chorale. Usually has to bring a guest; his wife Kristi doesn't seem interested." He stopped, watching Alice again. "Ellie told me that night how strange it was, seeing someone she'd loved so long ago. I asked her if there was still a spark. She said, 'I fear it's possible.' She meant that word, 'fear.' She still loves Woodie, of course."

"Of course," Alice said. "Do you think she saw Roger…again?"

The waiter brought dessert menus. "Lemon cream," Alice said.

"Warm gingerbread for me." After the waiter left, Francis said, "I know she saw Roger again because I saw them together. Up at Chimayo. I had a meeting with a group of Chimayo artists. Ellie and Roger were in the gallery there. They didn't see me. I sure didn't want to intrude, either." Francis glanced up at Alice. "Roger was admiring Ellie more than the art."

"When was this?"

"Just last month. The middle of May." He gave her a half-smile. "They left in separate cars."

Ellie didn't tell me about this last trip to Santa Fe, did she? Sneaking around, Alice thought. Like in high school. Both of them over seventy and still—what? Was Roger still in love with Ellie? "I fear it's possible," she'd told Francis. And Ellie, so loyal to her Woodie, what did she feel?

After dessert Alice and Francis settled the bill and exchanged contact information. "Let me know," he said, "if you want any help on Baumann's work, or current values. If you need an appraisal for the estate, I can point you to a decent appraiser or two. If you just want to talk turkey, no charge. Happy to help."

"Thanks, Francis."

And off into the night they went, he one direction, she another, still with her mind on Ellie and her bittersweet encounter with Roger.

As she reached her car, the phone rang. Files. "It wasn't the horse that killed Ellie."

Not the Horse?

Oh, lord. She got into the car, started the engine, locked the doors. "Not the horse?"

Files filled in details. "No. According to the medical examiner in Austin, the head wound wasn't made by that horse you found. The wound's not the size or shape that a horseshoe might make, and, besides, we found no sign of human hair or blood on the samples from the horse. The newel post on the stairs was a candidate, but we found no signs she fell down the stairs. The medical examiner thinks the victim was struck from behind by something curved and heavy, likely wood. Furthermore, we found tiny blood spatters on the wall by the staircase and on the stairs. That indicates she was struck more than once, which is consistent with the skull fractures. We're not sure about the weapon."

The weapon. Therefore not an accident. "You haven't found anything likely?"

"No. We're still looking. She was killed where you found her, we think. No sign she was moved."

Killed in her own house…by someone known to her? By a stranger who invaded, then put the horse in the house to confuse the evidence?

"When did she die?" Alice asked. The cool skin, no pulse, head had stopped bleeding…

"The medical examiner thinks she was dead by about three," Files said.

She missed her board meeting, Alice thought. No way she'd miss that with the upcoming production.

"I need you to tell me more about the family," Files went on. "We know her son Don was there Monday, but he says he and his wife were both at work in Houston on Tuesday. We're waiting to talk to his wife, Danielle. We're also confirming Chuck and his wife were at their jobs in Dallas, which is what they say."

"You might want to talk to Judith Strong, the cleaning lady. She told us last night she'd overheard some hot words on Monday morning between Don and Ellie."

"Ah. About?"

"Apparently, Don wanted some of his inheritance early. He wanted Ellie to sell the Wildflower Central farm and split the money between him and Chuck. Also, according to Judith, something else Ellie said also upset Don. You'll want to ask her about that." She gave him Judith Strong's phone number. "Plus, remember after the crime scene team left, I noticed a picture was missing from the dining room wall? It's got value; during our inventory we found a policy insuring it," Alice said. "But Judith Strong said it was still on the wall on Monday when she was cleaning, after Don left."

She could hear him typing notes on his keyboard. On that chaotic afternoon at what was now officially a murder scene, Files hadn't asked, and she hadn't had a chance to explain, why Ellie had made an appointment with her. Until Alice had a chance to talk to Valerie Ames, she felt a strong wave of reluctance to unearth a story that Ellie had kept deeply buried.

But this was a murder investigation.

Alice took a deep breath. "You asked me about the family. Ellie recently told me she got pregnant at seventeen, and the families wanted the two teenagers to stop seeing each other and put up the baby for adoption. That's what they did. Later each married, each had at least one child. The adoption's been secret until very recently, when two things happened. The adopted child hired a genealogist to find her parents, and the birth father's grandson wanted to learn about his own DNA and any DNA relatives."

"Okay, you need to download all this for me. Can you come in the office tomorrow morning?"

"Not tomorrow. I'm in Santa Fe. I've got to secure Ellie's second home up here."

"How long?"

"I drove to Santa Fe, so… I could be back day after tomorrow." She heard shouting in the background, heard someone yell, "Hey, Files!"

"Gotta go. Call me." He hung up.

She put the car in gear and drove slowly back to her room at the El Rey Court, where she locked her door and put the chain on. Fear like a gray fog rolled in around her as she thought of the violence of Ellie's death and the intruder at Moon Mountain. Generally, Alice felt fearless, impervious, undaunted, or tried to persuade herself of that…but now and then she thought: a single woman alone on the road?

*****

Restored the next morning by a strong, fragrant cup of coffee, so rich the bubbles were dark, she persuaded herself. Determined. Undaunted. Forget fear, she told herself. She stopped on Cerrillos Road for a to-go breakfast burrito and proclaimed herself even more undaunted after a bite stoked with chiles and cheese. As she drove up Moon Mountain, her plan was to finish her inventory by ten, when the security folks reached the Moon Mountain house, then maybe ask Francis Blake about Baumann experts.

No Jeep was visible on Ellie's stretch of road. Alice was not interested in being visible either. She unlocked the garage door, parked the Discovery inside, and lowered the garage door. From the garage Alice toted into the house two bankers' boxes intended for any financial papers or valuables and left them by the washing machine. She checked the front door and back door: both still locked. She chained the back door; she'd exit via the garage.

The adobe house was silent.

First question: how to get into the attic, where Ellie found the mystery box? Alice wandered through the small house again, scrutinizing ceilings. The living room, dining room, and master bedroom boasted the traditional ceilings of *vigas*, with big logs running across from wall to wall, and smaller straight sticks—*latillas*—making a herringbone pattern between the *vigas*. Nope, no pull-down attic door in the garage. She peered in the hall closet, the two baths, the pantry, the laundry, the guest room. Plain white sheetrock ceilings. Frustrated, she returned to the master bedroom closet and scrutinized the ceiling. Nothing. Back in the small guestroom she again opened the closet, narrow but several feet deep. The white painted ceiling featured molding surrounding the top of the shelving. The molding ran all the way around the ceiling. She looked harder. The ceiling was not sheetrock: it was painted wood.

She went back to the garage. No stepladder. Laundry room: only a two-step kitchen stepstool. Something niggled at her brain. Back to the guest room, where she examined the artisanal ladder by the desk, hand-made of cottonwood, tied with rawhide strips. She removed the

Hopi baskets and put them on the desk, then carried the ladder to the closet, leaning it against the back wall.

She climbed up, placing her feet gently on each rung, hoping the rawhide thongs could hold her weight. At the top she pushed up hard with her hands. The painted wood ceiling rectangle finally yielded. She slid it aside, then climbed cautiously up to the next-to-last rung, levered herself up with her arms, and crawled into the attic.

She sneezed. The attic was dark, dusty, with a floor of splintered planks. It wasn't a true attic—merely a small wooden platform, extending over part of the kitchen ceiling and a slice of the guest room ceiling. On the kitchen side of the platform, what looked like the kitchen hood vent ran up to the roof. On the sides facing the house interior, the platform was open. Wiring and pipes ran along the sheetrock ceilings above the hallway and baths, with vent pipes rising from the bathroom ceilings to the roof.

The only ambient light came up through the *latillas* over the living and dining rooms and master bedroom. Alice crawled to the edge of the platform. To her amazement, through the spaces between some of the more irregular *latillas* she could glimpse narrow slivers of the rooms below. As she turned to crawl back toward the access opening, she saw a dark shape in deeper darkness where the rear of the house met the platform. She turned on her phone flashlight and shone it toward the shape. The dust was disturbed on the planks of the attic floor around it. Flashlight in hand, she crawled over to a square package, almost invisible in the black tarp folded around it. The shape inside felt like a box.

Feeling like a child in a fairy tale, crouched beneath the roof, she unfolded the tarp, old and crackling, and gently tugged aside an old wool blanket. Her phone flashlight played on the outside of a fine-grained wooden box about eighteen inches square, lighting up little painted figures dancing in a pueblo plaza, hoeing corn in a narrow field, hunting on mountainsides, feeding a fire. The landscapes ran around each side of the box. She leaned over, enchanted: were the landscapes spring, summer, winter, fall? The box lid bore the dawn sky; the bottom, a moonlit night.

No lock on the metal latch. Holding her breath, and using the blanket to avoid fingerprints, Alice lifted the heavy wooden lid. Inside a brown accordion folder she saw sheets of heavy cream-colored paper, each standing vertically in a separate manila folder, protected by a sheet of tissue. The first and second folders, though, were empty. Using the blanket, she carefully extracted a woodcut print from the third folder, catching her breath as she recognized the colors so distinctive of Baumann: mustard and parakeet green, gold cottonwoods, a blue stream. The next sheet silhouetted a mountain peak against the deep cobalt sky. After those two, Alice counted five more folders, each with a painting separated with tissue from a matching print. She would need to photograph each carefully. Behind the prints in each manila folder stood thin rectangular pieces of wood, about a quarter of an inch thick, separated by scraps of fabric. Again using the blanket, she carefully picked one up. It felt surprisingly light. She marveled at the complex carving. With her flashlight she tried to imagine the print from its inverse. Paint smudges—an astounding yellowish blue-green—still stained the wood. The next slab was smudged with orange, the next with black. At the back of the box she saw more blocks.

She closed the lid and sat back, thinking. If indeed these were Baumann's work, Ellie was right: there'd be plenty of money. What to do next?

She heard noise downstairs. Footsteps, voices. Someone had unlocked the back door, which she'd chained shut. She heard shoulders banging against the wooden door as someone tried to break the chain. "Go get the bolt cutter!" Footsteps running away.

She absolutely could not be found up here, could not let someone see what Ellie had left hidden. Panicked, she crawled to the access opening and pulled up the cottonwood ladder, desperate to prevent noise. She laid the ladder on the platform. She crawled to the painted wood ceiling rectangle, placed one edge silently on one side of the opening, then gingerly let it down to close the ceiling opening. It fit perfectly. She let out her breath. But what if the intruders guessed? Found the secret entry to the attic?

A loud snap of the chain; the back door slammed open. "Got it!"

Now their voices were coming up through the *vigas* ceiling. Were they in the dining room? She heard them opening the buffet, pulling open drawers, slamming them shut.

Her frightened brain came back to life. She turned on her phone, began recording sound.

"Nothing here. I'll try the living room." That was the first voice. Male, youngish.

She heard footsteps going toward the fireplace, moving books on the shelves. Same voice: "Nothing." The voices came closer, back in the kitchen, then in the hallway, fading away toward the master bedroom. She heard drawers open, slam shut, heard the bathroom linen closet door and drawers slamming.

"What's this room?" A second voice, right underneath her.

"Guestroom maybe." The first voice, the one who told the other to get the bolt cutter.

She held her breath, praying they'd be as hasty here as elsewhere.

The first voice said, "We gotta check the garage, too."

Alice flinched. Her car!

She heard a vehicle outside, crunching up the gravel drive.

"Who the hell is that?" said the second voice, anxious.

Footsteps ran back into the living room, then thudded back to the study. "Let's get outta here. It's a Santa Fe Safety truck."

Alice had almost forgotten. Security people at ten.

She heard the intruders hurrying out the back door. The first voice said, "Don't leave the damn bolt cutter! Get it!"

Then what? She could faintly hear boots skidding down the rocky slope behind the house.

Alice hastily rewrapped the blanket around the box, and the tarp around the blanket, and videoed the bag sitting on the platform. In the light from her cell phone she glimpsed another package in the darkness where the roof joined the platform—an irregular oblong also wrapped in a dark tarp, with what looked like small wooden legs sticking out. But no time for furniture now. What she needed was Ellie's mysterious box. She managed to pry up the tight-fitting wood rectangle, bruising her fingers, and slid the cottonwood ladder to the floor. Already she heard heavy footsteps rounding the back of the house, and two men talking. "Yeah, they want motion detectors inside and also outside. Where's that lawyer?"

"Supposed to meet us. Let's get the ladders out of the truck."

Alice tugged the wrapped box to the access opening and balanced on the ladder. Though the precious prints and carved woodblocks were light, the wooden box itself was heavy. No wonder Ellie had left the treasure box in the attic: alone in the house, she couldn't risk falling off the ladder with that awkward parcel. But Alice had to get it down. She laid the wrapped box on the closet floor, climbed back up the ladder, felt for the wood rectangle, and tugged it back into place.

She managed to get the box to the garage. She locked it in the Discovery, tried to brush the sweat from her forehead, assumed what she hoped looked like a composed expression, and opened the garage door.

"Hi, guys," she said to two startled men in the driveway by a white van with a large blue SFS logo on the hood. One burly, one wiry, they both wore Santa Fe Safety shirts. "I'm Alice Greer. Thanks for coming."

They introduced themselves: the burly one was Brian, the wiry one was Wayne. They told her they'd begin outdoors, then work on the interior.

"I'll let you get started," she said.

She went to the back door and took a picture of the dangling ends of the broken chain lock. If anyone asked, this is why she needed to secure the house. And any treasure within it.

Now what? She called the Santa Fe police, reported the second intrusion and asked for someone to come take fingerprints from the busted lock. "Yes, I called last night. I think the same guy was back. With a buddy."

How the hell to get this problem box safely back to Coffee Creek? She loved a road trip, but what if, driving alone, she had a flat tire? Engine trouble? She knew no safe haven in Santa Fe. Would any Santa Fe bank let her waltz in and rent a huge safety deposit box without already having an account? Maybe if her own bank called on her behalf? She picked up her phone to call her friend Miranda at Madrone Bank in Coffee Creek. The receptionist said, "She won that company prize, a trip to Antarctica! Left last week! No phone service right now!"

Hmmph.

Alice walked outside. Wiry Wayne was adjusting a ladder against the front eave of the house. Burly Brian, biceps bulging, lugged two bags of equipment up the driveway.

"Your company's bonded, right?" she asked Brian.

"Of course." He sounded faintly offended.

Maybe one of them would like to ride shotgun to Coffee Creek, Texas?

Wayne spoke from halfway up the ladder. "I can do it if the boss says it's okay. What'll you pay?"

She called Wayne's boss Ryan, at Santa Fe Safety. Yes, he could spare Wayne for two days, if Wayne was willing, and if she'd get him on the first plane back from Austin. Yes, Wayne looked mild but was capable. He made twenty-five dollars an hour.

She told Wayne the rules: (1) she ran the show; (2) she chose the route; and (3) under no circumstances was he to touch, open, or any way mess with the box.

Wayne agreed.

Short of renting a Brinks truck, it seemed like the safest bet. However, she decided she'd do the driving.

With respect to her fiduciary duties as executor, in trying to get Ellie's treasure box back to Coffee Creek, she had the uneasy feeling she was making up procedures as she went along. She retrieved the box from the Discovery, took it to the kitchen, found some rubber gloves, and asked Brian and Wayne to step in to witness her video. She liked the idea of having their shirts, proclaiming "Santa Fe Safety," on record. As they watched, she opened the treasure box on the kitchen table and, with the two men in the background, carefully photographed the contents of each folder. She noticed the prints in the third and fourth folders included a title, a penciled signature—"Gustave Baumann"—and a charming orange hand-heart symbol. The rest did not. Were these really Baumanns? Originals that hadn't yet seen the light of day? Unfinished versions? What were they?

"Thanks, guys."

"Those look kinda familiar," Wayne said.

"Have you ever seen the Gustave Baumann house over on Camino de las Animas?"

His forehead wrinkled. "Oh yeah, we had a field trip there in high school. He'd painted stuff all over the inside of the house. Weird."

"I don't know if they're genuine or not, but this is what you're escorting to Coffee Creek."

"Cool."

Burly Brian and Wiry Wayne began installing interior cameras.

✱ ✱ ✱ ✱ ✱

Time for more phone work. She went out in the back yard and called Francis Blake, who sounded glad to hear from her.

"Francis, if I wanted to ask about some art that might be by Baumann, who would know?"

After a moment, he said, "Now you've got me curious. I'd have thought all the Baumanns are catalogued and spoken for." Before she could answer he said, "Wait a sec. This is about Ellie, isn't it? But not *The Bishop's Apricot?*"

"Right. Some...some prints."

She wouldn't mention the treasure box quite yet.

"I tell you who'd know," Francis said. "Clare Graham, over at St. John's College. And he's in his office this week, finishing a summer seminar. Want me to call him and tell him you're coming?"

"Yes!"

Francis called back in five minutes. "Graham is waiting with bated breath. His giant ego is so flattered he may be insufferable." He told Alice where to find Graham's office at the college.

Alice still had to contend with her hot potato—the box. She confirmed that Brian and Wayne were out of earshot and called the clerk at the El Rey Court. Could they put a box into safekeeping for her? Yes, for an hour or two, if it was too big for the room safe.

She told Wayne she'd call about departure time. He seemed eager to assist. Maybe overeager. She hoped he didn't expect to talk to her for eleven hours or to choose the radio stations.

At the El Rey Court Alice dropped off the hot potato. "Remember, just a couple of hours," the clerk warned.

Momentarily relieved of responsibility, she climbed back into the car and headed up Camino de Cruz Blanca to the St. John's campus. She'd always wondered what it would be like to study the Great Books course, the basis of the St. John's undergrad curriculum, and was curious to see the campus. She lucked into a visitor parking slot and made her way up the placita, the campus mall, past a large koi pond. At the end she found the colonnaded Fine Arts Building. The wall directory inside announced Professor Clare Graham occupied Office 202.

Graham answered her knock. Medium height, vigorous gray hair and bushy eyebrows, sharp blue eyes behind reading glasses. Blue denim shirt, paint-stained, sleeves rolled above his elbows. His office smelled like sharpened pencils, charcoal, oil paints. A bookcase sagged with art books. An easel stood by the window.

Alice had thought carefully about what to say about Ellie's attic find. And what not to say.

"My client Ellie Windom died this week. Her woodcut print of *The Bishop's Apricot* is missing. It's got Baumann's signature and that orange hand-heart symbol." On her phone Alice showed him the photos of the print's description and print number from the insurance policy and invoice. He expanded the pictures, looked at them carefully.

"Well, it's got the print number, and you say it has his hand-heart symbol and signature," Graham said. "Not one of the earlier prints, but still valuable. I'd have to see it to be sure it wasn't some sort of clever forgery. Technology these days gets creative."

"If it's real, what's the value?"

"Market goes up and down. For a signed print, anywhere from several thousand to over twenty, depending on rarity and condition." The sharp eyes examined her. "That all you wanted to ask me? Any gallery dealer in Santa Fe could tell you this."

She hesitated. Perhaps a little misdirection was in order. "My client lived in Coffee Creek, Texas. Part of her estate includes some prints that might or might not be original Baumanns."

"You've got photos?"

She looked at him, thinking. "I'll show you a couple."

She thumbed her way to the pueblo scene print, with children playing in the plaza. He held the phone close to his eyes, expanding the picture, moving it here and there. Then he looked up at her. "This is one I've never seen. It sure as hell looks like a Baumann, but I'm not familiar with it. I can't give you any opinion without seeing it in person.

I see the signature…but no print number." He shook his head. "Hard to put a value on this."

"What if there are matching woodblocks?"

He leaned toward her. "Are there? Are you serious?"

"I'm not sure yet."

He leaned back in his chair. "You need to be very, very careful. Provenance is everything in art. So I hope you're documenting everything."

She nodded.

"And where are you keeping these? I assume there are more than one."

She nodded. "Trying to keep them very safe."

Again, sharp eyes measured her. "If people know you've got hold of unknown but genuine Baumanns, all these years after he died, they'll be in hot pursuit."

"I hope not too hot," Alice said.

"Could be hotter than hell."

She stood up. "Thanks very much, Professor Graham."

"Call me Clare. Listen, I want a chance to see these. Will you let me have first shot? Francis may have told you. Baumann's my life study. The man's talent…his colors…his craftmanship, his freedom, his precision…he never ceases to amaze me."

She liked this passion. "His pictures grab me, especially the Santa Fe ones," Alice admitted. "There's a fierce beauty to the landscapes. And those colors make the pictures take wing."

"So, can I have first shot at any authentication?" Graham pressed.

"I have to safeguard the artwork first. Could you look at the other furnishings and art in my client's house on Moon Mountain? And would you travel?"

"Yes, and no charge for travel. Coffee Creek, you said."

"Great. I must go."

Back in the car she called Francis to thank him for connecting her with Clare Graham and tell him she'd be leaving.

"He's already called me, all excited," Francis said. "Listen, are you driving back alone?"

"No. I've got a guy from the security company to ride shotgun."

"Ah."

She drove slowly through campus, enjoying the hilltop views. Oh to be a student again…spring term was over, summer session about to begin. In the dorm complex, young people ambled past, talking, laughing, with a couple throwing frisbees on a dorm lawn. Music blared from an open dorm window. On the way back to the college entrance, her eye was caught by a vehicle in the student parking lot to her right. She slowed, turned into the parking lot. Yes, a two-door olive drab Jeep Wrangler with Rubicon emblazoned on the spare tire cover on its rear. Pretty sporty, with a convertible soft top and what looked like plastic windows for the back seat, and the bright blue and orange Utah plate…including the number eight. She didn't know a soul from Utah; no one from Utah was involved with Ellie's estate. Santa Fe streets were full of Jeeps. This particular Jeep in the student parking lot might never have parked on Ellie's street. Still…the young voices of the intruders at Ellie's: could they be students?

What, at this pricey college?

She reminded herself that the first lone intruder had apparently returned with a buddy and a bolt cutter. They'd busted the door chain. They weren't after the usual loot—hadn't grabbed electronics, hadn't looked for jewelry. They'd searched for something specific.

What had Graham said? "You need to be very, very careful."

She loved the exotic feel of Santa Fe. Colors, history, desert, mountains. She wanted to talk more with Francis Blake, download the full story about Ellie and her meetings with Roger Preyer. Ellie hadn't told her everything, hadn't come close to telling her everything. From the little Ellie had said, Alice wanted to learn more about Roger Preyer, his wife Kristi, their son, their grandson. Santa Fe had a lot to tell her.

But something about the broken chain told her it was time to get the hell out of Dodge.

Chapter Seven

A Faint Warning Beep

R ight on time, at six on Friday morning, Wayne met her in the parking lot at the El Rey Court, carrying a small gym bag. The El Rey had provided sandwiches and drinks for the road trip. Alice told Wayne she did not intend to stop for anything except gas and a bio break. "It goes without saying that the box stays in the back, untouched," she said.

"Right," Wayne said, and belted himself in the front seat.

He started to reach for the radio.

"I like to listen to Bloomberg or NPR on the road," Alice said. "Especially in the morning. For the afternoon I've got a good audio tape on the Black Death in Europe. Really fascinating. Or you can just read, if you want. I hope to have you at the Austin airport by seven tonight." Was that too drastic? No, Alice thought, I'm not running a tour bus.

Wiry Wayne looked stunned but settled back as Alice listened to Daybreak Asia, the Asian-British accents capturing her as always. They left Clines Corners, cutting southeast toward Roswell. She watched the gas gauge. "We'll stop in Roswell. Gas and bio break." He nodded.

Two and a half hours later she picked the largest station in Roswell with, she hoped, the cleanest restrooms, and pulled into a gas pump. "Why don't you take first turn?" Wayne said. "You can just leave your stuff here, phone and keys and all. I'll watch everything."

Alice felt a faint warning beep, deep in her midbrain. She patted her pockets to be sure she had phone and keys. "That's all right. I'll be quick." She got the pump running with her credit card, then left for the restrooms.

Oh, no. A line. She stood awhile, shifting from foot to foot, then grabbed the first available stall. When she emerged from the restroom area, she glanced out the big plate glass windows toward the pump islands and stopped dead.

Wayne, one eye on the gas station front door, stood at the rear of the Discovery, its tailgate lifted. He'd put his gym bag on the asphalt, unwrapped the box and lifted the lid, and was fumbling in the folders holding the prints. Alice hurried to the station front door and held it open while peering back in to call "thank you" quite loudly to the cashier. In the few seconds that took, by the time she turned around, Wayne had shut the tailgate and was standing by the open front passenger door, earnestly staring down at his phone.

Alice marched back and smiled. "Your turn." She wanted him gone.

The instant Wayne disappeared into the station she reached in the open passenger door, retrieved his gym bag and unzipped it. No print, no woodblock. Instead, two pistols and one pair of presumably clean underwear. Alice doublechecked the interior pockets, gingerly lifted the pistols and underwear to be sure nothing lay beneath, and zipped the bag shut. She planted the bag atop the gas pump, jumped in the driver's seat, checked the rearview mirror and accelerated out of the parking lot, heading back north.

North, because she refused to abandon her plan to protect the treasure box until it was safe. North, because with her cargo she could not drive alone nine more hours through empty country where, in case of accident, no help lay. She'd checked the rearview mirror a dozen times while focused on staying close to the speed limit, when her cell phone rang.

Kinsear.

"How are you?" she said, a bit resentfully, assuming she was about to hear about fresh raspberries on Bainbridge Island, whales leaping offshore, Olympia oysters with perfect mignonette sauce, and a sunset backdrop.

Instead she heard, "Hush a moment, Carrie. I'm sorry, honey."

"Ben?" she said.

"Alice?"

"Are you okay?"

"No. Carrie broke her ankle yesterday. She's on crutches and in pain. We're going to start home, if I can figure out how to get her comfortable in the car."

"Oh no! What happened?"

"Rock climbing accident. Not a compound fracture at least, but no fun."

"Ben, I'm so sorry. That's a rotten way to celebrate high school graduation."

His voice sounded heavy. "Believe me, I know. Listen, Silla says you're in Santa Fe. Are you okay? I just called for sympathy."

"I'm fine. Sounds like you've got a car full of misery though."

"It's pretty uncomfortable for Isabel because I've got to lay the front passenger seat flat for Carrie. But we'll manage."

Wait a sec, Alice thought. Isabel? An idea blossomed in her head. "Listen, Ben, I seriously need someone to ride shotgun. Can you send Isabel to Santa Fe? Or I could pick her up in Albuquerque."

She heard Kinsear talking in the background, heard a muffled "you do?"

He came back on. "Alice, she's begging me to put her on the first plane."

Alice had met Isabel under difficult circumstances, had watched her take charge in a life-or-death situation when catastrophic flooding hit Coffee Creek. Alice had learned Isabel was, in frontier parlance, "someone to ride the river with."

"That's great news."

"I just wish I could change places," Kinsear said. "Poor Carrie."

Alice heard Isabel's voice in the background.

"She says she'll be in the flight that gets into Santa Fe about three today if that's okay, and she's up for whatever."

Which is why Alice finally had a smile on her face as she sped back toward Clines Corners. But she couldn't go back to the comfort of the El Rey, as Wayne might expect. After serious thought, she called Francis Blake. Fellow lawyer; needed to protect his reputation, since he served on the Desert Chorale Board; was at least non-slimy in law school; and knew and cared for Ellie Windom.

He answered immediately.

"Francis, I hired a guy from Santa Fe Safety to help me get those prints back to Coffee Creek, but he was too eager to get his own mitts on them."

"Mmm. I wondered about that."

"Why'd you wonder?"

"I just didn't like the idea of you traipsing off with some guy who might get an original idea. But you've always struck me as pretty… independent, so… You ditched him?"

"Yes. So now I'm racing back to Santa Fe. Kinsear's daughter Isabel's flying in this afternoon. She can drive back to Coffee Creek with me and those prints. I don't think it's a good idea to go back to the El

Rey Court, so I'm wondering—could you take in a couple of strays tonight?"

"Sure." He didn't miss a beat.

Inside, Alice sighed with relief.

"And as long as you're here," he added, "I don't know if Isabel would be interested, but the Desert Chorale's got a concert tonight. I've got extra tickets. And they're singing some of 'The Road Home.'"

The Desert Chorale. Where he and Ellie went when she was in town. Alice had heard their "I'll Be on My Way…" and "I'll Be Seeing You." Close harmony, unusual chords, voices exchanging musical themes, life, death, love, beauty. "That sounds wonderful. Like a respite, after all this pain over Ellie." Well, minus the death part.

Francis told her how to find his house, on Calle Peralta, a cul-de-sac off Old Pecos Trail.

Then a small bell jingled in her head. Desert Chorale, where Roger Preyer held season tickets. Yes, she wanted a respite, but she'd also like to lay eyes on Roger Preyer.

And talk to his daughter, Valerie Ames. Start filling in the picture. But she had to keep watch over the box.

*****

Alice cruised north up U.S. 285, contemplating the options. She felt pretty cocky about escaping Wiry Wayne until halfway back to Santa Fe. Then ahead in the oncoming lane she saw a faintly familiar white van speeding toward her, with a faintly familiar blue logo on the hood. As it whizzed by, she read "SFS" on the hood and door. And surely that was Burly Brian in the driver's seat, glaring straight ahead and gripping the wheel.

Her mind raced. Had he seen her? Had he seen her car at Ellie's house? Maybe only when she opened the garage door? Would he remember a green Discovery?

She blinked, trying to remember. Maybe he would.

If he was on his way to retrieve Wayne and his gym bag—and why else was he en route to Roswell on a Saturday morning?—were they a team? Wayne must have called him immediately.

Still angry, she thumbed "Santa Fe Safety" into the phone and called.

"This is Ryan, Santa Fe Safety."

"Alice Greer," she said grimly. "You told me Wayne was capable."

"What's wrong?"

"He did exactly what I told him not to do. Opened the tailgate, opened the cargo and was getting some of it out. So he's off the job."

"What do you mean? You're supposed to fly him back here from Austin!"

"He had his gym bag handy and was pulling out part of what I'm transporting. I saw he had two guns in the bag, so I don't know how the hell he expected to fly back from anywhere. He definitely breached our agreement. I ditched him." She thought a second. "He didn't report back to you, did he?"

"No."

"Well, I just saw his buddy Brian heading south in your van, presumably on the way to pick him up. Did Brian tell you he was taking your van to pick up Wayne?"

"No."

"So given you don't know what these two guys are doing, are they still your employees?"

"Look, Ms.—Greer, right? I've got to look into the situation."

Alice's blood pressure rose. "I need to know right this minute whether you are still taking full responsibility for security at 1702 Overlook? Can I trust you for that? Or should I be on the phone to the Better Business Bureau? Get on social media?"

He spluttered and muttered and reassured Alice that he'd take both men off the job immediately and be very sure the house stayed secure.

"Otherwise," she said, "I know my fellow trusts and estates folks, and bankers, and of course real estate agents, would be highly concerned to know they can't leave a client's house in your hands. So I have to know you can be counted on. Can I count on you?"

"Yes, ma'am! You can indeed!"

Grr, she thought, hanging up.

One more hour to Santa Fe. She called Silla. "Where are you?"

"I'm out at the stable, exercising Miss Priss." Miss Priss was Silla's current barrel-racing ride. "How's Santa Fe?"

"A little too exciting. I think I've found Ellie's treasure. I thought it was too risky to drive back alone with it but screwed up on my first choice of escort." She explained the ditching of Wiry Wayne. "Anyway, I'm gunning it back to Santa Fe, and I want to call Valerie Ames. Someone should call her; I mean, Ellie was her mother. Can you get me her phone number? She lives in Austin."

"I'll find it." Silla hung up.

In five minutes she was back. "Wow, Alice. Ellie Windom's baby girl's done all right for herself."

"What?"

"She's the new associate dean of the College of Arts and Sciences at UT, and according to the *Austin American-Statesman* she's being mentioned as possible interim president since the old prez has resigned. Have you got something to write with? No, never mind, you're driving. I've got the UT directory. I'm texting you her home phone, office phone, and cell."

"Thanks. Everything okay at Ellie's house there?" Alice asked.

"Yes. The security system's working. Any word from the police yet about Ellie's death?"

Alice reported what Files had said. "They've exonerated the horse."

"Of course," Silla said. "That horse was terrified, but it loved Ellie."

"The pathologist thinks Ellie was struck from behind with something heavy, curved, and possibly wooden. According to Files they haven't found a likely weapon. She was killed in the house. She wasn't moved from elsewhere."

"I'd like to get my hands on whoever did this," Silla said. "So, when are you coming back?"

Alice told Silla about Carrie's accident. "I asked Isabel to join me in Santa Fe while Kinsear drives Carrie home. She and I are spending the night in Santa Fe with an old acquaintance, Francis Blake. If we leave early enough, we could be back by seven tomorrow night." She paused. "Hey, Silla. I don't want to leave the box alone. Where's a good place in downtown Santa Fe to grab take-out for dinner? I'm thinking New Mexican since Isabel's been up in the Northwest with all those oysters and raspberries."

"What about The Shed, over on East Palace?"

"Perfect." One hand on the wheel, one on the phone, she texted Francis: "We're bringing supper."

He responded: "I'll eat anything."

This Hot Potato

Alice found Isabel waiting outside at the little Santa Fe airport. Isabel had Kinsear's height, his dark wavy hair, and his laughing eyes. She was attracting interest from everyone on the sidewalk. The two women looked at each other, grinning.

"Another adventure, right?" Isabel said, tossing her suitcase in the back seat.

"Yes." But not too much, Alice hoped. "We need to stop by The Shed to pick up tonight's dinner. Our host claims he'll eat anything. How about you choose for us?"

"Oh, yeah! I accept the challenge." Isabel studied her phone for a few minutes, then called in a menu including poblanos rellenos, posole, and salad. "We'll pick it up in about—" she glanced at Alice. Alice mouthed at her and held up two fingers. "Twenty minutes."

They chattered on the way from the airport to downtown Santa Fe and picked up supper. Then, with the back seat full of aromatic containers, Alice fell silent, preoccupied with the possibility of another theft attempt by either the intruders at Ellie's or by Wayne and Brian. She called Francis: "I need to stash my car and some art from Ellie's. Do you by chance have a lockable garage? And a safe?"

"Yes to the garage. The safe's pretty small." When Alice turned into Francis's cul-de-sac, she saw he'd parked his car on the street. He waved the Discovery into a built-in garage, which he locked. He hauled their suitcases inside and down the hall to a guestroom with twin beds and a view up toward Moon Mountain.

Alice thanked him. "I haven't seen you in over twenty years, and you've blithely taken us in. Along with this hot potato, Ellie's box. Where's your safe?"

"My office." He'd turned a bedroom into an office. The safe was built into the closet wall. "It's eighteen inches square. Should be bigger than most Baumann prints."

Well, Francis would know.

He and Alice returned to the Discovery, hauled the box back to his office, and placed it on his desk. He stared hungrily at the box, then looked at Alice. "I feel like the kid in *Treasure Island.*"

"But I've got to get home with all this," she retorted. "And before we stick them in your safe, tell me the combination."

He laughed, handed her an index card and a pencil, and dictated the sequence. She wrote it down, watching intently as he opened the safe. Then she tenderly lifted the manila folders out of the box and slid them into the safe.

"Alice! These are the basswood woodblocks?" He gently lifted one of the loose blocks by a corner, scrutinizing the paint smudge and the carving. "Do they match the prints?"

"I don't know yet." She lifted the stack of woodblocks into the safe. They just fit.

He relocked the safe. "Satisfied?"

She heaved a sigh. "I'll never again agree to serve as executor for someone with a second home. But you and I are doing this for Ellie."

He nodded. "Listen," he said. "The concert starts at eight. It's after five. How about a glass of wine so I can download your adventures on the road today?"

"Okay. And we can warm up the entrées."

They found Isabel in the living room, riveted by the landscape paintings. Long vistas, purple mountains, the loneliness of the big sky country. "Are these yours?" she demanded.

He reddened. "They are."

"Wow."

He turned to Alice, steady eyes boring into hers. "Okay."

She told him first about the intrusions at Ellie's. "One at night, one the next morning before ten, in broad daylight." She paused. "I wondered if they were students. From their voices I'd say they were young males…not looking for the usual expensive electronics…but something specific. They skedaddled when the Santa Fe Safety truck arrived. By then I'd found the box of prints, which I think is the secret treasure Ellie hinted at. I filmed the contents with the two security guys in the background, watching. I thought we needed a record of the inventory, and the security company's bonded…Then, thinking about driving home alone, not that I mind driving alone, I worried about the box. What if those young intruders followed me, tried to run me off the road? What if, I don't know—I had an accident and the box went missing? The security company boss said I could borrow one of his employees for two days, a guy named Wayne. But when we stopped for gas in Roswell, I spotted Wayne opening the box and starting to pull out a print. He tried to cover it up, but I decided the better part of wisdom was to leave him at the station and get back to Santa Fe to find a reliable companion. Hence, Isabel! She's saved my bacon before."

Isabel's eyes grew rounder and rounder during Alice's tale.

Francis's eyes didn't waver. "So tell me about the prints. You didn't let me peek."

Alice waited, thinking. "Okay. I'll show you the photos."

* * * * *

Francis fell silent after seeing the pictures on her phone. "You know Baumann ground his own pigments, made his own colors?" he said finally.

"I've read that," Isabel said.

"The different wood carvings with their different ink colors had to be placed on the paper in order, and overlaid perfectly," he went on. "His precision…" He went silent again.

They enjoyed a convivial dinner. Isabel regaled Alice with tales of the Kinsear family's trek through America's northwest until the point when Carrie tumbled off the rockface. Then, before it was time to leave for the concert, Isabel announced she'd stay to guard the box. "In my pajamas," she said. "Armed with a book and the poker."

"Lock the doors after us," Alice warned. She and Francis left for the Desert Chorale.

* * * * *

Francis had close-up tickets on the left side of the front row. He leaned toward Alice, commenting on the program, mentioning favorite piec-es, favorite soloists. The singers, in black dresses and tuxes, marched in to applause. The house lights dimmed. As the first notes sounded, Alice felt her whole body melting into the deep attention required by close harmony. She felt worry leave her shoulders, felt the weight of the executor's duties dissipate, felt her soul focus on beauty.

At intermission Alice stood in the lobby with Francis, smiling to herself at the Santa Fe crowd. Plenty of college kids, mostly sitting together in the back rows, exuding youth, talent, and hormones. Maybe some were in the music program at St. John's, she speculated.

The older audience members definitely made a Santa Fe statement. On the women, long dresses, vaguely hippie-ish. Ornate scarves and shawls in brilliant colors. Longer hair. Dangling earrings. The men sported silver curls brushed back on their collars or beyond, rugged canvas jackets, two buttons undone on their shirts, striking turquoise bolo ties. One dark-haired man in a pale suede jacket caught her eye. He stood by the bar with a glass of prosecco, surveying the crowd like a prince waiting for tardy courtiers. He lifted both his glass and an eyebrow at her and offered a smile of invitation. When she didn't respond he waggled an eyebrow again, then blithely rejoined the women near him.

She turned toward Francis, wondering why she felt so "judge-y judge-y," so annoyed by the man. She was puritanical about concert attendance. You went to hear the music, right? To throw yourself into the warm vibrations, the exquisite harmony, the cunning lyrics, the amazing voices that some people could offer the world. Not to troll the bar. Oh, Alice, so judge-y... Beyond Francis she caught sight of a tall man standing alone near the entrance, his hair white at the temples, dressed in a conventional navy blazer, studying his program.

Francis nudged Alice. "The guy by the door? In the blazer? That's Roger Preyer."

Well. Now or never. She looked up at Francis. He raised an eyebrow. "Want to meet him?"

She nodded, sliding a business card out of her purse and pocketing it.

"Roger!" The tall man lifted his head. The lines around his eyes, his mouth, were sad, but when he saw Francis, he broke into a smile.

"Francis!" He started toward them. The men shook hands.

Francis said, "Kristi didn't come tonight?"

Preyer raised his eyebrows. "Believe it or not, she did. She's here somewhere talking to friends. I expect she'll leave after intermission, though." A small smile. "Always in two cars—story of our lives."

"Roger, meet Alice Greer, an old law school classmate. You're living in Coffee Creek now, right, Alice?"

She nodded, watching Preyer's face. His gray eyes lit up. He leaned forward, looked intently at Alice. "Coffee Creek? You may know a friend of mine, then. Ellie Windom?"

Alice stood stock still. "I do. But…"

"What?" His face froze. "Is she okay?"

A male singer, in his tux, sidled up to Francis. "Mr. Blake? Do you have just a moment to talk about the fundraiser?" Francis turned and focused on the singer.

Alice, seeing Roger's face, took him by the arm. "Let's go outside for a moment." She steered him out the auditorium entrance, away from the chattering crowd indoors. Outside, a cool wind rustled the trees. In the east the rising moon lit the indigo sky. Alice shivered and pulled her shawl tighter.

He turned to her, eyes intense. "What is it?"

He and Ellie had just found each other after half a century. She couldn't think of a soft way to give him this news. "Roger, I'm so sorry to have to tell you. Ellie's dead."

"Ellie?" His face paled. "Dead? Not Ellie! What—what happened? Was she in an accident?"

"I'm afraid not." No way to sugarcoat it. "She was murdered."

"Murdered?" The finality of the word knocked Preyer back on his heels. He stared at Alice as if hoping for a different word. "*Murdered?*" His face collapsed in shock, then anger. "What—how did it happen?"

"She was at home. Someone hit her on the back of her head."

He stood, just shaking his head, eyes staring through Alice. "Who did this? Some—some intruder?"

"The police don't know yet. They're still investigating."

Alice slipped the business card out of her pocket and handed it to him. "But if you want, I'll keep you posted on the investigation. I'm Ellie's executor; I'm here to secure her house on Moon Mountain. I understand you and Ellie have seen each other recently. If you can help…or if you want to talk about Ellie, will you call me?"

The lobby bells began to bong softly, signaling the end of intermission.

Alice took Preyer's arm and walked him back inside, glancing sideways at his set face. Foreign service experience…surely he'd had bad news before. But maybe not like this. Francis joined them, watching Preyer with concern.

A shadow fell across Preyer's shoulder. "Roger! I just wanted you to know I'm taking off now." A peremptory voice from a pretty blond woman, with the high tan and eye wrinkles of a desert golfer. She was speaking to Roger, but staring at Alice.

Francis said, "Kristi! Meet my old law school classmate, Alice. She's visiting from Coffee Creek."

"How nice." Kristi Preyer's tone did not match the sentiment.

"You and Roger have children?" Alice asked. What imp made her do that?

"Of course, our son Randall," Kristi said, lifting a proud eyebrow. "He's about to launch a startup. His son, our grandson Beau, is in college. He's a champion lacrosse star." She turned away, saying over her shoulder, "Okay, I've had enough Chorale. Bye, Francis."

No goodbye for her husband and certainly none for Alice. Francis and Alice watched Kristi stride out the lobby doors, crossing the entry patio behind the suede-jacketed man and others.

At her side Roger stared down blankly, unseeing, at his concert program.

Alice touched his hand. "I'm here to secure any valuables at Ellie's house. My…young friend Isabel's helping." She watched Roger's face, waiting for some flicker showing he knew about Ellie's find in the Moon Mountain house.

Roger stood very still, his face expressionless. That must be how he managed negotiations abroad, Alice thought. Don't give anything away.

"How long do you plan to be here?" he asked.

"Not a minute longer than necessary," Alice said. She needed him to rise swiftly to the bait. "Francis is generous, but we'll leave as soon as we can, probably before mid-morning tomorrow." Make it easy… "We'll be working at Ellie's house tomorrow by eight. We'll put our car in the garage so as not to interest the neighbors. Could you stop by?"

Preyer nodded slowly. "Yes." The lobby bell rang insistently. He said, "Time to go in," and walked back into the auditorium.

Francis looked inquiringly at Alice. "Tell you after the concert," she said.

She felt sickened by the apparent emptiness between Roger and Kristi Preyer. Lord, what if marriage did that to her and Kinsear? She shuddered as she paced down the aisle to the front row. Before this night ended, she needed more music, more subtle dissonances, finally resolving into chords that could sooth the ache in her heart.

* * * * *

Isabel, pajama-clad, was peering around the curtain on the front window when Francis and Alice returned. "No burglars!" she declared, brandishing the fireplace poker. "I was armed and prepared!"

Francis laughed. "It's cool here in June. Let's have a fire so you can use that poker. Warm fire, cold prosecco." Over a nightcap, with piñon smoke perfuming the air, Francis posed some tough questions.

"Why do you need to talk to Roger?"

Alice took a sip of prosecco, letting the bubbles tingle, deciding what to say. This was Ellie's secret, and Roger's. But she needed Francis's help, and Isabel's, on Ellie's behalf.

"I can't share this with either of you unless you agree you'll be helping me on Ellie's behalf. And you can't disclose this. Either of you."

"Of course." Francis nodded. Isabel did too.

"They had a child together, as teenagers. Their parents urged them to put the baby girl up for adoption."

Francis lifted an interested eyebrow; Isabel looked surprised.

"That was a common solution then," Alice said. "The kids would forge ahead with college, no one would know, and Roger and Ellie would stay apart for the rest of their lives."

"But it didn't work out that way, did it," Francis said.

"No. Fifty years later, as you know, Ellie and Roger encountered each other here in Santa Fe. When his grandson did a DNA test looking for blood relatives, Roger discovered his birth daughter's current name and whereabouts. He told Ellie. I don't believe she and her daughter have actually met, but she told me she wanted to give her daughter something of value, hinting at a discovery in her Santa Fe house. I assume that's the box of prints we found. Francis, did she or Roger tell you any of this?"

"No—only that they'd been high school sweethearts. Like I said, when I saw them, he seemed riveted, intense, almost enthralled to be with Ellie again. She seemed more cautious." His eyes narrowed. "Alice, do those prints in my safe have anything to do with Ellie's death?"

"I don't know. But the police have determined she was murdered."

"Do they have a suspect?"

She shook her head. "I don't know. They asked me for info on her family members."

"So who were these young intruders who left Moon Mountain empty-handed?"

"You tell me."

She hoped Roger would rise to the bait and drop by Moon Mountain tomorrow morning. How far had he and Ellie gone, in reconnecting? Had they jointly agreed to contact Valerie? Did Roger know about the box in Ellie's attic? If so, did he know who the intruders were? Why was Kristi so icy, so suspicious?

Meanwhile, Silla had sent her that phone number in Area Code 512. Too late right now, but first thing tomorrow she'd call Valerie Ames.

Faint Tang of Mystery

Saturday morning, seven a.m. Mountain Daylight Time. An hour later in Austin.

"Valerie Ames."

The voice was calm, cool, pleasant, matter of fact.

Alice had thought long and hard about what to say to Ellie's birth child. The voice threw her off. Too calm!

But of course Valerie mightn't know her mother was dead.

Or mightn't care.

"My name's Alice Greer. I'm a lawyer in Coffee Creek. I represent the estate of Ellie Windom. Do you have a moment to talk?"

Silence.

After a few seconds the voice said, "The *estate* of Ellie Windom?"

"I'm sorry to tell you that she died last Tuesday."

"Last *Tuesday?*"

Was she concerned about the day itself? Or the delay in telling her?

"I wasn't sure if the Coffee Creek police had let you know."

The voice sharpened. "Why would the police let me know?"

"They asked me for contact info for Ellie's family members. Ellie had mentioned you." Well, that was partly true; Ellie had told Alice that Valerie now lived in Austin and that she wanted to give something to Valerie. From ferreting in Ellie's "Family" folder Alice had learned that Valerie had attended one of Ellie's plays.

"But why the police? What happened?"

"The police believe she was murdered."

"*Murdered?*"

People keep saying that, Alice thought.

After a moment, Valerie said, "Who did it?"

"I don't know."

"When did it happen?"

Why did Valerie want to know when? "Sometime Tuesday afternoon. She didn't show up for a three o'clock appointment she'd made with me. I stopped by around five and found her. She was already dead, from blows to the back of her skull."

"Blows to the…" Silence. "Oh, God." Alice waited. "Three days ago. Three days! I—I wish I'd had a chance to meet her. I did attend one of her productions but didn't…waltz up to introduce myself." She paused. "I loved my Mom and Dad—my adoptive parents, James and Joyce Lewis—very, very much. They gave me everything. The best parents ever. They weren't jealous or insecure. I knew I was adopted, but I had no interest in finding my birth parents. Still, when I was about forty-five, my parents told me their names. They thought the day might come when I'd want to find them."

"Are your—are Mr. and Mrs. Lewis still alive?"

"No. They were killed in a head-on collision on vacation in Minnesota five years ago."

"I'm sorry," Alice said. "They sound like remarkable people."

"They were." Alice heard a sigh. "And they were right. When I got to Austin, I tracked Ellie down. I didn't contact her, but I drove out to Coffee Creek to watch one of her theater productions because…I was curious. That night, she was so vivid, so engaged with those actors, I decided that someday I at least wanted to hear her story, in part so I could decide what to tell my own children. I wasn't ready that night. I'm still not sure what to tell my kids. If anything. They also lost their dad in that wreck." After a pause, Valerie said, "Now Ellie's been snatched away before I could make up my mind. Again."

Alice felt tears rise…and blinked them back. She thought Ellie would want her at least to tell Valerie she'd been thinking of her, but she also had to protect Ellie's confidential communications. "I've got a limited role as executor, Valerie. I just want you to know that Ellie had you on her mind, but she died before we could meet to—to make any decision." In the background someone was saying, "Professor Ames? Excuse me, Professor Ames?"

Alice hurried on. "Right now I'm in Santa Fe to secure Ellie's house here, but I'll be back in Coffee Creek tomorrow night. Can we meet?"

"Yes. Sorry, someone's here I've got to talk to." Click.

Alice hung up, wondering what it was like to learn your own very young birth parents gave you up. When did Valerie find that out? At seventeen, did she know that at that age her mother was pressured to give her up for adoption? Did she wonder what it was like for Ellie to be seventeen and pregnant the summer after freshman year, by another teenager, with their respective parents wanting desperately for them to have a chance at college, to have the freedom to explore options and choose a future, without struggling as teen parents?

Did she wonder whether Ellie ever thought of her, at Christmas, or on her birthday?

And Valerie's children—where were they? She should have asked.

*****

Francis helped Alice and Isabel stow their luggage in the Discovery and gave them go-cups of some excellent coffee. Alice hugged him.

"Keep me posted," he said. "If you get in trouble on the road…I'll head your way."

Alice nodded. "Thanks." She meant it.

Before breakfast the trio had opened the safe and admired the prints again. Francis made Alice match the prints with the pictures on her phone before she loaded the brown expansion folder in the box. Then they rewrapped the box in its blanket and tarp. From the garage Francis produced two straps with a ratchet mechanism, fed the straps through metal tie-down loops in the rear of the Discovery, lashed the straps firmly around the box and tightened the ratchet. "Like tying a ribbon around a big present," Francis said. "That'll slow someone down."

Eight a.m., with a long drive ahead. But first, Moon Mountain.

*****

The morning felt fresh and cool, with that faint tang of mystery Santa Fe always held for Alice. She and Isabel sped up Moon Mountain, parked the Discovery in Ellie's garage, and locked the garage door.

"What a cool house," Isabel said, wandering into the living room. "Okay, what's my job?"

Alice handed her one of the empty banker's boxes. "We'll load Ellie's papers in here. Check the desk in the master bedroom. Put documents on the bed and we'll video them first. If you find jewelry, same. Also, let's check the kitchen drawers for any correspondence or notes."

But Alice's mind was on that mysterious parcel she'd spotted under the eaves in the attic, with maybe chair legs sticking out. She'd just check it. She returned to the guest room, moved the cottonwood ladder to the closet wall, and pushed up the white wooden rectangle in the ceiling.

Soon she was sneezing attic dust. She crawled toward the dark package where the roof met the attic platform.

It felt bulkier than she'd thought.

"Isabel?"

"Where are you?"

"Up here! In the attic! Above the guestroom!"

After a moment Isabel's head appeared in the attic opening. "What are you doing?"

"Help me. Can you get this down the ladder?" Alice put the tarp-wrapped package on the edge of the opening.

Isabel, at five foot ten, had no trouble getting the package down.

Alice followed her and replaced the ceiling panel

"Let's take a look."

They laid the oblong package on the kitchen table, by the window looking out over Santa Fe, glinting in the morning sun below. Now, heart thumping as she saw the paint on the legs sticking out, Alice took a video of Isabel unwrapping the tarp, then unfolding the old blanket inside.

"It's magic," Isabel said.

On the table lay two wooden children's chairs, each painted a distinctive creamy yellow, each with different figures dancing up and down all over the chairs, the slats on the back, the legs, the arms. The top rails, the "ears," and the arms were hand-carved, with curving lines. Alice took another video while Isabel tenderly turned the chairs, showing the scenes—children playing, mountains and waterfalls, deer, pueblos—on the fronts and backs and on the seats and beneath each seat.

Frivolous, fanciful, and as real as any fairy tale.

"Any child would love these chairs forever," said Isabel, eyes shining. "You'd feel like, if you sat in your little chair, any wish you made would come true."

Alice turned the chairs upside down, searching in vain for a signature, for the orange hand symbol. She found nothing. But she too felt the magic. The way the green and gold cottonwoods rippled along the chair rails, above an azure stream, the way the deer bounded across the endless mesa, the perfect sizes and utter absorption of the children playing in the plaza…

She chided herself. What if she hadn't gone back for a second look?

The two women jumped when the doorbell rang. Isabel hastily rewrapped the chairs while Alice answered the door.

Roger Preyer, tall in his sweater and down vest, stood beneath the portal. He walked in slowly, gazing left and right. He took a deep breath. "Ellie's house," he murmured.

"You've never been here?" Alice asked.

He blushed. "I've driven by, a couple of times. Like a lovelorn teenager."

"I'm glad you came. Isabel and I need to leave soon for Coffee Creek. So, let's sit." She waved at the leather armchairs in the living room and watched his face as he took in the landscapes on the wall.

He turned to her, eyes serious, intelligent. "You wanted to talk to me. I want to talk to you. too. But you first."

"Tell me about the last eight months, since you and Ellie first ran into each other. At a Baumann exhibit, right?"

"Right." He nodded, a faraway look in his eyes. "I saw her first. I stared. I wasn't sure I could believe my eyes. After all these years! Then she saw me watching her and…I don't know, it was like the tractor beam in *Star Trek*, pulling us together. We went outside, talking, looking at each other, laughing…her voice sounded the same, her eyes were the same, I *felt* the same, this bubbly feeling. Kind of like being drunk. Like I could say just anything and she'd laugh and give me that great smile."

He shook his head. "I didn't want to leave. Didn't want to go home." He looked up at Alice. "You met Kristi last night."

"Right."

"It's embarrassing to say, but there's nothing left." He tapped his heart. "I've tried hard to take good care of Kristi, tried really hard. She likes her social status, but she always wants more money. Money's really important to her—maybe the only thing she wants from me. That could be my fault. All those years in the foreign service, all the overseas posts, all the secrecy for some of my assignments…she might've been bored, I don't know. Too much golf, too much bridge. Some of the tours were hard duty, even dangerous. She didn't want to join me. Sometimes we'd be apart for a year.

"But sitting in the garden at that gallery talking with Ellie, just as if we'd never been apart, I realized how empty my life is. I love our son, our grandson…but that's all I have. Ellie had just lost Woodie. There we sat, alone together."

Alice realized that Roger's feelings had galloped far ahead of her imagination. "Were you thinking of leaving Kristi?"

He nodded. "Yes. I still am. Just seeing Ellie again made me come alive, when I felt like I was nothing but a scarecrow. Empty. A straw man. I can't go back to that. It's unbearable, that Ellie's dead, that just when I'd found her, I lost her again."

That's what Valerie said, Alice remembered.

"But it's made me think. I've decided to do something different with my life. I've talked to a lawyer here, nice guy, Francis recommended him. There's plenty of money, even if Kristi will never believe it." He paused. "It's unearned money. My parents owned some desolate ranchland out in the Permian Basin. Turns out it's right on top of shale oil. I didn't work for it, and I don't need it. It's just sitting in a trust."

Alice felt stunned. She'd seen Roger as passive, willing to stay for form's sake in an unhappy marriage. "You're—you're thinking divorce?"

He nodded. "Yes. Or at least separation. It's not the first time. I started to leave Kristi years ago, when I came back from my last tour, in Ukraine. Came back to what? Nothing. But we retired to Santa Fe. I've got Desert Chorale, a book group, volunteer work at the community college. I teach some seminars there on foreign relations. Plus our son Randall's in Albuquerque, and our grandson Beau's at St. John's."

At St. John's? Alice sat up. "What year?"

"He's a senior." Preyer went on. "Maybe I'll just move out. But my life's going to change."

"What about Valerie Ames?" Alice said. "Tell me about that."

His face broke out in a smile. "Unbelievable. I never knew where she was, what her name was. Ellie and I talked about that back in November, at the Baumann exhibition. Then at Christmas my grandson, Beau, asked for a DNA test. He wanted to find some blood relatives.

I'm an only child, so's Kristi. So he turns up this girl in Chicago who shares about a quarter of his chromosomes. They'd both agreed to share DNA with close relatives. They got in touch…and the Chicago girl, now moved to Austin, turns out to be Valerie's daughter Anna. Of course Beau came to me, eyes wide. I told him the score. Furthermore, the Chicago kid's got a twin sister, Tania. I got online and did some research, plus I still have friends in the foreign service, et cetera. Bottom line, I found Valerie."

"Did you contact her?"

"Yes. I wrote her."

"Did you talk to Ellie about this?"

"I told Ellie her name, that she'd gotten a job in Austin." He stopped. "Ellie lit up like a Roman candle. She said she wanted to give Valerie something of value. She knew she couldn't permanently infuriate her two boys, couldn't do something radical, but she wanted to do something significant for Valerie."

"Did you, too?"

"Yes. I love the idea. We talked about it. We thought it should be with no strings attached, no expectations for ourselves; we just wanted a chance to show her—now that we've found her—that we never forgot her, that we always prayed she'd have the love she deserved, that we were just kids ourselves…" He made a face. "I don't know that I'll ever get a chance to tell her I wish we'd done something different. Still, it would fill a hole in my heart if she'll let us show her that we never forgot her."

Isabel slipped quietly into the room. Alice introduced her, then went on.

"What about your son? Randall, right?"

"Yes. Randall—he seems pretty chill about Valerie. But Kristi went ballistic. Unfortunately, Beau spilled the beans about Valerie to Randall, who mentioned it to Kristi."

"You'd never told her about Valerie?"

"She's not the forgiving sort. So, no. Besides, she wants us to sink a pot of gold into Randall's startup. His software company's going public. Fine. I still want to give something to Valerie."

"And Randall's okay with that?"

"Yes. Kristi wouldn't be, but she doesn't need to know. Randall's got venture capital coming in. He doesn't even need us, though I'm glad to help him. Thing is, Kristi wants a piece of the IPO. That's something she'll enjoy mentioning at parties." He shook his head. "Sorry I sound so judgmental. Pretty tacky."

She wondered about Beau. "Your grandson, Beau—does he know Ellie owned a house here in Santa Fe?"

Roger frowned. "No. I didn't tell anyone her Santa Fe connection." He looked at his watch. "Whoops. Nine-thirty. I've got a meeting at the community college. I'm glad we got to talk before you leave." He looked straight at Alice. "Drive safely. I'll be seeing you." And he was gone, giving a wave to Isabel as he hurried out the front door.

"Wow," Isabel said, wide-eyed. "Now I wish I'd been at the concert. Is his wife like an ice carving?"

Alice sighed. "Yes. Frozen with fear, perhaps. Maybe she has been for a long time. People crippled by jealousy, people fixated on getting what they see as their share of money…they swim in a sea of fear. Fear that some other child is loved more and will get more money, fear that they won't get the money they think would make them feel properly valued. Fear's a powerful motivator. At least, that's what I've experienced in my law practice." She looked at her watch. "We've got to get out of here. Let's stash the magic in the back of the Discovery and lock up."

The wrapped-up chairs fit perfectly on the floor between the front and back seats.

Before leaving, they checked every window, every door. Alice called Santa Fe Security; Ryan answered. "What's the story with Wayne and Brian? Are they still on your payroll?"

"No, ma'am," he said.

"So I can trust you for the security at the Moon Mountain house?"

"Yes, ma'am."

"Okay, we've armed the security system here," she said. "We're about to head out. You'll call if there's any blip, any question, any hint of intrusion, right?"

"Yes, ma'am."

He'd sure as hell better. Maybe she'd ask Francis to drive by the house a couple of times, too. When she got back to Coffee Creek, maybe she'd get a duplicate key made for him and send it, just in case.

"It's nearly ten. Let's get going." Alice buckled her seatbelt. As she and Isabel rolled down the driveway, Roger's "I'll be seeing you" reverberated in her mind. When?

Off the Map

"What a relief," Alice said. She passed a poky gray minivan inching its way down Overlook and sped downhill. "No Rubicon Jeep and no Santa Fe Safety truck following us." She and Isabel crossed under Interstate 40 and merged into the eastbound traffic.

She'd opted to take I-40 east to Santa Rosa instead of U.S. 285 south to Roswell. She hoped Wiry Wayne had lost interest in her and her cargo. Even if he hadn't, maybe he'd expect to find her on U.S. 285 again. Where she wasn't. The interstate gave her options—exit south toward Encino, or exit at Santa Rosa for Fort Sumner, or…

She handed the map to Isabel. "I'd say, U.S. 84 to Fort Sumner, then east to Clovis and Texico."

They sipped the coffees Isabel had brewed in Ellie's kitchen. Isabel attached her phone to the sound system and played some tunes, many new to Alice.

Alice loved driving alone, especially across these golden hills with their sudden arroyos, their abrupt drop-offs, their vistas, the everchanging sky. She and Isabel had a history now, had built some trust. She felt comfortable in the music, and in the silence, which lasted for several miles.

Then: "I didn't tell you about this boy I met," Isabel said.

"A boy?" Alice glanced sideways, catching the little smile at the corner of Isabel's mouth. A humorous, tender mouth that reminded her of Kinsear. "Where'd you meet him?"

"At the library. Cramming for finals." Isabel had just finished her sophomore year at UT.

"How do you meet someone in the library? I thought it was verboten to chit-chat in there."

"I was in the stacks at the Perry-Castañeda Library looking for the exact book I needed for my final paper on ethical models in decision-making. Just as I got to that bookstack…just as I was getting to the right section…this guy yanked my book right off the top shelf."

"Another psych major?"

Isabel grinned. "Yep. He's a couple of years ahead."

"So who got the book?"

Isabel's grin widened. "I got it nine to five, he got it nights."

"Aha. So you had to…to meet every day."

"So we could discuss the book, of course. And exchange possession."

"What's he like?" Alice's guess was a smart ass, like her dad.

"He's a smart ass. A smart smart ass."

"Meaning interesting?"

Isabel nodded. "Not boring after five minutes. Pretty interesting."

"Interesting meaning also attractive?"

Isabel laughed. "How'd you guess? What is it about interesting men that makes them attractive?"

"Are they attractive because they're interesting?"

"Interesting because they're intellectually challenging?"

Yes, Alice thought, exactly. Her own standards for a lifetime companion involved someone she respected, someone who stayed interesting, someone who smelled right, someone with nice hands.

"So he smells good?" Alice blurted.

"Oh, yeah."

Alice smiled, staring down the long lanes of interstate ahead, watching the signs flash past. Next exit in five miles at Santa Rosa. She was traveling about 79, 80, like most of the traffic. The limit was 75. Alice liked to see a minesweeper ahead of her here and there, someone going faster than she was, someone the watchful trooper would choose to nab instead of her…

"His name's Sam Brody. He's from Menard, out in the Hill Country."

Well, Sam Brody. If Isabel's thinking seriously enough about you to mention you, you better be good to her. Or I'll…

She stared again at the rearview mirror. The gray minivan had settled in behind her, several hundred yards behind. Several cars had passed it, then passed her. She slowed down to 75. C'mon, buddy, you can pass. The minivan slowed too, maintaining its distance.

"Isabel, can you see who's in that minivan behind us?"

Isabel twisted around, squinting through the rear windshield.

"Two guys, I think. Driver's kind of hefty."

"Uh-oh. Watch them."

"I can't quite tell…other guy's maybe on the phone. Like, one elbow cocked. But I'm not sure."

A silver Lexus cruised slowly past Alice and blinked its intention to move back right. It's only half a mile to the Santa Rosa exit, Alice thought. As soon as the Lexus moved right, she stood on her accelerator, passed the Lexus and sped ahead over a hill.

"The minivan's in the left lane, trying to catch up," Isabel warned.

The sign at the hilltop said next exit, Santa Rosa. Alice was down and out the exit before the minivan could get out of the passing lane.

They wheeled into the T&D Truck Stop and parked behind the store.

"I'm pretty sure that was Wiry Wayne and Burly Brian," she told Isabel. "I hope they think we've exited to get on U.S. 84 to Fort Sumner."

"But we're not?"

"Nope." Watching the road for a gray minivan, they crept back through the store parking lot, turned back on 84 going north, then turned east onto a smaller road, New Mexico 156. Isabel clutched the map. "You go on this road for ages, then it wiggles, makes a right-angle turn south, then another right-angle turn east, and goes through some small towns. Are you aiming for Clovis?"

"Yes."

The new highway took them through empty land, golden grass, endless ranches, a few antelope here and there. Tiny roads left and right led off...to where?

"Off the map," Isabel said.

"But no sign of Wiry Wayne and Burly Brian," Alice said. They rejoined U.S. 84 east of Fort Sumner at Melrose, with Clovis the next big town. Not far ahead, Alice could see a gray minivan toiling along. She slowed, wanting to keep the minivan in sight, but hoping Wayne would be peering forward, not backward, hoping that at this distance he wouldn't recognize the Discovery. Had he really been on the phone? Talking to...?

"We could turn south in downtown Clovis onto U.S. 70 and lose the minivan," Isabel offered. "Then turn around and dodge back east. You'd have your pick of roads in Texas, like U.S. 84."

Alice was riveted now on the rearview mirror. A dark Jeep, not black, maybe olive drab, had appeared, staying a sedate distance behind her. No other cars behind her. Just steady Eddie, in the Jeep.

But New Mexico must have had hundreds of Jeeps. Dark ones. Olive drab ones.

Besides, the Rubicon 8 didn't know what her car looked like. Right?

As she considered the issue, wrong. She'd left her car parked right across from Ellie's the night she arrived in Santa Fe. The night the hoodied guy jumped off the back porch. What made her think he couldn't see her car?

But why would the kid intruder, or intruders, follow her out of Santa Fe?

Same reason they were in Ellie's house in the first place.

But who told them what to search for?

That last question was key. She didn't know the answer.

Meanwhile, she sure as hell did not want to be caught alone with Isabel in empty country. For some reason, the Jeep seemed even more threatening than Wiry Wayne and Burly Brian.

"Alice," Isabel said in a quiet voice, "have you no armament?"

"I do," Alice said. "Under the seat."

Isabel rooted around and came up with the packet containing Alice's orange plastic flare gun, plus three remaining flares.

"This is it? This is all we've got?"

Alice nodded. "In the right hands, it brought down a helicopter." She remembered Mr. Navarro saying calmly, "You must hit the rotor." That was after he'd carefully taken aim and brought down the sniper-carrying helicopter on the lonely road.

Isabel raised her eyebrows and began scanning the instructions on the flare gun packet.

"Does Wiry Wayne et cetera know how to find you in Coffee Creek?"

Alice had wondered about that. "Not at home. But Santa Fe Safety has my phone and the office address."

"I'll call Silla. Those bozos might head there even if they aren't following us." Isabel gave Silla the rundown while Alice watched the rearview.

Had the Jeep inched closer? Yes.

"Isabel. How soon can we turn off this road and go south?"

"At the main intersection in downtown Clovis, you turn right on U.S. 70. You're behind the minivan, so if it misses that turn, but the Jeep doesn't, you can try a maneuver from U.S. 70 and take a little road to Muleshoe to lose the Jeep. Okay, there's the sign for U.S. 70!"

Without signaling Alice hurtled right onto U.S. 70, quickly dodged right onto a small side road and turned around again, stopping the car behind a lone cottonwood until the Jeep flashed by on U.S. 70, heading south—yes, an olive drab Jeep, with Rubicon emblazoned on the spare tire cover. Yes, an "8" on the license plate with some blue, some orange. Then she re-entered U.S. 70, staying well behind the Jeep.

"Turn left now!" Isabel ordered.

"You're kidding?" But Alice did turn left, onto a road about the width of her driveway.

"This little baby will take you straight across the Texas line to Lariat. You can get back on U.S. 84 there."

I hope you know how to read a map, Alice thought, dutifully speeding straight east.

She and Isabel heaved a joint sigh of relief as they crossed the Texas line. To celebrate they pulled off at a picnic area marked by a solitary tree, the only tree visible for miles around. They opened the car doors in the international signal for what Alice had heard the French termed a "pipi rustique." Back in the car they high-fived. In Lariat their driveway-sized road entered the four-lane divided emptiness of U.S. 84, and Alice responded by goosing the accelerator. "We can make some decent time now."

"Next stop, Muleshoe," Isabel said. "If you want the direct route, we'd stay on 84 through Lubbock and then southeast through Slaton and Post. Home of Grape Nuts, right? Then decision time: we hit I-20 at Sweetwater. From there you can go south to Wingate and Winters and then 83, or take the interstate to Abilene and get off there."

"I like going south from Sweetwater to find 83, and I don't think anyone will expect it," Alice said.

"Hey! U.S. 83 goes through Menard!" Isabel said.

"Have you ever been to Sam Brody's place in Menard?"

"No. His family has a ranch outside town."

"What do they raise?"

"Goats."

Alice laughed.

"Goats are ecologically sound!" protested Isabel.

"I like goat cheese, I promise." After a pause Alice said, "Do you know the way to his ranch? Is he there by chance?"

"Yes. He texted me the directions. And yes." Isabel blushed.

"Good."

"Why?"

"Because even if we managed to lose the minivan and the Jeep, they might be waiting for us at the end of the road."

They waved at the Mule Memorial in Muleshoe. "Wanna stop?" asked Isabel. "Selfies?"

"No. I'm with the donkeys, not the mules."

The flat cottonfields stretched on forever. No antelope, no mystery. They got gas in Lubbock, and Alice took the wheel again. After Lubbock U.S. 84 entered rough hills broken by the north and south forks of the Double Mountain Fork of the Brazos, with wind turbines, long curves of railroad, fields full of oil equipment. In Sweetwater they ducked under I-20 and took the road to Wingate and Winters. Now the hills were covered with wind turbines, and the highway wound between the high hills, so that ahead through the windshield the huge white turbines seemed to Alice to bob up and down. It was like driving in an arcade game.

In late afternoon they found themselves nearing the blessed limestone of the Edwards Plateau, with its live oaks, cedars, and hidden springs. Alice could feel herself relaxing. At five-thirty in Ballinger they missed the turn onto 83 and had to swing twice around the elegant Courthouse Square. Alice's phone rang: Kinsear. She put him on speakerphone.

Simultaneously each asked, "Where are you?"

"Dad, we're rolling south from Ballinger," Isabel said.

"Pretty country, right? Well, Carrie and I made it past Grand Junction. We'll spend the night in Raton, if we're lucky. If not, Colorado Springs."

"How's Carrie doing?" Alice asked.

"She's okay. Feels like crap. Looking forward to learning how to use crutches, right, Carrie?"

"Yeah, Dad." Carrie's voice, faint.

"How's your trip going?" Kinsear asked. "With Isabel riding shotgun?"

Alice laughed. "She's got strong map skills."

"I'm feeling large and in charge, Dad!" Isabel said. "We lost a couple of unwanted companions. Through clever maneuvers."

Silence.

"Some guys that are too interested in our cargo," Isabel added.

Silence. Then Kinsear said, "Mind explaining that to me?"

"Well, Alice found this amazing art in her client's house, but somebody else seems interested in it too. Without having a right to be interested. But don't worry, Dad, I read all the instructions on the flare gun."

Alice took him off speaker.

"I think it'll be fine, Ben," she said. "We needed to bring Ellie Windom's valuables back to Coffee Creek."

"That's a lawyerly response if ever I heard one," he said. "Dammit. Well, can you please call me when you are safely wherever you're going?"

"Absolutely. We need to get to Coffee Creek and get this box into the office safe, but we've got options, like stopping in Menard, or stopping at your ranch in Fredericksburg."

"I wish I were with you," Kinsear said.

Alice could tell he meant it.

"I do too." She meant it as well. "We should be fine. It's about three hours from Ballinger to Coffee Creek. We'll be home just after dark, unless I get to meet Isabel's friend in Menard."

"Isabel's friend? Who's that?"

She glanced at Isabel, whose eyes sparkled with mischief and maybe something more.

Then she envisioned her office, dark and empty, on Live Oak Street in Coffee Creek. Dark and empty, except for Silla…

"Sorry, gotta go, Ben. Love you."

She ended the call and turned to Isabel. "Remind me what you told

Silla?"

"I told her about the box, and she said she'd wait for us to get there."

Silla, waiting for them. Alone.

"We need a plan." Alice called Silla. Busy signal. Alice had gone from smug and self-satisfied to terrified and guilt-ridden in ten seconds. If anything happened to Silla…she'd never forgive herself.

Perfectly Calm Here

Silla finally answered the office phone: "Perfectly calm here."

Alice discussed the possibility that two, or possibly four, guys might show up at the office, looking for Alice's cargo.

"I'm prepared. They'll have their work cut out for them," Silla said.

"How prepared?"

Silla emitted that expressive "tsk" she sometimes used when irritated. "Alice, don't worry, and don't drive fast, okay? I've got reinforcements. Stay calm."

Alice knew Silla could deal with idiots, roughnecks, angry opposing counsel…could race aggressive horses around tight corners at flat-out speed…surely she could deal with Wiry Wayne and Burly Brian, if she knew what they planned. Or with the youthful intruders at Moon Mountain—again, if she knew their intentions. She didn't, and Alice didn't.

Neither pair might show up.

Or both.

Plan accordingly. What if Silla hadn't accounted for all possibilities?

"What if the minivan and Jeep arrive at the same time?" she asked Isabel.

"Won't they be surprised."

"Unless…when you saw Wiry Wayne maybe on the phone, he was talking to the Jeep?"

"They won't be splitting the box," Isabel retorted. "Wayne and Brian probably see this as their ticket out! Out of being proles with ladders! Didn't Wayne tell you he'd been to the Baumann house? He's got some notion of the value. But he didn't know until after you…"

"Showed them what was in the box. You're right. The Jeepsters, though…someone told them what to look for. They've tried twice. They have some backing somewhere. I don't like that."

"Do you think someone talked? That Professor Graham?"

"He knew I was working for a client…and he knows Francis. You're right, I did mention Ellie's name when I showed him the insurance policy on *The Bishop's Apricot*. One of those things you say, and then instantly wish you hadn't. Dammit." She shook her head. "But Graham wants the appraisal work…surely he knows not to let his

competitors know about this. He won't get hired if he's too chatty."
She thought about Francis, with his clear appreciation of Baumann's
skill. "I don't think Francis would talk either. He knows we've got a
murder on our hands."

"I don't know," Isabel said. "The art community would be pretty
jazzed about newly found Baumann prints. Probably all Santa Fe
would be talking."

Alice nodded.

"What about Roger? He knows about Ellie's desire to make a
gift…does he know about the prints?"

"I didn't ask him flat out. He and Ellie talked about the gift to
Valerie…but he didn't ask me about Ellie's proposed gift, or look
around the house like 'where's the treasure,' did he?"

"No. Why *didn't* he ask you about the gift to Valerie? Why didn't
he ask if you as executor were following through on that?" Isabel
asked.

Hmm. Good question.

Their tires hummed on the blacktop. "Almost to Menard," Isabel
said. "It's so teensy, you'll miss it if you blink. Turn left on Highway
29. The entrance to Sam's ranch is just past the intersection. Look,
Alice, why don't we ask him to meet us right at the end of the drive? I
know you want to get to Coffee Creek. We could use another body!"

Alice smiled in spite of herself. "We could indeed. You could ride
with him if you promise to stay right behind me!"

"Deal."

*****

Alice admired what little she saw of Menard, whizzing through at
dusk. She made the turn onto Highway 29 and turned right into the
drive Isabel indicated. She braked and put the Discovery into park.
She clambered out, stretching after the long siege in the driver's seat.

Isabel was out the passenger door before the car was fully stopped.
Standing at the ranch gate by an elderly cream and brown Bronco was
a rangy twenty-something with a one-sided smile and eyes only for
Isabel, who was looking up at him from under her lashes. Without

looking at Alice she said, "Alice, meet Sam Brody. Sam, this is Alice Greer."

He tore his eyes away, extended his hand to Alice's outstretched hand, bowed slightly and said, "Ma'am."

She liked the humor in his face. He'd do better with Isabel, equipped with humor. Alice noted the roughout boots, the clean, well-used jeans, the overall air of competence, of being generally ready. Hmm. Could be serious.

"We're going to follow Alice to her office," Isabel told him. "I'll explain on the way. You've got gas?"

"I've got gas."

"And we can stay at Alice's, I think, or drive back to my place at Fredericksburg."

"If all goes well, and we get the baby locked in the office safe, maybe we could all have dinner at the Beer Barn," Alice offered. "With not many beers, of course."

"Okay, let's roll." Isabel opened the passenger door on the Bronco. Alice backed around the end of the driveway and pulled back onto Highway 29 heading for Mason, then Fredericksburg, then Coffee Creek…maybe two hours to go. The Bronco's headlights swung into place behind her.

She picked up her phone to call Kinsear just as it rang. Kinsear. "I was about to call you," she said. "So you haven't met Sam Brody? Friend of Isabel?"

A deep short chuckle. "Not yet. Will I?"

"I predict yes. Where are you?"

"South of Colorado Springs, about to stop for the night. Carrie needs a break. We should be back in Fredericksburg tomorrow afternoon. Okay, are you gonna tell me why Isabel's reading instructions on the flare gun?"

"Two sets of yo-yos tried to follow us. I think they're both after Ellie's surprise artwork."

"But you lost them?"

"Yes. They could be waiting at the office in Coffee Creek. Silla says she's ready, but we're bringing reinforcements."

"I don't like this one bit."

"Isabel's with Sam. They're following me. It'll be fine. Gotta go, it's getting dark. Hey, we're on the Texas Forts Trail!"

"If you're where I think you are, off that ridge to your left is the San Saba River valley," Kinsear said. "I've wanted to show you that area. It feels much less settled, much wilder, than some of the Hill Country. Maybe that's just my imagination, or maybe it's the wild history out there. Don't contribute any more wildness, okay? Call me when you can."

* * * * *

Alice glued her eyes to the darkening road, thinking of Silla alone in the office. She liked the idea less and less. Finally, she called Raptor Cellars. Maybe she could get Eddie LaFarge, former pro football center, to leave his wine cellar for a minute.

No answer.

She slowed and turned onto U.S. 87 at Mason, watching the Bronco's headlights follow her, then south across the Llano River and up the hill from the river valley. Ninety minutes to Coffee Creek. Now it was too dark to see Enchanted Rock, the mysterious red granite bulge in the earth's limestone crust, looming to the east. She tried Eddie again. No answer. She tried Silla's cell. Damn! Was she already too late? She sped up. If any roving trooper caught her…

Ahead on the right glittered the neon signs and retro gas pumps of the Hilltop Café. Music beckoned but…she promised herself that, if this all worked out, she'd come back, spend the evening at the Hilltop with Kinsear and the night at his ranch, just outside Fredericksburg.

Now she was on Main Street, trying to make every light heading east on U.S. 290, the Bronco close behind. Fifty-five minutes to Coffee Creek.

As she accelerated, leaving the city limits, her phone rang. Silla. Breathless. "Sorry I couldn't grab my phone, Alice. We were busy."

"We?"

"Where are you?"

"Just passing Stonewall!"

Bad connection. Static, squeaks. "Silla?"

"Sorry…need to charge…" she heard… "we've got to…start…fire…" Fire? Her phone made its "giving up" squawk.

Fire? Surely the office wasn't on fire? All those documents? She and Silla diligently kept paper files of key documents and also scanned everything to the cloud. All her client files, work product, everything on her computer was backed up…wasn't it?

She redialed Silla. No answer. Thoughts grim, Alice sped through Johnson City and made the turn toward Coffee Creek. Fifteen minutes to go…

Come on, she told herself, gripping the wheel, taking the curves on the uphill side of Cow Creek. The Coffee Creek Fire Department is mere blocks from the office. Silla would call the fire department in a heartbeat. But hanging on to the wheel with one hand, she speed-dialed her best friend.

"Alice!"

"Listen, Red, I got a weird call from Silla. Could you call Coffee Creek Fire Department just to be sure there's no fire at my office?"

If she lost her office, where the hell could Alice put the box? She'd counted on the enormous relief she'd feel once she stashed the Baumann prints and woodblocks in her safe, her antique safe, six feet tall, black and gold, bought from the old Coffee Creek Cowman's Bank and bolted to the joists beneath the closet in her conference room. But if the office was on fire?

Eighty, said her speedometer. The Bronco was riding her bumper. Almost there. She signaled for the City Hall exit into Coffee Creek, raced down Tenth Street heading east, turned left on a cross street and slammed on the brakes for the stop sign at Live Oak. The Bronco's brakes squealed behind her. She saw the gray minivan parked across the street, empty, in front of the rental house she'd recently bought. Her office was to the right, past another small house and the old post office property, now dark and vacant.

What the hell was happening at her office?

She saw smoke, but…

Alice pulled slowly around the corner onto Live Oak, heart thumping.

Roped and Tied

A vast black iron barbecue smoker sat at her curb, attached to a tan pickup that now blocked her driveway. Her office lights were on but paled in comparison to the Christmas lights strung across the top of the smoker.

Unmistakably, that was Jorgé Benavides, an owner of the Beer Barn and Alice's favorite client, sauntering across the grass, carrying two beers. Silla, red ponytail flashing in the Christmas lights, took one of the beers and saluted Jorgé with it.

In the street at the curbside smoker, enormous in his chef's apron, tongs in hand, stood Conroy Robinson, still as intimidating as when he'd played in the NFL for ten years as pulling guard on Eddie La-Farge's right side. Alice couldn't recall putting a picnic table in the office's front yard. Perhaps it had arrived in Conroy's pickup. Part of the excellent service….

Two lawn chairs were planted in her driveway. She squinted. Each was occupied. The chairs bounced and wiggled, as if the occupants were trying to get the chairs to dance.

Her phone beeped. Text from Red: "No fire reported at your office."

The neighbors had an RV parked in front of their house. Alice backed up and parked the Discovery in the driveway of the old post office, separated by an unruly hedge from Alice's office property. Sam and Isabel parked the Bronco across the street. They joined Alice as she reached the smoker.

"Alice!" said Conroy, in his soft bass voice. He lifted tongs in salute. "Welcome home! Hey, these ribs are very close to done!"

"Conroy? Eddie?" Alice watched in happy amazement as Eddie backed out of the pickup cab lugging two baskets and carried them to the picnic table. Silla and Jorgé emerged from Alice's office front door carrying a cooler labeled "Beer Barn."

"Hey, Alice! You know these jokers?" called Eddie. He waved a thumb at the driveway.

Burly Brian and Wiry Wayne, roped and tied, glared resentfully at her from the lawn chairs.

"We've met." She glared back at them.

"They're under lawn chair arrest for breaking into your office,"

Eddie said.

"Tell me what happened!"

Silla grinned, saluting Alice with her beer. "I'd asked Jorgé to bring the beer for this little party. He and I were inside your office with the lights out, waiting, when the gray minivan drove past at about three miles an hour. Looking for your address, I guess. They left it down the street."

Alice nodded.

"Conroy and I parked the barbecue rig back by the Courthouse, watching," Eddie said. The Courthouse was a block east of Alice's office. "We saw the gray minivan creeping toward your office. After these two jokers got out, we boogied up the street. Quietly."

"With catlike tread," Conroy added.

"They'd already sneaked through the gate into your back yard."

"So then what?" Alice asked.

Silla jumped back in. "Jorgé and I heard them messing around at the corner of the house. Turned out they'd cut the wires on the security system. Then they broke the window on the back door and unlocked it. They made it through the kitchen and into the hall, carrying their gym bag. We came screeching out of your office and gave chase, and they ran out the back door." She held up her phone. "I've got pictures. By then Conroy and Eddie were waiting in the front yard." She shook her head in admiration, looking up at the two ex-NFL players. "I will just testify that these two guys haven't lost a step. They laid some pro moves on those two losers. Sat on 'em awhile too."

Eddie and Conroy grinned at each other. "Sometimes I miss the old days," Conroy said. "A little contact sport now and then gets the blood moving, doesn't it?"

"And," Silla said, "the gym bag, Alice. Two pistols, wire cutters, various tools." She waved her phone. "More pictures. There's the bag, over by the skinny one."

Sitting in the driveway by Wayne was a gym bag that looked very like the one she'd deposited on top of the gas pump in Roswell. Alice walked over to examine the lawn chair occupants. She admired the way the two men were tied to the old tubular aluminum lawn chairs, arms roped to the chair arms, legs roped to the chair legs, torsos roped to the chair backs. Workmanlike knots.

Brian had a bloody nose. The blood looked black under the street-light. Since he couldn't use his arms, he'd wiped his bloody nose on his T-shirted shoulder. Wayne, eyes miserable, kept sniffing. He looked about to cry. Was that an incipient black eye?

Alice turned to the watching friends. "We should call the sheriff and get these guys charged with breaking and entering and attempted burglary. Armed burglary, given what you found in the gym bag. Obviously, felony charges. Also, they crossed state lines to get here. Maybe federal charges, too?" Alice said. "Conspiracy to commit interstate theft?"

She stared down at the lawn chair boys. Wayne wouldn't meet her eyes. Brian finally did, then looked down again.

"Hope you've got insurance, because I'm suing for repairs."

Their eyes widened. "Didn't think about that, did you?" she snapped. She pushed harder. "Is this a frolic of your own? Or are you two working for someone?"

The two men looked sideways at each other.

"Look, I know you're after the prints you saw at the Windom house. Right?"

They looked down. Finally, "It was his idea!" Brian muttered, nodding at Wayne. "He looked up the prices. Said we could clear a hundred thou."

"All you and the Internet, Wayne? Or did you stop by a gallery in Santa Fe? Talk to a dealer?"

When Wayne didn't look up, she turned to Brian. "Who'd he talk to, Brian? Some gallery staffer? Someone up at St. John's?" Just double-checking on Graham...

"Someone at a gallery downtown," muttered Brian. "Just off the Plaza. Darryn, something like that."

"Does Darryn get to sell the prints?"

Brian looked up, blinked.

Wayne tried to elbow him, but succeeded only in rocking his own lawn chair.

"Darryn takes a cut of the purchase price, then pays you two?"

Brian nodded.

"I don't suppose ol' Darryn committed to pay your legal bills, did he? For criminal defense and also for civil damages?"

Wayne sagged. Brian looked at him.

"Didn't think about that, did you, asshole!" Brian hissed. "Another of your great ideas after getting us fired in the first place!"

Alice's temples pounded with rage. Then, looking at them in the lawn chairs, thinking of Conroy and Eddie sitting atop their prey, she thought, if I weren't so mad, I could laugh at these two idiots. But I'm still too mad.

She remembered her manners. "Jorgé, Silla, Eddie, Conroy. I can't thank you enough. True friends! Let me introduce Isabel Kinsear and Sam Brody. Isabel rode shotgun all the way from Santa Fe, and Sam joined us in Menard. Sam and Isabel, meet Jorgé Benavides, Eddie LaFarge and Conroy Robinson. Sam, meet Silla. She and Isabel are already comrades."

The three men shook hands with Isabel and with Sam, whose eyes had gotten wide. He stared in awe at Eddie and Conroy. "Wow. Wow! Eddie LaFarge and Conroy Robinson? My mom won't believe this. She's such a fan."

Silla hugged Isabel. "Good to see you again, girl." They'd met three months earlier when Isabel had acted as paralegal for a case involving Alice's neighbors on the creek.

Alice remembered the Jeep. "None of you have seen an olive drab Jeep prowling past? Utah plates, 'Rubicon' model?"

They shook their heads no.

"You're sure?"

They nodded.

"Hey, folks, hate to interrupt," Conroy said. "But these ribs have reached the state of perfection. They are ribs of nirvana. Alice, they will soothe your troubled soul."

"Should we let the prisoners have a rib?" Silla asked.

Eddie untied the workmanlike knots on the right arm of each man, first moving the gym bag away from Wayne's chair. Then he put a paper plate on each man's lap, with ribs, potato salad, slaw.

The rest gathered at the picnic table. Alice realized that she and Isabel had barely eaten all day. The two looked at each other and laughed, each with an orange chin from Conroy's secret rub, each with a small pile of bare bones on her plate. And potato salad. "My grandmother's recipe," Conroy said. "Only thing I'll say is, add a little pickle juice." And coleslaw. "I put fresh mint in it," Conroy said.

Alice wished Kinsear were there to press Conroy for more recipe details.

"Before we call the cops, Alice, come see the damage these guys did." Alice followed Silla through the gate into the back yard, furious at the broken window, the cut wires on the security system. "The security people will be here in the morning," Silla said, "and I called your guy Tonio, who said he could fix the broken glass and maybe put a grille inside the back door."

"Good idea," Alice said. But now she worried as they made their way back into the front yard: what to do with the box tonight? Take it home? Maybe Sam and Isabel will come too, she thought, somewhat reassured. She so wanted the contents of that box safely locked in the trusty old safe in the conference room closet in her office, so wanted the responsibility off her shoulders, at least for a while. The magic chairs—well, they wouldn't fit in the safe. Maybe she'd just lock them in the conference room closet.

She heard commotion on the other side of the hedge, heard an engine roar, saw Sam running into the street.

"Hey!" shouted Sam. He raced toward his car. "Isabel! Come on!"

Alice dashed into the street. Across from the old post office, Sam and Isabel climbed into the Bronco, started the engine, u-turned, and raced down the block after a dark Jeep. "Rubicon," mocked the tire cover.

Panicked, Alice ran up the old post office driveway. The Discovery's tailgate, bent and scarred, stood agape. The straps holding the box were slashed. The box was gone.

Kolaches

E ddie, Conroy, Silla, and Jorgé hurried to the street, watching the Bronco disappear around a corner.

"What's going on?" Silla said.

Jorgé jogged over to the Discovery with its gaping tailgate. "What the hell, Alice," he said. "Someone jimmied your car open?"

"I know. I feel like an idiot," she muttered. She knew she should have stashed the box in the office safe immediately, before questioning Brian and Wayne, before eating ribs, before checking the damage to her office. She yanked open the rear car door, peered between the seats, and sighed in relief. At least the Jeepsters hadn't grabbed the magic chairs. She turned to her friends. "Well, locked in the back was the box Isabel and I carted down here from Santa Fe—part of Ellie Windom's estate that I've got to protect. Besides the lawn chair boys, there was another pair of guys we couldn't identify who broke into Ellie's Santa Fe house twice, looking for something. Now they've got it."

To her embarrassment, she burst into angry tears.

"Don't worry," Silla said. "Isabel's on their tail."

Alice's phone rang in her pocket. Isabel, breathless, car noise in the background. "They're on Highway 71, going east toward Austin. We're behind them, staying back so they don't spot us. I'll call with updates. Don't worry, Alice. They'll be sorry they ever messed with that box."

Whoever they were, they weren't on the way to Santa Fe. So who…? Then Alice felt a wave of pure terror: Kinsear's daughter was speeding across Texas after two unknown quantities, bold enough to steal a box out of Alice's car when she was just a hedge away. "Isabel, promise me, whatever you do, don't speed!" she yelled into the phone. "Be careful!"

But Isabel had hung up. Oh, God, if Isabel died in a high-speed chase, Alice would never forgive herself…

She took a deep breath. Then she walked back to her front yard, called the Coffee County Sheriff's Department and asked for Detective George Files. Miraculously, he was on duty on Saturday night. "George, help. Kinsear's daughter and her boyfriend are chasing the guys who just robbed my car of a client's very valuable artwork. Remember Isabel?"

He did, from the flood case.

"She's in an old cream and brown Bronco, Texas plates; they're in an olive drab two-door Jeep, soft top, 'Rubicon' on the rear, Utah plates with an eight. Heading east on Highway 71 toward Austin. Can the DPS be on the lookout for them?" The DPS, Texas Department of Public Safety, had highway jurisdiction.

"It's Saturday night. There may be some troopers out, at least between Bastrop and LaGrange." That stretch was a known speed trap. "I'll see who's out there."

Alice thanked him. As she reported what he'd said, she glimpsed a smirk on Wayne's face.

Brian hissed at him through his teeth. "Stop it!"

"Don't think that lets you two off the hook!" she snapped. "Now it's your turn!"

* * * * *

Only five minutes after Alice's call to the main desk, a mild-mannered, middle-aged deputy, name tag Arnold Stowe, climbed out of a Coffee County Sheriff's Department SUV. He tipped his hat, introduced himself, and raised his eyebrows at the roped-up prisoners.

"Hey, we fed them supper," said Silla in indignation. "They hardly deserved Conroy's ribs after what they did. It was magnanimous on our part, given that they'd cut the wires on the security system and broke the back window and—"

Alice introduced herself and the rest of the group.

"Anywhere we can sit down, ma'am?"

"Yes, at the picnic table. By the way, Deputy Stowe, have you had supper? Because there's leftover ribs and potato salad and slaw."

"And my banana pudding." said Conroy's deep voice. "No commercial pud, man. We're talking my homemade custard. My mama's recipe."

Stowe took statements from Silla and Jorgé, and Eddie and Conroy. Then Alice had to describe how she'd met the two men in Santa Fe, show the pictures of the box with the two men watching her video the prints, mention that she'd spotted Wayne opening the box in

Roswell and that Brian had come to get him, and state that their boss had reportedly fired them. Yes, the prints might be valuable. Yes, the two men might know of their potential value. Yes, they had followed her down from Santa Fe. There was a second witness, Isabel Kinsear. No, Isabel couldn't give a statement right now… Alice gave him Isabel's contact information.

Silla took him to see the cut wires and the broken window. When they returned to the picnic table, she said, "Don't forget the gym bag, sir. That's what they were carrying when they broke in. We saw two pistols in there."

"You didn't touch them?"

"Of course not."

"I think I got it all," said the deputy, glancing at Alice. He noted the contact information of all those present. "Now if you're serious about the barbecue, I had Cheetos from the vending machine for dinner. So…"

"I'll make you a to-go plate," Silla said, deftly ladling ribs, slaw and potato salad onto paper plates and covering them with other paper plates. "Okay if we get the security system and the window fixed tomorrow morning? Do you need pictures or anything?"

"I'll send someone over first thing in the morning, when it's light," he said. Then he called in for reinforcements. Another pair of deputies appeared in a cruiser. Eddie and Conroy helped untie the prisoners. The officers handcuffed them, took the gym bag, and disappeared back down Live Oak toward the jail at the Courthouse.

Isabel and Sam had been gone about forty minutes. Alice kept looking at her phone, waiting to hear from Isabel. She knew Kinsear was expecting a call but dreaded having to tell him she'd not only lost the box but that his elder daughter was careening down a highway after the thieves.

Bing! Message from Isabel: "They're passing the Austin airport going straight east on Highway 71. We're behind, lying low."

"Don't speed!" Alice texted.

Eddie and Conroy packed up the picnic table, tied down the rig, and hugged Alice goodbye. She felt her eyes fill with tears and pretended they hadn't. "Thank you."

Jorgé carried the Beer Barn cooler back to his car, came back and hugged both Silla and Alice. "Thank you so much, Jorgé," Alice said.

"My pleasure. Always exciting, Alice, being your client." He grinned and left.

She started to say, "What if those guys had shot you and Silla?" But she could hardly bear the thought.

"Okay, boss," Silla said. "I'm gonna lock up. Are Isabel and that young man staying with you tonight?"

"Yes," Alice said. "I expect they are."

"I'll come in for a while tomorrow morning. We've got to deal with that Smutbuster lawsuit against the Library Board. The president asked you to call her on Monday. Plus, one of Ellie's sons called with questions about the estate process. Shouldn't we set up a conference call with them? Also, did you finish your CLE requirements?"

Alice shut her eyes in horror. "No."

"You can listen on your car audio. Hand me your phone."

Alice reluctantly handed it over. Silla darted into the office. Alice saw lights on in her workroom. In a few minutes the lights went out and Silla trotted back out the front door. She handed Alice her phone and a thumb drive. "I downloaded that riveting estates and trusts annual update program on both these. Listen on the way home. You've got one more day of grace."

"Thanks, Silla."

Alice's phone rang. Isabel.

"Alice, we're in LaGrange." LaGrange was a small town east of Austin, about eighty-five miles from Coffee Creek, with a long history and many residents of Czech heritage. Alice was partial to the jerky at the LaGrange Smokehouse.

Isabel sounded flurried. "Listen, they're stopping at the Weikel! Gotta go!" She hung up.

The Weikel! A roadside emporium famous for its fruit and cream kolaches, simultaneously rich and light, utterly delectable. The original small Czech bakery had morphed into a vast gas station complex with a large store containing glass cases of tray upon tray of strudel, sweet rolls, pigs-in-the-blanket, and especially kolaches: cherry, apple, apricot, peach, lemon, cream cheese, and Alice's favorites—prune and poppyseed. Although if apricots were in season, she went with apricot.

In her mind Alice saw the young hoodied dude leaping from Ellie's back porch. Yes, that guy would want to stop at the Weikel, would probably get pigs-in-a-blanket and, oh, cherry or apple. Her faves were the traditional Czech. She realized she was drooling, even after those ribs.

"Where are they?" Silla demanded.

"At the Weikel!"

"You think she'll bring us back some kolaches?"

"Those guys *stopped* at the Weikel."

Silla got a faraway look in her eyes. "The Weikel. You can park in front or around at the side…"

"Or out at the pumps," Alice added.

"Those guys in the Jeep probably need to pee…"

"That'll be inside, at the back," Alice remembered.

"Then they'll have to walk back past those glass cases full of ko-laches…"

"Right," Alice said.

"Do you think they locked the Jeep?"

"Didn't have much in the way of doors, that Jeep. It had a soft top. I think those side windows are just zipped in."

"So…?"

They stared down at Alice's silent phone.

*****

"Can you hear me?" Isabel on the phone, breathless. "We got it!"

"You did? Oh my gosh." Alice put her on speaker. She and Silla stood, heads bent together, staring down at the phone as if they could see Isabel. "Are you okay? Where are you? What happened?"

"The Jeep stopped at the Weikel. You know how you can park in front or on the side by the gas pumps?"

"Yes."

"Those guys parked on the side. We stayed back behind them and watched them both go into the store. *Both* of them." Isabel wasn't impressed with their behavior. "Pretty dumbish."

"And then?"

"We snuck right up by the Jeep. I got out and followed the Jeep-sters into the store so I could keep an eye on them, slow them down if necessary. Sam got the box out the side window of that Jeep in ten seconds and put it in the Bronco and drove around to the other side of the store and texted me where he was."

"Yes!" Alice said.

"So I stayed inside, staring at the kolaches until the guys came out of the men's room, one at a time. The first guy of course had to order kolaches. I've got a good picture of him, face riveted on the baked goods in the display case. I also got a shot of the other, the one with curly hair. I'll send them to you in just a sec. I heard the second one say, 'Hey, Draco, get me two cherry ones and a pig-in-the-blanket.'"

Alice would have been so surprised if he'd ordered poppyseed. But…Draco?

"It looked like the curly-haired guy was going to head outside, so I beat him to the door, beat feet to the far side of the Weikel, jumped in the Bronco, and we took off."

"They didn't see you?"

"I don't think so. We were on the other side of the building. Plus, you know how when you leave the Weikel, you have to do that weird loop under the highway to head back toward Austin?"

"Right."

"Well, we were speedy but quiet in our departure, and nobody followed us so far as I can tell. There must've been a wreck behind us, though. We saw an ambulance and some state troopers pulled over. We're already nearly to Smithville."

"And the box looks intact?"

"It's still wrapped up tight. I don't think they had a chance to open it."

Alice let out a huge sigh of relief. But she couldn't relax until she had Isabel and Sam safely back and under her roof. With the box.

"It's maybe an hour from Smithville to Coffee Creek," Alice said. "You remember how to get to my house? I'm going to be a nervous wreck, pacing the floor till I see you two!"

Isabel laughed. "It's been a long day. We should be glad the Weikel was still open. If it had been closed—no kolaches to tempt those guys—we might not have had the same luck."

Alice shook her head at the realization that it was still Saturday. From Santa Fe to Coffee Creek…and, for Sam and Isabel, to LaGrange and back…

"A very long day. Will you please text me your progress and confirm no one's after you?"

"Yep." Isabel hung up.

Silla and Alice looked at each other. "Told you she'd get it back," Silla said.

Alice nodded. "But how much can I tell her dad?" Then, "Silla, I can't thank you enough…" She stopped, searching for adequate words.

"Are you kidding? I wish every day were equally exciting. But let's bail. Tomorrow's almost here."

*****

Driving home, listening to her CLE download while the broken latch on the tailgate of her Discovery banged at every bump in the road, Alice realized she hadn't looked at Isabel's pictures. She'd forgotten to ask if Isabel got the plate numbers on the Jeep. She wondered about the Jeep's destination, if not Santa Fe.

The creek road was dark and empty. As she neared the gate leading to Ellie's house, she slowed, glanced up at the house. Also dark and empty. She hadn't heard a word from Files: had he found the murder weapon yet?

After she passed through her own gate, Alice pulled up Isabel's message attaching pictures. The first—oh, Isabel, bless you—showed the Utah license plate. All digits, including the 8. Then came the box thieves—one with dark curly hair poking out from under an Astros ball cap, one with straight sandy hair, staring intently through the glass at the kolaches. Both slim, T-shirted, twenty-ish…students, that's what they looked like.

Eleven-thirty. An hour earlier in Colorado. She parked, unlocked her house, turned on all the outside lights to welcome Isabel and Sam, and called Kinsear.

"Finally," he said softly. "I'm whispering because Carrie's asleep."

"What a day," Alice said. "Your Isabel and her friend Sam saved my bacon." She recounted the smoky surprise they'd found at the office, with Wayne and Brian riding lawn chairs, then the awfulness of finding the box gone, then the rapid departure of Sam and Isabel, in full cry, and their coup in the Weikel parking lot.

"I was so angry with myself," she told Kinsear. "All that time and effort to get the box to the office and then…"

"Oh, come on, Alice! Dealing with two sets of rascals at once? But you say Isabel and this boy got it back?"

"Yep. They should be getting here in the next twenty minutes."

"Who are the dudes who broke into the Discovery?" Kinsear asked.

"Maybe students at St. John's in Santa Fe. Their Jeep looks like one I saw in the student parking lot. They were headed toward Houston, stopped at the Weikel, and left the box unattended in the Jeep. According to Isabel, it looked unopened. I hope she's right." She paused. "So, I guess I'll try putting Sam in John's room and Isabel in Ann's?"

Kinsear snorted. "Well, for starters. I need to meet this Sam guy."

"You do."

They were both silent.

"I miss you—"

"I wish we were—"

They both laughed. "I can't wait to see you," she said.

"Same. Let's figure it out tomorrow. But how about you up the ante on phone calls? You're in deficit mode right now. Maybe tomorrow you won't be gripping the steering wheel and driving too fast to call me."

"Okay. Sleep tight. I love you."

She went back out into the dark night and finished unloading the car, grousing to herself about the busted lock.

Back inside she checked the hall bath—yes, decent towels. She checked her kids' bedrooms. Yes, clean sheets. She turned on the bedside lamps.

She found an open bottle of zinfandel in the refrigerator and

poured a glass and sat down at the kitchen island. The wine tasted…
delicious. She sat, sipping, letting images rise in her mind: Ellie's face,
talking about that moment she realized how nice it felt to sit with
Roger…her own scramble into the Moon Mountain attic…Roger
Preyer's grief, as he stared blankly down at the concert program. Then
the rush, hightailing it across New Mexico and Texas, dodging the
minivan, dodging the Jeep, all this frantic anxiety—all for Ellie Windom. Who shouldn't have died. She lifted a glass and said aloud, "To
Ellie. Client and friend." And added, mentally, I will by God find out
who killed you. And I will get in touch with your birth daughter. I
promise.

Then she saw headlights in the driveway. Now to deal with her
lover's daughter, and the daughter's…well, she'd soon know.

*****

"I've put you in my son's room," Alice said to Sam. "Isabel, I put you
here, in Ann's room. Bath's down the hall."

They thanked her and threw their bags in their rooms.

"Are you hungry? I've got Blue Bell Cookies and Cream. And
some Dulce de Leche."

Their faces lit up. Back to the kitchen they trooped. The box,
still in its blanket and tarp, sat on the kitchen island where Sam had
deposited it, next to the wrapped-up chairs. Alice had gone around the
house and checked all the locks, twice. She planned to carry the box to
her bedroom.

When all three were ensconced at the kitchen island, spoons in
their ice cream, Isabel said, "Here's what I think is weird, Alice."

Alice looked up.

"Those guys had the box, in its same blanket and tarp, just sitting
in the back seat of the Jeep."

"With the seat belt around it," Sam said. "Sorta. Wouldn't have
held it for a second if they'd turned over."

Alice shuddered. The hand-painted box, the prints, the delicate
basswood woodblocks…

Isabel went on. "It's like someone told them, 'Go get this'…well, maybe they didn't know what they were looking for. 'Go get this package.' But that someone didn't really tell them enough that they could appreciate its importance or value. I mean, if I'd spent the effort they did, two break-ins and an eight-hundred-mile chase, I'd want to know why."

"And if they couldn't lock the Jeep at the Weikel, which, I mean, zip-off windows, I'd sure as hell have left someone to watch it," Sam said.

"So they just considered this a lark," Isabel concluded.

Isabel and Sam finished the ice cream, giving their spoons a final lick, smiling at each other.

"I've got to go in early tomorrow," Alice said, suddenly lonesome for Kinsear.

"We'll head to Fredericksburg," Isabel said. "Meet Dad and Carrie when they get home. Give Dad a break from taking care of Carrie."

"And introduce him to Sam!" Alice said, grinning. "I've already told him you two saved my bacon, going after the Jeep."

Chapter Fourteen

Let's See How This Goes

Sunday morning; no traffic. At the office Silla was supervising the security system repairs. Alice carried in the box and carefully deposited it by her desk, then went back to her car and carried in the magic chairs. She plopped down at her desk and sighed, turning on the computer, intending to finish watching her CLE video. But she spied welcome distraction: front and center on her desk sat the complaint filed against the Coffee Creek Community Library Board by Mary Ellen Stokely, aka (at the library at least) Ms. Smutbuster.

Alice flipped to page two to learn what had drawn Ms. Smutbuster's ire this year. Last year she'd tried to ban *Captain Underpants*. This year?

"You're kidding," she breathed. *Harry Potter*, all volumes? Ms. Smutbuster wanted the books banned for including magic and witchcraft, sexual references, violence, and characters using "nefarious means" to attain goals.

Alice's blood pressure soared. Two years ago Ms. Smutbuster had complained about Susan Cooper's Arthurian fantasies; the library had spent hours dealing with her. Last year Ms. Smutbuster had filed her own lawsuit, reportedly unable to find a lawyer to take her case pro bono. Ms. Smutbuster was still an unknown quantity to Alice. When Alice served initial discovery requests on her (demanding that Ms. Smutbuster identify offending passages, explain her legal theories, and list potential witnesses and experts), and Ms. Smutbuster didn't respond within the required thirty days, Alice filed a motion to dismiss. Ms. Smutbuster withdrew her complaint before Alice ever met her.

This year, Ms. Smutbuster had found a lawyer—Edmund Fleischer, a man Alice knew vaguely from Rotary. Alice glared at the complaint, tired of these annual fire drills, tired of the stress it caused the librarians and the Library Board. She hammered out a brief answer to the lawsuit and served her initial request for disclosures, along with a request to depose Ms. Smutbuster and a discovery demand for Smutbuster to list all books she'd either read to her own children or, in the last five years, allowed her children to check out of a library.

She emailed her drafts to the Library Board president for discussion on Monday. Then she leaned back and closed her eyes, imagining questions she could ask at Ms. Smutbuster's deposition…about magic…and magical thinking…Cinderella…Santa…could be a lot of fun…

Silla stuck her head in. "The security guys have finished, Alice." She stared at the packages on the floor. "Hey, is one of those our treasure box?"

"Yes. Plus some hand-painted chairs. Let's get this stuff stowed in the safe." Alice carried the box to the conference room and laid it on the table. Silla pulled open doors to the conference room closet where the heavy antique safe resided.

Silla helped remove the tarp and blanket. An involuntary "oh!" escaped her as she saw the butter-yellow painted wood, the dancing figures. She turned the box gently from side to side. "I see," she said. "All four seasons. Alice, what a treasure."

Alice lifted the latch.

First, inventory. She and Silla gently pulled out the folders containing the prints and spread them on the table. The first two were empty. Silla lingered over the third folder, brilliant yellow cottonwoods and a mountain stream. "*Chama Stream*," said Silla. "I'd like that on my wall." She opened the fourth folder. "Scary! *Deception Peak*."

Alice showed her the photos she'd taken at Moon Mountain. They matched each photo to a print. "Seven photos of seven prints," Silla said. "How come the last five folders also have these vivid watercolors of the same scene? And why no titles?"

"No idea."

"Forward me those photos for the file," Silla said. "But what about these two empty folders? And the loose woodblocks at the end?"

Alice shook her head. "Already empty when I got the box. Okay, let's tackle the woodblocks."

Per Francis, each block was used for only one color; most prints involved at least four blocks. Alice gazed at the two empty folders. "Let's assume the unassigned blocks belong to those folders. Maybe each folder gets a blue, a green, a gold, a black. Maybe a rose or orange?"

"But we have no idea what the pictures are supposed to be," Silla pointed out. "And some blocks show no paint."

"True."

"You think we're missing two prints but maybe have the blocks for them?"

"Maybe," Alice said. "These two folders just represent our best guesses."

They repacked the box and loaded it into the safe. Alice pushed the heavy steel door shut and spun the combination lock. She stowed the wrapped-up chairs in the corner of the closet.

Silla shut and locked the closet doors.

They looked at each other. Silla frowned.

"Yeah, but can you think of a better place?" Alice asked.

"The office safety deposit box?"

"Too small," Alice said. "So's my personal one."

"What if I hire us a security guard?" Silla said. "For night duty. An off-duty cop maybe. Just for a month."

"Good." Alice was tired of playing security guard.

*****

Silla stuck her head back in Alice's doorway. Alice gratefully hit 'pause' on the CLE video.

"Chuck Windom's on the phone. Ellie's older son. He and his brother Don are talking to Ellie's pastor about the memorial service. He wants to know when Ellie's body will be released. I'm transferring him to your phone."

Coffee County had transported Ellie's body to the Travis County medical examiner in Austin. Had the medical examiner finished with the body?

She picked up the phone. "Hi, Chuck."

Chuck Windom sounded tired, uncertain. Alice felt a wave of sympathy. Burying our mothers…we don't get much experience for that.

"Mom always said she wanted to be cremated," he said. "Like my dad was."

"I'll check but it may be two weeks before that can be scheduled," Alice said. "With cremation, in a murder investigation, before the body's released, the police have to be sure they have whatever evidence is needed."

"Oh."

"But if you're having a memorial service, that won't matter, right? The family will get the ashes later."

"I guess so."

"I'll check back with Detective Files for you. Will the service be at Holy Spirit Episcopal, like Woodie's?"

"Yes."

She switched gears, told him security measures were in place for both houses and that she and Silla were completing an inventory. "Given the original artwork in both houses, it's probably wise to have an appraiser for each. Unless you and Don are already in full agreement as to who would get what."

There was a pause.

"Get appraisers, please." And he hung up.

Hmm. An insight into brotherly love? Family dynamics?

Alice left a message for Files asking about release of Ellie's body. Then, grumbling, she finished the last two hours of her CLE video. "Silla, could you send in my CLE report? I'm street-legal now."

Next on the list: she needed to meet with Valerie Ames. She called.

Valerie Ames sounded distant, preoccupied. "Do we need to meet today? I'm preparing for some meetings tomorrow at UT."

"It would help if we could meet today." She wanted a sense of Valerie Ames before she met with Ellie's sons and their families. Just part of being prepared. "It shouldn't take long."

Valerie Ames gave Alice directions to her house and hung up.

At least on Sunday the traffic won't be so bad, Alice thought. Let's see how this goes.

Who Was the "Someone"?

Valerie Ames lived off Seventh Street, close to Lake Austin Boulevard, in a renovated two-story on a street where some imaginative gentrification had occurred. Alice opened the gate in a low stone wall and crossed a courtyard to an entry framed by big Mexican pots filled with blue and purple salvia.

The front door opened. Alice's heart stopped. Valerie was a younger dead ringer for Ellie, with Ellie's intense brown eyes, dark hair, dramatic eyebrows, graceful hands…yet this woman was not a drama teacher but a self-possessed college dean with an air of self-command. Same thing, perhaps.

"Come in." Valerie led the way to the living room.

Alice took in the vivid art on the walls, the folk art sculptures, the comfortable sofas and chairs in the living room. Maybe Valerie Ames was secretly fun-loving and welcoming? But today, all business, and probably wondering why Alice was there.

Valerie sat in an armchair, waiting for Alice to speak.

"I'll bet this is high on your list of weird experiences," Alice said.

Valerie gave a short laugh. "Along with hiring a genealogist to find my birth parents? And then finding them, just like that. Yes."

Alice couldn't help herself. "You look so much like Ellie!" After a moment she added, "I can't believe she's gone."

"Me either," Valerie said. "I'd made up my mind that at some point I'd have to take the plunge and meet her, if that's what she wanted. I told myself the world's too big for me not to reach out to her, and too small for me not to bother. But now she's gone. And you're here. You said this was a murder investigation. Do the police know who killed her?"

"Not yet."

"When you called before, I couldn't believe she'd died on Tuesday. That morning I got a package from her. I want you to see what she sent." She stood and disappeared down the hallway, then returned with a large flat overnight delivery box, already opened. She pulled out the contents, individually wrapped in bubble wrap, and handed them to Alice.

On top, a woodcut print of a night scene, about a foot square, titled *Moon over Taos Village*. Alice unwrapped the second: another woodcut print, all blue sky and little figures in a pueblo square, called *Children at Chimayo*. Both bore Baumann's signature and the little orange hand-heart. She pulled back the bubble wrap on the third, still in its frame: *The Bishop's Apricot.*

For a moment Alice couldn't speak.

"They're wonderful, aren't they," Valerie said.

"You got the package Tuesday morning?"

"Yes. About ten-thirty. It was a complete surprise."

"Was there a note?"

"Yes. Very short. She said she loved *The Bishop's Apricot* and hoped I would too, and would I give the other prints to my children. My twins, Anna and Tania, are juniors at Austin High. Well, I picked up the phone and called her. One of my rules is, life's too short not to say thank you. I didn't get her but left a message. I figured she'd worry if she didn't hear, since she'd sent the box overnight delivery. Her phone number was on the box so I had no excuse for not calling. I admit I was glad to leave a message, because I really wasn't ready to talk to her. I mean, what do you say when your mother gave you up for adoption?" Her eyes met Alice's. "I'm glad now that I called."

Not as glad as I am, Alice thought.

"Then she called back. I was in the car, driving to UT. I barely had time to say 'thank you' when she said, 'Oh my, I've got company. Someone just walked into my house. May I call you back?'"

"That's exactly what she said? 'Oh my, I've got company. Someone just walked into my house'?" Interesting phrasing, Alice thought. As if Ellie knew the "someone" who'd walked in and wanted to make that "someone" aware Ellie was alerting her telephone caller to the arrival. "What time was that?"

"Maybe twelve-thirty."

"She didn't say who'd walked into her house?"

"No. She sounded a little surprised."

"She said she'd call you back?"

"Yes. But she never did."

Files will need to hear this, Alice thought. He'll want to see the box and the note. Before she could speak, Valerie said, "Look, Alice. I wanted to thank Ellie Windom for this gift. But I want no further involvement with her family. I'm not interested in meeting her kids. They probably feel the same way—shell-shocked. I've got to think about my own kids' needs at this point. They know nothing about Ellie or any of the rest of this."

"The police will need to hear about her call to you. And they'll want to see that overnight delivery box and her note, to figure out a time line."

"Right. Of course I'll talk to the police. But I'm hoping for minimal involvement. I've got a lot on my plate right now, with my new job, and I still don't know what I'll tell my own children." She gave Alice a long look. "You understand, I'm sure."

Alice nodded. "You've helped me. I wanted to meet Ellie's daughter. I wanted to tell you she'd been thinking of you in the days before she died. She obviously took matters into her own hands in making this gift." She thought for a moment. "Valerie, I assume you're familiar with the artist who made these prints?"

"Somewhat," Valerie said. "From Santa Fe, right?"

"Right. I know you'll want to keep them safe, but you might also want them appraised. They may be pretty valuable." Alice hoped she'd take the hint. Meanwhile, she thought, at least I've done what I can to fulfill Ellie's wishes. And I've met a pretty impressive woman, for what that's worth. She stood up, smiled.

So did Valerie. "Thanks for taking the time, Alice. I'm glad we've met. Sorry, but I've got to head to the office."

"Me too." Alice said goodbye.

On the way back to Coffee Creek, she called Files and left a message about the overnight delivery. He had Ellie's phone…which might contain key evidence, of Valerie's message, of Ellie's call to her.

Who was the "someone" who'd walked into Ellie's house?

Maybe She'd Win the Lottery

Monday morning. On the way to the office Alice dropped off the Discovery at the collision repair shop and picked up a nondescript white loaner car. The clerk squinted at the Discovery. "Didn't we just fix your Discovery maybe two months ago after that woman rammed you?"

Alice sighed. "Yes," and climbed into the loaner…redolent of stale fast food. She stuck her head out the window. "Can you please put a rush on my car?" she called to the clerk.

✻ ✻ ✻ ✻ ✻

"Coffee's up," Silla called when Alice pushed open the office door.

"Silla, I need some help." Alice briefed her on the visit with Valerie. "So the day before she died, Ellie sent Valerie by overnight delivery not only *The Bishop's Apricot*, still in its frame, but two other unframed prints."

Silla blinked. "Aha," she said. "Did she show you the two prints?"

"Yes. Let's get that box out of the safe."

In the conference room, they unlocked the safe and lifted the box onto the conference table. Alice pulled out the two groups of unassigned woodblocks.

"One print's called *Moon over Taos Village*. It's got mountains in the background. The other's called *Children at Chimayo*, with kids playing on a pueblo square," Alice said.

"What about the colors?"

"*Moon over Taos Village* is dark, lots of blue, except for the moon. *Children at Chimayo* has the ocher pueblo and bright little shirts on the children."

They laid the woodblocks on the table, scrutinizing the delicate carving.

"I see mountains there, right?" Silla pointed at one woodblock. "Does the pueblo scene have mountains?"

"I don't think so." Alice moved the mountain woodblock to her left. "Children here," she said. "See their heads?" She moved that woodblock to her right.

Slowly they separated the blocks into two groups.

"An expert could second-guess us," Alice said. "But I think those two prints likely came from these blocks."

They re-stowed the woodblocks and relocked the safe and closet. Silla turned to Alice. "Those prints were already gone when you found the box in the attic in Santa Fe!"

"Yep." Alice laughed. "That Ellie! I bet she brought them with her when she flew back from Santa Fe, maybe the last trip, and left the box in the attic."

"Then sometime last Monday she lifted *The Bishop's Apricot* from her dining room wall," Silla added.

"After Don left." Alice was remembering the harsh words Judith Strong overheard. Did that trigger Ellie's decision? "Then she hauled off and sent all three pieces to Valerie Ames. Can you find that receipt?"

"Sure." In two minutes Silla was back with the folder of items from Ellie's car. She and Alice peered at the paper receipt showing Ellie had delivered the box to the overnight company on Monday for delivery in Austin on Tuesday morning.

"Well, those three items should have an asterisk, if we list them on the inventory. Speaking of which, are we nearly done with our draft?"

"Just about. I've included financials, personal and real property, and tax valuations. What about appraisals?"

"Can you call Mackie Appraisal about appraising the Coffee Creek real estate and house contents as soon as possible? I'll call that Santa Fe art prof about the Santa Fe house."

"Yes."

Silla disappeared to her work desk, and Alice called Clare Graham in Santa Fe.

"Hey, I thought you'd ditched me! Am I still in line to be your appraiser?" he asked.

"You told me you wouldn't charge for travel to Coffee Creek to appraise these possible Baumanns, right?"

"Right."

"Can you also handle art and furnishings in the Santa Fe house? This week?" She stewed for a moment but decided it was worth the risk—she had the box and the chairs. "I'll give you the alarm code."

"Yes. I'll start on that today and head your way tomorrow."

A wave of relief. With appraisals underway, she could submit the inventory to the court on time.

Now to deal with Ms. Smutbuster. She called Jean Elder, president of the Library Board.

"Those drafts you sent, the answer, the discovery requests—they look good to me," Jean said. "Last time that woman backed down, but she didn't have a lawyer. What about this time?"

"This time if she won't drop the suit, she'll have to be deposed."

"At the deposition will you ask her whether it's okay to believe in Santa, and fairy godmothers, and talking animals, and the tooth fairy?"

"Yes, indeed. We need to depose her on video. It costs more, but I think it'll be worth it."

"Okay. Listen, can we treat this as a library fundraiser and sell tickets?"

Alice laughed. "I doubt it. Depositions are supposed to be public. Still, there may be some entertainment value."

She told Silla, "Let's file our answer to the Smutbuster petition and serve the discovery requests."

"Will do. Hey, I called Holy Spirit Episcopal. Ellie's service will be this Friday at two o'clock. Shouldn't we send flowers?"

Alice nodded.

"There's an obit in today's *Austin American-Statesman.* Sounds like the family wrote it. Plus you should see the Community Theater's Facebook page. Huge tribute to Ellie, plus video clips from some of her productions." Silla shook her head. "What a woman. And now Woodie's gone, and we're left with those two boys."

"Theoretically, grown men," Alice said. "Can you call and check whether they want to meet later this week?"

She wondered if Valerie would watch for the obit in the Austin paper, then debated letting her know about the service. No. Presumptuous.

She was emailing the obit to Francis Blake when Silla reappeared at Alice's door. "I called Chuck Windom. He said Don and Danielle want to meet Friday at noon. They're driving from Houston that morning."

"But the service is at two!" said Alice, scandalized. She'd assumed they'd drive straight to the church to meet with the pastor. "Oh well.

You've already sent them Ellie's will and our probate letter, right?"

"Of course," Silla said.

Silla routinely sent beneficiaries Alice's detailed form letter on the probate process, including the executor's obligations to submit the will and application for letters testamentary to the probate court, take the executor's oath, locate and secure real and personal property, pay and collect debts and costs, submit a sworn inventory, deal with tax returns, and distribute any remaining assets to beneficiaries.

"Well, maybe we'll have some draft real estate appraisals by Friday. We can discuss those."

Alice had met the brothers and their wives at Woodie's funeral. Maybe the Friday meeting would be short, peaceful, and businesslike, with no disputes, no acrimony.

And maybe she'd win the lottery.

C h a p t e r   S e v e n t e e n

That Creepy Feeling

A t seven-thirty Tuesday morning the vet's truck crunched down Alice's drive. Alice had risen early to lure the burros into their pen, offering carrots while making a "tck tck tck" noise. She watched as the vet and her assistant gave the burros their equine encephalitis shots and their worming medication and examined their teeth and their hooves. "They look healthy," said the vet. "Maybe they could stand to lose a little weight."

The donkeys snorted and exited the pen. A tight group of three, never more than seventy feet apart, the burros patrolled Alice's property, disdaining certain grasses, relishing others. Alice sometimes wondered if the neighbors minded Big Boy's early morning bray, his salute to the dawn. The burros gave a pass to wandering deer, turkeys, and jackrabbits, merely gazing at them with dispassionate eyes, but Alice was aware that after the burros took charge, she never saw stray dogs or coyotes on her land.

Maybe she should consider a guard burro for the office. No further theft attempts had occurred, but she'd heave a sigh of relief when the box in her safe, and its contents, were safely off her premises.

The vet team departed. By eight-thirty Alice was back in her office, preparing for a morning meeting with family members trying to hash out a conservation easement on their long-held family ranch. By nine-thirty, ten family members were huddled in the conference room scrutinizing the survey and the draft agreement limiting development. By eleven Alice had elicited general agreement on a revised draft. One cousin balked at what his relatives wanted, insisting he'd rather have cash, but the matriarch gave him a meaningful look and said, "Sugar, you need to get in the boat with the rest of us." He'd huffed.

On her way out the door the matriarch hugged Alice. "I'll get him signed up," she whispered, and marched out.

Alice found these projects both challenging and frustrating, given that individuals comprising a family had to reach agreement on an emotion-evoking topic: family land. But she felt satisfaction when a family could stay connected by engaging in stewardship that benefited their land. She smiled as all ten relatives exited the office. With the last one gone, she sought refuge in the kitchen.

"I'm starving!" Alice said.

"Hey, don't forget your Library Board lunch meeting at noon," Silla said. "'No rest for the weary or the wicked,' as my high school English teacher always said."

Alice yanked open the refrigerator, grabbed an apple and a pair of cheese sticks, and marched off to her car.

The meeting was blessedly brief. The Board thanked Alice for agreeing to defend the Smutbuster suit. "Can you make her stop suing us?" asked one member.

"I'm not a miracle worker," Alice said. However, she hoped this time Ms. Smutbuster would discover litigation wasn't as much fun as she expected.

When she returned to her office, Silla called from her work room. "Clare Graham will be here early tomorrow. He said he's finished looking at the Santa Fe house art and contents. He's flying into Austin tonight. I've booked him into the Tea Garden House."

"Great. What about the woman appraising Ellie's Coffee Creek property?"

"I'm meeting her at Ellie's house in thirty minutes with a key."

Progress. She wanted appraisals before the family showed up Friday at noon. She worked away, returning phone calls, following up on client requests.

At five-thirty her phone rang. Kinsear.

"What's going on?" she asked.

"Sam got those girls to spend the afternoon playing every card game they know. Right now it's a vicious game of Spades."

"He's still there?"

"Still here. I kind of like him. He leaves tomorrow morning, so I'm at the grocery store scaring up dinner. The steaks look pretty good. Can you join us?"

"Thanks, but it's book group night. Still…" She sang into the phone, "You were always on my mind…you were always on my mind…"

Silla called from the front door. "Hey, Alice, I'm leaving for Ellie's."

"Thanks!" Alice called after her. The front door closed.

Then to Kinsear, "How's Carrie doing?"

"She had follow-up appointments this morning. She's healing well."

Movement outside caught Alice's eye. Through her office window she saw a dark gray Audi pull slowly to the curb. For a moment nothing happened, then a tall man wearing a navy blazer emerged from the driver's side, gazed up and down the street, and turned his face toward her front door. Roger Preyer, blank-faced. She'd last seen him Saturday in Santa Fe at Ellie's house. What was he doing at her office?

"I've got a guest," she told Kinsear. "Gotta go. I'll call you after book group."

Roger Preyer almost stumbled on her front steps as she opened the door. He looked up at her, blinking. She saw age spots on his hand as he grabbed the porch railing.

"Roger?"

He straightened. "Alice. Sorry to stop by so late. It's probably a bad time."

"No, come in."

He stood in the entry hall. "I'm on my way to Austin… from Roswell." That was an eight-hour drive.

"Roswell? Not Santa Fe?"

He looked shocky, pale, unfocused.

"Come sit down," she said, leading him down the hall to the conference room.

He sank into a chair. "Thank you."

Six o'clock. "Let me get you something to drink." She hurried to the kitchen for a bowl of ice and a pitcher of water. Had he eaten? She grabbed the cheese sticks from the fridge and stuck them on a plate with some crackers. She deposited ice, water, and the cheese plate on the conference table and sat down. She considered her guest, then opened the credenza and brought out a crystal tumbler and a bottle of Talisker single malt.

His face brightened.

"Just one cube of ice, please. Thank you very much." He took a sip.

"Why were you in Roswell?"

"I had to spend last night there. My car…the brakes failed. You know Highway 285?"

She'd just traveled that road. Hills, curves, arroyos…out in the middle of nowhere.

"What happened to your brakes?"

He shook his head. "It was very sudden. I was an hour north of Roswell. One minute everything was fine, the next minute—I had to brake for a curve, going downhill, and they just quit. I mean, nothing."

"What'd you do?"

"Pumped the brakes to the floor, grabbed the gear shift, tried to shift into a lower gear…went off the road trying to steer up a rise so the car would slow down." He shook his head again. "Barely missed an arroyo, you know how hidden they can be."

She nodded, envisioning trying to steer, trying to shift to a lower gear, trying to find a safe spot to land, all in a second or two…

"But I got the car stopped. I called my auto service folks. Took an hour for anyone to get there. I saw maybe one pickup go by, that whole hour I was waiting. Anyway, the wrecker arrived, loaded up my car and me, took us to Roswell. Didn't take the mechanic there more than five minutes. 'You've lost all your brake fluid. Master cylinder's empty,' he said. But then when he tried to refill it, he found a big leak in the rubber line from the cylinder to one of the brakes. Brake fluid puddled on the garage floor."

"A leak in the line?"

"He replaced the line that was leaking. Filled up the master cylinder. I paid and left. By then I had to find a motel in Roswell. Today I didn't have any problems, although I held my breath every time I had to slow down."

He took another sip of Talisker. Alice watched. His cheeks were pinker now; he looked more himself.

"What's bringing you to Austin?" Maybe Ellie's memorial service?

"I'm staying with an old buddy at the LBJ School at UT Austin," he said. "Grant Hines. He works on some of the social media analysis they're doing there." The Lyndon Baines Johnson School occupied the elevated ridge along Red River Street, east of the main campus. "We're having a mini-reunion, I guess you'd say. He and I spent some interesting hours together when we were both assigned to the Kurdish territories. He's invited me several times. I finally decided to take him up on it."

Was a mini-reunion the only reason? Alice was trying to frame a not-too-intrusive question when he heaved a sigh and said, "You're awfully nice to let me come in unannounced. Thank you. I've wanted to talk with you, with someone objective. Lately I've been wondering… I've had the strangest feeling…" He stopped.

"What?"

"You'll think I'm losing it. I have the strangest feeling someone's watching me." He glanced at her. "You know when someone's been in your kitchen and moved the measuring spoons to the wrong spot?"

Alice nodded.

"In my study…really, no one uses it but me. But I've still got my old habits, from my days in the service. A hair stuck on the outside of a drawer. Pens and pencils in a certain order. One notebook at an angle in the drawer. Maybe a receipt sticking out in a stack of papers. A couple of times I've thought someone's been in there. And I must say"—here he lifted his head with a steely glance at Alice—"when I've had those thoughts before, I've usually been right. Someone has been watching me." He turned the crystal tumbler in his fingers, meditatively. "Not just in my study, but around Santa Fe. A couple of times at the community college, where I teach a night course. A couple of times on the plaza downtown, just strolling."

"But have you figured out who? Or why?"

He shook his head no.

"It's another reason I'm glad to visit Grant. If I'm losing it, he'll tell me. Maybe we old…old embassy types…" Was he about to say "old spies"? Alice wondered. "Maybe we just stay paranoid." He took a sip of Talisker. "Paranoia doesn't mean…"

"…doesn't mean you're crazy," Alice said.

He laughed. Alice smiled back, glad to see some expression other than the blank stare he'd offered when he came into the office.

Suddenly he stood. "I feel much better. Thanks, Alice." He turned to her, looked into her eyes. "Listen. I'll be there Friday. But I won't talk to anyone. Don't worry. I'll honor Ellie, then disappear." He smiled. "I know how to do that."

She walked him to the door. "Drive safely."

Was Roger losing it? Dementia? Could someone be watching him? But who, and why? Alice could think of no reason. But she knew that creepy feeling, the feeling of being watched …a feeling it was unwise to ignore.

Chapter Eighteen

Here's Another Mystery

At eight on Wednesday morning Clare Graham was already pacing around the conference room in jeans and blue denim shirt with rolled-up sleeves, clutching a cup of coffee, when Alice arrived. He turned to her, eyes sharp above his reading glasses, and lifted the cup in salute.

"I've been up since five," he said, without preamble. "Wide awake, waiting to see those prints. I was prowling up and down your sidewalk when your assistant got here." He put the coffee cup down and rubbed his hands in anticipation. "Lemme at 'em!"

Alice laughed. "How was the Tea Garden House? Did they offer breakfast at five?"

"It's a great place. Thanks for putting me there. That M.A. character … she's a trip."

Alice's friend M.A. and her friend Val had bought the elegant Tea Garden House near Alice's office and transformed it into a successful B&B. M.A., a retired biology teacher, possessed a tart tongue and excellent recipes.

Alice unlocked the conference room closet. Clare Graham stood at her shoulder. She turned around and shooed him back to the far end of the room. "No peeking!"

Then, standing so he couldn't see the dial, she entered the combination and opened the safe. She pulled out the painted box and put it on the table.

"Let me see," he said. He looked at all sides, at the top, at the bottom. "Spring, summer, winter, fall," he muttered. "Night and day."

When he stood back, Alice lifted the lid. She spread out the two empty folders, the two with prints and blocks, and the five that also included paintings.

Graham pulled out his phone. He photographed the contents of each folder, then began dictating his notes. "Folder three. Signature and hand-heart symbol. No print number. Traditional pencil dots surround the printed area. Deckle paper, feels right. Colors…" He sighed. "Viridian. Lapis blue. Gold. Orange. Blue and viridian trees…"

Alice sat at the other end of the table, working on her laptop. She'd hired him; but she didn't want to leave him alone with those prints. Silla brought more coffee. Graham examined the prints and the woodblocks in each folder, standing at the table, dictating his notes. She heard him say, "Folders five through nine include a gouache."

"What's gouache?" she asked.

"That's painting with water color with extra pigments added, so the paint adds texture and intense color. Baumann often—not always—started his print process based on a gouache painting. His gouaches are intense, color-wise, but the woodcut prints based on the gouaches are even more intense. It's mysterious, but I think for some reason his prints have more impact. Let me show you."

From folder five he pulled out the painting and a matching print and held them up before her. "There. See that? On your left is the gouache, on your right you've got the woodcut print."

Alice liked the brush stroke and the texture of the paint on the gouache. But Graham was right: the print was even more intense.

He went back to work.

Finally, he looked over at Alice, who looked back at him.

"What do you think?" she asked.

"I think you have the blocks for each print, plus some extra blocks. I think the prints may all be authentic. But they're new to me. If Baumann got this far with each print, why didn't he print more copies, numbered prints, as he normally would?" He shook his head. "That's a mystery."

"Are they rejects? Are they flawed?"

"We have just one print from each set of blocks, so I don't know," Graham said. "He was picky. Maybe he just didn't like these? Maybe he put them away for another day? Maybe he wanted to re-carve the blocks? He did that sometimes."

He pointed at the box. "But here's another mystery. Did he paint this box? And why are the prints in here? What's the story?"

"It was in the attic of the Moon Mountain house our client bought decades ago," Alice said. "Wrapped in an old blanket and then in an old tarp. She apparently discovered the box there. I'm not sure precisely when." She went back to the closet and brought out the two children's chairs. "These were also in the attic. Also wrapped up."

Graham's face broke into a smile. "Charming. I wish I were small enough to fit in one."

"I don't know if they were meant for specific children," Alice said.

Graham peered at the legs and feet of the chairs. "No wear here," he said. "You'd have wear from a wood floor, a tile floor. Maybe they were always on carpet? Or maybe never used. And no signature."

He sat back down at his laptop and started working. Alice worked at hers. Occasionally Silla brought more coffee.

Finally: "I'm looking at comparables," he said. "I think these could be Baumanns. The pigments and the designs alone could convince me. I'm not sure why five have gouaches and two don't. But value? Where the print is signed, with his hand-heart symbol, that's one thing. Especially where it's numbered in a series. Where it's not…" He pointed at the box. "And what about prints that haven't been seen before? The whole provenance question requires a hefty deduction." He stood up and gently turned the box back and forth, examining the progression of seasons painted around the sides. "But the box itself is unique. The fact that you've got the carvings as well as a print of each adds value."

He sat down again at the laptop. "I'll have to give you a range, Alice."

She nodded.

He pushed his glasses up on his nose. "It could be anywhere from twenty thousand to two or even three times that."

"You said 'range,' not random numbers. Can't you be more specific?"

"Not unless we start shopping these around."

Her eyes widened in horror. "You can't."

"I know."

"Can I have a draft of your report by Friday morning?"

"Certainly on the contents of the Santa Fe house. On this box… I'll try to give you something conditioned on getting further info." He looked around the table at the chairs, the box, the folders, the prints, the woodblocks. "Here's another deduction, one I can't put in my range, but one you should consider—the cost of keeping these safe."

Damn. A girl could get burned, trying to hold onto these hot potatoes.

Graham lowered his eyes to the laptop and began typing.

Alice's phone pinged: text from Roger Preyer. "Alice, please call. Additional info."

She texted Silla in the next room: "Come sit with Graham for a sec so I can make a call."

Chapter Nineteen

Guess What, Ol' Buddy

From her office Alice called Roger's cell. He sounded short of breath.

"Alice. Thanks for calling back. Listen, you know what I said…that strange feeling of being watched?"

"Yes?"

"I told my buddy Grant about the brakes. Grant's ex-CIA. He got that narrow-eyed look and asked to see the old brake line. Usually, I don't keep my used car parts, but for some reason I kept that failed brake line, threw it in the back of the car. Grant took a look. He showed me where the rubber in the line was cut part way through with a razor or a very sharp knife. If you look before and after the spot where it split, you can still see the straight-line cut."

"Holy cow," Alice said.

"Then Grant got under the car to check the other brake line. 'Guess what, ol' buddy,' he said. It was cut too … not quite as deep, so it hadn't split. I guess one failed line didn't make the mechanic suspicious enough to check the other line. But Grant concludes someone sabotaged the car."

They were both silent.

"Do we know where?"

"Maybe in the parking lot at the community college, where I taught last Friday afternoon. Or Saturday morning, when I parked the car to hike around Moon Mountain." He gave a short laugh. "Friday night, at the Desert Chorale concert. Or Sunday, parked downtown at church, for all I know."

"But who, Roger? Assuming the sabotage happened last week or this week, who knew you were about to take a road trip?" Where he'd be alone, miles from help…where he might have lost control, might have flipped into an arroyo, hit a tree, broken his neck…

"I've been thinking about a trip to Austin for a while. But as to when, I decided only last week."

"Who else knew?"

"I'm trying to remember. Friday, Saturday, Sunday? Busy days."

Was someone trying to prevent him from seeing Valerie? Or attending Ellie's memorial service?

"Did you decide to come after you saw the obituary this past

Monday?" Alice asked.

"No, I was already on the road, early Monday."

Ellie's obit didn't hit the paper until Monday, so those two theories didn't quite work. Not much for answering questions, was he? Like why he'd come to Austin. She didn't think it was only to see his friend Grant.

"I need to go," he said. "Grant's following me to the mechanic to get that other brake line replaced." He hung up.

Alice sat for a moment in her office, then called Francis Blake. Roger's friend…he deserved to know about the brakes.

"I'm sitting here with Clare Graham, Francis," she said. "He's looking at the prints right now."

"Is he behaving?"

"Fairly well. Listen, I just had a call from Roger Preyer."

"Sitting with Clare Graham, talking to Roger Preyer, and calling me. You've got three fifths of the poker group right there."

"Clare too?" Good grief.

"Yeah. When he pushes his glasses up on the bridge of his nose…"

"Yes?"

"He's gonna bluff."

"Well, listen." She told him about Roger's brake issue. "So who in Santa Fe would want to hurt Roger?"

Francis was silent for a moment. "You're assuming it's someone in Santa Fe." Another silence. "Maybe so, but…he's well liked here. You know, not a joker, pretty serious, but good in meetings, good on committees, generous giver. Cutting brake lines? That sounds like the kind of crap some low-life would pull. I don't think Roger's offended any low-lifes."

"Who knew he was about to leave for Austin on a road trip?"

"Not me. And I saw him Friday, with you."

"I saw him the next morning at Ellie's and he said he'd be seeing me…but not two days later."

Several seconds passed.

"Does his wife know?" Francis asked. "About the brakes?"

"I don't know," Alice said. "Surely he's told her."

"Mmm." That was noncommittal. "What does Clare think about that box of prints?"

"He's providing a range. Hasn't given me the numbers yet. He's curious about how long they've been in Ellie's Moon Mountain house."

"He's not the only one. But he likes them? Thinks they're genuine?"

"A cautious 'maybe,' with qualifications."

"Will you keep me posted? Not just about the prints, but…" His voice slowed. "That worries me about Roger."

"Yes."

"Before you hang up—any word on who killed Ellie?"

"Not yet."

Alice said goodbye. She stared blankly out her office window. Ellie dead. Roger's car sabotaged.

She picked up her phone again, called Files, got voicemail. "Can you update me on the investigation of Ellie Windom's murder?"

He called back almost immediately. "I was about to call you. Right now we're at a stand-still, without a murder weapon. Since it's a homicide, the medical examiner's releasing the victim's personal effects to us."

"Yes?"

"The medical examiner found a folded paper in her back pants pocket, pretty wet and wrinkled. Blood stains, body fluid. Looks handwritten. Because it was fragile, they've sent it to the Questioned Documents section for examination. They're going to compare the handwriting to the samples of Ellie's handwriting on her wall calendar, her kitchen notepad, her planner. They think they can get it to me soon, with the rest of her personal effects."

"But what's the paper?"

"I guess we'll find out when we get it. I'll call you."

Silla stuck her head into Alice's office. "Where are we on our draft application for probate of will and issuance of letters testamentary for Ellie's will? We need to get that sucker filed in the probate court so you can take your oath as executor and get rolling."

Alice thought about the folded paper, handwritten, stained, in Ellie's back pants pocket. Maybe nothing, but the fact that the medical examiner wanted to confirm it was Ellie's handwriting rang alarm bells. She remembered how intently Ellie had listened at their meeting. "Let's hold off until after Ellie's service on Friday."

On Thursday she headed to Coffee Creek, thinking about the Friday meeting with the Windom boys and their spouses. Draft agenda: hear whether her sons agreed or disagreed on the disposition of Ellie's real estate and other assets; explain the process and the application for probate and appointment of the executor; discuss the preliminary appraisals and inventory. She closed her eyes for a moment—unsafe on the creek road—imagining possible outbursts at the meeting. Oh, well. It was work, which paid the bills, kept the lights on, though she'd prefer Ellie to be alive.

Which made her think of the costs Ellie's estate was running up. She called Red to see whether she needed to order another round bale for Ellie's two horses and the pony. "Yes, you do, at least by the end of next week," Red said. "Two horses and a pony, I bet they'll go through that round bale in three weeks."

Ellie's will would pay for maintaining the horses…but she could already imagine Don on Friday, carping about the cost.

C h a p t e r   T w e n t y

Who Has a Key?

Friday morning. Silla and Alice had finished preparing for the noon meeting with Ellie's sons, Chuck and Don, and their wives. Instead of their traditional Friday boots and jeans, both women wore suits and heels, ready for Ellie's memorial service at two p.m.

Silla poured them each a mug of coffee. "It's hard to believe we're going to a memorial service for Ellie just eight months after her husband died. And that she was murdered, for God's sake." She paused. "I admired both of them. Woodie was such a nice guy."

Alice remembered Woodie before his stroke, sitting in her conference room, smiling at Ellie, carefully reading his revised medical directive, then signing.

"Ellie's sons weren't much comfort at Woodie's service. You remember she was in tears when she came into the church?"

Alice nodded. She remembered Ellie's face, still teary, as she led the family into the reserved pew.

"The vicar's wife told me Don picked a fight with Chuck just before the service, when the family was meeting with the vicar."

"Nice." Alice hoped Don wouldn't do the same today in her office. "At least Chuck and Joanne were civil at the reception. Though their boy Max stuck close to you."

Silla tossed her head, red ponytail bouncing. "Who can blame him? He was desperate to escape his relatives."

"Oh, boy." Alice took a deep breath, thinking about today's meeting. "We've got an hour. Is everything ready?"

"All laid out in the conference room. Graham sneaked out without finalizing his appraisal, though. He stamped every page 'DRAFT.'" She handed a copy to Alice, who immediately noted he'd omitted the box and chairs.

At five till eleven Alice, at her desk, watched a Lexus SUV pull up to the curb. Chuck, dark-haired, dark-eyed, erect in a navy suit, helped Joanne from the passenger seat. She was petite, with laugh wrinkles by her eyes and brown hair in a casual bun. She wore a charcoal linen jacket and skirt. Their son Max, eyes on the office door, also wore a dark suit. He'd lost his round teen-age cheeks, looked downright handsome.

Silla took Chuck and Joanne to the conference room, where coffee and their documents waited. Max hung back. Alice heard him say, "I don't need to be in that meeting." He followed Silla to the kitchen.

Alice joined Chuck and Joanne. "You've got copies of the will, some real estate appraisals, and preliminary inventory lists in your stack. Are we expecting Don's family too?"

Chuck nodded.

Joanne glanced briefly toward Chuck, then down at the documents, then at Alice. "We're supposed to meet the vicar at Holy Spirit at one. We'll need to grab a quick bite before then."

"I'll leave you two alone to look at the documents." Alice went back to her office.

At eleven-fifteen Don's family still hadn't arrived.

At eleven-twenty Alice returned to the conference room. Chuck was pacing the floor, looking at his watch. "My brother's never on time for anybody," he muttered. "Guess he's just too important."

"Want to start going over the documents?" she asked. "I'd prefer to have you and Don together for part of this discussion, but I can go over things separately with Don when he gets here."

Chuck returned to his chair. "My first question is whether the police have got any idea who killed my mother."

"I talked to Detective Files on Wednesday. He says they're still trying to find the murder weapon."

"So weird. For someone to kill my mother. Bashing her on the head! Of all the things I was afraid could happen to her—falling off her horse, tripping over a stage prop—that wasn't one." Chuck looked down at the documents. After a moment he said, "I have no questions about the will. It's clear."

"What about the real estate?" Alice picked up her set of the real estate appraisals. "Her house, the rental house, the feed store, the Santa Fe house." Chuck found his set. "We don't need final decisions yet, but I'll need your thoughts." They began walking through the papers.

Eleven-forty.

Noisy footsteps in the hallway.

Silla opened the conference room door.

Don Windom and Danielle strode in. Don was six foot two. Alice figured he enjoyed being taller than his big brother. Since Woodie's funeral he'd lost some hair on top and gained some weight, partly disguised by a visibly Italian suit. Danielle herself was nearly six feet tall, with blonde hair cut gamine style, dressed in a sleeveless bright pink jersey sheath that showed off athletic legs and sinewy arms. She wore a heavy silver and turquoise necklace, a multi-carat diamond on her hand. Her eyes darted around the room. She arranged herself in the chair next to Don and offered a smile to the room.

"Started without us, huh?" Don scooted his chair closer to the table. "Couldn't wait for us to get here from Houston?"

"We drove down from Dallas, baby bro," Chuck retorted.

Alice turned to Don. "We haven't discussed the real estate yet. Do you have any questions before we get started?"

"No. Except I don't see why she went to the expense of making you executor."

Alice had expected that one. "It's not my preference; in fact, when she asked me, I told Ellie that, if she was serious, she needed to hire another lawyer to revise her will to add me as executor. Otherwise I wouldn't do it. In fact, that firm still had the original of her will," she said. "But she said she wouldn't wish that burden on either of you. After serving as Woodie's executor, she thought her estate, with all the real property, would be tougher to deal with. She worried about inconveniencing you two, in Houston and Dallas."

"I could've handled the executor gig without a bit of trouble," Don grumbled, shooting a skeptical look at Alice. "Nothing to it. Just paperwork. Fill in the blanks, right?"

Oh, right, Alice thought.

"I bet Ellie didn't want fighting between her two boys," Joanne said with a small smile.

Alice smiled back. "Don, any other questions about the will?"

He shook his head no.

"Let's talk about the real estate decisions you'll need to make, about Ellie's house and acreage, the old feed store and a rental house in Coffee Creek, and the Santa Fe house, as well as the Wildflower Central retail store and fields. You've got appraisals in your papers." She waited while they found their copies, then went on. "First, what about her house? That's first in your stack. You see the appraised value and the annual taxes."

"Sell it," Don said.

"I may want to keep it," Chuck said. "Not sure yet."

"What about the horses?" Alice asked. "Will either of you want them?"

"Broken-down old nags," Danielle scoffed.

"Didn't Ellie and Woodie want their horses cared for, like for life?" Joanne asked.

"Yes. They're getting daily visits," Alice answered.

"   That's expensive!" Don said. "I mean, how much hay do those animals eat?"

Alice was glad she'd asked Red. "A round bale should last about three weeks."

"And costs how much?" Don demanded.

"Ninety to a hundred and ten dollars. So we'll likely order another round bale next week."

Alice looked from one man to the other. "Okay, how about the old feed store and the rental house in Coffee Creek?"

Don was leafing through the appraisals. "They don't produce much rent. Looks like they could need big-ticket repairs. I say sell them."

"I'm still thinking about those as well," Chuck said.

Not making much progress here. Alice foresaw plenty of conflict ahead. Ellie was smart to ask a third party to serve as executor. "Okay, Wildflower Central," Alice said. "Does either of you want to keep operating it? Or sell the business and the property? Or sell only the business but lease back the property? The appraiser says the current store manager might want to buy the business. He gave you some ranges to think about." She wondered if Don would again argue for immediate sale. She remembered Ellie's housekeeper, Judith Strong, saying she'd overheard Don demanding that on his last visit to Ellie.

"Sell it. I've got no interest in a wildflower business. Not much upside." Don stared at Chuck.

"I might be interested in selling the operation to the current manager, and leasing back the property. Got to run some numbers,"

Chuck said.

Alice picked up the next appraisal. "What about the Santa Fe house?"

"Old, small, needs a ton of renovation," Don said. "Sell that puppy."

"I'm not sure about that," Chuck said. "I'll need more time to decide."

"By the way," Alice said, "while I was in Santa Fe, there were two attempts to burglarize your mom's place. Some kid was there when I arrived, ran out the back door. The next morning when I was checking inventory, two guys broke in. They used a boltcutter on the back door chain, but"—she looked at Don, at Chuck—"both times, whoever it was had a key. Who has a key to the Santa Fe house?"

"Ellie gave us each one," Chuck said. "Joanne's got ours. Right, honey?" She nodded, pulled out her key chain, held it up.

"I've got ours." Danielle reached in her purse, pulled out a key.

Silence around the table. "Well, I've got Ellie's," Alice said. "Please give some thought to who else might have one." No response.

"Did they take anything?" Don asked.

"I don't think so." She looked at Don, then Chuck. "Back to real estate. How long will you need to decide what to keep?"

"Maybe a month," Chuck said.

"A *month*?" Don slapped the appraisal packet on the table, glared at his brother. "Listen, Chuck, we need to get these properties on the market! I'm looking for income here! I'm not sitting around waiting a month for you to sharpen your pencil and play with your calculator!"

Here we go, Alice said to herself.

Chuck stared back, frowning. "What's the rush? Mom just died, man! Very suddenly! I'm still in shock. These are big decisions, and I want time to think them through. Look, we're talking about the house we grew up in. I may indeed want to keep it."

"It's after one," Alice said, glancing at the wall clock. "What if we set up a conference call about Ellie's house and the Santa Fe house in, say, ten days? Since no one's living in either house, I'm more concerned about those. Will that work, Chuck?"

He nodded.

"But the Santa Fe house—you haven't said a word about the value of all the contents, the art!" Danielle burst out. "That group of…that collection of art!" She stopped, looked at Chuck, at Joanne.

"Draft inventories detailing the contents of the two houses, Coffee Creek and Santa Fe, are in your stack, with preliminary values. The first one's for the Coffee Creek property."

Danielle reached into Don's document stack, found the packet titled "Inventory," and flipped it open. She and Don leaned over it. Don lost interest and looked up. Danielle's blonde head stayed bent over the paper. "Where's that one picture Ellie always said she liked, some tree in Santa Fe?" she asked. "I don't see it."

The Bishop's Apricot?" Alice looked around the table. "Ellie gave that away, before she died."

Silence around the table. Joanne looked at Alice, a question in her eyes.

"It's ours! Part of our inheritance!" Don said. "She can't do that!"

"Why couldn't she do that? Make a gift to someone?" Joanne countered.

"We ought to get it back!" Don's face was red. "Who'd she give it to?"

"She gave it to a woman in Austin," said Alice. She steeled herself, feeling like she was about to lob a grenade into her own meeting. "Her birth daughter."

Joanne's jaw dropped. "Birth daughter?" she whispered. "Ellie?"

"Say that again?" Chuck asked. "Our mother had a daughter?"

Alice had thought about this. She hated revealing Ellie's confidence. But Ellie had insisted on making this particular gift, a gift that would inevitably need explanation.

"Ellie gave up a baby to adoption when she was barely eighteen. That adopted child is now over fifty. They've been in touch. Ellie wanted her to have that picture."

"But it's worth money!" Danielle burst out. "She can't just give things away!"

Chuck frowned at her, then turned to Alice. "Who was the father?"

"A young man at West Point. As a cadet he couldn't marry, and

Ellie's mom wanted her own daughter to go to college. She herself had struggled as a single mother. They had no money."

They digested that. Chuck sat stunned, his eyes still on Alice, his mouth slightly open. Joanne had a faraway look in her eyes. "Poor Ellie! That must have been so hard."

"She should've been more careful!" Danielle said.

"Oh, come on!" Joanne retorted.

Alice couldn't stop herself. "Ellie was just seventeen when she got pregnant. You realize it wasn't until 1965 that the Supreme Court ruled in *Griswold v. Connecticut* that contraception was legal for *married* women?"

"Who cares? I still don't see why she can just haul off and send a valuable picture to this woman," Don growled. "I say we get it back." He looked at Danielle for affirmation.

"That print's worth about seven thousand," Danielle hissed, her index finger scrolling down the inventory page.

"Ellie was entitled to make gifts," Alice said. "It was her print."

"She should have kept it in the estate!" Don barked. "What do you mean, Mom was 'in touch' with this person?"

Silla shouldered open the conference room door and set a platter on the credenza. The scent of ancho, pasilla, cilantro filled the room. "I ordered tacos from Flores, thinking you need a bite before you head for Holy Spirit." Max followed Silla, carrying an ice bucket and a six-pack of flavored club sodas.

"Good lord!" Chuck looked at his watch. "We're supposed to meet the vicar in fifteen minutes!"

A scramble toward the credenza; the poof! of carbonated drinks popping open; a crunching sound; a general lowering of blood pressure.

"Thanks, Silla," Alice said in a low voice. She saw no reason to answer Don's question, much less identify Valerie. They'd also run out of time before discussing the contents of the Santa Fe house, including the box's contents: that issue still loomed.

In ten minutes the conference room was empty except for Silla, messy paper plates, napkins, forks, and soda cans, and an unclaimed taco. From the front door Alice watched Don and Danielle climb into a white Lincoln Navigator.

She sighed in relief and returned to the conference room. She and Silla collected the trash in a plastic bag. "You and the tacos staved off World War III," Alice said.

"That Danielle's a tough date, isn't she?" Silla commented. "Keeps herself in shape, though. Max says his Aunt Danielle's a real gym rat."

"By the way, where was Don and Danielle's son? Drake?"

"Well," said Silla, "*apparently…*" "*Apparently*" usually signaled she was about to share new gossip. "*Apparently*, according to Max, Drake is not attending his grandmother's funeral. Chuck and Joanne were 'appalled.' Max's word."

"Why didn't he come?"

"Max said his Uncle Don told his parents that Drake had to finish a late term paper for a course. Max's parents thought that was low-rent since Ellie's been paying his tuition. The least he could do was show up at her service. Max said a friend told him that Drake was about to flunk out anyway."

Interesting. "Where's Max in school?"

"Southern Methodist, in Dallas," Silla said, hoisting the plastic bag and heading for the kitchen.

Alice's cell rang: Francis Blake. "You're probably about to leave for Ellie's memorial service, right? I read about it online."

"Yes," Alice said. "After surviving the first meeting with her sons about her estate."

"The joys of law practice. Listen, have you heard from Roger?"

"Not since he told me about the brakes."

"I bet he'll be there today. I'm just wondering when he's coming back."

"For your poker game?" Alice asked.

"Well, poker's actually this coming Wednesday. But I was going to try to get him out for dinner. Speaking of being out for dinner, I saw his wife Kristi last night at Cafe Piñon, having dinner with Billy Menger."

"Who's that?"

"He's the guy who was eyeing you from the bar at the Desert Chorale concert. Suede jacket, fancy boots. Remember?"

"I didn't think you'd noticed."

"Well, you didn't seem interested, so I didn't introduce you." He paused. "Billy wanted to join our poker night, but we had to say no."

"Why?"

"Too much casino."

"What do you mean?"

"He plays a lot, up at Tesuque and other casinos. That's not our deal."

"Explain that to me." Alice wasn't sure what he meant.

"Word is he's run up some debts. He used to brag about all the free drinks and hotel rooms he got, but a guy I know went with him to Tesuque and found out Billy lost his comps there. Same story at a casino in Albuquerque. Losing a lot at casinos, that's bad juju. In a friendly poker game, you don't want to worry about whether the loser's gonna pay."

Alice furrowed her brow. "He and Kristi are friends?"

Silence from Francis. Then, "I don't know."

Alice wasn't sure what to do with that info. Not her business, was it? She certainly wouldn't pass it along. She did promise to get in touch with Roger and hung up.

Silla popped back in the conference room. "Ready to head to Holy Spirit?"

"I'm going to sit in the back so I can see who shows up," Alice said.

Silla nodded. "Could be interesting."

At My Departing

"**W**ow. Last row in the parking lot," Silla said.

Alice had asked her to drive. She still didn't have her Discovery back. "That white loaner smells disgusting. I hope my clothes don't smell like the inside of that car."

"When does the repair shop finish with your Discovery?" Silla asked.

"They're still waiting for the replacement tailgate."

Holy Spirit sat on a hill off the highway. A throng stood in the warm June sunshine flooding the courtyard between the parish hall and the church, waiting to enter the sanctuary. A welcome afternoon breeze rustled the trees around the courtyard. Alice and Silla joined the slow procession, stood in line to sign the register, then chose seats at the far end of the last pew on the right-hand aisle. Even in the back row, Alice smelled the penetrating sweetness of the star lilies banking the steps to the altar.

Alice kept an eye on the incoming crowd, wondering if Valerie Ames had changed her mind. Would Ellie's daughter, with her startling resemblance to Ellie, join the gathered mourners?

Movement in the center aisle caught her eye. A tall figure in a navy blazer stood facing the altar for a moment, then took a seat at the other end of their pew.

Roger had said he'd come.

Music now. Predictable, measured. Not vivacious, not sparkling, not Ellie…but sonorous, controlled, age-old. The crowd quieted. A side door opened at the front of the nave. Chuck, Joanne, Max, Don, and Danielle filed in and sidled into the reserved front row.

Alice picked up a prayer book from the pew rack. "Lord, thou hast been our refuge…" began the vicar, reading from Psalm 90, and a traditional service began. Alice turned to the Order for the Burial of the Dead. Order, indeed…a human attempt to bring order after disorder, perhaps the worst disorder, murder of one human by another. Predictability itself felt comforting.

She glanced at the bulletin, felt further reassured at the absence of any speeches offered by the family of the departed. Memorial services where all the children and best friends, and sometimes volunteers from the congregation, approached the lectern to share their feelings made her nervous, even though the comments, whether practiced or not, were often both apt and moving. Perhaps they were too moving, Alice wondered, chastising herself for her habit of avoiding, or trying to control, emotional reaction. But after today's office meeting, she thought speeches by Ellie's family might carry the whiff of hypocrisy. Honestly, would Don rather have his mother back? Or cash?

The readings continued. Then the vicar said, "An offering of music from some of Ellie Windom's students and actors."

A quartet moved to the lectern—two dewy-faced girls Alice had seen in Ellie's staging of *A Midsummer Night's Dream*, plus a gawky Romeo, and…Tommy Long. They sang, unaccompanied, the ancient Sarum hymn, almost five hundred years old, "God be in my head, And in my understanding…God be at mine end, And at my departing." Some polyphonic genius had taken strands of four-part harmony, pulled them apart, wound them back together. At the end, the soprano, alto, and tenor voices joined in a sustained chord, and softened and held it while Tommy Long, the bass, sang the powerful, slow, descending tones of "And at my departing." Contrary to her intention, Alice felt tears rise. Covertly she groped for a tissue.

She thought Ellie herself had looked too sorry, too surprised, lying there on the entry hall floor, to have felt, while dying, the comfort of the old words "at my departing." Ellie wanted to live, not die. This was not her chosen "departing." Alice wiped away another tear and clenched her jaw, swearing she'd find out why Ellie looked so surprised, so sorry. Murder so foul…

The vicar spoke of Ellie: her energy, generosity, devotion to students. He told the congregation of a new scholarship fund established in Ellie's honor by the Community Theater. Tommy Long, Alice thought.

She peeked down the row at Roger's stern profile. The congregation shuffled and stood for a hymn. The vicar prayed for "all thy saints." Wouldn't Ellie laugh, to think of herself as a saint, Alice thought. Finally, the benediction. As the echo died away, Alice and Silla hurried out the side aisle.

"I'll go make an appearance in the parish hall, shake hands with the family," Silla said.

Alice caught up with Roger by the fountain in the church court-yard. He looked at her, his face bleak. He was folding his handkerchief, putting it back in his suit pants. His eyes were red.

"I'm so sorry," Alice said.

"Who killed her, Alice?"

She shook her head. "I don't know. Yet."

He took a deep breath and let it out, gazing around the courtyard at the people moving out of the sanctuary and into the parish hall.

"I had hoped…" he began. "I had dreamed of a new life."

"With Ellie?"

He nodded, staring off in the distance.

Maybe that hope, that dream, precipitated his visit to the Santa Fe divorce lawyer? Maybe that was why Ellie looked so surprised, so sorry? But now?

"Francis called," she ventured. "He was curious when you're coming back."

Roger looked at her, his face now neutral, controlled. "I don't know." He looked deep into her eyes and said, finally, "Thanks, Alice."

She wanted to ask more questions, wanted to persuade Roger to talk longer, but he nodded, turned, and left for the parking lot. She watched the tall figure disappear down a row of cars.

"Ready?" Silla joined her. "Honestly, Alice, those people—Don and Danielle—do not know how to act. They basically abandoned Chuck and Joanne. They don't seem to appreciate that people are wait-ing in line in the parish hall to say something nice about Ellie to her offspring." Silla unlocked her truck. As she and Alice climbed in, she added, "I need to stop by Ellie's on the way back to the office. I told Red I'd check the horses today. I want to be sure that high school stu-dent of hers is taking good care of them."

"Okay," Alice said. "Take me to my stinky car at the office, and I'll go with you."

* * * * *

Alice, then Silla, drove through the gate and up to the graveled area behind Ellie's house. Silla popped out of the truck, took off her heels, stomped her feet into cowgirl boots and headed directly to the corral, carrying a bag of apples.

Alice stayed outside the gate, enjoying the breeze, the sun, and the sight of a barrel-racer conversing in the horse language she spoke so well…a language unknown to Alice. The two horses and the small pony responded, clustered around Silla and the apples with an air of relief.

After her colloquy with the horses, Silla disappeared into the barn. Alice stood looking across the gravel drive at Ellie's house, yellow crime tape still flapping around the Dutch door to the kitchen. Silla emerged from the barn carrying brushes and announced that Red's employee was performing acceptable work. She brushed each horse and the little pony, gave each another apple, then turned on the water spigot next to the barn and topped up the horse trough.

"I ordered another round bale. It'll be delivered Thursday. They've got plenty until then."

"Good," Alice said.

Silla opened the separate gate from the corral into the fenced pasture, then exited the corral, chained the gate, and re-locked it with the hefty combination lock Red had added.

Both turned as they heard Ellie's driveway gate creak open at the bottom of the hill. A white Lincoln Navigator sped up the drive, spraying gravel. The driver braked and parked behind Silla's truck.

What were they doing here?

Danielle, in large sunglasses, emerged from the driver's seat and strode toward Alice and Silla. "What are you two doing here?"

Don followed. "You guys billing for this? Patting the ponies? Padding the bills?"

"Oh, come on," Alice said, forcing a half-smile. "Silla's doing her quality control check on the student who's tending the horses. What about you two? What are you doing here?"

Don looked at Danielle, who had walked over to the corral gate. "Danielle said she wanted to look around, be sure everything was okay." He looked at the police tape on the door. "We don't need to go in. In fact," he looked down at his heavy gold wristwatch, "we need to head back to Houston."

So Don didn't want to go into the house? Didn't want to see where his mother died? Alice was puzzled—but thankful she didn't have to tell Don he couldn't cross the police tape, couldn't enter his mother's house. Given this morning's meeting, she was glad not to have the distasteful experience of following family members through the house watching that no treasured memento beloved by one heir disappeared into the pocket of another. She wanted all heirs to have a fair shot...

Danielle was still standing at the corral gate.

"Honey, we've got to go," Don called.

Danielle finally turned and walked past Alice and Silla to the car. "I have no idea why Ellie wanted to keep that murderous horse of hers. Or Woodie's broken-down old nag or that ridiculous pony," she said, looking back at the corral. "Such a waste of money. Now if they were serious horses, like the ones I used to jump..."

Alice couldn't think of any appropriate response that wasn't offensive. No one had suggested Ellie's horse was anything but well-behaved. She said nothing, but watched Danielle hit reverse gear, sending the car back toward the barn, then forward, roaring back down the hill. Alice watched as the Navigator turned left and sped back toward Coffee Creek and the highway to Houston.

"Was that weird? Strange? Peculiar?" Silla said. "Why were they here?"

Alice shook her head. "No idea."

"What do you think they'd have done if we hadn't been here?"

"Good question."

✳ ✳ ✳ ✳ ✳

Alice rolled down the windows in the white loaner as she left Ellie's, heading up the creek road toward home. Her phone rang. Kinsear.

"Alice. It's Friday night."

"Yes, and I don't have a date," she said.

"I'm totally stir-crazy. What do you say Isabel and Sam and I come over for dinner? We'll bring everything. I barbecued some ribs and made M.A.'s potato salad and coleslaw."

"Wow! But you're going to leave poor Carrie alone?"

"Um, no, we thought we'd bring her along. She's been cooped up all week."

Alice's first time to meet Carrie. She felt some trepidation. But the house was clean-ish. Emphasis on the ish. If she had an hour…

Kinsear went on. "Isabel and Sam have some ideas they want you to hear."

"Sounds great. Can you get Carrie up and down my front steps?"

"Sam can. He just picks her up. Likes to show off for Isabel."

She laughed. "Come on, then!" She hung up and stood on the accelerator, thinking—check the bathrooms, shut the closets, scoop up the magazines, make iced tea, put out some hors d'oeuvres—what else? Oh, yes. Take a deep breath.

* * * * *

Carrie had lighter hair and softer features than her big sister Isabel, but the same clear hazel eyes and a lopsided smile.

As promised, Sam carried her from the drive into Alice's ranch house. He deposited her in a leather chair in Alice's living room, which opened off the kitchen. He dragged over a footstool for her injured ankle, still in a cast. Isabel brought in Carrie's crutches.

"How's that ankle doing?" Alice asked.

"Much better, thanks. On Monday I get a walking boot."

"That's good news."

Alice gave Sam a quick hug, then hugged Isabel, noting the sparkle in her eyes when she looked at Sam. "At dinner we want a full report from you on everything," warned Isabel. Then she led Sam out onto the deck, where the afternoon sun lit up the creek valley. "That's where we crossed during the flood," Alice heard Isabel tell him. "When we had to rescue those people. Dad strung a rope across, the creek was so high."

Alice glanced at Kinsear, unloading food in the kitchen. Right after that memorable flood, he'd proposed to her, out in her treehouse. She wondered if Isabel and Sam were thinking, maybe even talking, long term.

She suddenly realized they'd all left Carrie alone, staring at her phone. Kinsear said she'd decided on Rice, in Houston, for freshman year. Alice sat down next to her. "I hear you got into Rice, A&M, and Texas. That's really cool. What made you decide on Rice?"

Carrie looked up. There was a nanosecond of uncomfortable silence before she answered. "I like the house system there. I'll be assigned to a house all four years. That means I'll get to know a bunch of people with different majors and different interests who get involved in house activities, like drama."

Alice nodded. "That sounds appealing. Have you already chosen your courses?"

"Not yet." She offered nothing further, looked back at her phone, then, fairly politely, at Alice. Alice felt the secret wall of adolescence clicking into place.

Kinsear rescued her. "Where are the serving spoons?" At the kitchen island he'd arranged the potato salad, the coleslaw, and now, with a flourish, his barbecued ribs.

"They smell fabulous." Alice snitched a tiny brown bite of meat. "Oh gosh." She reached for another piece.

"My own rub, my own sauce," Kinsear said. "The product of years of intense research."

Alice smiled as she dabbed sauce off her chin.

Isabel and Sam came inside to set the table. They put ice in the glasses and poured iced tea. Kinsear got a beer out of the refrigerator. This feels homey, Alice realized. Why had she dragged her feet so long, putting off meeting Kinsear's girls, putting off any decision about her future with him?

Oh, well. That was past. This is now, she thought, and felt a brief moment of peace. She never felt complete peace, though, except when her children, John and Ann, were safely under her roof. They'd be home in another two months when their summer jobs ended.

Ribs, potato salad, coleslaw. After the happy sighs died down, Isabel raised a hand. "Okay, Alice. Where are we on the box? On Ellie's murder?"

Alice recounted some of the story. "As to Ellie's death, the sheriff's department still has no murder weapon and no suspects. I saw Roger at the memorial service today—he sat in the back row. By the way, someone sabotaged his brake lines when he was driving down here from Santa Fe—his brakes failed somewhere north of Roswell."

That roused Isabel. "Who would do that to Roger? Some ancient enemy from back in his foreign service days?"

"He didn't give me any idea." Alice picked up her third rib, surveyed it with appreciation. "This is a nicer gathering than the one in my office this morning, with Ellie's sons and their wives. Pretty tense."

"Any sign of 'Draco,' the guy in the Weikel?" asked Isabel.

"Nope. We didn't discuss the box you rescued, or the contents. We ran out of time, because the Houston contingent was late."

"I don't suppose anyone there showed up in the Jeep?" Sam asked.

"No. White Lincoln Navigator."

Sam whistled. "Pricey."

"Matches Don's wife's ring," Alice waggled her eyebrows.

"Do they make that much money?" Kinsear, getting down to basics.

"Hmm." Alice didn't know. Don was certainly focused on cash. "He's with a Houston mutual fund, oil and gas related. She's assistant to a wedding planner."

She changed the subject. "Sam, you've just graduated, right? What's next?"

"I've got to make some money this summer. I'll be driving a truck for an oil field company out west of Menard, in the Permian," he said. "That's what I did last summer—made enough for books, tuition, and rent. Then in September I start grad school at UT."

"In?"

"It's a joint program between psych and the AI faculty," he said. "Really cutting edge in both areas."

Isabel, listening, broke in. "Sam, send her a link to the website where your senior paper was published." He blushed but nodded.

Alice decided she'd definitely read it. "Please do send it, will you?"

By nine Sam had picked up Carrie and toted her out to the Land Cruiser. Isabel hugged Alice and ran out the door. Alice kissed Kinsear, then kissed him again and sniffed his neck. Yes, he smelled right. But he had to go home tonight.

When the house was empty Alice walked out onto the deck, stared up at the darkening summer night, and watched the first stars come out. In less than a week the summer solstice would arrive. She wished she were somewhere above the Arctic Circle, alone with Kinsear, celebrating the longest day and shortest night of the year.

Instead, she thrashed all night dreaming of meetings where she couldn't come up with the right phrase, the right answer, to some mysterious question. What was the question?

Stained Codicil

iles called while she was driving to the office Saturday morning.

"I've got that document back from the Questioned Documents section," he said. "The one we found in Ms. Windom's pocket. Can you come over? I'm here until noon."

Virtually all the Courthouse parking slots were empty on a perfect June morning. Alice parked and darted into the Sheriff's Annex and asked for Files.

He came down the hall to get her and walked her back to his small, crowded office. Alice sat down on the institutional metal chair in front of his desk.

"Take a look, and you'll see why I need to talk to you," he said, pointing to the evidence packet on his desk. Inside its own plastic envelope she saw the once-folded paper from Ellie's pocket, now wrinkled and stained brownish red and yellow but with Ellie's angular writing and flashy capitals still visible.

"Here are two copies, printed so you can read past the stains. The documents people think they're pretty accurate copies."

Alice picked up the sheet he handed her. At the top she saw in blue ballpoint ink, in Ellie's handwriting, her own name: "Alice Greer, for my file."

Then she read, "I, Ellie Windom, make this codicil to my current will. From the box in my attic in Santa Fe, which I believe may contain Gustave Baumann woodcuts, I leave to my grandson Max the print titled *Chama Stream* and to my grandson Drake the print titled *Deception Peak*, and to each the woodblocks belonging to his print."

Alice turned the page, where the writing continued:

"Second, to my daughter, Valerie Ames, who will not otherwise inherit from my estate, I have given, or am giving, my woodcut of *The Bishop's Apricot*, and to her twins, also my grandchildren, from the box described above the two prints titled *Moon over Taos Village* and *Children at Chimayo* and the woodblocks belonging to those prints.

"Third, to the New Mexico Museum of Art I leave the remaining five prints of the Pecos River area, the related materials, and the box and painted wood items.

"Finally, to Judith Strong, three thousand dollars."

Aha, Alice thought. Solomonic wisdom from Ellie.

Below she saw Ellie's signature and the date: the Monday before she died.

"So what do you call this?" Files asked, brown eyes fixed on her. "This is your area, right? Wills and trusts?"

"It's a holographic will. Handwritten, signed and dated."

"Is it valid?"

"Looks like it."

"There aren't any witness signatures. No one notarized it. Don't you have to do that for a valid will?"

"Not for a proper holographic will. I believe it's valid under Texas law," Alice said, feeling a bit as if she were taking a law school exam. "It sure looks like Ellie's handwriting, Ellie's signature. Whether anyone will challenge it—that's another story." But now, she thought, perhaps the New Mexico Museum of Art would want to defend Ellie's gift.

"So, what do we do with this—this hologram?" Files said.

Alice laughed. "It is like a hologram. A holographic will is like a recording of that person appearing right in front of you and producing her handwritten declaration of what she intends." She sobered, looking at the stained and wrinkled original in the plastic bag. "For you, given the stains, I guess it's evidence that Ellie wrote it before she died. The location—her back pocket—and the note at the top may indicate she intended to bring it to me for our three o'clock meeting. I'll have to present it to the court along with her current will." Normally she'd file the original with the probate court. "Can you get me an affidavit from the Questioned Documents people saying they confirmed it's Ellie's handwriting?"

"Yes. But listen, does it give us a motive? Help us figure out who killed her?"

Alice looked up. "Did you ever ask Ellie's housekeeper—Judith Strong— about the hot words she overheard between Don and his mother? That was the same day as the date on this."

"Yes. She heard him trying to get Ellie to sell Wildflower Central. Ellie apparently refused." He looked at the notes he'd taken. "She also heard Ellie say something about grandchildren, like 'leave everything to the grandkids.' She wasn't quite sure about that last bit."

Alice remembered the look on Ellie's face, the look of mingled frustration and irritation, when Ellie sat in her office that Sunday afternoon. "Judith told me she heard Ellie say that." She glanced down at the codicil. "But Ellie didn't do that, did she. She just made specific gifts to two grandchildren, two other grandchildren she'd never met, and her birth daughter, Valerie Ames. And a museum. And her housekeeper."

"What about this Valerie Ames? Does she have a motive? I mean, she was adopted, but she's still Ellie's daughter."

Alice sat back in the metal chair, thinking. "If the lawyer who drew up Ellie's will was right, and the adoption order said Valerie could not inherit from her birth mother, then…no. Ellie told me there was such an order. But I haven't seen it, and the adoption took place over fifty years ago."

"What if Valerie didn't know about the adoption order? What if she thought she could inherit, just like the two sons?" Files leaned forward, ball-point pen poised over his notebook.

"Well, Ellie's codicil should wipe that out. Ellie named Valerie as her daughter but says she won't inherit under the will," Alice said.

"So Valerie could challenge the codicil, wanting to inherit like the two sons?" Files asked.

Reluctantly, Alice nodded. Valerie had made it crystal clear that she wanted nothing to do with her half-brothers…but wasn't that a different question from inheriting a third of her mother's estate?

"What about the sons?" Files was taking notes.

"They might challenge the codicil because it gives away potentially valuable woodcut prints."

Files stared down at his notes, then up at Alice. "But here's this codicil, folded and stashed in Ms. Windom's back pocket. If the killer knew about it, and didn't like it, wouldn't the killer have taken it?"

Alice's imagination took her to Ellie's kitchen, to Ellie turning from her phone call with Valerie to a person who'd maybe walked right into the kitchen. She thought about Ellie's clothes, and why someone might stash a single folded sheet in her back pocket. She thought about Ellie's decision to write that codicil, after their meeting the Sunday morning before she died. She pointed to the codicil in the evidence bag. "Did you find any prints besides Ellie's?"

"Nope."

"I don't know," she said, finally. "I have to ask again—have you found a murder weapon yet?"

He frowned, shaking his head. "We've searched that place several times…the ditches by the driveway, the pastures…nothing."

She lifted her copy of the codicil. "I'll need the original for the probate court. And that affidavit."

He nodded. "Thanks, Alice. I'll get both to you on Monday." He unfolded his long legs, stood up, walked her back to the front entrance.

She made her way slowly back down the Courthouse sidewalk to the loathsome loaner, musing on the vagaries of wills and trusts law, thinking of Files's list of suspects.

Ellie deserved better than having her children on that list.

* * * * *

The office held little appeal on Saturday afternoon. She left her copy of the stained codicil on Silla's desk with a note: "Files promised to give us the original on Monday with an affidavit that it appears to be her handwriting, to add to our application for probate. Let's file as soon as we can." She wondered how the beneficiaries would feel, opening their copies, about the stains on the codicil.

Feeling at loose ends, Alice made herself work awhile on questions for the Smutbuster deposition. She kept looking at the blue sky outside and finally threw down her legal pad. She should send thank-you baskets to Eddie and Conroy and Jorgé for their help catching Wiry Wayne and Burly Brian, still, per Files, in the Coffee County jail. She could rummage for some tights in the yoga bag hanging on her office door, take herself to yoga. Come on, Alice, you could just sit cross-legged on your office floor and meditate, couldn't you?

Instead, she grabbed for her phone when the message signal bonged. Roger: "Alice, tonight at the LBJ School, a State Department guy's lecturing on foreign interference with social media. My friend Grant arranged it. I can get you seats if you want." She thought for a moment about Sam's grad student focus and Isabel's interest in human motives, then forwarded the message to Isabel and Kinsear. Both responded immediately. "Can Sam come too?" Isabel texted. Alice replied to Roger: "Yes! Four seats."

Well, at least she'd see Kinsear. Somewhat cheered, she revised a few Smutbuster questions, then headed out of Coffee Creek down the creek road toward home. She glanced up automatically as she neared Ellie's gate. A familiar red pickup sat in Ellie's driveway. She veered off the creek road, pushed in the code at Ellie's gate and parked behind her best friend, Red, the horse whisperer.

Red, in jeans and boots, had herded the equines out of the corral and back into the pasture. She chained the pasture gate, then the corral gate.

"Saw your truck," Alice said.

"I told my high school kid I'd take weekend duty, Saturday and Sunday." Red pulled a bandana from her rear pocket and wiped sweat from her forehead. "I know these horses miss Ellie."

"How do you know what they're thinking?"

Red shook her head. "I just try to think like a horse."

Alice looked downhill. The horses and the stubby pony stood in the sun, peacefully cropping grass. "Do you always put them back in the pasture? They don't stay in the corral at night? Or the barn?"

"It's not cold, it's not wet, the grass hasn't dried up yet, and I like them to get plenty of pasture exercise. So they get a hay snack, then go back to the pasture. They've got another water trough, down by the windmill."

Red re-locked the corral, spinning the dial on the combination lock.

Alice stood for a moment, looking from Ellie's house, with the flapping crime tape, to the horses. "Can't the horses tell no one's living here now? Don't they feel lonesome? Uneasy?" That's how she'd feel, outside at night without a roof over her head.

"This time of year, they don't need to be cooped up in a stall." Red dusted her hands on her jeans. "You have any plans tonight?"

"Kinsear and I are taking his daughter Isabel and her boyfriend to a lecture in Austin at the LBJ Library."

"Isabel's got a beau? Do you like him?"

"I do. And she does. Most important, I think her dad can tolerate him."

"I've got to boogie," Red said. "I'll be back here in the morning."

Alice turned her car and started down the drive, followed by Red in her truck. Kinsear, Isabel, and Sam would pick her up in an hour. She hoped this outing wouldn't bore them to tears.

Chapter Twenty-Three

Alice Is a Noticer

To Alice's astonishment Isabel and Sam had packed a "car picnic" for the drive to Austin for the lecture at the LBJ Library. "Because we won't have time for dinner," Isabel said in a serious tone. "No dinner means I fidget in my seat and think only of food. So we brought provisions." She opened the small cooler on the back seat.

Sam handed two sandwiches wrapped in waxed paper up to Alice. "One for you and one for Mr. Kinsear. Veggie cream cheese. Homemade by Isabel. Chips too," he said. "Barbecue, vinegar, chili pepper, or regular?"

Alice grinned. "Regular, please." Alice was tickled by the fact that the young people had packed food for their elders. Had even made veggie cream cheese. Again, cozy, domestic. This pair was moving fast. Now she heard them privately murmuring to each other in the back seat...a delightful sound. She resisted the urge to peek at them.

Kinsear kept his eyes on the road. "Anything new on Ellie's death?" he asked, his voice low.

Alice told him about the holographic will.

"Whoa," he said. "Sounds like a law school exam. And this was in Ellie's back pocket?"

"Yep."

"So she had it—or stashed it—when her visitor arrived."

"Sounds likely," Alice said.

"But you still don't know who showed up?"

"Nope."

"And no murder weapon?"

"Not yet," she said. Was Files still searching, or had he given up?

As they exited the MoPac Expressway into the neighborhoods west of UT, Isabel piped up from the back seat. "Hey, Alice? What's Roger's involvement with this lecture?"

"He's staying with an ex-CIA guy he knew back in his foreign service days, Grant Hines. Hines has connections with tonight's speaker, who's with the State Department—an assistant secretary for security."

"Spies," Isabel concluded.

The sun was just setting above the hills west of Austin as they turned from Red River Street into the vast parking lot that served the long, low arcades of the LBJ School of Public Affairs. Behind the LBJ School loomed the imposing white LBJ Library. The two buildings overlooked most of the UT campus. As the four exited the parking lot, they passed an official-looking black sedan with tinted windows. Two men in dark suits stood by the sedan, their sunglasses glinting in the late sunlight. Alice noted their earbuds and the "U.S. Government" license plate and elbowed Kinsear. "State Department security?" she asked.

"Looks like it."

They crossed under the open arcade below the LBJ School and toiled up the long concrete ramp, with its occasional steps, to the LBJ Library courtyard entrance. "I never feel like I get the rhythm of these steps," Alice said to Kinsear.

"Maybe the architects thought it was an allegorical way to reach a presidential library," he answered. "It's a long hard pull, but the view from the top's awesome."

"Maybe so," she puffed.

"I'd say the top of the ramp's at least fifty feet above the ground."

They reached the courtyard at the top. Alice tugged Kinsear's sleeve. "Stop." They gazed west toward the cedar-covered hills of the Balcones Escarpment, the uplift that separated the black dirt of the plains to the east from the spring-riddled limestone of the Edwards Plateau to the west. "You can see why Austin calls those hills the 'violet crown.'"

"I love these long June sunsets," Kinsear commented. "It won't be dark for at least an hour."

"It's almost the summer solstice," Alice said.

They crossed the courtyard and entered the glass-walled lobby, joining a mixed crowd of students wearing jeans and carrying backpacks and slightly more formally dressed Austinites. The crowd slowly moved downstairs and stood in line to check in. A fresh-faced student scanned a list, then handed Alice four tickets.

The auditorium was filling fast. "Big crowd for a Saturday night in June," Kinsear commented.

"Summer school starts Monday," Sam said. "I heard a lot of

buzz about this lecture before the term ended. Foreign interference in social media, embassy security…sexy stuff. Plenty of people at UT are studying the impact of misinformation and disinformation online."

Kinsear found four seats on the aisle, half-way down. Isabel, then Sam, then Alice, then Kinsear edged into the row. "Thanks for letting me have the aisle," Kinsear said.

"Otherwise, your legs encroach on my space!" Alice retorted.

On stage a young man checked the podium mike. Alice recognized the tall figure standing on the floor looking up at the stage, speaking to an attentive sixty-something man in blazer and slacks. The tall figure nodded, turned and walked up the aisle. Roger Preyer. Alice waved.

Roger smiled as he reached their row. "Didn't know if you'd make it." He greeted Isabel, who introduced Sam. "Glad you're here."

"Was that Grant Hines you were talking to?" asked Alice.

"Yes. He's the reason we got this speaker. They worked together. Embassy security."

"We saw some security detail outside," Kinsear said. "Earbuds and all."

Roger nodded. "This speaker's pretty important. Not someone we'd want to lose."

Somewhere a bell bonged. A spotlight lit the podium. "Gotta go." Roger walked back down to the first row and sat down next to Grant Hines.

The dean of the LBJ School tapped the podium mike, and the evening began. The dean introduced the State Department official, who paid compliments to the evening's hosts and gave a short summary of his talk. A screen descended above the stage, and the program began. Using the slides projected on the screen, the speaker highlighted techniques used to spread—and detect—offshore disinformation. Alice peeked at Sam and Isabel. Their faces were rapt.

Thirty minutes flew by. The dean approached the podium. "We'll have a short intermission, then …"

Alice heard nothing more: Roger, face bleak, lips pursed in

a straight line, came striding fast up the aisle, eyes riveted to his phone, with the face of a man who'd received the worst news.

"Something's really wrong," she told Kinsear, standing and squeezing past him. She trotted up the aisle after Roger. Kinsear followed with Sam and Isabel in close pursuit. Roger had already reached the top of the stairs to the lobby. Alice grabbed the handrail and climbed as fast as she could. Across the lobby she spotted Roger, dialing his phone. Still holding it, he pushed his way outside into the red light from the setting sun. Alice saw two almost identically burly men dressed all in black—boots, long-sleeved shirts, ball caps, and wraparound sunglasses—hurry out the door behind him. One crowded up to his left side, the other to his right. Surprised, Roger struggled to get free. The two men crowded him, marched him across the courtyard toward the long ramp down to the sidewalk.

"Roger!" she yelled. One of the black-shirted men looked back, then hustled Roger onto the ramp. Kinsear and Alice ran for the ramp, dodging the startled guests streaming onto the courtyard for intermission.

"Stop!" roared Kinsear. Each of the two black-shirted men, already clutching Roger's arms, grabbed at his legs. Caught between the two men, Roger twisted and kicked.

The assailant to their left now had one arm around Roger's waist and one around his leg and struggled to lift Roger, as he twisted and kicked, toward the top of the wall along the ramp—fifty feet above the ground. Kinsear launched himself toward the assailant, grabbing his legs, causing him to hit his head on the concrete top step of the ramp and go limp. Sam tackled the attacker on the right, dodging his booted kicks, while Isabel tore Roger's arm free from the man's grip. Alice grabbed Roger's phone, which flew out of the mix. Two men in dark suits, white shirts, and sunglasses thundered across the courtyard onto the ramp, nearly knocking Alice over, and swarmed onto Sam and Kinsear, pinning their arms behind them, with Roger crushed beneath. The attacker Sam had tackled wriggled free and ran down the ramp.

"Hey!" yelled an outraged Kinsear. "We're the good guys!" He rolled over and glared at the dark-suited men. "Who the hell are you?"

"Who the hell are you?" demanded the taller of the two.

"Roger's friends!" yelled Alice. "Go catch that man who ran down the ramp! He tried to kill Roger!"

But the man had disappeared into the shrubbery below.

Sam rolled sideways, freeing Roger, who scrambled to his knees, then stood.

Alice, kneeling on the hard concrete, peered at the closed eyes of the man Kinsear had tackled.

"I think his bell's rung," Kinsear said.

The shorter of the two dark-suited men, blond, crew-cut, flashed a badge. "Federal agents. State Department security. Watching out for Roger Preyer, among others."

Alice glared at him. "Kind of late to the party."

Isabel scowled up at the taller man, who'd grabbed Sam from behind. "You gave Sam a bloody nose and let the attacker get away!"

The taller man lifted an eyebrow and pulled out his phone. He called campus security, asking for an immediate search of the area. "Guy dressed all in black, long sleeves, long pants, boots, black cap, just ran down the ramp from the LBJ Library. Attacked a former State Department rep." He halted, listening. "Well, call the Austin Police Department too. ASAP." Alice heard him say to the blond agent, "Campus loses jurisdiction once the perp makes it across Dean Keeton." Alice realized the assailant might have made it across Dean Keeton Street, immediately adjacent to the LBJ Library, before the federal agent finished his call.

Roger turned to Alice. "I've got to call Kristi."

Alice handed him his phone, asking "What happened? Who called you?"

"I got a text that Randall was in an accident, was in a hospital in Santa Fe." Randall, his son, his only son.

"Who sent the text?" This from the taller of the two security men, serious, dark-haired.

Roger looked down at his phone. "I don't know who. I didn't recognize the number. I tried to get Randall, but the call went to voicemail." He dialed his phone. "Kristi. Is Randall okay?" He listened. His face cleared. "Oh, uh…someone sent me a message. Said

Randall was in an accident, was in a Santa Fe hospital. I couldn't get him on the phone." He listened. "No, I'm fine. Maybe Wednesday."

Roger hung up. "As far as Kristi knows, he's fine." Roger punched in another number. "Randall? Is that you? You okay?" He looked at Alice, nodded. "I was just checking. Are you in Santa Fe?" He paused. "Okay, see you this week. Give your mom a call. Love you." He shook his head. "He's fine. He's not even in Santa Fe; he's at home in Albuquerque."

Roger turned to the two security men. "Classic. Lure me outside with a fake call." They frowned, nodded.

"That kind of message," Alice retorted, "that your child is in the hospital—any parent goes straight into panic mode. You have to respond immediately. But…who were those guys?"

The two agents stared at Roger. Alice speculated that the narrowed eyes on the blond agent were supposed to warn Roger—don't divulge classified information.

"No idea," Roger said. "I've never seen them before. Here's the text I got." He held out his phone to the agents. "They didn't say which hospital in Santa Fe. St. Vincent, Presbyterian…?" Roger shook his head. "What a dope. A real friend would tell me which hospital."

The blond agent scribbled down the number. "We'll check."

Roger put his fingers in the ripped shoulder seam of his blazer, furrowed his brow, took off the blazer, folded it over his arm.

A bell rang. Intermission would end soon. The curious crowd at the top of the ramp finally turned and trailed back into the building. Nothing to see here…

"Well!" Isabel said. "That was exciting."

Roger looked at her. "Thank you, Isabel." He shook Sam's hand. Sam flinched, but only slightly. "Oh," Roger said. He handed Sam a clean handkerchief. Sam wound it around his abraded knuckles.

"Alice." To her surprise, Roger hugged her. "How did you know?"

"I saw your face. I knew it had to be your child or your grandchild…" Later she thought, why didn't I say "your wife"? The thought that Roger's dreadful news concerned Kristi had not crossed her mind, had not risen to the terrifying level of "child" or "grand-child." Hmm.

Roger thanked Kinsear. "You've wrecked your jeans."

Kinsear looked down. He'd worn old jeans, now with new rips at the knees, and a decent blazer. "Always fun to see if I still remember how to tackle."

A campus security guard hurried up the ramp, followed by two men in Austin Police Department uniforms.

The State Department security men cornered the police and beckoned to Roger. Roger gave them a version of events that Alice couldn't hear. The police handcuffed the still-groggy prisoner to the ramp handrail and called in an APB for his escaped colleague. Then Alice, Kinsear, Isabel, and Sam gave their brief statements and provided contact information. The agents looked on as the police marched their prisoner down the concrete ramp.

The bell rang again. End of intermission. "I've got to go back," Roger said. "There's a reception later. Are you all…do you want to come back in?"

Alice looked at Isabel, Sam, Kinsear. They didn't blink, just stared at her.

"Thanks for the tickets, Roger," Alice said. "I think we'll get some Mexican food."

Roger laughed in spite of himself.

Finally, Alice thought. He has finally laughed.

She hugged him. Then she took him by his now unblazered shoulders. "Are you riding home with Grant?" He nodded. "Because whoever sent that message…"

"Knew I was here. Yes, I know. I'll be very careful, Alice." He tilted his head toward the waiting agents.

"Well, maybe," she said, still dubious.

"Listen, I've met Valerie. I'll tell you later about that." Before she could frame a question, Roger turned and walked back across the courtyard to the library entrance, closely escorted by the two agents.

The western sky was orange now, streaked with dark violet. Streetlights flickered on across campus. From the courtyard Alice could see the law school building where, once upon a time, she and

Kinsear had studied. Those days felt far away. A soft breeze rattled the stiff leaves of the live oaks on the lawn below, carrying the indefinably pleasant fragrance that Alice always recognized…Austin. She remembered her first flight home from college, getting off the plane and smelling Austin air. Home! Once again Alice tried to analyze it… blooming shrubs, a touch of cedar, the scent of limestone, the smell of water…and something astringent. Live oaks? As usual, she failed to pin it down.

"Okay. What sounds good? Polvo's? Maudie's? Hecho in Mexico?" Kinsear paused. "Fonda San Miguel? La Condesa?"

"Salsa bar at Polvo's," Isabel declared.

"No objection here," Sam said.

"Gee, Alice," Kinsear said, dusting off his jacket. He took Alice's hand as they started down the ramp behind Isabel and Sam. "You do take us to the nicest events."

She rolled her eyes. But her mind was on Roger's text message… the kind guaranteed to bring a parent, a grandparent, dashing out of any event, without looking left or right, desperate to get in touch with the beloved child, the precious grandchild.

Who sent that text to Roger?

Someone who knew he was in Austin, at the LBJ Library, at this particular lecture. Someone who knew two attackers were poised in the courtyard. Yet his brake lines were cut somewhere in New Mexico. Who wanted to kill Roger, and why?

And that throwaway line—he'd met Valerie. She tried and failed to see how that meeting could trigger this attack.

Chills ran down her spine. Once again, she'd dragged her own loved ones into danger. But they wouldn't stand by, watching men heave Roger over the balcony.

Kinsear, maybe aware of her silence, put a warm arm around her. "If you hadn't seen Roger's face, Alice…"

She looked up at him.

"If you hadn't said 'something's really wrong…'" He nodded at the concrete wall of the ramp. "Roger could be lying dead down there."

"Alice is a noticer," Isabel said over her shoulder.

"Some humans are," Sam said. "Some aren't. And then there are those who notice but stand back."

"Not our way, I hope," Isabel said. "Okay. Am I going to have the shrimp fajitas? Or the tacos al carbon?" Holding hands, arms swinging, she and Sam started down the ramp.

Alice liked that. "Our way."

On the way to Polvo's Isabel spoke up. "So who knew Roger was at this lecture on disinformation? Were those black-shirts after him because of his foreign service work? Like, Putinesque assailants?"

Sam grunted. "The one who got away cussed me out, called me *hijo de puta.*"

Alice knew that one. Son of a whore. So, more local than, say, Moscow or the Middle East. Maybe homegrown.

Chapter Twenty-Four

Don't Make Assumptions

Late Sunday morning, all alone. Alice fixed herself a second latte, grinding the beans, making espresso, frothing the milk. Her ritual coffee provided caffeine and comfort but didn't allay her worry about unfinished business with Chuck and Don Windom. They'd rushed out of her conference room on Friday trying not to be late to their mother's memorial service, before Alice could discuss the inventory of Ellie's Santa Fe house… including the precious box found in her attic. The next morning Files had shown her the handwritten codicil found on Ellie's body. She needed to tell Chuck and Don that, under the codicil, not only their sons but two other grandchildren they'd never heard of would be receiving a print from the precious box, with the box, its remaining contents and two hand-painted chairs going to the New Mexico Museum of Art, along with three thousand to Judith Strong. And that Alice would be notifying Valerie, the four grandchildren, the museum, and Judith Strong that they too were beneficiaries.

She didn't look forward to that discussion. Ellie's sons were stunned enough to hear Ellie had a birth daughter and more stunned to hear Ellie had been in touch with her. Alice remembered Chuck's round eyes, his mouth agape.

Oh, yes, there's so much we never know about the secret lives of our parents. Alice often thought of questions she'd like to ask her own parents. Questions she'd never asked, maybe never *wanted* to ask, while they were alive. She and Red had once discussed that over late-night wine, proposing possible questions they wished they'd asked…maybe.

Red came up with, "Did you ever wonder if your mother ever, in her whole life, loved someone else?"

Alice said, "Did you ever wonder what was the worst thing they ever did?"

Red said, "I'd like to know—now—what they were most ashamed of and never told." She paused. "Well, maybe I don't want to know. Same with 'did they actually like, not just love, their children?' No to that one."

Alice asked, "Why didn't I ask them to tell me their earliest memories? What they remembered of their own parents and grandparents?

What was their most frightened moment?"

And so on. Did they believe in life after death? What would they do differently now that they know what it's like to be dead? What advice do they wish they could give their children now that they can no longer give it? Because, frankly, Alice would be grateful for such advice. She also wondered what advice she could give her children before it was too late.

She shook these thoughts away, standing on her deck taking in the sunlit valley below. The summer air smelled green and glorious. She could stop by the office for a while…maybe call Red to see if she was at Ellie's, taking care of Ellie's horses. Maybe she'd even help—so long as Red didn't assign her any tasks like putting a saddle or bridle on a horse. Maybe she and Red could go to the afternoon yoga class and then stop somewhere on Ranch Road 12 for pizza and artisanal beer, sitting outside at a picnic table under a live oak.

She tugged on yoga pants and a top, grabbed her mat and marched out to the loathsome loaner. Thank God, if the collision shop kept its word, tomorrow she could retrieve her Discovery. She just had to survive twenty-four more hours driving this tuna-fish can, which smelled like tuna fish…among other things.

Alice was halfway to town on the creek road, almost to Ellie's, when her phone rang.

Red, her voice high and tight. "Alice? Listen, can you come over to Ellie's? I found something weird…in the corral. In the haystack."

"What?"

"I'm not sure. You need to see. It's—weird."

"I'm turning onto Ellie's drive right this second."

Red had parked her red truck in the pole barn, next to Ellie's old Mercedes. She stood grim-faced by the round bale of hay in the corral.

Alice flung open the tuna-can's door and hurried over.

"Look." Red pointed at what looked like the end of a smooth pale wood baton, about an inch and a half in diameter, several inches of it poking up at an angle toward the center of the corral from the curved side of the half-eaten round bale.

"I started to pull it out," Red said. "I thought, what the heck is that? A horse could get hurt! Then I saw some…some…something on it." Alice lifted her eyes to Red's. Red's blue eyes were scared. "A darkish stain. Like … I don't know," Red said. "I just know it doesn't belong in this hay bale."

Alice speed-dialed Files. Sunday morning. No answer. She left a message. "We're at Ellie's. My friend Red found something odd in the hay bale in the corral. A piece of wood. She says it's stained."

He called back immediately, demanding details. Then, "Don't touch anything. I'm on my way."

Alice stared unseeing at the barn, remembering Kinsear's arrival in her kitchen one winter night. He'd brought pizza sauce, dough and toppings, declaring, "Romantic Friday dinner! How about if we try out my new pizza stone on your grill?" He'd assembled the toppings and slapped the ball of pizza dough onto a floured cutting board, only to discover the dough was still partly frozen. "No problem," he said, snatching up Alice's long rolling pin…a pale wooden baton, eighteen inches long, smooth and strong. Then he'd whacked the frozen dough into submission. Bam! Bam! Bam! When the ball of dough yielded, Kinsear triumphantly rolled it into a circle. The pizza? Smoky, spicy, delicious. But she still remembered the loud whacking, echoing around the kitchen.

"Doesn't the end of it look kind of like a rolling pin?" Red asked. "You know, the French kind?"

Alice nodded.

That ball of pizza dough was no match for the rolling pin. And for a skull? Alice shuddered, remembering the pool of blood beneath Ellie's head.

Files and Joske sped up the drive, followed by a second car with two crime scene techs.

Alice and Red walked out to meet them. Alice introduced Red. "She and her helper have been checking on Ellie's horses since Ellie died."

"You've met Assistant Detective Alan Joske," Files said. "Meet our techs, Ann Hayden and Rocky Cruz. They probably skipped church this morning hoping to sleep late. Didn't work out, did it, Rocky?"

The dark-haired young man smiled briefly, but his eyes were on the hay bale.

Alice said, "Red started to pull out that…that piece of wood"—she pointed—"but she stopped."

"I held it only by the end," Red said.

Ann Hayden took Red's fingerprints. Rocky Cruz entered the corral and circled the haystack, taking pictures.

Alice and Red stood on the bottom rail of the corral watching the two detectives and the techs examine the hay bale. Finally, the two techs carefully removed the baton with a large amount of surrounding straw and put the entire assembly into a large evidence container. "Let me see this baton, or whatever it is," Files said, leaning over them.

Hayden gently pushed back enough straw that all could see the eighteen inches of bare wood. "Stains," said Hayden. "Maybe blood and something more. Looks like someone wiped the wood before shoving it in the haystack. Didn't wipe it very well. See how the stains are smeared?"

"Funny place to put a murder weapon, if that's what we've got," Files mused. "But you know the rule, don't make assumptions. We'll know more after we get test results."

"That looks like my rolling pin at home," Alice said from her perch at the corral fence.

Files looked at her, then at Ellie's house, then at the Dutch door leading inside, then back at the evidence container. "Ah," he said. "Could've been Ellie Windom's. Right out of her kitchen."

Alice said, "Judith Strong might know. Ellie's housekeeper, remember? She told Silla and me that something was missing."

Files lifted an eyebrow at Joske, who was taking notes. "Let's get her back in." He looked back at Alice. "Maybe I'll borrow your rolling pin, if you're sure it looks like this one."

The techs walked slowly around the corral, scrutinizing the dirt, the fence, the chain over the gate to the pasture, the padlock on the corral gate to the driveway. "Ms. Windom was killed thirteen days ago, right? Was the round bale close to new then?" Rocky asked Files.

Red spoke up. "It was. The horses have eaten it way down. Another bale's coming on Thursday."

"It would take some strength to shove that baton into a new hay bale," Joske said.

Alice thought about that.

"Assuming someone shoved the baton deep enough into that bale, deep enough where it couldn't be seen, the horses probably ate some of our evidence. Maybe some hay with fluid residue," Files said, shaking his head. "To think this was right here, when we were searching the house, the ditches, the pastures, the barn…"

To think it was right here the day Ellie died, when the horse ran back into the corral and I chained the gate, Alice thought. Right here the afternoon of Ellie's memorial service, when Silla and I stopped by to check the horses. Right here, the whole time.

How odd, though, to shove a murder weapon—if that's what it was—into a hay bale. To leave it where it could be discovered. Why wasn't it carried away, thrown off a bridge, burnt in a bonfire?

Alice turned to say something to Red but noticed how white she was, how withdrawn.

"Red," she said, putting her hand on Red's arm. "Let's get out of here. They don't need us."

Red said nothing, just nodded, staring blankly into the corral at the techs, still working.

Alice tried again. "What about the noon yoga class, then maybe lunch? As a reward?"

Red's eyes refocused. She turned to Alice. "Deal. Let's go eat lunch at that new place on the creek road. Picnic tables and an egg salad sandwich." She paused. "I've got yoga togs in the truck. I'll grab 'em. We can take your car."

Alice nodded. She was glad Red hadn't opted for pizza. Bam! Bam! Bam! She squeezed her eyes shut, trying to exorcise the memory.

*****

Two hours later, sweaty and virtuous after a demanding class and an undemanding picnic table lunch, with a beer, Alice and Red climbed back into the loaner and headed north up the creek road. As they neared Ellie's drive, Red leaned forward in the passenger seat, squinting through the windshield.

"Who's that?" Red pointed.

Alice whipped the wheel to the right, punched the gate code into Ellie's gate, and parked directly behind a white Lincoln Navigator.

She hopped out, followed by Red.

Don Windom's wife, Danielle, stood at the corral gate, scanning the barn, corral, pasture. She gave them a quick look, turned back to the corral, then spun and seemed to start toward Ellie's house for a moment, where crime scene tape flapped across the Dutch door, then stopped and walked slowly back across the graveled area toward them, blonde hair glinting in the sun, eyes hidden behind designer sunglasses. Skinny jeans, tank top, fancy suede ballet flats. She was rattling keys in one hand.

"Were you looking for something?" Alice asked.

"No. Thought I'd stop by Don's old home place. Nice day so…so I thought I'd scout some new wedding venues."

"All the way from Houston on Sunday afternoon?"

Danielle paused. "Less traffic on Sunday. Coffee Creek's got a venue or two. Not really worth the trip though."

Snob, thought Alice.

Red asked, "Which one did you visit?"

The sunglasses turned toward Red. "Creek House." She gave Alice's loaner a dismissive look, then: "I need to head back. Don will be getting anxious."

"Okay. Safe travels," Alice said. She walked back to the loaner, watched Danielle climb into the Navigator, then backed the loaner into a space in the pole barn.

The Navigator sped past her and down the drive, paused at the gate, then turned left toward the highway back to Houston.

Alice rejoined Red in the corral where Ellie's horse, Woodie's horse, and the pony stood peering into the corral from the pasture. When Red unlocked the pasture gate, the three equines trotted in, nudged each other into place at the remains of the round bale and began munching. Ellie's horse showed no trace of the terrorized animal someone had locked in her house. Watching the horses, Alice felt almost contemplative…or maybe it was the yoga. Or the beer? Alice had discovered she felt oddly peaceful when she patted her own donkeys. When they moved closer, leaned against her, enjoying a pat, she always felt her own breath slow and deepen, felt her eyes close, felt one with donkeys and pasture. At least for a moment.

The sun slanted across the pasture, across the corral. A mockingbird sang from the top of the telephone pole by the barn. Mockingbird aria, theme and variations, Alice thought.

"These horses are doing fine." Red's voice changed. "Hey—I guess Danielle did climb into the corral."

"Hmm?" Alice was still focused on the mockingbird, beak sharp against the sky.

"Danielle climbed in here."

"How do you know?"

"She dropped that tissue." Red pointed to the bottom edge of the bale on the side facing the barn.

"Huh," Alice said. She didn't think the crime techs this morning would've left even a scrap of paper. But the image of Danielle climbing into the Navigator popped up…with a little hay on one of her suede flats. Reflexively, Alice tiptoed past the pony and picked up the pink tissue, holding it by one corner. Why? she asked herself. Danielle's not a suspect.

"So what was she really doing here?" Red asked. "Drove all the way from Houston to check out Creek House?"

Alice frowned.

"I don't know," she said at last. "Maybe that tissue just blew in. Anyway, she was at work the day Ellie died. The police already checked." Alice looked back at the house, crime tape still waving from the Dutch door. "Maybe she went inside. Or tried to. Then we showed up." Those jingling keys.

But still…why did Danielle bring Don here, the afternoon of Ellie's memorial service?

Why was she here today?

In the loaner she found the plastic folder of rental documents. Better than nothing. She dumped out the documents and poked in the pink tissue.

Chapter Twenty-Five

Knowledge Is Power

On Monday Silla met Alice at the office front door and handed her a mug of coffee. "Call Clare Graham, that Santa Fe appraiser. Urgent, he says."

Alice dropped her briefcase by the desk, grabbed a tablet and pen, installed herself in her chair, and called Graham.

"Hey, Alice. I've got news." His voice sounded vibrant, excited.

"What's up?"

"I got curious about who owned Ellie's Moon Mountain house before her. I found the deed in the property records. Did you know the house used to belong to Agnes Dietz?"

Alice remembered the deed from Ellie's file folder. "Right, she bought it out of the estate of Agnes Dietz."

"Yes! Do you know who that was?"

"No."

"She was a character, one of those intense, talented women who wind up in Santa Fe."

"Tell me!"

"Well," Graham said, "she was German-American. Grew up in New York, with money. Arrived in Santa Fe around 1954. Per the property records, she bought the Moon Mountain house in 1956. Early on, she opened a bookbinding studio for art books, but hiking became a passion. She hiked the desert, the mountains, rivers, canyons. She published one book of petroglyph photos she'd taken but refused to tell people where they were."

"Interesting woman," Alice said.

"Did I say she was heartbreakingly beautiful?" Graham went on. "Didn't wear makeup, dressed mostly in chinos or hiking shorts and a sombrero, red bandana, beat-up Swiss hiking boots."

"Sounds like you knew her?"

"I met her at a gallery opening in 1985, when I first came to Santa Fe."

"Was she wearing her sombrero?" Alice joked.

"No, but she always wore those hiking boots." He stopped, started again, voice confessional. "I was twenty-two, and she took my breath away. She somehow glowed, like she was radioactive. She rarely smiled, but when she did everyone stopped talking and just stared. By then she was fifty-something, a power in the Santa Fe art scene. So far as I know, she never married, had no children…I never heard of any living relatives. The New Mexico Museum of Art was after her for a big donation, but somehow they got crosswise, and she withdrew her support."

"Wonder what happened?"

"I tried every which way to find out," Graham said. "Never got a straight story. But I think it involved work by Baumann. The museum has a big collection of his prints."

Gustave Baumann… "Tell me more," Alice said.

"Baumann died in 1971. I'm sure Agnes Dietz met him," Graham said. "He and his wife were beloved in Santa Fe. They built a marionette theater in their living room; he carved the marionettes. After I saw the deed, and realized Agnes had owned the house, and thought about the charming box and chairs, I began wondering if Agnes put them in the attic herself."

"When did she die?" Alice asked.

"1987. She fell on a solo hike up Deception Peak." He sighed. "Broke my young heart."

"Ellie bought the house from the Dietz estate in 1989."

"Right," Graham said. "So when did Ellie find the box?"

Alice didn't want Graham raising questions about Ellie's entitlement to that box.

"My impression was she found them on one of her Santa Fe trips after Woodie died. But they're definitely hers," she said. "The deed from Dietz's estate included house and contents." She wondered if Ellie ever got a bill of sale listing whatever the "contents" were. Maybe in the sales contract?

"Working on this appraisal made me start pondering Agnes Dietz again," Graham said. "The more I think about Dietz's wealth and her art scene connections, the more possible it seems that the box and its contents have definite connections to Baumann."

"Ah." Alice said.

"You know I'm bothered that some of those prints aren't signed, aren't numbered, aren't titled. The subjects are typical of Baumann, but I've never seen them before, and I thought I'd seen them all. That could lower their value. But something occurred to me that might go the other direction. I'm leaning toward revising my appraisal for the Santa Fe house contents."

"Revising it upward?"

"Cautiously, but yes."

Should she mention Ellie's codicil, giving four woodcuts to her grandchildren and the rest to the New Mexico Museum of Art? No, not until after she filed the application for probate of the will and codicil and sent notice to all beneficiaries. Clare was an inveterate gatherer of information in the Santa Fe art world…and probably a spreader too. Knowledge is power.

"Listen," Graham said. "Poker night's this Wednesday. Francis Blake says Roger's still in Austin. When's he coming back?"

"No idea."

They said goodbye.

Agnes Dietz. Ellie Windom. Two dynamite women.

Explosive, apparently.

*****

Alice sat at her desk, her stomach churning in the way it did when she knew she was dodging an unpleasant obligation. She needed to reconvene the Windom brothers to tell them about the codicil Files had given her on Saturday morning—the day after her Friday meeting with them before Ellie's memorial service.

She sent Chuck and Don an email saying new information had come to light; the police had found a codicil to Ellie's will. Could they be available for a conference call this afternoon? She attached a copy of the codicil.

She'd have to explain the box and the chairs at the same time. Which would mean stirring up a hornet's nest—explaining the gift to Valerie, four grandchildren, and the New Mexico Museum of Art, as well as Judith Strong. Don, at least, would resent any reduction of what he expected as his share of the estate, especially after Clare Graham's "upward revised" appraisal. Up until now the box hadn't been mentioned, right?

Would Valerie challenge the codicil? Claim she was entitled to a third of the estate? Alice hoped not.

"Hey, Alice." Silla popped her head around Alice's door, red ponytail swinging. "Listen, I'm still putting together the exhibits for our application for probate. Aren't you supposed to be on your way to Library Board? It's nearly noon!"

Alice stood up in relief and grabbed her handbag. Library Board sounded better than the afternoon conference call with Ellie's sons.

"Oh, and I've set up your call with the Windom boys at three." Silla waggled her eyebrows.

"Thanks so much." Alice put a little bite in her voice.

"And here's your copy of Ms. Smutbuster's lawyer's objections and responses to your discovery questions. Just got here. I'll forward it to the Library Board."

"Thanks again." Alice gave the response a quick look. "She's barely providing any documents! Can you set up a time for us to review them and get copies made?"

"Sure."

"And let's get a deposition date set. Say a week after we see their documents."

Grr, Alice thought, stomping off to the loathsome loaner. As she sped to the library, she tried to smile a few times into the rearview mirror. Otherwise, my smile muscles will atrophy...

Instead, her jaw dropped as she turned into the library driveway. Along the stone sidewalk leading to the library entrance marched fifteen or so mostly middle-aged men and women carrying signs. "Ban Harmful Harry!" "Ditch Damaging Books!" "No Fiendish Anti-Family Fantasy!" "Protect Our Youth!" Alice parked in the small parking lot and started back toward the library, feeling her blood pressure rise. She pulled out her phone and took a video.

When she reached the front sidewalk, three marchers stopped and blocked her way. "Shame!" they yelled. "Ban Potter! Stop damaging children!"

"Don't block my way, please," Alice said.

A burly woman with an angry face shouted "We have a right to be here!"

"But not to block the way into the library," Alice repeated. "Please move off the sidewalk."

"Who's gonna make me?" The woman leaned closer to Alice.

"I'll call the police right now if you continue blocking free entrance to the library." Alice felt her heart thump and her blood pressure rising into the red zone. Keep calm, she told herself.

"Okay, Wanda," said another marcher. "Back off a little."

"All the way off this sidewalk," Alice said, pushing her luck. "No blocking access for library patrons."

Wanda backed up six inches, still on the sidewalk. Alice lifted her phone. "I'm ready to dial," she said. "I need you to stay off the sidewalk. You're welcome to march along the street."

At that moment an elderly Buick carrying an elderly couple inched toward the sidewalk. The white-haired man who was driving parked the Buick, then came around the front of the car to open the passenger door. He helped out a silver-haired woman with a cane, who gazed with a puzzled face at the marchers.

"Why don't you like Harry Potter?" she asked. "My grandchildren love those books!'

Wanda snorted but moved into the flower bed by the sidewalk. Alice followed the silver-haired grandmother as she tapped her way into the library. She felt eyes on her back all the way. She wondered if one of the marchers might be Ms. Smutbuster.

When she emerged from her Board meeting an hour later, the marchers were gone, but the loaner's windshield was cracked.

Alice turned on her heel and went back inside to find Olive Gregg, the imposing head librarian. She told her what had happened.

"In the parking lot?" The librarian beamed a conspiratorial smile, then turned and called softly into a small office behind her. "Gene?"

A mild-mannered, middle-aged man emerged.

"Gene's our in-house genius," the librarian said. "Online books, Internet requests, you name it. Gene, can you see if someone attacked a car in the parking lot this afternoon? The last ninety minutes?" She turned to Alice. "What color and make?"

Alice told her. Gene disappeared back into his lair. He beckoned Alice. She leaned over his shoulder watching video from the closed-circuit system. "There!" she said.

"Someone trashing your windshield?" he said. "Looks like one of those marchers. I saw her this morning. Hang on, I'll make you a duplicate."

The day was improving.

On her way back to the office, Alice stopped at the collision shop to turn in the loaner and pick up her Discovery. It didn't smell quite hers yet—smelled like paint, polish, cleaner. But the new tailgate opened and closed smoothly. When she saw the bill, her jaw dropped. Her deductible was high…but so was the bill. "I'm sorry," said the cashier. "That tailgate assembly is pricey." Well, Alice thought, I've got an idea who should pick up the cost.

She told the cashier about the loaner's library adventure. "I've got a video," she offered.

The cashier shook her head. "Don't worry yet. I'll tell management what happened."

Alice climbed into her Discovery. Then a thought struck her. She climbed back out and buttonholed the repair garage manager. "Can you load my busted tailgate into the trunk?"

"Sure." Then he gave her a look. "Most customers never ask."

She said nothing.

"But you're the boss." He maneuvered the dented door into the rear of her Discovery.

Ye gods, she thought. I've still got that conference call with the Windom boys.

* * * * *

At three p.m. sharp Alice saw Chuck's face pop up on the screen.

"Let me guess," he said. "Don hasn't deigned to join us yet."

Alice smiled, but only with her mouth.

"This color picture you sent of both sides of the codicil," he said. "Those stains…they freak me out."

"The medical examiner found it in your mother's hip pocket," Alice said. "Unfortunately…"

"Yeah," he said. "Okay, I'm texting Don. I'll read it again while we wait on him."

At three-ten Don's face appeared on screen. "Market's just closing," he said. "Oil's up. Can't let opportunity slide."

"It closed ten minutes ago, Don," Chuck said with asperity.

Alice jumped in before Don could declare war. "On Saturday morning Detective George Files received your mom's personal effects from the medical examiner's office. Those included the hand-written codicil found in her back pocket. Because of staining the medical examiner sent it to the Questioned Documents section. That section made the enclosed copy that I sent you."

"But what does this mean?" Don burst out. "She already had a will. Can this handwritten piece of paper change it? There's no notarization, for sure."

She was surprised he said nothing about the stains.

"Texas recognizes holographic wills," Alice said. "If the testator—the person making the will—writes it completely in his or her own handwriting and signs it, it can be valid. No witness is needed. And as to her will, this codicil makes no change except what's specifically addressed here: her gift of *The Bishop's Apricot* to her birth daughter and specific woodcuts from a box she had in her Santa Fe attic to her four grandchildren: your boys, and her birth daughter's two children. She's giving the box, the remaining woodcuts in the box and two children's chairs to the New Mexico Museum of Art. And three thousand dollars to Judith Strong."

"Three thousand dollars? To the housecleaner? Why? And what about this box in the attic?" Don interrupted. "How come she never showed it to us? How much is it worth? Wouldn't it be part of dad's trust? She couldn't get rid of his assets, could she?"

Gee, you wanted her to sell Wildflower Central, Alice thought. "Actually, she could. But the Santa Fe house was your mother's separate property, bought in her name with her funds. Your dad agreed."

"Well, what about this box? If that came along later, why don't Chuck and I get it?"

"Her deed to the house indicates it includes both house and contents." She needed to ask the lawyer who'd drafted that deed for a copy of the sales contract…

Chuck broke in. "Don, what's your problem? What's wrong with

Mom making a gift to the museum? Or a gift to your son and my son? Or this birth daughter? Who's apparently our half-sister."

"What's wrong? We're first in line! She's reducing what we thought we'd get! I don't know about you, but I'm counting on it!" Don insisted. "How much are these woodcuts worth? You may be giving away a ton of dough, Chuck!"

"I'm not the one giving it away," Chuck said. His voice was harsh. "Our mother made a gift. Why do you think she's wasn't entitled to do so? Besides…" he paused. "Didn't she already do it?"

"Yes," Alice said. "Your mother sent *The Bishop's Apricot* and two woodcuts to her birth daughter before she died. She memorialized that in the codicil, giving the specific name of the woodcuts."

"Where's this box?" Don asked.

Alice felt an odd wave of reluctance. "It's been placed in safe-keeping," she began. Her office door opened. Silla.

"Excuse me, Alice, the library called. They need help. Said it's urgent."

"Chuck, Don, I'm sorry, but I need to deal with an emergency," Alice said. "Do you have any other questions?"

"You haven't said how much these damn prints are worth!" Don.

"I'll forward the original draft appraisal of the house contents to you, from Clare Graham. For the box and contents, he's provided a range from twenty thousand to two or three times that, depending on whether or not Baumann's the artist, and that's not clear. Some of the prints are unsigned. Graham said he may revise it higher."

"But the museum would get the biggest share?" Chuck asked.

"Yes."

"That's cool," he said, "if they'll name it after Mom. Can we make that happen?"

"Easy for you to say! I want my share of the cash!" Don cut in. "When's Graham going to give us a solid number?" Then in a different tone, "What if we challenge that codicil? I don't think Mom was playing with a full deck."

"There was nothing wrong with Mom!" Chuck snapped. "Don't you start that crap!"

"Gentlemen," Alice said, "I'm sorry to cut this short. We can reconvene later this afternoon or in the next few days when convenient for you, to discuss Graham's appraisal and also your positions on family real estate."

"Give me two more days on the real estate and set up a meeting. I'll have my answers," Chuck said.

"Sell it all!" Don said. He hung up.

"Thanks, Alice," Chuck said. "Tell Silla to email me about meeting times. Bye."

Whew. Alice wondered why Don was so vehement about getting cash. Didn't mutual fund advisers make good money? Danielle had a job…only one kid to put through school…

"Silla? What's up?"

Silla stuck her head around the door, eyes flashing. "The head librarian called. Mrs. Gregg. She was furious. Whoo-ee! Those marchers scared the second-graders who were visiting for their library field trip. Apparently, the school bus parked behind the building. When the children came around the side of the building and started toward the front sidewalk with their two teachers, the marchers rushed toward them, waving their signs and yelling. The teachers tried without success to clear the way, but by then the kids were freaking out. One little boy was crying and hiding behind his teacher. The teachers marched them all back to the bus and called off the field trip."

Second-graders. Alice called Mrs. Gregg.

"I want a restraining order, Alice." Her voice was icy. "Those people…those heartless people…scaring little kids at the library, for God's sake! The Board agrees."

"Did anyone take pictures?"

"Gene got some good shots." In steely tones she added, "Including crying children."

"Do you have any names, any phone numbers, for these marchers? Is this an organization, an association, or just a motley crew?" The lawyer for Mary Ellen Stokely, aka Ms. Smutbuster, had filed the lawsuit on her behalf as an individual, not an entity.

"I didn't recognize any of those people. Gene got some first names. He's checking our library card records to see if there are first-name matches. Then he can try a Facebook search, comparing online pictures to the pictures he took today."

Wow, if none of these characters are actual library patrons, that won't improve their case. "Okay," she told Mrs. Gregg, "For a TRO we need to ask the court for specific relief. These folks have First Amendment rights—but not to block, not to impede, and certainly not to frighten. What if we ask the court to require them to stay in the parking lot and not to impede anyone's access to the library or parking for library patrons? They'll complain, but everyone who drives in and parks will see their signs."

"Okay. And no bullhorns," Mrs. Gregg said through clenched teeth.

"Bullhorns?"

"I kid you not."

"Do you have tape of that?"

"Yes, on Gene's video. We could barely hear ourselves think."

"I'll need copies of Gene's pictures and videos. And I need to know the name of the group, if there's a name. Any possibility that one of those people is Mary Ellen Stokely?"

"I've got Gene on that. His pictures are on their way. I'll follow up on identities. I'm pretty sure one of those signs mentions the name of the group." Mrs. Gregg hung up.

Lord love a duck, Alice thought. She called the Board president: "File it," she barked. Alice began a request for a temporary restraining order or TRO. She might use the video of crying children not only at the TRO hearing but also at the Smutbuster deposition.

She stopped drafting for a moment, her heart speeding as she thought of her sins of omission, the tasks not yet done: she still needed to pin down what "contents" meant in Ellie's deed to the Santa Fe house. She left her desk and asked Silla to run that trap for her, see if she could find the sales contract in Ellie's papers, see if the lawyer for Agnes Dietz's estate was still around.

"Will do," Silla said. "Hey, Files sent over that affidavit from the Questioned Documents section. I've got your application for probate of the will and codicil ready to go."

"Hallelujah." Alice scanned the affidavit. "This looks good." Given the rumbles from Don about the codicil, she definitely wanted the judge to see an affidavit indicating Ellie wrote it.

Alice checked the exhibits, reread the application once more, and signed. "Thanks, Silla. After we file, let's send each beneficiary the documents and our probate letter. Email plus certified, return receipt requested."

"Wonder what they'll think of the stains on that codicil?" Silla asked. "Stains from when she died." She shook her head. "Filing something like that in court feels indecent. Too close to the bone."

Alice shuddered, remembering Ellie's body.

Another loose end should be on the to-do list, but she couldn't think what.

Her phone rang. Roger.

"I may head back to Santa Fe this week and didn't want to leave without telling you about my visit with Valerie," he said. "Do you like Japanese food? I managed to get a booth at Uchi for seven-thirty." The request was low-key, but his voice trembled with hope.

"Yes," she said. She drafted madly on the TRO request until seven, matching her text to Gene's pictures and video. She'd file first thing tomorrow. She threw her drafts into the Discovery and sped out of the office onto the highway toward Austin, watching for the exit onto Lamar, eager to hear Roger's story.

Chapter Twenty-Six

Worth More Dead Than Alive

Roger had gotten the best booth, in the rear corner at Uchi. Alice was jealous; he'd taken her favorite seat, back to the wall, so he could see the whole room. But not a bad idea, given he'd nearly gotten heaved off the terrace at the LBJ Library.

He stood to welcome her, smiling steadily. Blue blazer, blue button-down. "I'm glad you could come."

"Me too! This is a treat." Hot green tea appeared before her, gracefully arranged.

"I'm very fond of Japanese food," Roger said. "I was stationed in Japan for a year. You do like sushi? Sashimi?"

"Yes, except for shrimp," Alice said. "And tamago. And no eel. Just raw fish, please!"

"Shall I order for you then?"

She nodded. He rattled off a list to their waitress. Miso soup, seaweed salad, then the lovely fish… "Sapporo beer?" he asked. She nodded again. What a luxury, to have someone choose, and choose just what she wanted.

As the waitress scurried away, Alice looked Roger in the eye. "So many questions," she said.

"Shoot."

"What's the scoop on your black-shirted assailant? The one who didn't get away?"

"Austin police say he's from Albuquerque. Albuquerque police have his prints on file. They suspect he's got organized crime connections. All he'll say is that he and the other guy were hired by a man at a bar near Kirtland Air Force Base in Albuquerque. Half the cash up front, the rest when they finish the job."

"He's not out on bail, is he?" Alice asked.

"No, he's a flight risk. Thank goodness."

"But the other guy?"

Roger shook his head. "No idea who he is or where he is. So my buddy Grant suggested precautions."

"Such as?"

He thumped his chest. An odd sound…

"Ahh." Alice grinned. "Kevlar vest?"

Roger nodded. "Pretty hot, in June. But I promised Grant I'd wear this and a helmet when I drive back to Santa Fe. No helmet inside Uchi, though."

Alice spotted the helmet next to him on the bench.

Miso soup arrived. Seaweed salad. Icy Sapporo.

Alice took a sip of the beer, closed her eyes happily. Then she said, "Why did the man in the bar want you disposed of?"

Roger stared back, nodding gently. "Good question. Before he totally quit talking to the Austin cops, the guy in jail let slip that he and his buddy were told I was worth more dead than alive."

Worth more dead than alive?

"The police asked who my life insurance beneficiary was. It's Kristi, and of course she'd never do something like this."

Hmm. "What about a ghost from your past? Maybe you've got information from your days overseas, like in Ukraine, that someone wants to erase?"

"Grant wondered about that. He's run some traps with his agency friends. They haven't heard any rumors." He picked up his chopsticks and deftly scooped up a bite of seaweed salad.

Alice did the same, appreciating the crisp seaweed, the fragrant sesame oil.

"But hiring someone at a bar in Albuquerque? That's odd," she said. "Do you think those two guys also sliced your brake lines? Which happened while you drove away from Santa Fe, right?"

"Yes. Skillfully done, so they'd blow out on a highway."

Miso soup, savory, salty.

"You said you'd had the sense in Santa Fe that someone was following you, watching you," Alice said slowly. "When did you first notice?"

He sat, chopsticks poised, gazing just past Alice, remembering. "I met you Friday, at Desert Chorale. I had that sense of eyes on my back at least two days earlier."

"Was APD able to learn when your ninja buddies got hired?"

"Good question. I don't think they did."

Alice shook her head, puzzled by the whole scheme.

Elegantly sliced tuna sashimi arrived, followed by the first of their sushi, arranged on an earthenware platter shaped like a leaf. Roger signaled the waitress for two more Sapporos. Alice sighed in contentment.

After a decent interval, Roger wiped his mouth. "I want to tell you about Valerie."

Alice nodded as she maneuvered a slice of sashimi into her soy sauce and into her mouth.

"I got her on the phone in her office at UT and told her about my grandson's voyage into the DNA and ancestry websites. I told her I'd be in Austin for Ellie's memorial service. I said I would like to meet her, at least briefly."

Alice sat spellbound, imagining this conversation. "Did she want to see you?"

"No. She told me she loved her adoptive parents—that they were her true parents, and her kids' true grandparents. She admired them, loved them, cherished them, and didn't need any other parents."

Similar to my first conversation with her, Alice thought.

Roger went on. "I persisted. I said I understood and had no intention of foisting myself on her. But I wanted to honor her in some… some noninvasive way, as Ellie and I had discussed the last time we were together. There was a long silence. I thought she'd hung up. Finally, she said we could meet for a coffee at Maudie's on Lake Austin Boulevard."

Close to her house, Alice thought. On her way home.

"How'd that go?" she asked.

"I was waiting in the parking lot. She looked so much like Ellie I recognized her immediately. We found a table inside by the windows. Know what she wanted to hear about?"

"What?"

"How Ellie and I reconnected. I told her we hadn't seen or heard from each other all those years and then—like a bolt of lightning—we recognized each other in Santa Fe. She hung on every word. Especially when I said that we'd not only lost Valerie herself, and the chance to raise her: we'd lost each other, all those years." He lifted his eyes to Alice. "I think that's when she softened, just a bit."

"Did she tell you about her children?"

"Yes. Her daughters are juniors at Austin High. I asked Valerie if she had 529 college savings accounts for them. 'Of course,' she said. I told Valerie I'd like to make a small contribution to those accounts. At first she resisted. But by then we'd moved from just coffee to Maudie's enchiladas and guacamole, and she wavered. I promised I'd do nothing more, would like to meet her children at some point, if she or they had an interest, would be glad to send them each a letter, if they didn't object."

"What did Valerie say?

"She wants more time to think about any contact with the kids. But she finally agreed to the money. Both kids are bright, both will likely go after graduate degrees. I told her I wanted them to have a chance to travel as part of their education. I've learned so much myself from living outside my native land. That made sense to her. I said if this money let them learn other languages, other customs, learn to see from more than a single point of view, it would be worth it. And that it would be generous on her part to let me do it." He paused. "That last bit helped, I think."

Then he knotted his eyebrows. "My challenge was to get it done while still alive, especially after that attack at the LBJ Library. I'd met with my lawyer, changing a trust, dealing with drafts, signatures, notarization…I could imagine another brake line incident on the way home, you know?"

Alice nodded, thinking of the vast lonely spaces Roger would cross, driving back to Santa Fe.

"I wanted to prevent anyone from stopping me. So I went to the bank today and wired fifty thousand dollars into each 529 account." He poured more tea for Alice, then poured more into his tiny china cup, then grinned at her.

Alice felt her own face break into a huge smile. "Good for you!"

"It's done. Finished. On the way out of town, I'll stop at Ellie's place, on that creek road north of Coffee Creek, just to…to tell her. Tell the air in her pasture that I've done what we agreed. Then—head northwest."

Alice watched him, the calm face, the air of reserve, the faithful blue blazer, the appropriate blue button-down—his uniform, really, for decades. All unimpeachably correct, but masking a man of quiet competence and steely determination.

"So you'll be home in time for Wednesday night poker? Clare Graham was asking."

"Yep. By the way, have the police have made any headway on Ellie's murder? Valerie wondered and I couldn't tell her."

"I don't think so." She should call Files for news on that stained baton, that…rolling pin. "Did you tell Valerie that someone's made two runs at killing you?"

He frowned. "Why would I tell her that?"

Alice couldn't think of a reason.

They slid out of the booth. Roger collected the helmet. In Uchi's entry way he strapped it on, then walked Alice toward her car. Alice looked at the fashion combo—blazer and helmet—and almost laughed but stopped in her tracks. "On second thought," she said, "I'm walking you to yours." And did. As Roger drove out of the parking lot, he lowered the window and waved.

"Good luck Wednesday night!" she called.

See You at the Courthouse

Tuesday morning. The sunrise woke her at five-thirty. Kinsear called as she took her first sip of her ritual coffee, espresso, foamy hot milk.

"Carrie's off her crutches," he reported. "Still stomping around in a boot. She's pretty cranky."

"Well, it's her right ankle, isn't it? She can't drive. That's a serious drag." Eighteen and can't drive, stuck out at the ranch…

Alice said a little prayer for Kinsear and another prayer of gratitude that she herself wasn't having to play Nurse Ratched. She revered the heroism of Florence Nightingale—indeed, of all nurses—but she herself lacked patience for the convalescent process. Sure, she could handle emergencies: she'd tied a tourniquet on Jordie's arm after his tractor accident, doctored earaches and sore throats, raced her kids to the ER when they'd fallen out of trees. But she knew she'd be a dreadful nurse. She didn't cut herself any slack, either. If she scraped her knees falling off the bike, twisted her ankle on the tennis court, her dad always said, "Rub dirt on it, and keep playing." She still said it to herself. Just figurative dirt, of course…not real.

Kinsear asked about developments on Ellie's murder. She told him about Red's finding the stained baton in the round bale in the corral. "I think it's Ellie's rolling pin," she said. "Like mine. No handles."

"That would be pretty cold, to bash someone to death and then stick your weapon into a hay bale," Kinsear remarked. "Also weird."

He invited himself for Friday night. Alice sighed happily as she hung up the phone.

* * * * *

The east was still pink and gold as she turned south on the creek road heading toward Coffee Creek. No traffic this early. As she topped the hill approaching Ellie's place, she saw a car at the gate. Still a distance away, she pulled onto the right shoulder and stopped. Roger stood at the gate, straight-backed, unmoving, gazing up at the house. As she watched, he turned, climbed into his car, backed out of the gate entrance, and pulled onto the creek road heading south. Alice waited a decent interval, then followed slowly behind, thinking about his pilgrimage to Ellie's and his determination to do what he and Ellie had promised each other. As they neared Coffee Creek, she watched him turn onto the highway heading west, then made her own turn onto Live Oak Street.

She was mentally listing her office to-do's when a flash of pink on the car floorboard caught her eye. The pink tissue from Ellie's corral, still in its plastic bag. On impulse she parked at Courthouse Square next to the Sheriff's Annex. Would George Files be in? She dialed his direct line.

"Files."

"It's Alice Greer. I'm just wondering if you got any results on the rolling pin that Red Griffin found in the round bale at the Windom house?"

"The blood stains match Ellie Windom's blood group. DNA tests are still underway."

"Are there fingerprints?"

"Yes. Ms. Windom's and some others we haven't identified."

"When Red and I stopped back at Ellie's to give the horses their afternoon check, Danielle Windom was there. That's Don's wife."

"Where? In the house?"

"No," Alice said. "She was in the driveway. She said she'd driven over from Houston to check out some Coffee Creek wedding venues and just stopped by to see the house. Seemed distracted, looking first at the house, then the corral."

"Was she in the corral?" Files asked.

"Not when we got there. But after she left, we found a pink tissue by the round bale. I put it in a bag in case you wanted it." Sounded ridiculous. Who did she think she was, Ms. Crime Tech?

"You might as well bring it in," Files said. "It's hurry-up-and-wait time. Waiting on the lab."

She left the bagged tissue at the front desk in the Sheriff's Annex and drove the short block down Live Oak to her office. This morning: file the request for a TRO. Get going, Alice.

* * * * *

"Ha!" Silla greeted Alice as she opened the front door to the office. She pointed Alice to her worktable. "Double ha! Look at this!"

On the table Silla had laid out prints of Gene's pictures. She'd also found a Facebook account for Mary Ellen Stokely. And staring out from Silla's computer, in living color, was the Facebook photo of the subscriber, Mary Ellen Stokely. Her Facebook photo was a dead ringer for a marcher in Gene's photos.

"Hallelujah!" Alice said.

"But wait, there's more!" Silla scrolled down Stokely's page to a post describing "my hard work" for Protect Our Youth. Then she moved to the Protect Our Youth website, where a post showed both Wanda Slocom—Wanda who'd menaced Alice on the library sidewalk—and Mary Ellen Stokely.

"Thank goodness!" Alice said. "It's pretty hard to file a TRO when you can't specify who you're trying to restrain." She paused, thinking. "Silla…can you check out Protect Our Youth on the secretary of state's website? Who organized it? Who are the officers and directors?"

In two minutes Silla looked up from the computer screen and said, "Slocom and Stokely are president and secretary as well as directors. And guess what? Edmund Fleischer's also a director. The registered agent for Protect Our Youth is POY, LLC, a Texas limited liability corporation. Wait, I'm looking up POY, LLC too." Silla's fingers flew across the computer.

She looked up, face smug. "Get this, Alice. The sole member and registered agent of POY, LLC is…Edmund Fleischer."

"Holy cow. Smutbuster's lawyer? Which of those entities came first?"

Silla checked again. "First came POY, LLC. Then Protect Our Youth."

So Ms. Smutbuster's lawyer, who'd filed the lawsuit against the library on her behalf, had organized both the non-profit and his own LLC. Cozy.

By nine Silla was on her way to the Courthouse to file the request for a TRO, with a copy for Judge Sandoval. She confirmed with his secretary that the judge could be available to hear the request at four p.m. Alice called Mrs. Gregg, the head librarian. "Can you and Gene be at the courthouse at three-fifteen this afternoon? Judge Sandoval can hear us at four. I need you two to testify about the incident with the school kids and about the noise from the bullhorn, and identify the photos. We can go over the questions in Judge Sandoval's jury room before the hearing." They agreed.

Silla emailed a copy to Edmund Fleischer and sent a courier to hand-deliver a copy as well. Fleischer called Alice at once, blustering about First Amendment rights.

"Edmund, you represent Mary Ellen Stokely, correct?"

He agreed he did.

"Also the group Protect Our Youth? And its officers, including Wanda Slocom?"

"I do, and I'm proud to do so."

"In fact, you're the registered agent for Protect Our Youth, right?"

"That's irrelevant," he burst out. "These folks have every right to express their strong concerns about the Potter books, with their anti-family themes and ridiculous fantasies."

"You'd agree there are other rights involved here as well, wouldn't you? Library patrons have rights to unimpeded access to their library. School children have rights to accompany their teachers on field trips without being frightened and harassed," Alice said, gritting her teeth.

"Ridiculous exaggerations!"

"I'm eager for the judge to hear us," Alice said, standing at her desk as she did for fierce calls. "I'm eager for him to see the videos and hear the bullhorns."

"Bullhorns?"

"We'll have a witness to testify about his video of yesterday's marchers, including bullhorns."

"That's First Amendment speech!"

"Doesn't sound like you have any inclination to agree right now to keep your folks in the road, not on the sidewalk, and to stop using bullhorns. Am I right?"

"I'm not authorized to relinquish the constitutional rights of my clients," blustered Fleischer. "And I'm not sure I can be available today!"

"You'll need to be available. See you at the Courthouse at four." She hung up.

"Silla," she said, "Can you be there?"

"Yep."

*****

At three-ten she and Silla trudged up the worn limestone stairway leading to the third floor of the Coffee County Courthouse, inhaling the familiar odor of paper, files, and anxious humans. Alice pushed open the double oak doors to Judge Bernie Sandoval's high-ceilinged courtroom, empty except for the bailiff, who grinned at Silla. "I'll tell Judge you're here," he said, and vanished through the door into the judge's chambers.

Gene, the library tech wizard, arrived with Mrs. Gregg, the head librarian. Alice and Silla took them into the jury room and went over the TRO request. Alice quizzed Gene, who readily identified his photos and explained how he'd discovered the names of specific protesters. Mrs. Gregg was rock-steady on the obstructed field trip and disruptive bullhorn noise. "And the footage of the marcher whacking my windshield?" Alice asked.

"Got it right here," Gene said.

At three-fifty Alice and Silla commandeered their counsel table and ushered their witnesses to the oak pew behind them. Alice poured a glass of water from the ever-present water pitcher on the counsel table and did some deep breathing. Silla numbered the exhibits and organized a set for the court reporter and for Fleischer.

At four the courtroom doors burst open, and Edmund Fleischer hurried to the other counsel table, red-faced and sweating. He was large, with slicked-back brown hair and heavy glasses. He didn't greet Alice or Silla. Alice rose and walked over. "Alice Greer." Fleischer stuck out a damp hand, gave a half-hearted shake, squeezing only Alice's fingers—the male handshake-for-women, which Alice detested. She wiped her hand on her jacket.

Fleischer shooed the two women following him into the oak pew behind his table. Alice recognized both. She'd faced off on the library sidewalk with Wanda Slocom, a burly woman with an outraged face and permanently permed hair. Today she wore a sedate flowered dress.

Mary Ellen Stokely, with surprised eyebrows the only features on an otherwise bland face, was captured in one of Gene's pictures—holding a bullhorn.

The bailiff leaned around the door from the judge's chambers. "Everyone here?" The court reporter squeezed past the bailiff and sat in her appointed niche below the bench. Judge Bernie Sandoval, fifty-something and portly, strode in, climbed onto the dais, and settled in the leather armchair behind his desk. He looked down over half-moon spectacles at the assembled parties. Alice knew that penetrating brown stare from her probate cases. Coffee County lawyers failed at their peril to follow Judge Sandoval's rules: cut the chatter, get to the point, and never misstate case law. If you don't know, admit it.

"Ms. Greer, I believe this is your request. Proceed."

Alice began. "Your Honor, the Coffee Creek Library Board comes before you seeking immediate relief. We request that you enter an order effective immediately requiring persons protesting Harry Potter books at the library to refrain from using bullhorns and impeding or disturbing patrons trying to use the library. Our request attaches photographs and videos taken by library employee Gene Sharp, who's present today" (she turned and gestured at Gene, who stood and then sat back down on the hard oak pew). "Also present is Mrs. Olive Gregg, Head Librarian." Mrs. Gregg stood, looked the judge square in the eyes, and sat. "She will testify that the protesters frightened the second-graders during their field trip to the library."

Fleischer huffed to his feet. "Objection! Nobody prevented anything!"

The judge lifted a hand. "You'll have your turn in a moment, Mr. Fleischer."

Fleischer blinked and sat down heavily in his chair.

"Your Honor," Alice continued, "if you've had a chance to review our pleadings, you may already have seen from the pictures that the protesters blocked the sidewalk to the library entrance and confronted a group of second-graders and their teachers. You'll have seen the picture of the crying child behind his teacher, confronted by adults waving signs. Your Honor, First Amendment rights do not extend to frightening school children or to blocking ingress to the Coffee Creek Library.

Our TRO request also seeks to bar the use of bullhorns on grounds of nuisance. We'll have testimony on that as well. Your Honor, we were unsuccessful in seeking to settle with opposing counsel before this hearing. We've prepared a proposed order for your consideration, attached to the TRO request."

"I've read it. I've read all the pleadings. All right, Mr. Fleischer, if you have a brief opening statement, let's hear it. Then Ms. Greer can proceed."

Fleischer lumbered to his feet. "Your Honor, we are outraged at plaintiff's attempt to interfere with our rights under the state and federal constitutions. Peaceful assembly and First Amendment speech at a public institution such as the Coffee Creek Library are recognized as permitted."

"What about the library's claim concerning bullhorns?"

"Simply amplified free speech, Your Honor."

"What about the library's nuisance claim?"

"Exercise of free speech, Your Honor."

"How far does that extend, counsel?"

"I would think free speech trumps nuisance, Your Honor."

"You have case law on that?"

Silence. "I—I'm sure there is, Your Honor."

Oops, Alice thought. You'd better be right about that.

"At any rate, these peaceful protesters are merely exercising protected First Amendment speech. We deny the library's claims." He sat down.

Oops again, Alice thought. Where's his case law? She stood. "Your Honor, I call Gene Sharp."

Gene walked up to the court reporter, who swore him in. Then he took the witness stand. After preliminaries—name, job—Alice handed him six photographs. "Mr. Sharp, please look at the photographs marked Exhibits 1 through 6. Tell me if you can identify them."

"I took each of these at the library, during the protest," Gene said.

"Are any of the people in the pictures present here in the courtroom?"

"Yes. The two women behind Mr. Fleischer."

"Do you know their names?"

Gene flushed. "I heard the one in the flowered dress called Wanda by one of the others. I found her picture on the Protect Our Youth Facebook page, listing her as Wanda Slocom. I took the picture of the woman sitting next to her as well. I found her on the same Facebook page, listed as Mary Ellen Stokely."

"By the way," Alice asked, "did you check library records to see if either Ms. Slocom or Ms. Stokely has a Coffee County library card?"

"I did check. Neither one's got a card."

Alice glanced at Judge Sandoval. He'd raised one eyebrow and pursed his lips.

"Did you also take a video of the protesters using bullhorns?"

"I did. I saw and heard two bullhorns."

"And do you have video of a protester damaging a car in the library parking lot?"

"I do, from our security cameras."

Silla got the video screen up and running, where only Gene could see it. He identified his videos and the security footage of the woman bashing Alice's loaner.

"Your Honor, I move to admit the pictures in Exhibits 1 through 6 and the video and security footage as Exhibits 7 and 8."

"Admitted."

With the videos admitted and the screen visible to the courtroom, she asked Gene to describe what he'd seen.

"The protesters blocked the sidewalk when the old lady in the picture, I mean the elderly lady, tried to walk down it. She managed to get past. When the kids got to the library on the school bus and came around the corner, the protesters started toward them, and the teachers had to take them back to the bus."

"Did you see the little boy crying as the protesters approached?"

"Yes, he was hiding behind his teacher."

"What about the other kids?"

"Some looked really scared."

"What did the teachers do?"

"They talked, then hustled the kids back to the bus."

"And the video of the protester damaging a car?"

Gene explained how Alice asked him to check whether someone

had damaged her windshield and how he found the footage on the library camera.

"Your witness," Alice said to Fleischer.

Fleischer approached the witness stand. "The teachers could have marched those kids right into the library, couldn't they?"

Gene frowned. "As you see on the video, the protesters blocked the sidewalk. You mean like the teachers should've taken them into the library some way other than by going down the sidewalk? Or taken them in one at a time? Sorry, I don't understand."

Fleischer looked confused. "Answer the question."

Gene paused. "I guess the teachers could have gone and tried to get the protesters off the sidewalk, but then they'd be leaving the kids alone. Maybe they didn't want to do that. I mean, the kids were just second-graders."

"Move on, counsel," said the judge.

"Did you tamper with these videos?" asked Fleischer.

"No, sir," said Gene, surprised. "Tamper how?"

"Did you mess with the volume? Turn it up?"

"No. If you mean the bullhorns, that's what they sounded like."

Fleischer turned back to his chair. "No more questions."

"I call Olive Gregg," said Alice.

The head librarian marched calmly to the court reporter, said "I do" in her clear voice, and took the witness stand.

Alice had her identify herself: head librarian for the past fifteen years. "Is your office on the front of the library, facing the area where the protesters stood?"

"Yes."

"Did you hear the protesters' bullhorns through the walls or windows?"

"Yes. I couldn't hear myself think."

"Objection!" Fleischer said.

"I couldn't hear people who called me on the phone," Mrs. Gregg went on. "They couldn't hear me either. Plus"—lopsided smile—"the bullhorns set off my hearing aid. It squealed."

"The bullhorns interfered with your work?"

"Yes. Furthermore, they interfered with the ability of patrons to use the library as they like. They couldn't read in the reading room; it's on the front of the library, and the bullhorn noise came right through the wall. We've got students studying for summer school who gave up, said they couldn't concentrate."

"Objection, hearsay," said Fleischer.

"Let me rephrase," Alice said. "How did you know they gave up?"

"One of them rolled her eyes and slammed her book shut and said, 'I give up!'"

"Same objection!" roared Fleischer.

"So they gave the noise as a reason, whether or not that was their real reason?" Alice asked.

"Right."

Alice turned to Fleischer. "Your witness."

Silence. Then, "No questions."

Alice thought about calling Stokely, but decided to wait.

Fleischer did it for her. "I call Mary Ellen Stokely."

After being sworn in, Stokely testified that she was merely engaging in peaceful protest at the library to protect Coffee County youth from harmful stories based on ridiculous fantasy and magic, like talking animals and witches and wizards.

Alice's turn. "Ms. Stokely, you used a bullhorn during the protest, didn't you?"

"I…well, I held one."

"In fact, you were shouting through it, weren't you?" She got Silla to play Gene's video segment where Stokely, open-mouthed, was roaring into a bullhorn. "That's you yelling, isn't it?"

"Yes, but I was upset! This is important to me, the harmfulness of these stories!"

"I understand you have children. How old are they?

"Twelve and fourteen."

"Did you read to your children when they were younger?"

"Of course! So important, reading!" Mary Ellen Stokely smiled up at Judge Sandoval.

"You read them classics?"

"Indeed I did."

"You wanted to expose them to the great traditions in Western literature?"

"Of course. My children got a solid background."

"They're familiar with *Alice in Wonderland*?"

"Yes."

"The *Just So* stories by Rudyard Kipling?"

"Yes."

"Did you expose them to *The Lion, the Witch and the Wardrobe* by C.S. Lewis?"

"Yes."

"What about classic fairy tales by the Brothers Grimm? Like *Hansel and Gretel*?"

"Yes."

"Did you let them see movies based on the stories? The Disney versions, for example?" Alice asked.

"Yes, of course. *Sleeping Beauty, Snow White, Cinderella*."

"What about recent movies, like *Frozen*?"

"Yes. My kids know every song in that movie."

"Now, these fairy tales and movies we've mentioned often involve talking animals, don't they?"

"Well…maybe a couple."

"You recall the talking animals in Narnia, do you not, such as Mr. Tumnus?"

"I remember Mr. Tumnus, yes." Stokely frowned slightly.

"These same classic fairy tales and movies involve magic, don't they?"

"I don't know," muttered Stokely.

"Oh? What about the fairy godmother in *Cinderella*? The magic mirror in *Snow White*? A talking snowman and Elsa's magical ice powers in *Frozen*? The White Witch in Narnia turning Mr. Tumnus to stone? Those all involve magic, don't they?"

Stokely was silent, eyes shifting side to side, looking for an answer.

"Please answer the question."

"There's magic, but…"

"But you gave your children access to them, correct?"

After a moment, "Yes."

"Do you let your kids see *Star Wars* movies? Read *Star Wars* books?"

A long pause. Mary Ellen Stokely looked at her lawyer. He stared back.

"Please answer."

"Yes," the witness said to her lap.

"But you're not protesting *Star Wars*, are you? Why not?"

Stokely looked like a deer in the headlights. "Harry Potter…those books are anti-family." She took a breath. "They've got witches!"

"So does *The Lion, the Witch and the Wardrobe*, doesn't it?"

"Yes. I guess so," Stokely said. She looked like she wanted to say more but couldn't formulate an answer.

"Have you let your kids watch *The Wizard of Oz?*"

Stokely nodded.

"Please respond aloud so the court reporter can take down your answer, Ms. Stokely," the judge said.

"The child Dorothy faces not only witches but the supposed wizard, right?"

"Yes," Stokely said, her voice low.

"Switching gears," Alice said. "You're an officer and director of Protect Our Youth, correct?"

"Yes."

"How did you become part of that organization?"

Mary Ellen Stokely looked at Fleischer.

"He…my lawyer asked me…"

"Objection!" Fleischer said, turning redder. "Don't reveal client-lawyer confidences."

Interesting. "Mr. Fleischer represents you in your suit against the library, right?"

"Yes."

"He also represents Protect Our Youth, right?"

"Yes."

"Do you pay his legal fees?"

"Well, Protect Our Youth does."

"He also set up Protect Our Youth, correct?"

Stokely nodded. "Yes. He came up with the name and everything and asked us to be officers."

She'd answered before Fleischer could object.

"Ms. Stokely, you saw the library security footage played just now where a protester broke a windshield with a sign?"

"Yes."

"Who is the woman holding the sign?"

"Her name's Martha," Stokely said after a moment. "Martha Johnson."

"To your knowledge has she attended your meetings?"

"Yes."

Alice went on. "You're authorized as an officer to testify today on behalf of Protect Our Youth, as well as for yourself, correct?"

"Yes," proudly. Alice expected Fleischer to object but he seemed flustered.

"As a parent and as a member of Protect Our Youth, do you consider it's your right to monitor what your children check out from the library?"

"Of course!" Stokely said.

"Indeed, you consider it your responsibility as a parent?"

"Yes, indeed."

"Do you agree that the right to monitor your own children's library selections belongs to you, as the child's parent, not to the parents of some other child?"

"Of course! I should be the one..."

"I assume that is also the position of Protect Our Youth, correct?"

Stokely looked slightly confused. "Umm...yes."

"You agree that Protect Our Youth has no right to tell you what your children can or cannot check out?"

"Uh...well..."

"Let me restate. As between you yourself and Protect Our Youth, you believe the authority to decide what your children can or cannot check out of the library properly belongs to you, correct?"

"Well, yes."

"So if a parent wants to allow his or her child to check out Potter books, Protect Our Youth can't interfere with that parent's decision, right?"

"Well...I suppose not."

Fleischer hadn't had time to object.

Alice stopped. "No more questions."

Judge Sandoval stared out over his spectacles. "Anything further, Mr. Fleischer?"

"No, Your Honor."

"I'm granting the requested relief to the library, on the terms requested in the Order, which I will sign and enter this afternoon, effective immediately. Please note, Mr. Fleischer, that under the terms of the Order your clients may protest in the parking lot but may not block ingress and egress to the library and may not use bullhorns or make noise constituting a nuisance. I know you will convey that to your clients immediately." He looked over his half-moon glasses at the order, then back at Fleischer. "I will add to the proposed Order a requirement for Protect Our Youth to reimburse the cost of repairing the damaged windshield." He gave one rap of the gavel and left the bench for his chambers.

Fleischer picked up his briefcase, stood staring at the bench for a moment, then turned and left, followed by his clients.

* * * * *

The library team adjourned to the Beer Barn, where Gene bought beers for Alice, Silla, and his boss, the head librarian. They carried their drafts to the darkest corner of the Beer Barn's bar. Gene leaned across the table and high-fived Alice. The head librarian permitted herself a chaste but satisfied smile.

"I don't think we'll see those folks for a while," Mrs. Gregg said. "Alice, I'm so pleased with the judge's order."

"Me, too," Alice said. Thinking back to the hearing, she felt an idea forming. "Silla, let's get a copy of today's transcript."

Silla nodded.

Mrs. Gregg went on. "I especially like the part where, if the protesters violate the order and we have to enforce it, they have to pay our fees."

"Yep," Alice said. "If they do, I may raise my rates. From where they are now." She lifted an inquiring eyebrow at the head librarian.

"If they challenge the order, you can charge your normal rate.

Those poor second-graders," Mrs. Gregg said, narrowing her eyes and staring at her beer. "Seeing grownups acting that way! What kind of life lessons are they learning?"

Silla snorted and turned to Alice. "Maybe we should've added another instruction to the order. 'Get a life.'"

Alice couldn't help it. She laughed so hard she accidentally sprayed beer on Mrs. Gregg. Mrs. Gregg was all aplomb as she dabbed her chest with a napkin. "Appropriate celebration."

Petroglyphs

As usual, the brief moment of triumph in court disappeared in a heartbeat. On the way home, Alice's sins of omission—for actual paying legal work—assailed her. She could almost see bullet points popping up on the windshield.

First: get a glimpse of Agnes Dietz's will. The money from the estate—such as Ellie's purchase of the adobe house—who'd it go to? That beneficiary might try to lay claim to the attic artwork.

Second: doublecheck Ellie's Santa Fe attic. Was she quite sure she'd found everything? She'd had light only from her phone in that dark space and had been interrupted by the housebreakers. What if she'd missed some treasure? As executor, she couldn't screw up.

Third: find out whether Chuck wanted to keep any of the real estate. That would simplify matters.

Fourth: hire a trust and estates lawyer in Santa Fe to advise on New Mexico probate process.

As she turned into her driveway at seven-thirty, her cell phone rang. Don Windom. She tried to control her sinking feeling. Executors had a fiduciary duty to all beneficiaries, even the cranky ones. "Hi, Don," she said in her best neutral-yet-cheerful voice.

"Listen," he said. "This lawyer at my office says that if Mom's birth daughter wasn't precluded by the adoption order, she could claim an equal part of Mom's estate! Is that right?"

Alice chose her words. "She could try to do so, since the will itself didn't recognize her. But as we discussed in our meeting, Ellie's codicil recognizes Valerie Ames as her child, but also says she won't inherit under the will, and specifies what she will get. That may eliminate her ability to inherit a share under the will."

"But what if it doesn't?" Don sounded frantic. "What if she claims a third, and this whole estate is tied up for years?"

"I don't believe she'd succeed," Alice said. "But we've sent her the will and the codicil, and she's shown no interest in challenging either."

"I don't trust her for a minute." Unclear whether he meant his mother or Valerie. Don abruptly changed direction. "Aren't you supposed to be filing something with the court? Like an inventory?"

Alice bit her tongue. Beneficiaries often got emotional, got wrapped around the axle. "It's in process. The Coffee Creek appraiser's still taking inventory of property here."

"What about Santa Fe? What's happening there?"

"We're waiting for the updated appraisal." She took a chance. "Is there something specific worrying you, Don? We're well ahead of any deadlines."

"I just need to know what happens when, and what's going on in Santa Fe." He hung up without waiting for an answer.

Puzzling.

With Santa Fe now her top priority, she'd ask Francis to pick a lawyer who could hold her hand through New Mexico probate and—she hoped—explain what happened to Agnes Dietz's property.

She herself would crawl back up in that adobe house attic with a strong light.

And she was hungry. Right now, starving. Thinking of…what was that fancy Santa Fe restaurant where Francis saw Kristi having dinner with Suede Jacket?

She called Kinsear and reeled off her list of Santa Fe chores.

"I need a road trip," he said. "There's a meeting in Santa Fe I ought to attend. Let's leave in the morning. I'll pick you up."

"What about the girls?"

"Isabel's in charge of Carrie. No worries."

"And dinner?" Alice begged. "I heard of this new place…Cafe Piñon."

Once home she grabbed her suitcase, started packing.

* * * * *

Dawn—five thirty, birds competing for air time, wrens, titmice, cardinals, their music echoing in the treetops and below in the creek valley. The scent of old-fashioned roses filled Alice's porch—her beloved Star of the Republic, Mme. Isaac Pereire, Lafter, Souvenir de la Malmaison spilling pink rosettes down from a small pin oak.

The three donkeys stood shoulder to shoulder watching Kinsear's Land Cruiser as Alice hurried out of the house juggling her small suitcase, her briefcase, and two mugs of coffee. The air smelled of car exhaust, caliche dust, sun on burgeoning leaves.

"Road trip!" Alice said, sliding into the passenger seat. She kissed Kinsear. He kissed back.

She peered at a brown canvas lump in the back seat. "Your guitar?"

He nodded, with a proprietary air. "I've been playing some." He lifted an eyebrow. "That's why the girls were so thrilled I was driving you to Santa Fe. Maybe we can sing some on the way."

She remembered watching Kinsear play guitar at a law school student party, years ago. The black curls, the humorous baritone, the strong notes. "Not without coffee." She handed him his mug, then pulled out the map book. "Which way?" Alice loved to peruse a map.

"Let's go the fastest way. All the shortcuts."

Sipping coffee, listening to the morning news, watching deer start moving in the pastures, they were west of Abilene by nine, west of Lubbock by lunchtime, and crossing into New Mexico by early afternoon.

Alice scanned the horizon, watching for the first antelope. "What is it about the New Mexico sky?" she wondered. "Texas sky is big, but...New Mexico?"

"I know," said Kinsear. "Maybe it's the mountains in the distance, the mesas, the buttes. The transparent air." He turned to Alice. "How's our Roger?"

Save a man's life, he's yours, Alice thought. "He said he'd leave on Tuesday. We should call and see if he got back okay." She found Roger's number and put him on speakerphone. He sounded pleased to hear Kinsear's "Hey, man!"

"You're both coming to Santa Fe?"

"Yep," Kinsear answered. "Alice's got business to tend to."

"Hey, tonight's poker night. Can you get here in time to sit in?"

Kinsear glanced at Alice, who gave him a thumbs up. "Sure."

"Seven okay? Francis Blake's hosting tonight. Alice, you know where he lives?"

"Yes."

"You don't mind me stealing Kinsear for a few hours?"

She laughed. "He's ready for some guy time."

Roger hung up. Kinsear turned to her. "You're sure? What about our dinner reservations?"

"Let's move them to Thursday. What if we stop at Maria's on the way to the El Rey for a margarita and some blue corn enchiladas?" She sobered. "I'm glad you're going, Ben. I worry about that man. Can you ask whether, since he got back, he's had that weird feeling of being watched?"

Kinsear nodded, watching the road.

Alice dialed Cafe Piñon and changed their dinner reservation. "I won't mind another night at the El Rey with you," she said. "I asked for the same room, with the kiva fireplace." She peered again at her to-do list and called Francis Blake.

"Got a lawyer for you," Francis said. "Mike Cortez. He said he'd be glad to help you use the simplified probate process for Ellie's house. Here's his number."

Alice thanked him and called Mike Cortez.

Easy baritone voice, with a transplant accent. "West Texas?" Alice wondered aloud.

He laughed. "Amarillo. But I got here as fast as I could."

She explained about Ellie's house. "She lived in Texas but owned this one property in New Mexico."

"We can help," he said. "Let's clear conflicts. Anyone adverse?"

She thought for a moment. "Well, Ellie bought her house out of the estate of Agnes Dietz. I'll email you the deed. Hold on."

Long pause. "Let me check something," he muttered. "The return address for the deed is the Blenheim firm. I've heard of Agnes Dietz, but we didn't handle her estate. Let me check her will online and see if that was also the Blenheim firm. That'll take me a minute…" A longer pause. "Yes. So, no conflict here."

"You've got the will in front of you?" asked Alice. "Can you take a look at the beneficiaries?"

"Hmmm." Silence. "Kinda weird. Guess she had no family. She left everything but her house to the Archeological Conservancy, solely for protection of New Mexico petroglyphs."

"Cool. Do you represent the Archeological Conservancy?"

"No," he said. "Why?"

"First, I need to ask one more thing. What about the house?" Alice asked, listening intently.

"That's weird too. Proceeds from the house sale were to go to the

New Mexico Museum of Art."

"Do you represent the museum?" She held her breath.

"No. Again, why?"

"Clearing conflicts. In Ellie's house," she began, "I found a box in the attic with what may be Baumann prints."

"Wow." Then he said, "Oh. You're wondering if anyone knew those were there when your client bought the house. If, say, the museum would claim their value wasn't included in the selling price?"

"Yep," Alice said.

"Hmm. Well, we've got no conflict defending Ellie's ownership. Remember, the Blenheim firm handled Dietz's will and the estate sale. The museum would need to contact Blenheim, as Dietz's counsel, if there's any question about what proceeds the museum got under her will."

"Great." Alice agreed to stop by his office the next morning. Telephone handshakes and goodbyes.

Kinsear pointed. "Antelope off to the right."

"Ooh!" Alice so loved to see the almost invisible swift animals, disappearing into golden grass. "Are we nearly to Santa Rosa?"

"We are."

She turned to him. "Thank you for driving. Can we sing tonight after the poker game? By the piñon fire in our room? While I admire your winnings?"

"We can. I will, with my huge Boy Scout skills, build us a roaring fire before unlimbering the guitar."

"And then?"

"Hmm. We're dawdling." He sped up.

* * * * *

Six p.m. "Two margaritas, frozen, with salt," said the waiter, lifting them off his tray. "And two orders of blue corn enchiladas. More chips and salsa, sir?"

"Absolutely."

The waiter hustled away. Alice and Kinsear clinked glasses.

"You won't lose our motel money tonight, will you?" she asked.

"Hey, I thought you were paying! I drove!"

She grinned, watching him enjoy the enchiladas, imagining him sitting at the poker table, covertly watching the other players for tells. She remembered Francis Blake's comment about Graham. "Listen, is it fair for me to tell you what Francis said about Clare Graham? 'When he pushes his glasses up on the bridge of his nose, he's gonna bluff.'"

"Forewarned is forearmed," Kinsear said.

"Also, while you're playing a batch of cardsharps you've never met—except for Roger"— Alice asked—"will you please find out if Roger's okay? Is anyone following him?" She stopped, brows furrowed. "Who else is playing tonight? I count only you, Roger, Clare, and Blake." She texted Francis, then looked up. "The fifth is someone named Pepe Longoria, an administrator at the community college. Their usual fifth is out tonight."

"I'll ask." His eyes met hers. "And I'll watch."

* * * * *

The sky was still light, but dimming fast, when Alice dropped Kinsear off at Francis Blake's house. She'd made plans.

At the El Rey she checked in and carried in the luggage, including the guitar. Yes, the same room she'd had before, piñon logs in the kiva fireplace, ready to light. She checked emails. One from Files: "Prints and DNA on the wood baton. No match yet."

For a moment, she was standing outside the corral with Red, staring at the stained piece of wood, thinking of Ellie, the battered skull, the horse in the house.

She shook her head and went back to the lobby to wait.

Headlights swept the entry court and stopped. Alice ran out the door. A tall figure with tawny hair in an untidy bun and wearing a gorgeous pink scarf swept toward her.

"Margaret!"

"Alice!"

She'd met Margaret on the college tennis team. Margaret the Merciless, they called her. Margaret could slam a volley to her opponent's weak side, hit a forehand cross court, make her opponent race panting from one side to the other while she dominated play. Now she worked in development for the Santa Fe Chamber Music Festival.

The two women hugged.

"Okay, tell me everything. Why are you here? Why didn't you phone me first?" demanded Margaret.

Alice dragged her back to the El Rey's bar, with its outdoor fireplace. They planted themselves on the cushioned banquette by the fire. Where to start? She explained about Ellie's murder…the Moon Mountain house…then stopped abruptly. She couldn't share her client's secrets. "That's all I can tell you right now. I'm here with my…"—she'd never said "fiancé" before, and decided not to start now—"…my beau. Business meetings in the morning. Tell me about you."

Two hours later, they'd almost caught up. Margaret said, "Another thing I'm doing is chasing petroglyphs. They mystify me, they enchant me. I go out hiking, hoping to find a new one."

Petroglyphs. "Did you ever hear of a woman named Agnes Dietz?"

Margaret stopped, stared at Alice. "She died before I got to Santa Fe. How do you know about her?"

"I heard she published a book of her petroglyph pictures."

"She did," Margaret said. "Back before you and I were born. But it's the rarest book around. I've never found one. Believe me, I've tried."

"What happened to the books?"

"What I hear is, she changed her mind after the books were printed and bought back all the copies before they got distributed. Rumor is she had them destroyed."

"Was she afraid of people vandalizing the petroglyphs?"

Margaret leaned back, looking up at the stars. "Maybe that was part of it. I'm pretty secretive about locations I've found, too. No, my theory is she wanted to be the only owner of things. Even furniture!"

"What makes you say that?"

"A talented cabinet maker in town makes original furniture. I saved enough to order a table and asked him to show me pictures of his work. 'There's one design I can't show you,' he told me. I asked why, and he said, 'The woman who ordered it made me sign an agreement never to make a copy.'"

"And that was Agnes Dietz?"

"Yes."

A glimmer of a thought began to form…her phone buzzed. Kinsear. "We're winding up here. Can you pick me up?"

"On my way."

On impulse she turned to Margaret and said, "Come with me! You can meet Kinsear, and we'll drive back here for your car."

But as they turned onto Calle Peralta, where Francis lived, headlights raced toward her. She jerked the steering wheel hard right to avoid being hit. "What the hell?" said Margaret, staring back at the car.

Ahead Alice saw Francis, his head backlit by the garage light, leaning over a dark shape lying in the driveway. She saw Kinsear jumping into someone else's car. As it careened past, Clare Graham yelled out the driver's window, "Help Francis!"

"What the hell?" breathed Margaret again. Her head jerked back and then forward as Alice stomped the accelerator, then the brake, screeching to a stop past Francis's driveway.

Chapter Twenty-Nine

Why Are We Alone?

lice and Margaret raced up the driveway.

On Roger's head, the incongruous white helmet. Blood, dark on the driveway, soaked his chinos, seeped through Francis's fingers as he crouched, pressing on Roger's leg. "Got to stop the bleeding," Francis grunted. "Pepe's called an ambulance."

Margaret was already unfurling the scarf around her neck and thrusting it at Alice. "Take it!" Margaret said. "I'll hold his leg. Hurry!"

Alice wrapped the scarf twice around Roger's lower leg and pulled it tight.

A man Alice didn't know ran out of the open garage. "Ambulance is on the way," he said. "Two minutes, they said. Cops too." He stood at Roger's feet, face anxious.

Must be Pepe Longoria, Alice thought.

Francis didn't look up. Margaret and Alice leaned forward, watching Roger's leg. The blood flow diminished to a trickle. "You're going to be okay, Roger," Francis said.

A short "thanks" through gritted teeth. Typical Roger, Alice thought. Manners, even while covering the driveway in blood.

The far-off wail of an ambulance grew louder, closer. Suddenly headlights and flashing red lights swerved around the corner. Alice held onto the scarf, now soaked in blood, until two uniformed EMTs, one tall, one broad-shouldered, slipped to their knees next to Roger and took over.

"Gunshot?" The broad-shouldered EMT looked up at Alice, who looked at Francis.

"Yes," Francis said. "We'd finished our game. I opened the garage door. Roger started out. I saw the muzzle flash, over by the hedge. Three shots. Roger went down on the third. The shooter ran to his car and blew out of here."

Francis turned to Alice. "Clare Graham and your man Kinsear are chasing the shooter."

"This guy's wearing an armored vest," said the taller EMT. "And a helmet? What's the deal?"

"Someone's been trying to kill him," Francis said.

"Good thing he dressed for the occasion," said the taller EMT.

His fingers explored an area on Roger's vest. "Looks like at least one round hit right above his heart."

A Santa Fe squad car, siren blaring, blue and red flashers lighting the sky, pulled into the driveway by the ambulance. The driver jumped out, eyes scanning the scene. Her badge: Jana Jenkins. A dark-haired, baby-faced male officer climbed out of the passenger seat.

Officer Jenkins squatted next to Roger. "What've we got?"

"Guy's been shot in the leg," said the broad-shouldered EMT. "We need to get some blood in him right away."

"Christus St. Vincent?" she asked.

"Yes."

"Okay. Get going." The EMTs carefully loaded Roger into the ambulance and sped off, lights flashing.

Alice stood behind Margaret, texting Kinsear. "Where are you? Police are here."

Officer Jenkins turned to the baby-faced male. "Hanks, get everyone's contact info."

He pulled out a notebook, started taking information, first from Pepe, then Alice and Margaret.

Jenkins concentrated on Francis, who was wiping his bloody hands with an old garage towel. "All right, what happened here? Whose house is this?"

He stepped forward. "Mine. I'm Francis Blake. Five of us had a poker game tonight. When we finished, I opened the kitchen door to the garage and raised the garage door. Roger Preyer—the guy who got shot—was the first one out." He described the three shots. "The rest of us ran out. The shooter drove off, and two of our players chased after him. I was trying to stop the blood flow and Pepe"—he nodded toward the bald man standing in the garage—"Pepe Longoria called the ambulance and you guys."

"So you, Pepe Longoria, and the guy who got shot. Who's chasing the shooter?"

"Clare Graham—art professor—and Ben Kinsear. In Clare's car."

Alice texted Kinsear again. "Where r u?"

Officer Jenkins: "License plate on the shooter's car? Car model? Anything?"

Francis shook his head slowly. "Too dark. It was a smallish SUV, that's all I could see."

Margaret said, "I think it was a dark-colored RAV4. It almost hit us when we turned into Francis's street. Assuming that was the same car."

Officer Jenkins looked at Alice and Margaret. "You weren't playing?"

Alice introduced herself. "No, Kinsear texted me that the game was over and I could pick him up. I brought Margaret along. We saw Kinsear and Clare roaring out of here just as we turned the corner."

Jenkins tilted her head. "You mind telling me why the shooting victim's wearing a helmet to a poker game? Did he bike over?"

"No, that's his car," Francis said. He pointed to the Audi parked on the street.

Alice spoke up. "The helmet…" Where to start? "Roger just got back from Austin. At a lecture at the LBJ Library, two guys tried to throw him off the terrace. The Austin police caught one of the two men, but the other got away."

Jenkins cocked her head. "And the vest?"

"Belongs to Roger's friend in Austin, Grant Hines. After the library attack Hines made him wear a helmet and an armored vest." Alice paused.

"Hines just happened to have a spare military-style bullet-proof vest?" Jenkins inquired.

"My impression is Hines is ex-CIA."

Hanks scribbled that down.

"Roger knows the names of the Austin police involved," Alice offered.

"And why would"—Jenkins looked down at her notes—"Clare Graham and Ben Kinsear chase after the shooter?"

"We didn't get a good look at the car or the plates," Francis said. "We need to know who's after Roger."

"What're they driving?"

"Graham has an old Chevy van, silver." Francis said.

Alice's phone vibrated. Kinsear: "Going E on E Zia."

She handed the phone to Jenkins. "Here's where they are."

Sudden flurry of activity, with Jenkins on her radio. "Need support to locate shooter at Calle Peralta. Suspect in small dark SUV, maybe a RAV4, being chased by two idiots in old Chevy silver van, license…" She looked at Francis Blake.

"New Mexico, I think it ends in 007."

"Somebody give me phone numbers for the two idiots who are chasing the shooter," demanded Jenkins. Alice gave her both numbers.

Jenkins gave them an assessing stare, her eyes traveling from one to the next. "Normally we'd stay, but the backup squad car will be here in less than two minutes. They'll handle the crime scene. You four, touch nothing, you hear? Nothing!" She grabbed her radio again. Alice heard her say, "We're on a chase. You're handling the crime scene." She turned to the baby-faced officer. "Hanks, you're driving!" Jenkins tossed Alice's phone back, yanked open the passenger door, and jumped in.

Lights flashing, the squad car roared around the corner toward Old Pecos Trail. The street sat silent. Francis, Alice, Margaret, and Pepe Longoria stared at each other.

"What now?" Francis said.

Pepe left the bloodstained driveway and walked through the garage into the kitchen, then stuck his head back around the door. "Beer?"

Alice and Francis looked at each other. "No," they said, together.

"I'm going after Kinsear." Alice checked for a new text.

"I'm going to the hospital to check on Roger," Francis said.

"I'll follow Francis," Pepe said. He looked at Margaret. "I could drop you off."

"Nope. Alice, let's go," Margaret said.

"No!" Alice said. "I can't take you! That guy's got a gun!"

"I'm coming. You'll need a navigator." Margaret glared at Alice. "No way am I missing out on this."

As she and Margaret hustled to the Land Cruiser, Alice heard Pepe: "A poker night to remember."

✳ ✳ ✳ ✳ ✳

At an unsafe speed Alice urged the Land Cruiser south on Old Pecos Trail. "Get in the left lane," Margaret said. "That's East Zia coming up." The green light turned yellow. Alice ignored it, made the left turn.

Margaret studied Alice's phone. "New text. South on Old Santa Fe Trail. So stay in the right lane." Then, "Slow down! Turn at the light." Alice, going too fast, pumped the brakes and maneuvered the heavy Land Cruiser around the turn onto Old Santa Fe Trail.

The loose wind of a June night blowing through their windows brought the mixed smells of cooling urban asphalt and the pungent scent of chamisa.

"Dial 911, and tell the police where we just turned, in case Jenkins isn't linked to them yet," said Alice. "I thought we'd catch them by now."

Margaret made the call.

They sped past quiet businesses, doors shut, lights out. "Lots of stars," Margaret commented, peering up through the open roof. "Moon's not up yet." They sped on, with no sign of Jenkins and Hanks, no sign of Graham and Kinsear.

Her face lit by Alice's phone, Margaret said, "He's typing again. 'Left on Cloudstone.' Whoa, Nellie! That's the next turn!"

Margaret called 911 again, reported the new text.

Alice braked, then screeched left onto Cloudstone, heading uphill.

"Why's this guy going up toward Moon Mountain?" Margaret wondered.

"Moon Mountain?" Alice breathed. "That's a crazy escape route!"

"Agreed. Nothing but twists and turns. Hope I don't get carsick."

Alice braked for another uphill turn, her gut in a knot. "What the hell are Kinsear and Graham thinking? What if they get stuck in some cul-de-sac with this shooter?"

Ping! "Text," Margaret said. "Left on North Rimrock. Getting steeper. Listen, at the top this road's like a hydra—a bunch of driveways lead off to the mega-mansions. Stick with the street sign if you can." She dialed 911.

Alice's headlights picked out a street sign. She turned left up a steeper road then slowed for an S-curve that took the Land Cruiser higher up the ridge. Santa Fe lights sparkled below. The air was distinctly cooler. She and Margaret raised their windows.

"This makes no sense," Margaret muttered. "Where's this guy going? Where are Clare and Kinsear? And Officer Jenkins? Why are we alone?"

Chapter Thirty

Get Us Out of Here!

The road ahead split into identical dirt tracks, one continuing left along the ridge, one straight up. "Go left!" yelled Margaret. "I think!"

Alice went left.

The road split again, but rejoined around a small grove of trees. Alice careened around the trees. Two hundred yards ahead the road bent left, lit by a single safety light. "Big house past the light?" she asked Margaret.

"Million-dollar view. The higher we go, the more millions." To their left the hillside dropped steeply toward the lights of Santa Fe. Alice slowed to a crawl, puzzled that as yet she heard no engines, saw no cars.

A rattle of dirt and gravel hit the right fender. "Look out!" Margaret grabbed the dashboard. Alice stood on the brakes. A figure all in black skidded down the ridge on their right, almost under the Land Cruiser, then jumped up and crossed the road, arms pumping, running toward the drop-off. A gun shot rang out uphill to their right. The running figure jerked once and disappeared over the edge of the drop-off.

"Lord God!" breathed Margaret, frantically hitting the ceiling, trying to close the moonroof. "Get us out of here!"

"But whoever that was"—Alice's voice caught in her throat. Not Kinsear. The runner was shorter. Kinsear wasn't in black—jeans and chambray shirt, right? But…

Alice couldn't get Margaret shot. But if someone was there, bleeding? She backed the Land Cruiser against the cliff, then turned the wheels left, her headlights silhouetting every twig on the downhill side of the road. Nobody. And no body.

"I don't see anyone," Margaret echoed her thoughts.

Alice pointed the car back the way they'd come. As she reached the original road her headlights lit up a speeding black SUV rocketing downhill with no lights. She slammed on the brakes, skidding almost into the intersection.

"Yikes!" Margaret gasped. "The shooter?"

"Maybe."

Alice urgently needed to locate Kinsear, see for herself that he was safe. She wrenched the steering wheel left, turning up the winding road the shooter had just zoomed down. It curved sharply right, then left. Dust hung in the air, sparkling in her headlights.

"The micaceous clay of Santa Fe," Margaret said. "That's why it sparkles. Shouldn't we stop?"

Alice spotted another dirt track splitting off to the left, uphill and roughly parallel to the road where they'd heard the gunshot. The sparkling dust hung there too. Maybe…Alice took the left turn, the uphill ridge still on her right, another drop-off to her left, with Santa Fe's lights ever farther below.

"Looks like we're not going home quite yet, are we?" Margaret said.

Alice steered around a short bend. She heard squealing brakes. Through the dust ahead she saw a squad car shuddering to a stop, lights flashing red and blue, followed by a silver van. At the edge of the drive, overlooking the drop-off, sat a small dark SUV with one door hanging open. Jenkins and Hanks jumped from the squad car.

Alice parked.

Kinsear jumped out of the silver van, hurried to the Land Cruiser, opened Alice's door.

She fumbled her way out of the seat belt, slid her legs the distance down to the dirt road. Terra firma. A fierce, fierce hug. Thank you, Lord.

Jenkins and Hanks trotted over. Margaret climbed out of the Land Cruiser.

"Someone got shot. Down there." Alice pointed over the drop-off.

"Another shooting?" Jenkins grabbed her radio. "We've got another crime scene here! Where's our backup?" She stowed her radio, muttered something emphatic. She turned to Alice and Margaret.

"Okay. Why the hell are you two here?" she demanded.

"I needed to find Kinsear." Who rolled his eyes but smiled a one-sided smile.

Clare Graham walked over from the van.

"You say someone got shot?" Jenkins focused on Alice.

Alice pointed downhill. "We'd turned down that road below trying to find you. Then someone skidded down the hill…kind of standing up…right in front of us, we had to brake. We heard a shot from above, maybe from right here, and he went over the side of the road below."

"He jerked, like he'd been hit," Margaret said. "But we couldn't see him and someone above us had a gun, so…"

"So we turned around, and just as we got back to the main road this black SUV"—

"I think it was a Bronco," Margaret added.

—"zoomed past with no lights, going downhill," Alice finished. "So we drove up here looking for you. But we need to go back and see if that guy needs help. I think it was a guy."

Margaret nodded.

Jenkins turned around. "Hanks, we need an ambulance ASAP," she snapped. "And locate our backup! And APB for a speeding black SUV, maybe a Bronco, coming down or off Rimrock and Cloudstone." She turned back to Alice and Margaret. "The SUV you saw leaving the poker game"—she nodded her head at the car with its door hanging open—"could that be it?"

"Yeah," Margaret nodded.

"She got a better look than I did," Alice agreed.

"What'd the guy look like, the one you saw skidding downhill?"

"Black clothes," Margaret said. "A knit hat, pulled down. Couldn't see his face."

"Height? Weight?"

"Not as tall as Kinsear," Alice said. Thank God.

Lights behind them; police backup rolled in. Jenkins leaned in the driver's side window. "You're crime scene. That car"—she pointed at the small SUV— "might belong to the shooter on Calle Peralta. I'm going down below to look for a body." She motioned to Hanks. "You stay here, tell them what's going on."

She turned to Alice and Margaret. "Lead me back to where you saw the guy." She looked at Kinsear and Clare Graham. "You two can go. You'll just get in the way. Don't leave town."

"I'm coming along," Kinsear said. No objection from Jenkins.

Clare Graham put his hand on Kinsear's shoulder. "Any time you're around on poker night, just call." He walked back to his van.

With Kinsear in the back seat, Alice and Margaret clambered back into the Land Cruiser and turned around, followed by Jenkins in her cruiser.

Alice braked at the little grove of trees, leaving her headlights on, angling them up the slope. She and Margaret and Kinsear climbed out.

"Stay put," Jenkins said. "Show me where he came down the hill." She shone her Maglite on the ridge above. Alice and Margaret pointed.

"See those skid marks? Like he was skiing?" Margaret said.

"Boots, maybe." Jenkins squatted, swung the light back and forth, scanning the dirt drive. "Aha."

The three civilians spotted boot prints in the dirt at the downhill side of the road.

Carefully avoiding the prints, Jenkins edged off the slope into the brush, shining the Maglite downhill. "Broken bushes," she muttered. "Okay, I'm backing out of here and going down to the drive below, see what I can see."

"We'll follow you," Alice said. "In case you need…"

Jenkins nodded. She climbed back into the squad car, backed, and turned. They followed her down the main road to the next track to the right. Alice parked by Jenkins and angled her headlights uphill on high beam.

Jenkins scanned the hillside above with her Maglite. "Got him," she said.

Far below they heard an ambulance.

"Go back to the intersection here. Show them where I am."

Alice backed all the way to the main road and parked, flashers on. Kinsear got out. When the ambulance arrived, he waved it down toward Jenkins. He stuck his head back in the Land Cruiser and told Alice, "I'll see if they need any help." She watched him trot down the drive toward the ambulance. Halfway up the ridge where Jenkins stood, three EMTs were already at work, bending over someone on the ground, pulling equipment from their bags. Alice edged the car closer to Kinsear. They watched the EMTs carefully lifting the man onto the stretcher.

Jenkins waved the Maglite at Kinsear. "We're good!" she shouted. "Don't leave town!"

He saluted and trotted back to the Land Cruiser, climbed in. "Looks like he's alive," he said briefly. "Whoever it is. Maybe the guy who got away, in Austin?"

Margaret looked at Alice, then Kinsear. "Huh?"

"Long story. Requires wine," Alice said.

*****

Margaret navigated them back toward the El Rey. As soon as they got down the mountain, Alice called Francis's cell to ask about Roger.

"I'm on my way home from the hospital," Francis said. "They tell me Roger's fine. The bullet hit an artery in his calf. He's out of surgery. I got to talk to him right when he arrived at the hospital, but they won't let me see him now. Way past visiting hours."

Alice furrowed her brow. Was Roger all alone? What about his wife? "What about Kristi? Isn't she there?"

"I asked him when we got there if I should phone her. He said no."

"Why not?"

A pause. "I guess I can tell you. He told me before he went to Austin that he's told her he wants out."

Alice digested that. "Huh."

"Listen, did you guys find the shooter?" Francis asked.

Alice put the phone on speaker so Margaret and Kinsear could recount the evening's adventures.

"Wow," Francis said. "So the police might have the bad guy?"

"Yep. He seemed to be alive when the police told us to go home," Kinsear reported. They hung up.

At the El Rey parking lot, Alice groaned with relief as she abandoned the driver's seat of the Land Cruiser. She looked at her phone. Eleven-thirty.

She and Kinsear persuaded Margaret to join them at a table close to the glowing piñon fire in the welcoming courtyard. "Bar's still open," Kinsear said. "I'd like an adult beverage. You two?"

Alice and Margaret placed wine orders. "Red," said Alice. "Cabernet. No, Syrah."

"Pinot grigio," said Margaret. "A big glass, too, not one of those dinky ones."

Kinsear obliged.

For a few sips, grateful silence, apart from the faint rustle of cottonwood leaves in the cool night breeze. Alice shut her eyes, enjoying the fire's warmth.

Margaret moved closer to the fire, shivering just a bit.

"You'd be warmer if you still had that good-looking pink scarf," Alice said. "Sorry about that."

"Blood-red's not my best color," Margaret said. "It went to a good cause. Guys, what happened in Austin?"

Kinsear gave her the short version.

"Two villains from Albuquerque?"

"That's what the caught guy told the Austin police."

"Hmm." Margaret frowned.

"What?" Alice asked.

"Not a lot of people live up there where we were racing around tonight. Assuming Roger's shooter's also from Albuquerque, wouldn't he head back to Albuquerque? But if he was instructed to rendezvous with someone up on the mountain tonight—that's an if—and if that someone was from Santa Fe, it probably put the Albuquerque guy at a disadvantage." Margaret stood to leave. "Gotta go. Great evening. Haven't had this much excitement in years." She smiled the rakish smile Alice remembered from tennis matches. Kinsear walked her out to her car, then stopped on his way back to wave at the bartender for another pour.

"Question," said Alice, as he settled back in his chair, long legs crossed in front of him. "How did the shooter know where Roger was tonight?"

Kinsear nodded. "For that matter, how did he know where Roger was last week in Austin?"

The Syrah tasted like the night—dry and aggressive. The cottonwood leaves rustled overhead. She considered Kinsear's response. "What about the poker group?" Francis and Clare had asked her if Roger would be back from Austin for tonight's game…

"We're asking the wrong question," Kinsear said, finishing his wine. "The right question is, why does someone want Roger dead?" He stood and stretched. "Bedtime. You have the room key?" He leaned over. "Hey…wake up." He took the wine glass from her fingers. "Come on, sleepyhead."

At four a.m. she woke, remembering the right question: why kill Roger? But Roger wasn't her business. Ellie was her business. Alice slipped out of bed, made a pot of coffee on the motel's miniature coffeemaker as quietly as possible, checked messages, emailed her children, made a list. Meet Mike Cortez. Contact museum about codicil and New Mexico probate process. Maybe meet with Clare Graham: she was feeling uneasy about her appraiser. Climb up into Ellie's attic with a powerful flashlight. Then she would visit Roger.

Chapter Thirty-One

Watching the Rage Rise

When Kinsear emerged from the shower, she'd already forwarded Mike Cortez her draft letter to the museum and asked him to meet with her this morning at ten. She'd emailed Clare Graham asking him to meet at eleven to explain any significant change in his valuations of the box and its contents. But as she sipped her tepid and unsatisfying coffee, she realized she needed to check Ellie's attic before either of these meetings. She'd look like an idiot without certainty that she'd found absolutely everything there.

"What about breakfast?" Kinsear dangled the car keys.

"Yes! Why are you so dressed up?"

"Remember, I'm meeting people at ten about this year's Santa Fe Trail program and staying through lunch."

"But I've got to get to Ellie's first thing to confirm I didn't miss anything in the attic."

"How about if I drop you off, pick up breakfast and bring it back to Ellie's? Then you can take me to my meeting. Personally, I'm thinking huevos motuleños. But I thought you might want smoked trout hash? With poached eggs? And possibly you might share?" He lifted hopeful eyebrows.

"Yes! to the trout. And I might share. Ready?" Alice stuck her laptop in her bag and checked to be sure she had keys to Ellie's house and the code to the alarm system.

"Deal."

"Any other requests?" he asked as they left their room.

"I have total faith in your ability to provide the breakfast of my dreams. But I must have real coffee immediately," Alice begged.

They stopped at the coffee bar in the El Rey lobby. "Wait a sec," Alice said. She took her first sip. "Thank you, Lord." She took her second. Satisfied that the brew was rich enough, dark enough, fragrant enough to jump-start the morning, she followed Kinsear to the Land Cruiser.

* * * * *

A perfect June morning in Santa Fe. High sixties, variable breeze ruffling the tall cottonwoods in downtown Santa Fe. Those disappeared on the winding road to Ellie's, replaced by chamisa, stubby piñons, and some cholla cactus with its startling fuchsia blooms.

Ellie's street sat quiet in early sun. No traffic, no noise.

"Ellie had good taste," Kinsear remarked, taking in the view from the little adobe house on the side of Moon Mountain.

Alice lifted her face to the sun, thinking as she inhaled that the air felt almost effervescent. She patted her pants pocket to be sure she had her phone and the house keys, and grabbed her briefcase. "See you in a bit. Oh, wait. You have a good flashlight, I'll bet?"

Kinsear reached under his seat and produced a hefty Maglite. He checked the batteries, almost blinding Alice.

"That'll work. Thanks."

He backed out. She wondered if either the front or back door was chained. Maybe try the garage route. She unlocked the garage and, tucking the flashlight under her arm, hoisted the old-fashioned garage door with a suppressed grunt. She held it up, walked under it, then let it back down with a thump. She stuck the keys in her pocket with the phone and scampered toward the blinking alarm system to punch in the code.

Now the only noise she heard was the distant hum of the refrigerator. Ellie's house smelled vacant, but pleasant; she wondered if adobe somehow purified the air. A clay filter…

Okay, get this done. She trotted from the garage into the kitchen, then swung through the dining room, living room, and the master bedroom. All in order. In the guest bedroom she picked up the hand-made ladder with the rawhide ties knotted to each rung and placed it in the closet beneath the wooden rectangle that covered the ceiling opening. Flashlight awkward in her left hand, as before, she climbed cautiously up to the next-to-last rung, paused to turn on the flashlight and set it on the wooden platform above, then levered herself up with her arms, swinging up one knee, then the other.

She crawled onto the wooden planks of the platform. It was as small as she remembered: she had to crouch. She lifted the heavy flashlight and swung the beam slowly along the edge of the platform where the planks met the wall. Alice crawled closer, her kneecaps protesting at the hard wood. What appeared to be a dark shadow along that junction turned out to be a gap as wide and deep as her palm. She lowered the flashlight, shining it directly down the gap. Nothing but dust. She reversed direction. The beam lit up a small cardboard box, sticking out of the gap, about the size of a box of gift cards. Had she missed anything else? She ran the flashlight beam further down, reluctant to stick her fingers in the gap. She saw only a loose snakeskin and a dead scorpion. Turning, she carefully scanned the rest of the platform with the flashlight. Again, nothing but dust. She scooted around the edge, pointing the flashlight down to see if anything had fallen off onto the sheetrock below. Nothing.

She crawled back to the box, heart thumping, and examined it with the flashlight beam. It was indeed a stationery box, only about five by six inches, not too heavy, and closed with a couple of rubber bands. To her surprise, it wasn't dusty. Why not? She thought about that, rubbing her complaining knees, thinking. Should she open it up here?

She jumped at a sudden rumble below. The garage door. Someone had opened it…but not closed it. Way too soon for Kinsear—he'd been gone barely fifteen minutes. And Kinsear would be calling her name. She grabbed her phone and texted him—"SOS, someone in house"—and froze, listening. A woman's voice below, speaking an order into the telephone: "Call me."

Who? She pulled the ladder up into the dark attic, trying not to bang it. She hurried to replace the wooden rectangle in the closet ceiling, holding her breath as it slipped into place. She turned off the flashlight and clutched it tight, afraid to lose it on the platform.

Who was down there?

Someone strode through the kitchen, then the dining room…the living room…now back through the kitchen and into the hallway leading to the bedrooms. Suddenly, almost directly below, she heard a cellphone, on speaker: dial tone, then the electronic pings for the number. Alice didn't move, ears cocked.

"Hey! Listen. When you went to look in the attic at the Santa Fe house—how'd you get up there?" Pause. "Yeah, I know you had to leave in a hurry. But didn't you find a door?" Pause. "What about in the garage?" Pause, then hurriedly, "No, just curious, honey. No, I'm at work.

Gotta go."

She knew that voice. It had unpleasant connotations.

Alice had finished her search. She tucked her shirt tightly into her jeans and shoved the small box inside the back of her collar and down her back. Then she picked up the heavy flashlight, weighed it in her hand, considering her options. Hide?

No. The thought of being trapped up here…left for dead? No.

She heard drawers and cabinet doors slamming far down the hallway. Ellie's bedroom? Bedroom closet? Then closer. Linen closet? Hall bathroom?

Alice lifted the wooden rectangle from the opening in the closet ceiling, put it aside to her right.

She slid the ladder down the opening, resting it on her side of the ceiling opening, then braced her feet against the top rung. Okay. She lifted the flashlight in her right hand.

"Danielle?" she called.

Silence, then a thud of feet. Danielle's furious face appeared below her, eyes blazing. "What the hell are you doing here? This isn't your house! You have no right!"

"The house belongs to the estate. I'm the executor. You have no reason to be here."

Alice stared into Danielle's face, watching the rage rise in her eyes.

In a flash Danielle was on the ladder. In a fury she grabbed the butt end of the flashlight handle. Alice gripped it with both hands, then kicked the top rung of the ladder backwards. Danielle's head hit the sharp wooden edge of the closet ceiling opening. She shrieked as she fell, taking the ladder with her. She sprang to her feet, snatched up the ladder and stalked toward Alice.

"Alice! Alice, where are you?" Kinsear's voice. Feet pounded through the house.

Danielle whirled as Kinsear skidded to a stop at the guestroom door.

"What the…" he gasped. "Who's this?"

Danielle dropped the ladder and shoved him out of her path. He grabbed at her jacket; she yanked herself away and left him holding a faded jean jacket. He looked at Alice with wide eyes, then thundered after Danielle.

Alice stayed perched on the attic platform, unable to get down.

Outside, shouts and engine noise—screeching tires in the road.

Kinsear returned, picked up the ladder, and set it at Alice's dangling feet. Silently she handed him the flashlight, holding it by the flared end. "It's got her prints, so be careful." He laid it on the guestroom desk. Alice backed partway down the ladder, replaced the wooden cover in the ceiling opening, and stepped onto the guestroom floor. Kinsear gathered her in a one-armed hug.

"Holy guacamole," he said. "That's your *client*?"

"Nope. I represent the estate. That's the wife of Ellie's son Don, from Houston."

"What was she after?"

"Good question."

"And what the heck is this?" He patted the box under the back of her shirt. She untucked her shirt, grasped the box, and laid it on the desk. "Don't know yet."

Alice picked up Danielle's jacket and wrapped it cautiously around the flashlight. "I've got to take this to George Files. How did she get here so early? Drive all night?"

"Must've flown," Kinsear said. "Maybe the first morning flight from Houston to Albuquerque. She was driving a rental, anyway." He lowered his head and glared at Alice. "I drove up, found a strange car parked right in the driveway, and almost had a heart attack."

"You were in the nick of time," Alice said. "I wanted to ask her some questions, but she got so mad, so fast…"

"At least she didn't bash my car. I parked well behind her but she whipped that rental right across the yard when she left."

Alice sniffed. Did he smell, however faintly, of eggs, of fried plantain, of tortillas? "Ben!" she exclaimed. "What about our breakfast?"

"Oh, lord. The eggs will be cold." He strode out through the kitchen to his car.

They sat together in Ellie's kitchen by the big windows looking out toward Santa Fe and dived into their smoked trout hash and huevos motuleños. On the table lay the small box and Danielle's jacket, wrapped around the flashlight. Alice put the box in her briefcase. She found a clean plastic bag under the sink and carefully tucked it around the jacket and flashlight.

After a few bites Kinsear spoke. "Aren't you curious what's in the box?"

"Yes. I thought I'd open it in front of Mike Cortez, though."

"Good idea. Look, I'll trade you one of my fried plantains for a bite of trout hash."

She pushed over her plate.

Kinsear nodded at the bag holding Danielle's jacket. "You think she killed Ellie?"

Alice looked out the window at the limitless skies above Santa Fe. "I don't know. And I'll bet Don doesn't know she's here."

"What does that have to do with it?"

"She knows how to be somewhere she's not supposed to be." Alice took a breath, blew it out, remembering Danielle's fierce grip on the flashlight. "She sure meant to use that Maglite on me."

Chapter Thirty-Two

A Having Nature

A lice reset the alarms and locked the house.

"See what I mean?" Kinsear pointed at the car tracks running through the scanty grass of the front yard and through the shallow ditch at the road's edge. "That woman's dangerous."

Alice finally felt safe once she climbed up in the driver's seat of the Land Cruiser and slammed the heavy door.

She dropped Kinsear at the coffeeshop where the Santa Fe Trail program committee was meeting and wove her way through downtown Santa Fe to Mike Cortez's office in a renovated Territorial house on East Palace. "Oh, yes!" said a smiling receptionist. "Mr. Cortez is waiting in the conference room. Go right through that door. There's coffee and water set up."

Mike Cortez reminded Alice of Humpty Dumpty: egg-shaped, with some sparse strands on a bald head. But unlike Humpty, he looked sharply observant and generally benign. He offered a warm, strong handshake and pulled out a chair for Alice. "Can I get you coffee?" he said.

"Please." She settled into the chair, feeling better by the minute.

Cortez briskly outlined the applicable probate requirements and a tidy timeline.

Alice sighed again, this time in relief. "Sounds great. Let's do it."

"Now as to your draft letter about the codicil, to the museum," he began, "here are my suggestions." He passed her a marked-up copy. "I suggest we send it straight to Cynthia Logan. She's their counsel. I've known her at least ten years."

"What's she like?"

"Civilized. Smart, no-nonsense, but civilized. Always aware that bad behavior by anyone at the museum can do long-term harm."

Alice remembered the rumored spat between Agnes Dietz and some unnamed party at the museum. She mentioned it to Cortez.

"Interesting." He blinked, staring at his coffee. "Very interesting. So perhaps the museum will get a delayed gift from Agnes Dietz, via Ellie Windom?"

Alice opened her computer and set it up where Cortez could see it. She showed him the initial pictures she'd taken of the box contents, with the two Santa Fe Safety yahoos watching. "The codicil names four prints Ellie left to her grandchildren. Two folders in the box were empty of prints. I think their woodblocks are still in the box. I think Ellie mailed the two missing prints to her birth daughter but didn't take the woodblocks with her."

Cortez scrutinized the pictures of the remaining seven prints—two for the Windom grandchildren and five for the museum. "Baumann's signature on the first two, not the next five. So odd. Plus the woodblocks?"

"Right." She studied his face. "Did you ever find a bill of sale for house contents when Dietz's estate sold the house to Ellie?"

"No, but I think we argue it doesn't matter. The deed says 'house and contents.' The museum received the house sale money as Dietz's will specified. With this gift the museum winds up with even more value." He smiled at Alice. "Pigs get fat and hogs get slaughtered."

Alice liked his firm stance on behalf of Ellie. She pulled the small rubber-banded box from her briefcase.

"I found this today. Up in the small attic—just a platform, really—where the box and the chairs were. It might have fallen out of a tarp when I was wrestling with the packages."

"You haven't opened it?"

She smiled at Cortez. "Waiting on you, counsel."

She slipped off the rubber bands. They'd hardened with age. One broke.

"They've lost their elasticity. Like me," Cortez said. But he didn't take his eyes off the box. "Dietz died in eighty-seven. This box has been sitting in that attic for what, over thirty years? It's very clean…" He stood up. "Hang on a minute. Want some latex gloves?"

"Good idea."

When they were both gloved, Alice lifted the top.

Color photographs, still vivid but slightly faded. She lifted them out, spread them out in order. A photo of a river. Then a photo of a painting of the river. Then…a photo of a print apparently based on the painting, with the intense mustard and coral and green colors so characteristic of Baumann.

"That looks like the Pecos," Cortez said. He squinted at the picture. "But I can't tell the location."

The next trio showed a photo of a complex of ruined adobe buildings, then a photo of a painting on an easel of the buildings, then a photo of the print. Though the paintings were vivid, the prints felt more intense to Alice.

"Alice. You know what?"

She looked up. His eyes were wide.

"Those ruins look like the old customs house at the crossing on the Pecos! Down at San Miguel del Vado! You take State Highway 3 south of I-25."

She pointed at the next three. On the horizon, a tall church, white against the reddish dirt around it, with a photo of the painting of the church, then of the print.

Then three photos, showing first a field of lush green crops by a river, alongside an irrigation ditch, then a painting, then the print.

"*Acequia,*" said Cortez. "Irrigation ditch. By the Pecos, I bet."

Finally a trio showing a river canyon, the shadowy water running below red cliffs and golden cottonwoods against a deep blue sky, then the painting, then the print.

"I've been there," Cortez said. "That's a park on the Pecos. In fact, these five scenes all seem to be on the Pecos." He pointed at the canyon print. "I want that one."

"I prefer the custom house ruins," said Alice.

Cortez sighed. "These are amazing. Listen, the museum will go nuts."

"Hey. Look at this," Alice said.

The last photos weren't of landscapes, paintings or prints. Five showed the back of a spare figure in a hat, painting outdoors at a stand-up easel. "I can't really see his head," Alice said. "Can you tell what's he's painting?"

Cortez narrowed his eyes, brought the photos close to his nose. "Looks like these five scenes on the Pecos. Holy cow. C'mon, Agnes, give us a break," he breathed.

"You think she took the pictures?"

"And then kept them in her attic? Sounds like something she'd do. Reportedly she was…difficult."

He picked up the last photo: a head shot of a dark-haired young man in an open-necked shirt, inordinately handsome, looking away from the camera.

"Wow," Alice said. "Head by Michelangelo."

"But who the hell is that? It's certainly not Baumann. Isn't that the church in the background?"

Alice thought, I'll ask Clare Graham. He had a crush on Agnes Dietz… She sat up straight and turned to Cortez. "So you'll revise my draft to the museum to include the New Mexico process and schedule and send it to your colleague Cynthia at the museum? And handle our probate requirements? Ellie's sons haven't decided whether to sell the Santa Fe house. I'll try for a decision this coming week."

"You got it."

Alice stacked the photos in order and started to repack the box.

"You don't want to leave that with me?"

"No. I'm meeting Clare Graham. I hired him to appraise the art in the Santa Fe house, including the box of prints and the chairs. I want to hear what he says about these." She handed him the box. "Make yourself copies before I go."

He did.

Next stop: Graham's office at St. John's.

* * * * *

Graham was standing outside his office looking down the hallway when she emerged from the stairway.

"You look cheerful," she said.

"I just got back from the hospital, checking on Roger. He's doing okay, thank God." To her surprise he teared up, pulled a blue bandana from his pocket, pulled off his reading glasses, and wiped his eyes. "We could've lost him last night."

He took a big breath and smiled. "But okay! Show me whatcha got!" he said, ushering her to a chair by his desk. He rubbed his hands in anticipation.

Alice walked him through the photo triads, dealing them out on his desk like cards. His sharp eyes grew more and more intense as he scrutinized each group.

He turned to his computer, looking back and forth from his pictures of the box contents he'd appraised to the snapshots on his desk.

Then Alice showed him the snapshots at the bottom of the stack with the painter poised before his easel, looking at his subject.

"By God, that could be Baumann." Graham stood up and walked around in a tight circle, sat back down, pointed at the snapshots of the man painting. "Do you have any idea what this means?"

She waited, wondering if he'd see what Cortez had seen.

"You've got pictures of the artist standing and painting a specific place. The places look like they're all along the Pecos, south of Ribera. Like a series, maybe. You've got a gouache painting of that subject in the box. Then you have the print and woodblocks. You've got photos of each. But no dates on anything." He paused, waving a finger at Alice. "I want dates. I may take a trip out to Ribera, see what I can find out."

She laid the young man's head shot on the table.

Graham scrutinized the photo. "No idea who that is. But..." He picked up the photo of the white church, lit by slanting morning sun. "Don't you wonder who was standing by the photographer?" He pointed to three shadows, visible in the foreground.

Three...

"Let's get down to brass tacks," Alice said. She was feeling more comfortable with Graham now. Wiping his eyes about Roger…that was unexpected. Maybe the man did have a heart. "Did the box in Ellie's attic contain Baumann's work?"

"Maybe," Graham said. Then he shook his head. "And maybe not. The colors, subjects, styles —very convincing. The prints of *Chama Stream* and *Deception Peak* have Baumann's signature, but the Pecos works are unsigned with no print numbers and no hand-heart symbol. Yet they're accompanied by gouache sketches. Then these photos... they raise the ante."

"So how valuable are the contents of the box? Not counting the items Ellie gave her grandkids?"

Graham furrowed his brows. "Why not counting those?"

She reached into her briefcase and handed him a copy of the codicil. "It turns out Ellie left four specific prints, with their woodblocks, to four grandchildren. But the remaining box contents and the box and the painted chairs go to the museum here."

"But those prints she left the children," he muttered, "they're not part of this Pecos series. And if I recall"—he rechecked the photos on his computer—"they're only prints, with no gouaches."

Her thought exactly. "So in your opinion," she asked, "do these photos make the gift of the Pecos series more valuable?"

"Of course." No hesitation. "The museum could mount a whole exhibition based on these new works plus the photos. What are you worried about?"

"Suppose the museum still decides to challenge the codicil and claim it should get all the box contents? Agnes's will said only that the museum should get the *proceeds* of the sale of her house and contents." She'd argue the museum would get less if it demanded the worth of the house's "contents" as of 1989 but had no right to the contents themselves—which Ellie had bought.

Graham chewed his nether lip. "Look, Alice, for the museum to get hold of the photos plus the gouaches and prints is probably worth much more to the museum."

"So the museum won't demand the grandchildren's prints."

"Nah." He had a funny smile, wry and a little tender. "That Agnes."

"What do you mean?"

"Baumann considered himself a commercial artist. He made prints so the public—not just well-heeled collectors—could afford art. But what happened here? Think, Alice. It looks like Agnes Dietz acquired everything connected with each print—the gouache sketch if there was one, and the woodcut prints—and only a single print was made from each set of blocks."

"Seriously?"

"Yep. The blocks show almost no wear. I find no record of any other prints from these blocks. That may explain why the prints don't bear the usual print numbers." The sharp eyes met hers. "You ever read *The Forsyte Saga* by John Galsworthy?"

"I did."

"You remember when someone tells the infatuated young Jon that his lovely Fleur has 'a having nature'? Meaning she'd never share him.

He'd have to give up his wife and child."

Alice nodded.

"Maybe our Agnes was like that," Graham said.

Alice recounted Margaret's tale of the woodworker's table. Agnes wanted the original—the only original—no copies allowed.

"Agnes dropped me," he said, "after she saw me having margaritas with my girlfriend one night at Maria's. No more 'Hi, Clare dear.' No more invitations to events she was hosting. You were all hers or…you were nothing."

A having nature.

"But how did she manage to get hold of the box, the chairs, the prints, the woodblocks, the gouaches? Why'd she stick them in the attic crawl space of her house?"

"Baumann died in 1971. Agnes probably got the surprise of her life when she fell to her death in 1987. She was only in her late fifties. I bet she had a plan for her attic treasures, but who knows? I never heard a whiff of gossip about any of this." He shook his head, smiling a lopsided smile. "She was so beautiful, Alice. If you'd met her, you'd understand. But she was…inflexible. Unforgiving. Single-minded. Even so…utterly magnetic."

He cocked his head. "By the way, have you thought about what happens if either Ellie's birth daughter or Ellie's sons challenge the codicil?"

Of course she'd thought about it. She nodded, watching him think through the implications.

"That would be a mess. We don't want a mess, do we?" he asked. "The museum will favor the codicil." He gave her a sardonic look. "I'd encourage that."

"I have to be fair to all beneficiaries." She sighed. "Including the museum."

"Okay, Lady Justice. Thanks for hiring me. This is pretty fun."

"What about racing up the mountain last night in your van, with Kinsear, going after Roger's shooter?"

"That was pretty fun too, but oh, lord, what if Roger had died? Hopefully Roger's safe, now that the police have the suspect." Again he teared up, reached for his bandana. "Sorry. We've been friends a long time."

"Yes, what is it about that man? Francis seems to like him too."

"Roger's fair, he's funny, he's brave. But low-key. He's seen so much… When you're with him, you know he's ready for anything, has handled almost everything, dressed in his blue shirt and blazer. Courage personified, but disguised." Graham paused. "I've never seen him put himself first. Although now and then, he should."

"What do you mean?"

Graham shrugged. "Just sayin'."

Hmm.

Graham wanted to keep the photos. Alice promised him a set of copies.

As she walked to her car, Cortez called on her cellphone. "Talked to my friend Cynthia at the museum," he began. "She was circumspection personified but hinted at an unsubstantiated rumor that Dietz was attentive to a young museum employee named Broad. But he left suddenly for a job in Chicago when his wife was expecting their first child."

Alice filed that away. Now, the hospital, and Roger.

Signed, Sealed, and Delivered

R oom 329, Graham had said. She exited the hospital elevator, carrying a gift for Roger—a book of crossword puzzles. The elevator bank faced the nursing station. Bluegreen walls, fluorescent lights, brisk voices, various bings and bongs on the intercom. She stopped at the nursing station to make sure Roger was still in 329. "Yes," said the nurse. "He's down that wing." She pointed to Alice's left. "Last room on the left."

Alice made her way down the hall. Maybe she'd tell Roger he'd "dodged a bullet this time." Ha. Three bullets, actually. Moreover, he hadn't really dodged them. Plus, before the poker game there'd been the brake line sabotage, then the assault at the LBJ Library. Who wanted to kill Roger, and why?

For that matter, who killed Ellie, and why?

She frowned. Was someone out to eliminate both Valerie's birth parents? Maybe Valerie was somehow a key to the attacks?

Ahead of her a uniformed policewoman and man in chinos and jacket emerged from the last room on her left.

"Officer Jenkins," Alice said. "You're here to see Roger?"

"Yep." Jenkins introduced the detective with her. "You know the shooter's in the hospital too? Same floor, but as far apart as possible." She nodded toward the wing on the other side of the nursing station.

Alice's face must have shown alarm.

"No worries, we've got a guard on him. Thanks for helping out last night. You and your two…uh…"

"Idiots?" Alice supplied.

"They did a pretty decent job. We wouldn't have found the shooter otherwise. Okay, see ya." The two strode toward the elevator.

They'd left the door of Room 329 slightly ajar. Alice was about to knock when she heard voices inside.

"Listen, Dad, Mom said something weird on the phone. Are you really moving out?"

Alice froze.

Roger's voice: "Yes. After my…my friend was killed in Texas, I decided life was too short to live this way. Your mother and I…we don't have much in common these days."

"I know it's been…maybe…um…" The first voice fumbled,

stopped.

"No, listen," Roger said. "She won't miss me. Anyway, she's got a thing going with a guy from the golf club."

Alice backed away from Roger's door, wanting to hear more but maybe not to eavesdrop—at least not to be caught in the act. Just then a cart rattled down the hall toward her, steered by a fast-moving aide. The aide pushed the door wide open, singing out "Lunchtime! Meatloaf today! Sound good, Mr. Preyer?" She propped the door open with her cart and bustled in, rearranged his table, set down the lunch tray, raised the back of his bed, checked his water, and bestowed a smile.

Make your move, Alice told herself. She knocked. Roger, sitting up now, looked up and saw Alice in the hall. "Come in, Alice," he said. "Good to see you. Meet my son, Randall. He drove up from Albuquerque."

Sitting at the far side of Roger's bed was a forty-something man with thinning blond hair and gray eyes like Roger's. Software engineer, she remembered. About to launch his IPO. He stood up and moved to the foot of the bed to shake Alice's hand.

"When your dad gets shot, you show up," Randall said, with a wry smile.

"Alice showed up herself last night," Roger said. "Came to pick up her boyfriend at the poker game and wound up slapping a tourniquet around my leg. I remember that," he added, turning to Alice. "You keep on saving my life."

"Thank you," Randall said to Alice. "Dad told me what happened in Austin. Now this shooting, which scared the...well." He looked at his watch. "I hate to leave, Dad, but I've got a meeting at two back in Albuquerque. You wouldn't believe how many meetings an IPO involves. But I had to see you. Listen..." He moved back to the far side of Roger's bed. "Dad, are you going to be okay?"

Roger smiled. "Yes. Thanks, son."

Randall took Roger's hand, squeezed it, leaned over to give him a kiss on the head. "You're the best," he murmured. "The very best."

Alice felt a pang at her heart.

"Nice to meet you, Alice. Thanks again for that tourniquet." At the door Randall turned back and held Roger's eyes for a moment. "I'll do what you asked, Dad."

After Randall made his way out of the room Alice opened the gift bag and handed Roger the crossword book. "I don't know if you like these…"

"Love 'em. Put it on this table where I can reach it. It's sure better than TV. Thank you." He managed a real smile. "Sit, Alice. It's great to have someone to talk to." He pointed to the chair next to the door.

She pulled it closer and sat down, saying, "Okay, but only if you'll go ahead with your lunch. How're you feeling?"

"Not bad. Ready to get out of here."

"I saw the police leaving. They say your attacker's in a room at the other end of this floor, with a guard."

"Yeah," Roger said. "That freaked out Randall. The detective showed me photos of the guy they caught. I've never seen him before."

"Are they sure he's the one who shot you?"

"They said they found a recently fired gun, three rounds missing, in his car up on the mountain."

"But who shot him? Do the police know?" asked Alice.

He shook his head no. "They told me you and Margaret saw a black Bronco coming downhill, but they weren't able to locate it."

"So what's going on, Roger?" Alice asked. "Is this related to your work overseas?"

"Not that we know of." She took note of the "we."

"Who's 'we'? The royal 'we'?"

He laughed, shook his head.

"What about the guy in Austin?" Alice asked. "The one they caught?"

"He's still not talking. Won't say another word. The Austin police told the Santa Fe police they're beginning to think he's mobbed up. But what that's got to do with me, I have no idea."

"I thought the guy in Austin told the police that the man who hired him said you were worth more dead than alive."

Roger snorted. "Well, I've fixed that. I told you my parents left me that dried-up family ranch in west Texas that turned out to be part of the Permian shale oil play?" Alice nodded. Roger ate some fruit cocktail, made a face, swallowed. "While I was in Austin, I changed the trust beneficiary so the money's all going to the Science on a Sphere program at the community college here—a big check now, and future royalties. That way the kids in Santa Fe can visualize how precious our planet really is. Lord knows I don't need more money. And Randall's about to make it large from his IPO."

He reached for his water, but it was too far away. Alice handed it to him, noting the fine features, the set mouth.

"Giving that money away made me feel…lighter, somehow. I think I'll be back in Austin a lot." He sipped through the straw. "At least some good came of that trip."

"Coming to Ellie's service?"

He nodded.

"And getting in touch with Valerie?"

He smiled. "Oh, Alice. You can't imagine."

A nurse stuck her head around the door, then came in to check Roger's vitals. Alice stepped out of the room and stood staring out the window at the end of the hall while she called Kinsear to ask when his meeting would end. "Maybe thirty more minutes," he said. "We're thrashing out some details."

She looked up in time to see the nurse leaving and a dark-haired woman hurrying into Roger's room.

Valerie Ames.

A momentary flash of panic. But surely, she thought, Valerie's no threat to Roger?

She walked back to the open door. Valerie sat leaning forward in the chair on the other side of Roger's bed, gazing at him with her big brown eyes. Ellie's eyes. Alice heard him say, "How did you know? How'd you get here so fast?"

Valerie smiled. "Your friend Francis called me. He thought I'd want to know."

"And did you? Did you want to know?" His voice was almost inaudible, anxious, hopeful.

"You know I did. Oh, Roger. Quit getting shot at, would you?" She burst into tears. "I've just found you! I can't lose you!"

He reached for her hand, his face softening.

Valerie glanced up and saw Alice.

Roger turned toward Alice, face alight. "Alice! Come back in! You've met my—you and Valerie met in Austin, I believe."

The two women nodded at each other.

"Alice, what brought you up here?" asked Valerie.

"Talking to local counsel about probate for Ellie's house. Then last night…"

Roger jumped in. "Alice drove over to Francis's house to retrieve her boyfriend. He'd joined our poker game."

"But when I got there, Roger was lying in the driveway," Alice said.

"She put a tourniquet on my leg," Roger finished. "Thanks, Alice."

Valerie wanted the whole story. She made Alice tell some of the tale while Roger picked at his lunch.

"So your attacker got shot and is somewhere *here?* In this hospital?" Valerie looked horrified. "But you don't know him?"

"Never saw him before."

"So is he like a hired gun? From your past?" Valerie demanded.

"I don't think so."

Reluctantly Alice stood. Time to rescue Kinsear from his meeting. Her mind was spinning. "*Hired gun.*" "*Worth more dead than alive.*"

She said her goodbyes, told Valerie she'd be in touch, and slipped out of the room, gently closing the door. Police, Randall, Valerie, herself…Roger's room felt like Grand Central Station. She stepped back to her vantage point by the window at the end of the hall and texted Kinsear. "Ready?"

Across from the nursing station down the hall the elevator doors opened. Several nurses emerged, then a man who turned down the hallway toward her. Still unaware of Alice, the man, jaunty in boots and fringed suede jacket, walked slowly, checking room numbers, cradling in his arms a large translucent plastic bag that looked like it contained a square box. The man had a bounce to his step that reminded her…ah. The man who'd lifted a glass to her at the Desert Chorale concert. The man with the flirty smile, the knowing eyes. Suede Jacket, she'd named him. What had Francis said his name was? Billy Menger.

Billy Menger, the man Francis saw at Cafe Piñon with Roger's wife, Kristi. The golf club, was it, where she'd met him? The man Francis and Clare wouldn't allow to join their poker group. The man who'd lost his comps at the casino.

He owed the casino.

Roger was worth more dead than alive.

Through the semi-transparent bag she could make out the distinctive red cursive Krispy Kreme on the side of the box. She smelled the irresistible yeasty, sugary aroma of fresh doughnuts. The man was cradling the bag with his left hand; she couldn't see his right. He slowed his pace one room away, checking the room number.

Alice moved in front of Roger's door. "If you're here to see Roger Preyer, this isn't a good time," she said. "His…his daughter just got here. Flew in from Austin." She smiled. "So I left. That's why I'm out here."

"Oh," he said. "I can wait."

Alice suddenly realized mentioning Roger's daughter might be a fatal mistake. Could this guy be after Valerie?

"No, don't," she said, moving where she could feel the door handle in the small of her back. "It's obvious Roger really wants a private visit with her."

He shifted from foot to foot, impatient with this dense woman who unaccountably wouldn't get out of his way.

Alice remembered watching Kristi at the Desert Chorale concert, watching her leave, watching her follow this man out to the patio. Roger had told Francis he'd asked Kristi for a divorce. What if…

She heard herself say, "I expect Roger's telling her how he's given away his money."

The man tilted his head, looked puzzled. "Given away his money?"

"Yes, he's made a huge gift, all his trust money, I think, to the community college here. Says he doesn't need it and the school science program does." She babbled on. "It's for the Science on a Sphere project. So generous! The college must be over the moon!"

"His trust fund? That's what he gave up?"

"Yes. All that money from his parents. Isn't that cool?" Don't over-do it, she scolded herself.

"He's already finalized the gift?"

An odd question. "I think it's signed, sealed, and delivered." She couldn't stop. "I'm hoping there'll be a big reception now that…now that he's made this gift." Well, Roger wasn't her client. She couldn't get in too much trouble disclosing this, could she? Even if she was wobbly on details?

He turned away and stared out the hall window, a faraway look in his eyes. Then he turned back to Alice, switching gears. "I heard someone tried to shoot him. Anyone know who?"

"I think the police caught the man."

He looked up, startled. "Alive?"

What an odd question. Why would he care? Unless…

"I think so." In fact she knew so. If she looked down the hall past the nursing station, she could just see a man in uniform standing up, stretching his arms in the air, then sitting back down on a chair outside a room. She wouldn't mention that.

Suede Jacket looked directly in her face. "I know where I saw you. At the Desert Chorale concert. You were with Roger and Francis Blake."

She watched him filing that information, processing it. He rear-ranged his right arm. She noticed a small movement inside the plastic bag. Through the thin plastic she saw a dark round hole. Like a gun muzzle. Her stomach clenched. She ordered her eyes to meet his eyes, ordered her face to look pleasant, interested.

But she had to ask. "How'd you find out Roger was in the hos-pital?"

His eyes widened slightly. "Oh, I think… at the golf club. The grapevine, you know."

Roger just got shot last night. Pretty speedy grapevine, she thought.

Soft laughter floated out of Room 329. Abruptly the man said, "Tell Roger that Billy came by to say hi."

"I could give him the doughnuts later," she said.

Almost imperceptibly he tightened his left arm around the bag.

"Or you could leave the doughnuts at the nursing station," she added.

"Thanks." He turned and strode back toward the nursing station but stopped halfway there, apparently staring straight down the opposite wing, where the uniformed man sat outside a patient's room. Then he punched the elevator button. The doors opened; he disappeared, still holding the doughnut bag.

Alice didn't realize she'd been holding her breath until she heard herself exhale. But where was Billy Menger going? She ran to the "STAIRS" door, hurtled two flights down and burst into the hospital entrance lobby. She hurried to the door in time to see Suede Jacket disappear into a row of cars. She pushed open the revolving door and stood where she could see him climb into a black Bronco.

A black Bronco.

Last night she'd braked hard to avoid being hit by a black Bronco hurtling down the mountain.

No wonder he'd asked, "Alive?" The last piece fell into place.

The Bronco roared off, leaving a gray cloud of exhaust hanging in the clear air.

Her phone squawked. "Alice? This meeting's finally over."

Kinsear.

"On my way," she said, catching her breath. "Be there in ten minutes." But first...

When the Chips Were Down

The Land Cruiser was parked close to the hospital entrance. She hurried to the car and drove after the black Bronco. It turned out of the hospital grounds onto Harkle Street but slowed momentarily for a red light, then sped forward when the light changed. Alice, trying to catch up, strained her eyes for the license tag. "XTG," she said aloud. Those were the first letters on his plate. He was far ahead now, turning south on Arroyo Seco.

Alice, this is not your job, she told herself. "XTG. XTG," she repeated aloud. She made her way back downtown to the maze of one-way streets. Kinsear stood waiting outside the coffee shop. "I skipped lunch at the meeting," he said. "Can I treat? It's late enough we might find a table at Pasqual's."

Excellent idea. "XTG," she said. "Remember that." She slowed for pedestrians, avoided alarming Kinsear, and maneuvered her way triumphantly into a parking spot at Café Pasqual's.

As they entered Pasqual's, Alice snatched a cocktail napkin from the bar. She scribbled "XTG" on it and stuck it in her pocket. When the waiter pointed them to a table, she said to Kinsear, "I need to alert the Santa Fe police. Order for me, will you? Quesadillas barbacoa!"

She took her phone back out into the June sunshine, and finally, after several minutes, reached Officer Jana Jenkins.

When Alice began her report, Jenkins said, "At the *hospital?*" Then, "Who?" Then, "But why do you think…" Then, "You mean the car you saw coming downhill before Hanks and I got there?" Finally, "Repeat that tag number. What's the rest of it?" Alice confessed failure on that score.

Back inside beneath the ristras and colorful paper banners, Kinsear sat enjoying a draft beer and scooping up chips and salsa. The waiter bustled up with Alice's platter of fragrant quesadillas and Kinsear's cheese enchiladas. "Back to basics," Kinsear said.

After a few bites Alice poured out her morning story, starting with the last installment: the stream of visitors to Room 329. Including Suede Jacket.

"You think he had a gun in the doughnut bag?" Kinsear's black eyebrows rose higher than usual. "Alice, for God's sake, you shouldn't…"

"Shouldn't what? I had to keep him away from Roger."

He set down his fork. "Still…"

New topic. "How was your meeting?" she asked. "Got the program all planned?"

"Yeah. It's about the segment of the Santa Fe Trail that crossed the Pecos, down by San Miguel del Vado. You know, the falling-down adobe customs house on the river?"

Alice stared at him across the table, jaw dropping. "Ben—that box of photos Ellie had in her attic"—she took a breath—"those are snapshots where a guy who might be Baumann painted sketches and made prints of five sites on the Pecos. Including the customs house."

"You're kidding."

"I am not. Those are the photos and sketches and prints and woodblocks Ellie left to the New Mexico Museum of Art."

He leaned back in his chair. "Well! I'll need to tell the committee about that. What a draw that would be!"

"Assuming we have no litigation over Ellie's codicil," Alice said in her primmest voice. "I personally don't want litigation, but if the museum…"

"Are you trying to co-opt me? To pressure the museum?"

She grinned. "Of course not. Just advancing my clients' interests." She frowned. "All their interests, which is part of the problem."

Kinsear finished his enchiladas and said, "Listen. I need to get home. Can we bail out of here early tomorrow morning?"

"Yes," Alice said. "We've done what we needed at Ellie's. Mike Cortez's taking charge of probate. Clare Graham is finalizing the appraisal for the Santa Fe house—again. And Roger's still alive, though that wasn't our job."

"Poor guy. Lying there in the hospital, with hospital food." Kinsear ate his last bite of enchilada, then narrowed his eyes the way he did when he'd had an idea. "Listen, let's order dinner from here and take it by the hospital before we go out to eat."

"Let's get dinner for two in case Valerie's still there." Alice looked at the time. "I've got phone calls to make."

She looked at his face, the lines a little deeper than she remembered, the black curls a little grayer. The smile a little more ironic… aware of the gap between the ideal and the actual. A face she'd learned to count on. Especially when the chips were down. In this case, chips and salsa. She lifted her glass: "More road trips."

He lifted his. "More road trips."

"Your kids are okay?"

"They say so. Yours?"

"Ann and John won't be home until late August." She sighed. "You're so lucky. Yours are close. Mine are so far away."

"Part of the price of parenthood," Kinsear said. "You train them to be independent, and they grow wings."

"I miss them so much," Alice admitted. "I try not to drive them nuts, calling…"

The waiter appeared with their check.

*****

Back at the El Rey, Alice phoned Mike Cortez. He sounded proud of himself. "I've already touched base with the museum about the codicil," he said. "They're cautiously…well…"

"What?" She couldn't stand the suspense.

"Pleased. Also, get a decision from those Windom boys on whether they're keeping the house here so I can get started."

She dialed Clare Graham next. "I'm sending the final appraisal," he said. "It's still a range. Based on my tentative and non-gold-plated assumption that Baumann's the artist and that each print is unique, with no copies, the gifts to the four grandkids could be worth about ten thousand apiece. Maybe more. Because of the photos and the gouache sketches, I'm putting the Pecos prints higher, very conservatively, at twenty thousand each, plus five thousand for the box and chairs. Of course, I'm not guaranteeing their authenticity. If the artist's not Baumann, twenty thousand total. I'm emailing you now."

She called Silla. "Can you call Chuck Windom, ask what he's decided about keeping Ellie's real estate? Tell him and Don we'd like to meet with both of them next week."

"Got it. Also, the discovery responses arrived from Edmund Fleischer, Smutbuster's lawyer."

"Did she actually answer?"

"Yeah. You'll enjoy."

"What else is going on?"

"The usual. A couple of clients returned their will questionnaires, so I'm working on their draft wills."

"Great. What do you want from Santa Fe?"

"More of those piñon coffee beans."

"Done." Alice hung up. She'd missed a call: Francis Blake. She put him on speaker. "Alice, you're not going back tomorrow, are you?"

"Planning to. Why?"

"Can you and Kinsear come over for dinner? I've asked Clare too. We should talk before you leave."

"Well…" She gave Kinsear an inquiring look as he walked in.

"I'm roasting a leg of New Mexico lamb, and Clare volunteered chocolate cake," Francis added.

Kinsear said, "We'll bring the wine."

"Six o'clock." Francis hung up.

Kinsear turned to Alice. "We can always go out to eat, but don't we need to talk to these guys before we leave Santa Fe? We've got to figure this out about Roger. It still makes no sense."

Alice agreed. She canceled their reservations again. By five they'd finished packing for an early morning exit. Kinsear drove them to Pasqual's, and Alice collected dinner for two. "We'll get this upstairs to Roger before that hospital cart rattles in," she said.

They barely made it, scuttling into Room 329 at the hospital just as the elevator doors opened behind them, discharging the smell of institutional cooking.

Valerie and Roger looked up in surprise.

"We thought you might like dinner from Café Pasqual," Alice said.

She introduced Kinsear. He carefully unloaded a colorful plate of red-and-green-sauced enchiladas onto Roger's tray table. After Valerie put another pillow behind Roger's back to make him more comfortable, Kinsear presented a plate to Valerie and popped the caps off two beers. "The word is, people heal more quickly with adequate intake of chiles and cerveza," Kinsear said.

Roger laughed. Alice hid her surprise at how relaxed his face was.

Where were the cautious frown lines between his eyes, the tautness around the mouth? Valerie too: the tension in her face had disappeared.

"We've just talked and talked," Roger said.

"For hours," Valerie added.

"About nothing," he said.

"About everything." She smiled at him.

The door banged open.

"Well!" Roger's wife, Kristi, immaculate in a pale blue pantsuit, stood in the doorway, her mouth a bitter line. "I see you're having a party!"

Roger didn't miss a beat. "Kristi, you met Alice at the Desert Chorale. Meet her friend Ben"—

Kristi swept dismissive eyes over Alice and Kinsear and stared at Valerie. "And you are?"

"Kristi," Roger tried again, "please meet Valerie Ames."

Her eyes bored into Valerie's face. "Your…birth daughter, I believe you said? Here for the big money-giveaway?"

Shocked silence greeted her.

Valerie stood straight up, face like stone. "Roger's not allowed to give me anything."

"Oh, really?" Kristi turned to Roger. "I hear you're spreading money all over Santa Fe without one word to your wife! Giving away your trust fund!"

"That money's my business, not yours." Roger's voice was sharp.

"Apparently it's 'signed, sealed, and delivered'! That's what I heard! A big gift to the community college without consulting me at all! That's what I get after all these years with you!"

"Who told you the gift was 'signed, sealed, and delivered'?" asked Alice. "Who told you that?"

Kristi glanced at her. "Why do you care? It's not your business!" She turned back to Roger. "So it's true? It's official? You never said a word to me. How'm I supposed to hold my head up in this town?"

Roger said, "Don't worry. You'll still be able to keep your golf club membership."

Ooh. The first acerbic comment Alice had heard from Roger.

With four people staring at her, Kristi turned and swooped out the door.

Roger lifted an eyebrow and looked first at Valerie, then Alice and Kinsear. "I guess now you know why I'm doing what I'm doing."

Momentary silence. "Where will you stay?" Alice blurted. Not her business, but she couldn't bear the thought of Roger—still recovering from a murderous attack—depending on the tender mercies of Kristi Preyer.

"Don't worry. I'll be discharged tomorrow morning. I'm staying with friends till then."

Valerie spoke. "I'll get him settled in the morning. I'm spending one more night."

Alice heaved a sigh of relief.

"I know Alice will stay in touch, but let me know if I can do anything at all," Kinsear said, handing a card to Roger and one to Valerie.

"Safe travels," Roger said.

*****

Alice and Kinsear didn't utter a word until the elevator reached the lobby.

"Lord God," Kinsear said. "Let's go find Francis and Clare. We need to talk to those guys."

As they pulled into Calle Peralta, Alice pointed at the Audi in front of Francis's house. "Roger's car is still here! I wonder…"

Francis met them at the door, wearing his chef's apron. Alice said, "Roger's car?"

"Yep. He'll be staying in the guestroom until his new place is ready. I've already brought in his computer and all his luggage."

"Nice," Alice said.

"His son's going over to Kristi's while she's not there to grab some boxes of records he packed up."

"Roger's been planning this," Kinsear said.

"Mm-hmm. For a while."

The kitchen smelled like a Greek island—charcoal, thyme, red wine, garlic. The grilled leg of lamb sat proudly on a platter. "My specialty," Francis said. "The secret's the marinade."

Clare Graham, also aproned, carried bread, cheese, and olives to the kitchen island. Kinsear poured wine. They sat on stools around the island.

"Summer solstice," Francis said, lifting his glass. "Longest day, shortest night."

Alice told them about their mission of mercy, carrying dinner to Room 329, and Kristi's furious descent on Roger.

"Let's just say she's not anyone you want at your bedside when you're helpless," Kinsear said. "She didn't ask Roger how he felt, or what happened to him, or when he'd be discharged…"

"Or why someone shot him," Alice added. "Which is what I want to know. But wait, there's more. Roger's room this afternoon looked like Grand Central Station. His son Randall was there when I arrived. Then came Valerie Ames, his birth daughter. Then, while I was out in the hall, who do you think showed up?"

Graham and Francis glanced at each other, then back at Alice.

"Billy Menger!" she said.

To her surprise, they just nodded. "That's what we want to talk about," Francis said. "Tell me this: who knew Roger would be at my house for poker night?"

"His wife Kristi, presumably," Kinsear said. "And you two, and Pepe."

"Well, I've started this story wrong," Francis said. "I told you I'd seen Kristi having dinner with Billy Menger at Cafe Piñon, while Roger was in Austin. That's an expensive place. High visibility for the socially lofty. Also pretty tasty. But who knows"—he lifted an ironic eyebrow—"they could've been talking about recruiting a board member for the golf club."

"Speaking of the golf club, of which I'm a member," Graham said, "Billy Menger's got a condo out on the ninth hole. Kristi plays a lot of golf. He's often in the foursome."

"Still…" Alice knew plenty of golfers who enjoyed riveting discussions of bunkers and putting strategies with fellow players.

"Alice," Francis said, then stopped. "Look. They're an item. They've stepped over whatever invisible line there is between golf buddies and—you know, disappearing off the course at the ninth hole condos." He lifted his glass, for emphasis. "And we tried to tell you why we don't play poker with Billy."

"Too much casino," she said.

"So now we've had three attacks on Roger," Graham said. "I mean, Kristi could go ahead and divorce him if she couldn't stand another minute, right? But what if Roger's—"

"—worth more dead than alive?" she finished. "That's what one of the Austin assailants told the police. But today Roger told me he's giving away big bucks from his trust fund to the community college. And when I was trying to keep Suede Jacket—I mean, Billy Menger—from going into Roger's room, I told him that Roger's gift was 'signed, sealed, and delivered.' And when Kristi barged into his room just hours later, she was furious that the gift was, as she said, already 'signed, sealed, and delivered.' When I asked who told her, she wouldn't answer."

"But you know who she heard it from," Graham said. "Menger." He paused, then said, "The word at the golf club bar is that to pay back the casino, Billy might've gotten a loan from some of the hard guys in Albuquerque."

"If you mean loan sharks, that's dangerous company," Kinsear said. "They might've pushed him to the point where he had to hire some muscle to get the cash to pay them back…" He shook his head.

"But to get enough he'd have to marry Kristi. After Roger was dead," Francis finished.

"And he'd have to do it before Roger changed the trust beneficiary to the community college," Alice said, "which Kristi didn't know because he made that change while he was in Austin. So if the attack on Roger here at your house had succeeded, Kristi still wouldn't have gotten enough money. Which is why I told Menger that the gift was 'signed, sealed, and delivered.' So he'd quit trying to kill Roger."

"Ah," said Francis.

Graham nodded approvingly.

"Now she knows, though. So will Roger be safe?" Kinsear asked.

They sipped their wine and ate olives, faces thoughtful. "Roger will be here tomorrow morning," Alice said.

"Should I get security guards?" Francis asked.

"I dunno," Kinsear said. "Hopefully Billy Menger's the one in danger now. If the golf club rumor's true, if he's in deep with loan sharks, and the police now have the guy who tried to kill Roger, Billy's out of luck. He's a liability, especially if he talks."

Alice's phone vibrated. Caller: Santa Fe police. "Hello?"

"Officer Jana Jenkins here. Listen, a black Bronco with partial tag XTG just hit the overpass abutment north of Santa Fe, up by the Opera," she said. "The car's registered to a guy named Menger."

"Billy Menger? Is he dead?"

"Very. And before you ask, no, we don't know what caused the wreck." She paused. "There's a dent on the rear where he might've been hit, but we're not sure. Of course, it's also a classic suicide scenario."

Alice excused herself and walked out on Francis's patio to report to Jenkins what little she knew.

"Sounds like I need to talk to Kristi Preyer," Jenkins said. "Was she in on this?"

"I don't know," Alice said. "Maybe, maybe not." Because Kristi might've thought Billy Menger hung around her, asked to marry her, because he really loved her—not because he was desperate for Roger's money and assumed Kristi would get it if Roger died.

She put her phone away, walked back inside, and told the men about the wreck.

"It'll be a sort of negative clue, if no one else tries to kill Roger," Francis said. "If nothing else happens, it was all Billy."

"Or maybe, now that Kristi knows she wouldn't get all the money, there's no point in killing Roger," Graham said.

No one smiled. Kinsear poured more wine.

"To love—anyway," he said. "To Ellie. To Roger. To Valerie."

They lifted their glasses, chorusing "To love—anyway." But Alice's voice died away, and her eyes prickled with tears.

Later, driving back to the El Rey, Kinsear asked, "What's up? You hardly said a word during dinner." He glanced at her, eyes narrowed. "Wait. Let me guess. You're feeling…sorry for Billy Menger. Or maybe…you're feeling bad that you told him the deal was 'signed, sealed, and delivered,' and then—maybe—he decided to run his Bronco into a concrete bridge abutment."

Alice nodded.

"If you hadn't uttered those words, my bet is he'd still have run into that bridge abutment. Or been run into it. The jig was up. You can't wish away casino debts. They're not going to disappear. And if your life depends on the patience of people you owe gambling bucks to—at high interest—your life's not worth a plugged nickel."

Alice fumbled for a tissue and blew her nose. "When we get back," she said, "I'd like a margarita."

At the El Rey they ordered two margaritas and carried them to their room. Kinsear lit the piñon logs in the kiva fireplace, then pulled her close.

"We missed our romantic evening at Café Piñon," he said, kissing her behind the ear, then nuzzling his way down her neck. "But hey, Alice…" More kisses, warm, enthusiastic. "Let me help you out of these clothes." He held the small of her back with one hand, unsnapping her jeans with the other.

She kissed him back, reached up, began unbuttoning his shirt.

The logs crackled in the fireplace.

Chapter Thirty-Five

Strong Work

D awn found them barreling through Santa Rosa, angling southeast, amid golden pastures backlit by the rising sun.

"The last time I was here, Isabel and I were dodging the Rubicon Jeep and the gray minivan carrying the Santa Fe Safety guys," Alice commented. "This time I've got you."

"Were they in cahoots?" Kinsear asked.

"Not sure. I need to nail down the Rubicon boys, who jimmied open my Discovery and stole the art box."

"Sounds painful." A couple of miles blew past. "What do you need to know?"

"Were Wiry Wayne and Burly Brian—those are the two guys from the security company that was supposed to secure Ellie's house—in contact with the Rubicon boys on the drive down? Also, when the Santa Fe Safety guys screwed up burgling my office, how did the Rubicon boys know exactly where my car was, with the box inside? Did they plan to meet the Santa Fe Safety guys at my office in Coffee Creek to pick up the goods? And pay them off?"

Kinsear nodded. "Maybe the Santa Fe Safety pair did a deal knowing two security workers would never get away with trying to sell stolen Baumann prints for big bucks in Santa Fe. They needed to get rid of them fast, for a quick payoff." He tapped his fingers on the steering wheel. "But how did they link up with the Rubicon boys?"

"Maybe the other way around, and the Rubicon boys got in touch with them. I saw the Jeep my first night in Santa Fe, when I surprised an intruder—apparently with a key—at Ellie's. The next morning, I'd just found the box in the attic when two guys broke into the house—again with a key. I'd chained the back door, but they cut the chain with a bolt cutter. When the Santa Fe Safety truck pulled up to install the alarm system, I overheard them saying they needed to disappear out the back door. But maybe the Santa Fe Safety truck gave them an idea."

"So who are the Rubicon boys?"

"After hearing Danielle ask someone she called 'honey' whether he'd found the door to the attic, and after hearing her tell him she was at work—when she was actually on her phone, in Ellie's guestroom—I assume one of the Rubicon boys is her son, Drake. Look here."

Alice pulled up photos on her phone. "The Rubicon Jeep left my office headed for Houston. Your sweet Isabel got these shots of the boys inside the Weikel in LaGrange." She showed him the photos of the boys ogling the kolaches in the display case. "And I believe I've got fingerprints."

"Where?"

"On the busted tailgate of my Discovery, which is sitting in my barn."

"Oh, Alice," Kinsear said. "Strong work. Strong work!"

The sun was fully up in the east, glinting on windmills in pastures. "Look, antelope!" She pointed west, toward tiny graceful animals racing away across the grass.

"The problem is…" Alice began.

"Yes?"

"I dread pointing out that the wife of one beneficiary—Don—tried to hijack the valuables in the attic before his brother Chuck—the other beneficiary—could get wind of what was in the attic. Presumably, Danielle intended to rathole any goodies before they got inventoried."

"And Danielle's son was actually breaking into the Santa Fe house when you arrived that night?"

"I think so. It makes me sick."

Kinsear grunted in agreement. "He didn't come up with that idea himself."

"I've asked Silla to get Don and Chuck back to the office for a status conference. That way they can share the pain."

"Good lord, Alice. At least ask Roger if you can borrow his armored vest. Or buy your own—surely that's a deductible cost for a trust and estates lawyer."

Alice managed a small laugh. Then she wondered…maybe a bullet-proof blazer? No, that left her heart vulnerable. Better a Mao jacket. Could be chic. Maybe I should sell the jackets online, she thought. Or sell them at the bar CLE meetings for trust and estates lawyers. Get Isabel to help with marketing.

Thirty minutes from Coffee Creek, Alice phoned George Files. Friday afternoon; he was still at the office. "You haven't identified the prints on that wooden baton, that rolling pin, from Ellie Windom's hay bale?" she asked.

"Nope. You have a candidate?"

"If you're still there," she said, "could I bring by a flashlight Ellie's daughter-in-law tried to grab from me? Maybe you could check those prints?"

A pause. "Mind telling me where you were and why she tried to grab the flashlight?"

"In the attic of Ellie's Santa Fe house. Did Judith Strong mention she thought she heard Ellie tell Don she'd found something valuable in the attic so there'd be plenty of money for a gift to her birth daughter?"

"Something like that."

* * * * *

With Kinsear driving, they stopped only for bio breaks and gas and made it to the Coffee Creek Sheriff's Annex by five-thirty. Alice presented Files with the trash bag containing the flashlight wrapped in Danielle's jacket. "Always a pleasure, Alice," Files said. He didn't smile, but Alice thought the corner of one eye crinkled, just slightly.

Ten minutes later, when Kinsear and Alice reached Alice's house, Kinsear emerged from the driver's seat, stretched long arms and legs, and said, "Yes, I will have a cold beer, thank you."

"Can you stay for dinner?"

"I probably should get back to the ranch. My imagination's running wild with thoughts of Carrie unsupervised and Isabel and Sam frolicking around. Also unsupervised."

"Call first?" Alice suggested. She always appreciated the fact that her children didn't tell her things she shouldn't know. Or should know but didn't want to know. "It's Friday night. What makes you think they're home?"

"Okay. You're right. I'll stay for a while. But first I'll let them know I'm back."

Alice rummaged in the freezer for frozen brisket burgers. Kinsear thawed the patties in the microwave, then applied his patented mixture of chili powder and hot paprika while Alice sliced pickles and onions and lit the grill. Kinsear opened two bottles of Real Ale Fireman's #4. While they waited for the coals to heat, they took their glasses out on the deck, looking down at the creek, where, in the late western sun, birds looked golden as they flew down the valley.

"We are so lucky," Kinsear said abruptly. Alice leaned sideways, hugging him.

"Are you thinking of Roger?"

Eyes on the valley, Kinsear nodded. "Roger's spent all those years with someone who doesn't appreciate him. Doesn't even like him, apparently. That must feel so empty."

Alice watched a great blue heron flap west toward the sunset. She thought of Randall at the hospital, bending over Roger, kissing his father's head, murmuring "You're the best."

"His son loves him," she said. "Maybe his daughter will too."

The daughter he shared with Ellie...whose killer still walked free.

Always on My Mind

A lice spent Saturday at the office digging through the menacing stack of to-do's Silla had placed on her desk.

On top sat a sticky note: "Chuck and Don Windom say Monday's convenient for a meeting. They'll be here at two. Hope you didn't have plans. Also, the court set the hearing on your application for executorship and probate of will and codicil. I've docketed all the deadlines. Rock on."

Below, Silla had clipped together the draft wills for Alice's new clients. Alice tackled those first, thanking God for paying work and enjoying as always the process of making words say just what the client meant and the law allowed.

Next in the stack, printouts of updated appraisals for Ellie's real estate and personal property, including Graham's new numbers for the contents of the painted box. Alice flipped through them, then drafted a short agenda for her meeting with the Windom brothers. Following Ellie's death she'd sent them her detailed form letter on the probate process, fully expecting they'd barely glanced at it. At Monday's meeting she intended to go over her duties and deadlines: notify beneficiaries, locate and secure Ellie's real and personal property, notify creditors, pay and collect debts and costs of administration, submit the final inventory to the court, deal with any tax return, and distribute the remaining assets per the will. She sensed Don would argue for a cash distribution sooner than allowed. A dry agenda…but possibly a loud meeting.

She'd saved the bottom of Silla's stack for last—Smutbuster's discovery responses. Alice's eyebrows rose as she read. Had Fleischer even proofed this mess? Smutbuster claimed the Potter books caused children to desire magical powers. She feared her children might become Wiccans. As evidence, she claimed only that for Christmas her daughter requested a dress from a tony British retailer printed with the names of spells from the Potter books and that her son insisted on dressing as Potter for Halloween. Without Potter influence they might have chosen other outfits. Good grief, Alice thought. Such as Luke Skywalker? Or Queen Elsa? As to the books her children checked out from the library, Smutbuster's list admitted to scores of *Star Wars* books, dragon adventures books, and space fantasies.

Oh, Judge Sandoval, Alice said to herself. She couldn't wait to see his face at the next hearing. She began drafting a short motion asking the judge to dismiss Smutbuster's lawsuit. At the TRO hearing Mary Ellen Stokely had essentially admitted Protect Our Youth couldn't interfere with parents' rights to control what their own children could or couldn't check out. Her own testimony undermined her claims. Besides, didn't children passionately long to hear stories of victory over creatures who were far bigger (giants) or meaner (trolls)? Stories of loyalty and courage in dark hours? Because—Ellie's face rose before her—evil does exist.

"Silla, let's get rid of Smutbuster. Can you incorporate my cites to the transcript and exhibits in the motion? Then send a copy to the Library Board president and head librarian."

"Hoo boy," Silla said, swiftly reading the first pages. "I know Judge Sandoval can't wait to get rid of this case."

"How do you know that?"

"Friends with his bailiff," Silla said with her irresistible smile.

Nevertheless, Alice found herself dialing her daughter, Ann. As always, Ann's breezy "hello!" made Alice smile. Yes, Ann was fine. She'd met some cool people during her internship. One guy was kind of interesting. But the jury was out. She was having fun, learning lots, seeing all the sights D.C. had to offer.

"Are you singing anywhere?"

"Yes," Ann said. "Didn't I tell you? I got a summer gig substituting as soprano soloist in the choir at the Presbyterian church downtown. The lead singer's in Europe on a college choir tour."

"How nice," Alice said. "What about the preaching—any good?"

"Pretty interesting," said Ann. "I stay awake, if that's what you mean." Then Ann wanted to hear about Alice, Kinsear, the burros. "Love you heaps, Mom. Bye!"

Despite the fact that Ann had finished each Potter book just days after publication, Alice detected no indication that Ann had become Wiccan, however Smutbuster defined that term. Next she called her son, John, expecting on Saturday he'd be out with friends. "Nope, I'm at the office, Mom, with a project due Monday," he said. Yes, he really liked the job and the people. They'd offered him a position, but he was still thinking seriously about grad school. "Gotta go, Mom, love you," he said—before she had a chance to ask if he'd become Wiccan.

Of course, Alice herself was pretty enthralled with the life of trees...what did that make her?

Just as she was leaving the office, Chuck Windom called. "Listen, okay if I bring my wife to the meeting Monday?"

"Of course," Alice said.

"The thing is, Don's bringing Danielle. I thought I'd warn you. She's after him to get some cash from the estate right now. Don says she's got her eye on a house in West University."

West University was a highly desirable Houston neighborhood close to Rice University. The houses grew bigger and pricier every year.

Well. Be ready, Alice. She'd have to tell Don that she could make a preliminary cash distribution but only after meeting required deadlines.

*****

As she left the office, she shook her head at the odd mix of cases confronting a small-town lawyer. Sometimes crazy pro bono work like the Smutbuster lawsuit. Complex property transactions, wills and trusts, often involving tense family disputes. Then the image of Ellie's still body flashed before her. Her engagement letter didn't specify finding her client's murderer...but she'd promised her dead friend she would.

Meanwhile the familiar pall of unpleasant and inescapable obligation settled heavily on her shoulders. Dealing with an uncooperative beneficiary like Don felt uncomfortably like her old days in litigation, constantly on high alert against enemy attack. She took satisfaction in knowing she was doing exactly what Ellie had begged her to do—and she understood now why Ellie had been so insistent. But she also suspected Ellie's son Don would be happy to sue her at the drop of a hat.

Even the drive home on a summery June afternoon didn't raise her spirits. She surveyed her empty house, went out onto the deck, gazing at the trees and the blue streak of water below. Finally, she tugged on a swimsuit, rolling her eyes at her pale legs, and made her way downhill to the creek. A light breeze ruffled the clear bluegreen water. Alice tiptoed in, up to her knees, shivering as the cold water splashed her thighs. Upstream she saw the pale circles of fish nests in the gravel bottom and the tireless anxious fish patrolling the perimeters. Just another image of parenthood, she told herself. She envisioned herself as a fish, swimming around John, swimming around Ann, both children oblivious to the eternal worried presence of their mom. "You were always on my mind…" Alice sang. Just like Willie said. Then her feet found the edge of a deeper pool. She took a breath and jumped. Zowie! Frozen to her armpits. She swam, kicking to get warm, then walked upstream to inspect the rock wall by the creek where the maidenhair fern hung down. Yes. There it was. She floated on her back for a few minutes, then made her way to the creek's edge and climbed back up the hill.

The phone stopped ringing just as, still dripping, feeling marginally more in charge of herself, she walked back into the house. Message from Kinsear: "Call. I've got a proposition. Where are you?"

He answered her call on the first ring.

"I've got a meeting with the Windom boys Monday," she said. "Sounds potentially fraught." She explained what Chuck had said. "So I went down to check out the creek. What's your proposition?"

"Monday afternoon Carrie's got her last appointment with the orthopedist. Hopefully she'll get the boot off. Maybe that will improve her temper," he said. "Also, Isabel and Sam want a visit with you. So I thought, why don't we all gather at Alice's Monday night for barbecue? Which we'll bring, with all the sides?"

She gave a happy sigh. "That would be a loud yes," she said. "Yes, indeed. So how's everything?"

"Carrie in her walking boot is not a happy camper. She has to be driven everywhere, can't ride her horse, can't keep up with her friends. But hopefully this purgatory ends Monday."

"What about Sam and Isabel?"

"They spend all their time on the phone when he's not camped out here. He's working that oilfield job, then driving up from Menard to see Isabel every chance he gets."

Alice wasn't surprised—the two seemed mutually smitten, in an almost grown-up way.

"I feel better already, knowing you'll be here Monday," she told Kinsear. She hung up the phone, pondering the thought that he and she were also mutually smitten, in a rather grown-up way.

*****

Monday morning Alice found Silla at the office, arranging documents in the conference room. "All set," Silla said.

"Can you help me carry something?" Alice asked.

Silla followed Alice out to her car. Alice opened the trunk. Together they lugged in the Discovery's original tailgate, battered and dented, with its destroyed latch.

"Ah," Silla said.

"My five-hundred-dollar deductible."

They leaned the heavy steel door inside the conference room closet.

"You gonna tell them to quit messing with Ellie's assets?"

Alice nodded.

"I'll add that deductible to the executor's expenses to date." Silla whirled out the door.

"Also, please print full-size copies of the pictures I forwarded."

That should put the cat among the pigeons.

Chapter Thirty-Seven

That Lingering Whiff of Evil

Chuck and his wife, Joanne, arrived at two o'clock sharp. Silla settled them in the conference room with Alice's agenda and the updated documents.

Alice worked in her office until two-fifteen, then went to check on Chuck and Joanne. "This looks complete, Alice," Chuck said, pointing to the draft inventory. "Listen, I've decided to buy out Don's half of whatever he wants to sell. I'm interested in keeping a toehold here in Coffee Creek."

"What about Santa Fe?"

"I want us to keep that," Joanne said.

"Don may want to get his own appraisals," Alice said.

"Whatever." Chuck looked at his watch, let out an irritated sigh, and picked up his phone. "Don, where the heck are you? You're the one who asked for a two o'clock meeting."

Alice couldn't hear the reply, but Chuck's face tightened. "You're costing us time and money." He hung up.

"I'll be in my office. I've got some catch-up to do," Alice said.

At two-thirty the front door banged open.

From her office Alice heard Silla shepherding Don and Danielle down the hall to the conference room. Alice heard her say, "I've put refreshments on the credenza. Please help yourselves." She heard the tinkle of ice, heard the whoosh of soda cans.

Alice picked up the papers Silla had brought her, took a deep breath, and marched down the hall to stand at her place at the head of the table. Chuck and Joanne sat on one side; Don and Danielle sat across from them.

"Let's begin," she said, looking from Chuck, to Joanne, to Don, and then to Danielle.

Danielle dropped her eyes, then lifted her head and stared back, furious.

"The court set a date for hearing our application for probate of the will and codicil and issuance of letters testamentary. I fully expect the court will approve it, and I'll take my oath as executor," Alice said. "Beneficiaries are notified. We'll publish the notice to creditors. We'll have deadlines to meet, the major ones being our inventory and any tax filing. Please take a look at the list of financial accounts we've located. It's the top document on your stack. Do you notice anything missing?"

After a moment they shook their heads no.

"Take a look at the draft appraisals for the inventory."

Papers rustled.

"No major changes except for the art in the box found in Ellie's Santa Fe attic. As you know, five of the prints, with the accompanying water colors and woodblocks, go to the New Mexico Museum of Art. The remaining prints go to Ellie's four grandchildren."

"That's so unfair!" Danielle broke out.

"Why?" Joanne asked, leaning forward and facing Danielle. "Ellie could have left all that art to the museum! She could've left money too, if she wanted!"

Alice heard a phone ring at Silla's worktable, heard Silla talking.

"As executor, I'm bound by Ellie's wishes in her will and codicil," Alice said in her "opening statement" courtroom voice—calm, clear. "On my trip last week to Santa Fe, checking to be sure we'd found everything, I located photos of the Pecos art. Those should also go to the museum."

"Do the photos make the prints more valuable?" Joanne's shrewd question.

"The appraiser thinks they make the museum's Pecos prints more valuable, assuming the artist in the photos painting those watercolor sketches is actually Gustave Baumann. Which he has not confirmed."

Joanne again: "Do any other beneficiaries, like our sons, have any claim for the photos?"

Alice said, "The codicil says the materials 'related' to the Pecos art are part of Ellie's gift to the museum. So, no."

Joanne nodded. Danielle bristled.

Don glanced at his wife. "Look, Alice, let's cut to the chase. There's plenty of money in Mom's bank and brokerage accounts to cover debts and expenses, right? I want you to dole out some of the dough now." He smirked. "Dole out some dough!"

Danielle looked up from her phone and showed the screen to Chuck. "The bidding's going up on that house in West U," she hissed.

"Come on, Alice," Don said. "This is ridiculous!" His face reddened. "I need a check for at least a hundred thou!"

"Give it up, bro!" Chuck shot across the table.

Alice ordered herself to stay calm, control her voice. "I won't stand for any more interference with my duties."

"What are you talking about?" Don's face was scornful.

Alice felt her temples throb. She leaned forward, fists on the table. "Two days after your mother's death I was in Santa Fe to secure her house. When I got there, a break-in was under way, by a kid in a hoodie. The next morning, he and a buddy were back. They had a key and were looking for something specific. They just didn't know where to find it." She looked at Don, then Danielle. "I made recordings of their voices." Someone in the room moved, hearing that.

"That morning I found the art box of prints and woodblocks in the attic. On Saturday, with my college intern Isabel Kinsear, I drove back to Coffee Creek. When we got here two men were breaking into my office. We caught them. They're now in jail. While we waited for the police, two different guys jimmied open my car, grabbed the art box and took off… in a dark green Rubicon Jeep with Utah plates." She watched Don's face change at her description of the Jeep.

She walked over to the conference room closet and opened the doors. "Here's what the Rubicon boys did to my car."

"Holy cow," Chuck said.

Don slid his eyes sideways at Danielle, who sat motionless as if turned to stone.

Alice stalked back to the table. "Isabel Kinsear and her friend followed the Jeep. When it stopped in LaGrange at the Weikel, Isabel and her friend retrieved the art box from that Jeep. They also took photos of the two boys involved." She fanned out on the table copies of Isabel's photos from the Weikel: the Utah license plate on the Jeep, and the two box thieves, one with dark curly hair, one with straight sandy hair, staring intently at the kolaches.

"But that's Drake!" Joanne gasped, pointing to the sandy-haired boy. She looked up at Don and Danielle. "Isn't it?"

Neither Danielle nor Don answered.

Don's mouth hung open as he picked up the pictures, then put them back on the table. "I just can't believe…" He looked at his big brother. "Chuck, you don't think Drake would do something like that?"

Chuck's face indicated that yes, he did think Drake would do that. He folded his arms and glared down at the pictures, then at his brother.

"The deductible for my car repair was five hundred dollars," Alice said, passing out the revised list of estate expenses. "Under the circumstances it seems unfair for all beneficiaries to share equally in that cost."

Shocked silence.

"Don, that cost should be yours," Joanne said. "Your kid caused it."

"Here's the bigger point," Alice said. "The art taken from my Discovery belongs to the estate, not yet to any beneficiary. It's my job to keep estate assets safe until they can be properly distributed to the rightful beneficiaries under Ellie's will—*and codicil.* I will not tolerate any further attempts to interfere with my duties."

Don squirmed in his chair, opened his mouth a couple of times, but didn't speak.

"But there's more," Alice said. "I just returned from Santa Fe, where I needed to arrange local probate counsel for your mom's house there. I was in that house Thursday morning confirming we'd found everything in the attic when Danielle showed up. I heard her on the phone asking someone if he'd found the door to the attic...*when he was there before.*"

"But—Danielle was in Houston last Thursday!" Don burst out. He turned to Danielle. "You weren't—you didn't!" He looked up at Alice at the end of the table. "She couldn't have!"

"She was in Ellie's house. She had a rental car. She threatened me. My friend Ben Kinsear witnessed that. She ran out without her jacket." Alice turned to Danielle. "Danielle, I'll try to get your jacket back. The police have it."

"The police?" asked Joanne, her brow puzzled.

Chuck had sat silent. Now, his eyes fixed on Danielle, he spoke directly to her. "I get it now. You gave Drake a key. You sent Drake to look for whatever it was Ellie told Don was in the attic. Then you sent your son to break into Alice's car. What else?"

Alice stood motionless, watching rage mount in Danielle's face.

Danielle jumped up, pointing at Alice. "She's the problem! Your precious lawyer is trying to do us out of what's ours by right! Our rightful inheritance! She's trying to do what Ellie told Don—give it all to the grandchildren! She's in cahoots with that Valerie person who probably isn't Ellie's child at all! She's come up with fake low numbers on the damn artwork so you boys won't insist on getting the whole estate! Who knows what she's stolen from the attic?" She whirled around and grabbed an unopened glass bottle of club soda off the top of the credenza, holding it by the neck, and stood panting.

Don stood, trying to move Danielle back to her chair. She shook off his arm and started toward Alice, gripping the club soda bottle by the neck. "No, Danielle, calm down," he urged.

Alice heard voices in the office entry and then Silla's protest: "But she's in conference!" She turned, surprised, as the door opened and Files and Joske strode in. Another uniformed deputy stood in the hall, next to a wide-eyed Silla.

Alice started to speak, but Files held up a hand and moved toward the table. "I'm Detective George Files, Coffee Creek Sheriff's Department. This is Assistant Detective Alan Joske. We're here for Danielle Windom."

All eyes turned to Danielle. Her face was white, her pupils huge, her knuckles clenched on the club soda bottle.

"Danielle Windom, you'll need to come with us. We have a warrant for your arrest."

"Arrest for what?" Don sputtered. "Leaving her jacket in Santa Fe?" He turned to his wife.

Files didn't take his eyes off Danielle. "We're arresting you on suspicion of the murder of Ellie Windom."

Silence, then the room exploded. Chuck flew up from his chair, knocking it backward. "*Danielle? Murdered Mom?*"

Danielle lunged past Files toward the door. Joske sidestepped in front of her, grabbing her arms. Files yanked away the club soda bottle and snapped handcuffs on her wrists.

"On what evidence?" Don yelled. "What possible evidence? She wasn't even in Coffee Creek the day Mom died!"

"The evidence shows otherwise," Files said. "Including her prints on the murder weapon." He gave a quick nod to Joske, and the deputy walked a struggling Danielle down the hall and out the front door.

Don stood rooted in place, shaking his head, back and forth, eyes on Files. "You can't be serious! Danielle would never…I mean…" His voice broke.

Chuck spoke. "Her prints are on the murder weapon? What *is* the murder weapon?"

"We believe it's Ellie Windom's French rolling pin," Files replied.

"But maybe she helped Mom with—with a baking project some-time!" Don cried.

Face impassive, Files said, "Danielle Windom's fingerprints are superimposed over stains of blood and…other matter." He dug in his pocket and handed Don his card, then turned to Alice. "Sorry to interrupt this way, Alice." He picked up the confiscated soda bottle as he left.

Alice could think of nothing to do or say. She realized that, when Danielle lunged forward, she'd backed up and assumed tennis court stance, knees slightly bent, ready to move in any direction. Covertly, she straightened her knees.

"But Danielle was in Houston that day!" Don insisted, facing Chuck and Joanne. "She couldn't have killed Mom!"

"Like she wasn't in Santa Fe last Thursday trying to find valuables in Mom's attic?" Chuck retorted.

Joanne muttered something.

"What?" Don asked.

"I can't understand why anyone would murder Ellie…but *Danielle?*"

"Nobody's proved that!" Don said.

Chuck pointed at the battered tailgate of the Discovery. "Tell you what, bro. Alice's deductible for getting her car fixed comes out of your share. But right now, don't you need to work on getting a lawyer for Danielle?"

Don threw his hands in the air and rushed toward the door, then skidded to a stop. He turned to Alice. "Where'd they take her?" he asked.

"Right down the street. The jail's next to the Courthouse."

Silla was still standing outside the conference room. Alice caught her eye. "Maybe Silla will take her car and drive down ahead of you, show you the way. It's just a couple of blocks."

Silla nodded. "Come on. I'll show you."

Dazed, he followed her out.

Alice walked slowly back to the conference room table.

Chuck stared at the floor, shaking his head in disbelief. "Good lord. I've known Danielle twenty years. I was Don's best man! Drake and our son Max are cousins! They've opened Christmas presents together! They were all at our house last Thanksgiving! And she murdered Mom?"

Joanne sighed. "Innocent until…et cetera. The one I'm sorry for is Drake. Danielle involved her own son…"

Chuck lifted his head. "We've got to get going. I'll check to be sure Don found a lawyer. Alice, on the real estate topic, I want to buy Don's half of all the real estate except the home place. I don't know how he feels about it, but right now, after Mom's murder, I don't think I could bear to walk in the door again."

Alice nodded. She'd had the same thought. Still, maybe he'd change his mind.

Chuck went on. "But Alice…one more thing. Joanne and I have talked about it. We'd like to meet my…my half-sister. Valerie. Will you ask her if she'd be willing?"

"Of course."

"You can let it wait until tomorrow," he added.

Alice smiled. I've never had a beneficiary's wife arrested on suspicion of murder in my conference room, she thought. Law school did not prepare me for this. Must remember to tell Silla, no more big glass bottles.

"Maybe get Silla to burn one of those bundles of sage I saw on her windowsill," Joanne said.

Yes, Alice thought. Light that bundle of sage, open the conference room windows, get that lingering whiff of evil out of here.

She reminded Chuck to take his copies of the probate papers and walked them to the front door.

"Innocent until…et cetera." Joanne's words echoed in her head. She remembered Danielle's repeat visits to Ellie's house, and the crumpled pink tissue by the haystack in the corral. Alice very much wanted to hear what Files had found on the rolling pin.

Oh, the Trail of Tears

"That's the first murderer I've ever ushered into our conference room," Silla said, her voice uneven.

"Innocent until…" Alice repeated.

"Alice, get real. Did you see her grip on that bottle? That's exactly what she did to Ellie, but with a rolling pin," Silla retorted. "And you know it."

"It fits," Alice said. "Valerie Ames was on the phone with Ellie when someone came into her kitchen, someone Ellie knew."

"But what put Danielle in a killing rage?"

Alice shook her head. "Remember what Judith Strong thought she heard Ellie say to Don? Like maybe she'd leave everything to her grandkids?"

"But it was Ellie's money!"

"Yes. But you know kids…they live their life anticipating that little boost, that cash infusion, from their parents. No, they aren't *entitled*…but they have expectations."

"Ellie's not Danielle's mother!"

Alice thought about that. "Is it easier to kill your husband's mother?"

Silla made a disgusted face and whirled out of the room.

Alice couldn't wait another second. She called Files. "Okay, after that dramatic entrance and exit, don't you owe me an explanation?"

"Just the facts, ma'am, just the facts." Files at his driest. "Okay. The rolling pin in the hay bale bore traces of Ellie's blood and brain matter. It had been wiped, maybe with a tissue we didn't find. But the lab found Danielle Windom's palm-print, and fingerprints, both underneath and superimposed over the blood/brain spatter."

"What does that mean?"

"She repositioned her hand slightly, for the second strike, and again before she stuffed the rolling pin into the bale."

Alice cringed at "second strike." "What if Danielle claims she helped Ellie roll out pie dough?"

"No way. The palm print's not in rolling mode. It's in the same position as on that flashlight you asked me to test. The gripping-a-weapon position."

"Like the holding-a-bottle-of-club-soda position?"

"Yep," Files said. "That's a dangerous woman, Alice. Think about bashing your mother-in-law, then running outside and grabbing a horse and locking it in the house to disguise the crime. The lab's looking at the rope on the horse's bridle."

"Wouldn't Danielle's clothes be spattered with blood?"

"Yes, but we haven't found those yet."

"But the blood smell—wouldn't that send Ellie's horse into a frenzy?" Alice imagined Danielle grabbing the rope, the horse rearing, eyes rolling in its head, as she dragged it through the Dutch door into the kitchen. The very thought sent terror into Alice's soul. But apparently not Danielle's.

"Does Danielle ride?" Files asked.

"Oh, yes." Alice remembered Danielle's contempt for Woodie's horse—"broken-down old nag," she called it at their first meeting. "She mentioned she used to jump horses."

"That pink tissue you found by the hay bale? The lab found her DNA on it. Good thing you thought to preserve it…and bring me the flashlight."

"I just wondered why Danielle kept coming back to Ellie's. At first I assumed she was trying to get into the house, but I bet she was trying to retrieve the rolling pin from the hay bale. We kept interrupting—Silla, Red, Kinsear and I."

Files was silent, then said, "I knew Ellie. She taught my kid in high school. He won't forget playing Antony in *Julius Caesar.*"

Files hadn't mentioned knowing Ellie.

"He came to Ellie's memorial, with a bunch of kids from his year," Files added.

All those children Ellie inspired…all those years…while their teacher still thought every morning of the one child she couldn't find.

Alice blinked. "Will Danielle post bond?"

"My guess is no. The prosecutor will definitely oppose bail. Danielle's job's a godsend for someone who needs to manufacture an alibi. Driving around, supposedly scouting venues…"

Flight risk, thought Alice. Adept at being somewhere other than where she says. But oh, the trail of tears she left behind.

Alice drove home listing the things she needed to do before Kinsear and his kids arrived: set the table, make iced tea, check the bathrooms…but too late. Kinsear's Land Cruiser caught up with her as she drove through her gate. Oh well…

She smiled, watching Carrie climb out of the car—no crutches, no boot. A decent smile and hello for Alice. She got a hug from Isabel, who had a suspicious glow, no doubt engendered by hormones and the nearness of Sam, who also glowed when he hugged Alice.

"Looky here, looky here," Kinsear said, opening the tailgate.

The unmistakable aromas of barbecue, sauce, onions, jalapeños, pickles, and oak and hickory smoke wafted up from the wooden box in the back.

"Oh, honey," Alice breathed. "Is it Shade Tree?"

"Yep."

Shade Tree was a Coffee Creek legend, with its own Czech recipe for spicy sausage.

Sam hoisted the box and lugged it toward the house. Isabel scampered ahead of him to open the wrought-iron gate that kept the burros out of Alice's yard. Carrie followed.

Alice lingered on the driveway for a moment with Kinsear. She tiptoed and hugged him, grateful for the familiar citrusy tang of his aftershave, the blessed warmth of his arms around her, his very welcome kiss. She noted his tender, wry expression, a lifted whimsical eyebrow, as he watched his daughters and Sam chattering their way into Alice's house.

He looked back down at Alice. "So. Know how I got the news of the day? Not from you, counselor. I called Silla when you were on the phone. She announced the police stormed your conference room during a client meeting and arrested Danielle Windom for murder. New high? New low?"

"Awful." She looked up. "Files called her a dangerous woman. They found her palm prints and finger prints on the rolling pin. She moved her grip before the second strike."

"Oh, God." He blew out a long breath. "I thought property and estates law was supposed to be boring." He frowned. "What if you hadn't texted me that SOS when she showed up at Ellie's Santa Fe house?"

She had no answer.

A soft June evening breeze lifted the scent of hickory and oak and barbecue to their noses.

"Didn't the Greeks have a big barbecue honoring their dead, in the *Iliad*?" Kinsear said. "Let's do it." He strode through the wrought iron gate into Alice's house.

She closed the gate behind him and walked into noise, laughter, and music. Ellie would've loved it.

Chapter Thirty - Nine

To Love– Anyway!

The last weekend in August: Alice and Kinsear left the sweltering heat in Coffee Creek and checked into the El Rey again, reveling in the dry, cool air of Santa Fe. Kinsear carried his garment bag and Alice's suitcase up to the desk. "Same room as last time, sir. Here's your key."

They showered and changed. "The reception's at five," Kinsear reminded Alice, craning his neck and staring into the mirror as he tied his tie. "Okay, who do I not get to meet tonight?"

"I doubt you'll meet Don, with Danielle's trial a month away, and trying to get some help for Drake. Imagine having your mom on trial for murder. Also, I think Randall, Roger's son, is in San Francisco. His IPO's launching."

She'd tugged on a black sheath and was pushing her toes into high heels. "When did we last get this dressed up?" she asked.

"I don't know," he said, holding her shoulders, "but I like that dress. Okay, what's the drill?"

"Five o'clock reception at the museum, then meet for dinner at six-thirty at Francis's house."

"No speeches by you?" he asked.

"Hell no," she retorted. "But maybe a toast?"

* * * * *

Late sun lit the lofty hall of the art museum. Waiters swanned by with trays of prosecco, trays of hors d'oeuvres. Alice scanned the room, always tickled by Santa Fe fashion statements: long hair, long earrings, long dresses…bolo ties with cinnabar and turquoise, western shirts with tuxedo jackets, jeans, and polished boots. But no fringed suede jacket, she thought. Billy Menger would've wangled an invitation, but he was dead and buried.

A bell rang. Someone tapped a microphone. A fruity baritone welcomed the crowd. "The board of this museum welcomes all of you to the grand opening of the Ellie Windom Exhibit! We want to thank her family members gathered here, including Chuck and Joanne Windom, and Valerie Ames."

Alice's eyes widened. She looked around the room, trying to spot

Chuck. Or Valerie.

The baritone continued. "This gift, fifty years after the death of Gustave Baumann, of five heretofore unknown gouache sketches and woodcut prints of the Pecos Valley, is more exciting than we could ever have dreamed. We haven't confirmed the artist's identity. We're still in the authentication process, but I suspect you lovers of Baumann will immediately be attracted to the vivid intensity of the colors and the power of these works. Many of you will recognize the actual locations. We owe this opportunity to Ellie Windom, a member of this museum, whose bequest will enrich the experience of so many in years to come. Please join me in a toast to this extraordinary donor, Ellie Windom, and to her family members who are present." Cheers, huzzahs, clinking glasses. Alice groped in her bag for a tissue and felt her nose turning pink.

She and Kinsear edged their way to the dramatic display of the box, the children's chairs, and the five Pecos gouaches and woodblocks Ellie had donated. In the background the photos of the artist were projected on a large screen, with a voice-over describing gouache and woodcut techniques. Alice recognized Clare Graham's voice. Well, he did bill himself as a Baumann expert.

"Okay, I've hit the wall," Kinsear said in an undertone.

"Me too," Alice answered. Too many people, too many voices. They slipped out the door, found their car, and escaped.

* * * * *

As they turned onto Calle Peralta toward Francis's house, Alice flinched momentarily, recalling how she and Margaret barely escaped the shooter's RAV4 the night he shot Roger and left him lying in his own blood in the driveway.

Tonight festive lights hung from Francis's eaves. Francis, aproned, met them in the driveway. "We're gathering in the back yard," he said, pointing to a gate.

The back yard was welcoming: soft light from paper lanterns, music floating in the air from a Desert Chorale recording, one long table lined with hurricane lamps and candles. Clare Graham had set up an outdoor bar. "New Mexican champagne!" he said, handing glasses to Alice and Kinsear. "Look who's here!"

Alice turned and stared. Chuck and Joanne Windom with their son, Max. Alice's friend Margaret. Pepe Longoria. Lawyer Mike Cortez. Roger Preyer, with a twenty-something who must be his grandson, Beau. And next to Roger, Valerie Ames with two look-alikes who must be her twin girls. Hadn't Beau gotten this party started in the first place, when he got his DNA results?

The noise level rose, laughter rang out. Alice introduced Margaret to Mike Cortez, who asked Margaret to tell him the story of Agnes Dietz's one-of-a-kind table—which she forbade the designer to build for any other customer.

Alice stood talking with Valerie and Roger. Chuck approached and held out his hand to Valerie. "I'm Chuck Windom. I want to meet my sister," he said. Valerie shook his hand, eyes wide, then smiled. "I hope you won't mind," Chuck said. "I've switched the place cards around so we can sit together. Will that work?"

"Great."

Max and Joanne joined them, and Valerie introduced the twins and Roger and Beau.

Alice's smile was so big it almost hurt her cheeks. She backed quietly out of the group and found Kinsear. "Francis is serving New Mexico green chile stew," he said. "I think I've memorized his recipe." Kinsear, a notorious recipe hound, saw Alice's smirk. "Well, first things first," he said. "Sure, you've got your dramatic family reunion here, plus a dynamite new museum exhibit, but we've still got to eat. Now I've acquired a good green chile stew recipe."

Francis rang a fork on a wine glass. "Folks, this is a very special night. We have Roger here—recovered from Lord knows what all." Cheers. "We have Ellie's son Chuck and his family." Cheers. "We have Ellie and Roger's daughter, Valerie, and her children." More cheers. "We have art saved from oblivion and shared with the public by our beloved friend Ellie. Let's begin with a toast. To Ellie!—the one who brought us all here!"

Alice groped for her tissue again. At the far end of the table she saw Chuck and Valerie sit down together, already in conversation.

Could they, maybe, become like brother and sister? A few chairs away sat Roger, dressed as usual in his blue blazer and blue shirt. But he sat relaxed, laughing at a story Graham was telling. Maybe he'd turned a page too.

As dinner ended, and wine glasses were filled again, more toasts were made. Finally, Kinsear nudged Alice under the table in the way that meant, "Can we leave yet?"

Goodbyes, hugs, thanks, promises to stay in touch.

On their way to the car Kinsear said, "I thought you were going to make a toast?"

"Yeah, but there was so much—what—*relief* in the air, I decided not to. Chuck and Valerie were relieved finally to meet each other. Roger's relieved to be alive and relieved finally to have connected with Valerie. We're all relieved Ellie's exhibit's up. Hearts were lighter, right?"

"Did you have a toast in mind and decide against it?"

Alice nodded. "To love. So strong it pains our hearts. But to love—anyway!"

She was thinking about her own children, her beloved John and Ann. In two days they'd be coming down the escalator at the Austin airport, joking with each other, maybe scanning the crowd for her face. She'd have them in her arms again. The thought gave her a pang in the heart. What an odd expression. Maybe it meant a thump of love so strong the heart did hurt, for a moment. Worth it, though.

Tʜᴇ Eɴᴅ

ABOUT THE AUTHOR

Helen Currie Foster writes the Alice MacDonald Greer Mystery series. She lives north of Dripping Springs, Texas, supervised by three burros. She is drawn to the compelling landscape and quirky characters of the Texas Hill Country. She's also deeply curious about our human history and how, uninvited, the past keeps crashing the party.

Find her on Facebook or at www.helencurriefoster.com.

HEARING FROM YOU

Thanks for reading *Ghost Daughter!* If you enjoyed it, please consider rating it or putting a short review on Amazon. You readers who take the time to review books can and do make a difference in the success of a series.

Comments, questions or suggestions? Drop a note to thealicemysteries@gmail.com.

You can learn more about Alice and her adventures at www.helencurriefoster.com, and subscribe to the mailing list there, for updates and news about upcoming books.

This book would not have taken shape without invaluable information from Keith Clemson and suggestions from the amazing critique group and beloved book group. They have my heartfelt thanks. Any errors are mine.

To Judy K. Cohen for superb copy-editing, and Bill Carson for cover, design layout and sheer professional brio, thanks and more thanks.